ELEMENT

Hi Mary!
Merry Christmas
2007!

I hope you enjoy
the book.

Dec/21/07
Nic Beer

ELEMENT

CHRISTOPHER BESSE

Mundania Press

A Mundania Press Production
Mundania Press LLC
6470A Glenway Avenue, #109
Cincinnati, Ohio 45211-5222

To order additional copies of this book, contact:
books@mundania.com
www.mundania.com

Cover Art © 2007 by Anna Winsom
Book Design, Production, and Layout by Daniel J. Reitz, Sr.
Marketing and Promotion by Bob Sanders

Trade Paperback ISBN: 978-1-59426-474-0
eBook ISBN: 978-1-59426-473-3

First Edition • November 2007

Production by Mundania Press LLC
Printed in the United States of America
10   9   8   7   6   5   4   3   2   1

CHAPTER 1
RECON

"The darkness falls,
The bells peal,
Death take us all."

—Private Verlin Haydren, 4th Floren Marine Battalion,
at the Siege of Exdor—Terra earth year 1763 AD

Nothing moved in the alien night shadows, but the stillness and silence itself was a danger. It meant that whatever was following them knew that Jackson and his team were aware of their presence.

Mike Platoon's Wheel, Lieutenant Thomas Daniel Jackson, turned his head and let his eyes sweep the trail below him slowly and carefully, his Night Referencing Helmet (NRH) turning the shifting darkness into a holographic display of what passed for day on this strange, dark planet. He read the numbers off his display and cursed silently. Biological—nominal, infrared—nominal, electronic distortion—nominal, filter search parameters, random-passive—nominal; nothing! And that scared him worse than a full-redlined passband would have.

Jackson felt a whispering echo as his platoon level neural link went active. The neural link had been a major step forward in secure tactical communications systems and was ideally suited for recon teams. The neural energy was instantly translated into normalized speech patterns across the team's tactical net.

"I don't like this, Sir. We've been patrolling for four days with all active systems shut down and now, all of a sudden, we make signature contact. Two nights ago we picked up a return on the thoracic passband just as we settled in, then it disappeared until now and wham, we've got hard lock on a residual shimmer envelope when we shouldn't," Jeff Choi's thought echoed across the neural net.

"So what you're really saying," DeLuca broke in over the link, "is that we're ass deep in alligators in Indian country, and you think things are going to get ugly really quick. Is that it?"

"We were ass deep in alligators the minute we inserted," Jackson thought back in response. "Let's just see who these folks are, shall we, and we'll take it from there.

"Give me a suit check. Send the data stream now. I want sensor arrays in standby mode and all implants powered down. Nothing running but your thermal grid and HUD, all transmissions across the neural team net only. Chief, I want you to monitor the Hancock's command link and get ready to call for an extraction run if we make contact."

"Aye, Sir," the Chief responded.

Jackson watched as the numbers took shape in his mind and were instantly displayed across his helmet tactical display.

"Affirmative, all suits and implants nominal, no emissions. Neural network is set to team net, narrow band, standard battle format," Jackson confirmed.

Jackson knew his suit was working. Liquids moved through five kilometers of microscopic tubing, making it feel like a million Duvarian swamp ants trying to lift his body up and carry it away. He remembered the shock at the caressing feel the first time he had put a Bristol Dynamics class one recon suit on. Now he rarely noticed this second skin. The flexplate armor was as supple and oily smooth as a serpent moving through the grass, and it's bonded outer Chameleon coating could be used in passive or active mode, drawing power from the suit's tiny, nuclear power module.

On the left flank, Doc Hearst felt uneasy and exposed, as if something was watching them from the darkness above them. She carefully shifted her weight, trying to sink a little deeper into the dark ooze that seemed to bleed from the planet's surface.

"I sure wish I had my Class One assault armor on," she thought, and immediately regretted it as soft, chuckling echoes momentarily filled her mind from the other team members.

"Somebody forgot to set their privacy passband," Dyer whispered.

"What's the matter, Doc," LPO DeLuca thought back at her. "You miss all those servo manipulators and heavy plate armor the line grunts wear?"

Jackson had to smile grimly at DeLuca's comment. Suit technology had come a long way. During the 21st Century, several nations began developing suit armor to protect their armies. At first, suits were the exclusive domain of Special Operations teams. They had fully integrated electronics, multi-weapon platforms and high tech munition dispensing systems, all available at the tap of a chin control or retinal blink. So suited, a recon team could take on a full company of regular line grunts and their support elements. It only took a few years for the more developed nations to realize that they needed to extend similar protection and abilities to their regular forces or they would lose any tactical advantage, no matter how well trained their military forces were.

But that all changed, Jackson mused bitterly, when a desperate weapons technician with the Russian Twentieth Tanks released a low yield plasma discharge over an entire Chinese division at the Third Battle of Peking. They were slaughtered to the man because all their implants, nano enhancements and advanced acquire and engage electronics were disabled by the low energy pulse that radiated their position.

The two Russian regiments holding the line had descended on the helpless Chinese division that writhed and twitched like a bowl of squirming cockroaches, and put them to the sword in a crazed killing frenzy.

The slaughter at Peking-Three, Jackson thought.

After that, the focus on suit technology was stealth. Simply put, in the long run it was better to be invisible, get into knife cutting range, and kill them quick.

Bringing his mind back to the present, Jackson listened to the thought link and checked his suit. He was acutely aware that the ceramic deflection plating along the suit's dorsal line was not vibrating.

That's a good and a bad thing, he thought. Good because it meant he hadn't been illuminated, bad because it might mean that they had already been painted and were in the kill zone of whatever was stalking them.

"What do you have?" Jackson asked.

"Thoracic lock!" Choi's thoughts echoed across the neural net. "Confirm signature as thirteen Caldarian bio's, one unknown on point, running database on the unknown now.

"I don't know why they decided to close the distance here and now but they have. About 200 meters back and they know we're just in front of them by the way they're moving, and like I said, I had shimmer acquisition even before my passives picked them up."

"That's impossible," Jackson's mind whispered across the link.

Jackson scanned the bush around him and gestured to the dark section of trail across the narrow canyon to a point just before the switchback they had just walked. "OK, we're going to take them from here. I know it isn't the best spot but right now, this is all we've got. Hopefully they'll bunch up as they approach the turn but if these folk are who I think they are, their point element will probably flank the turn in anticipation anyway."

His team lay spread out in a ragged ambush line covering the trail across from their position. It was 40 meters across. The danger signal had come up the line from Choi. As rear security, he had been waiting and listening off the trail for two or three minutes at a time, then racing ahead to catch up with the team. Jackson's intuition told him they were in deep, serious trouble.

In eighteen months of bitter, bloody fighting, Jackson had learned to listen to that intuition. For one side or the other, the waiting and running was over. He and his team could run no further. This was the final jeopardy in a game of evasion that had begun two days ago when they got a twitch on the thoracic array. Last night, before dusk settled in, Jackson had located their Remain Overnight (RON) site, passing it and fish-hooking back to it just at dusk; so that anyone following would think their RON was 500 meters from where it actually was. Jackson's stomach felt empty, a reminder that their last meal, if field glop could correctly be called food, had been several hours ago.

Four days of eating patrol glop. His mind recited the training droid's litany of ingredients. A balanced meal of proteins, carbohydrates, vitamins and electrolytes, all tailored to each individual's specific tastes, heated by the body and eaten using either the nourishment dispensing tube or, if you were stupid enough to take your helmet off while on patrol, by slurping it straight from the pouch.

"It's times like this when I sure wish they could do this without hanging us out so far on a limb," Wicker said. "We always seem to pull the really long distance recons."

"All our resources are spread thin. The Ramillions have eight teams deployed in the Ortesian Rift, trying to interdict Caldarian troop transports coming through the corridor. And two Myloen deep insertion teams vanished without even a trace of residual DNA dust when something killed the Mylock and her escorting frigate, the Day Star. It doesn't matter how many high tech electronics they deploy, you and I both know that the only way to gather reliable, hard intelligence is to insert a recon team and let them do what every army since the dawn of time has done—find the enemy."

"Well, that's why they pay us the big bucks," Hearst whispered. "It's a good thing these Neural COM links are secure or we'd be crow bait by now," she added.

"Can't patrol in the dark with Chameleon mode on like we did in the old days, Doc," Chief Miller responded.

"Until now," Jackson thought. "At least, if what the spooks briefed us on is true. This of course raises an interesting question. Is there such a thing as truth in the intelligence business?" he asked the team in general.

"Rhetoric, Sir, pure rhetoric because we all know there is no such thing as an intelligent spook," Hearst's cynical thought echoed back.

Jackson felt dark, rippling laughter echo across his neural nodes and could sense the team's bow-string tight acuity as Hearst's anecdotal comment relieved some of the tension.

At 29, Jackson was still leading platoon recon teams. He had specifically been asked to stay at the platoon level by Captain Jim Ortello, commanding officer of SEAL Team One, Earth-Prime, and had agreed. The Confederate recon teams were desperately short of officers who could lead teams in the field and with their resources spread so thin, a man with Jackson's unique abilities was needed where he was.

At first glance, Jackson wasn't what people would think of as part of the varsity-elite of the Confederate armed forces. His brown hair was cut to the standard military length but all one had to do was to look into his deep, hazel eyes to sense that there was more to this man than what was first seen by the casual observer. He bore a confidence and casual lethality that said loud and clear, 'enter at your own risk'.

He was barely six feet tall and his frame was small but it hid a deadly litheness and whip-like suppleness that spoke of years of hard training and disciplined martial arts at the masters' level. It was rumored within the close-knit family of the teams that the knife scar Jackson carried low down on his left side was the result of an encounter with a Black Order hunter-killer team on his first deployment on Galdaris-One.

Jackson reached down with his left hand and tapped a small control node on his left thigh. A signal was transmitted to the other seven members of his team. He felt the locking lugs on his particle rifle latch into the battle lock position on his conformal pack and a small blue dot of light, low down in his HUD, informed him that the power source was switched off. Seven small, blue ID signatures appeared for a brief moment on his battle display, indicating that his team had followed suit.

The last goddamn thing we need right now is for a power pack to go active and start radiating a signature, he thought.

Suddenly Jackson tensed, and his eyes swung to the slope above the trail he was watching. Movement! Just a nuance but something was there. Jackson's eyes were drawn down and to the right. He worked the starlight filters on his helmet trying to gain more resolution on his display.

A spot of deeper darkness detached itself from the lighter background of the surrounding night and seemed to glide down the slope. The spot stopped, and Jackson's display went nominal momentarily as he lost target lock. He adjusted his filters again and swung his head. He felt his heart quicken as ghost-like, the rest of the hunter-killer team came into view.

He thought over the neural net and seven helmeted heads swiveled in the dark, in response to his terse command. Weapons came up and seven black-gloved hands moved to safeties and gently thumbed them off.

"I have lock," Doc Hearst whispered. "Tracking." She was holding the left flank and in the darkness her weapon slowly tracked on an invisible target. The eyepiece of her night scope was locked in the eyecup of her battle helmet. The target and acquisition features on her MP-225-N allowed her to lock and fire without necessarily bringing her targeting scope to the eyecup on her helmet but experience had proven that a shooter was more stable and accurate using the systems inherently built into the battle helmet. Where the acquisition and shoot system really shone was while patrolling. Snap shooting from the patrol position had saved more than one point man's life while allowing the team to roll out and outflank a hunter-killer team. Another part of her mind cataloged the hard edge of tension in Jackson's voice. It was feral and a savage elation took shape in her mind.

"Patience," she whispered to herself.

Jackson watched the Caldarian point man. He had gone to ground. His pulse quickened and his mind instantly began analyzing the tactical implications. Some sixth sense born in combat warned Jackson that whatever or whoever was walking point was uneasy and had sensed that they were being watched. An old memory flashed through his mind and he recognized that these were skilled and dangerous professionals stalking them in the darkness. "Point man just went nominal."

He felt the team's heightened acuity across the neural link.

Choi watched the data scroll across his helmet display. The scrolling stopped and he felt a cold needle of dread as he read the data.

"Unknown bio identified as Andorian, Sir," he whispered.

An Andorian tracker! "Shit," Jackson breathed.

"Why aren't they cloaked?" he whispered. "Something's wrong here. We're going to do this real careful and make sure we watch our backs."

"Whoever they are, they're definitely way too serious about their job," Hearst whispered. "Well spaced and spread out. I'd say they're definitely the varsity team. Fourteen against eight, not bad odds," she added as an afterthought.

"It could be worse, Doc," Dyer's thought echoed back. "It could be us in the kill zone." There were no comments.

"Robbie, I'm going to let them close it up as much as I can into the kill zone. I know they're close but with them spread out like they are, we're only going to get one shot at this before they realize what's going down, and then they're going to try and roll us up on the flank and break out. I want you to take out the Andorian first and I want your second shot on the COM man, if you get a second shot. He's two behind the one I think is the officer. In this dark it's hard to say. But the first shot goes to the tracker. Whatever else happens, take him out first.

"Chief, as soon as it starts, hit the transponder. That shuttle is gonna be coming in hot with no brakes and we're gonna be hauling ass to get the hell out of Dodge."

"Aye, Sir," was Senior Chief John Miller's only response.

Weapons Specialist First Class Robert Michael Dyer pressed the contact on his night scope. As it spun up, he placed the custom made eyepiece into the shooting cup of his battle mask and watched as his helmet display spooled the telemetry to his target. Everything came into sharp relief and he could see the Andorian tracker and the COM man clearly. His rifle was a fully automatic and optically integrated Tactical Operations 2351 chambered in .50 caliber. He could let his systems shoot for him, driving nails in the dark at a thousand meters but like most shooters, he preferred doing his shooting manually. He was a purest in the truest sense of the word and a perfectionist when it came to applying his particular deadly art form. His optical system had a built-in shine collector to dampen and absorb 'street shine', the tiny glimmer of detectable light from the reflected light off the forward lens of a light-intensifying night scope. The can or silencer pulled about three minutes of adjustment (MOA) but any silencer does that, and he simply made the proper adjustments to compensate. The rifle and scope were current issue, the stock made of the most highly advanced components in the combined Confederate inventory, overlaid with a composite chameleon skin to match his recon suit.

So, he thought wryly to himself, the Jarheads use the great, great grandchild of the 1996M40A3, and the army ranger teams use an adaptation of the M24 SWS (Sniper Weapon System). Dyer's weapon of choice was the Tango Operations 2351. He loved the big TO-51. It was chambered in .50 Cal and yet it was lighter than one of those ancient, heavy barreled sniper select M-16's in 5.56 that sat in heavy lexite museum cases in the run down, rusty range building in Coronado, California. He tapped in a command on his chin bar and checked the wind and humidity. He made a few minor adjustments and settled down to wait.

"Go to exotic places, meet new people...kill them," he whispered. His heavy weapon swung up, tracked and then settled. "I have lock," he confirmed a moment later. His finger took up the slack and he waited. He watched as the Andorian's head slowly rotated from side to side.

"One two hundred grain, urillium cored, armor piercing, tactical smart-point coming your way," he whispered. "It'll punch through your body armor, even that terrilium field armor you Caldarian recon bastards wear. And I hope you're just regular Caldarian legs and not Legion," he added as an afterthought.

Dyer was brought back to reality by Jackson's terse order. "When I blow the claymores, it's show time. Confirm!"

Jackson listened as each team member confirmed that they were ready. They were using conventional claymores, set 20 meters apart above the path that the Caldarian hunter-killer team was on. The problem was that because of the thick undergrowth and the way the Caldarian team was spread out, a lot of the claymores' lethal force would be absorbed by the thick underbrush.

Jackson allowed the point element of the hunter-killer team to move past the three claymores he had set in the brush above the trail. As the next three Caldarians moved into the kill zone, Jackson hit the clackers and blew the mines. The brush around him erupted as red tracers reached out and converged on the Caldarians. The three on the trail were shredded as they took the full force of the claymores.

Jackson noticed with grim professional respect that the Caldarian team reacted immediately, and the men who were not killed in the initial assault went to ground, while the trailing elements broke out on the left and tried to out-flank Jackson and his men.

You didn't expect this, did you, he thought. You were ready and you knew we had detected you but you didn't expect us to hit you here.

The Andorian's head exploded in a mist of red gore as the big .50 round took him in the right eye. The compensators steadied and the big rifle ejected and fed another round. Dyer shifted smoothly left, the sound-suppressed Tango-2351 coughed once more and the COM man went down, his chest turned to raspberry jam by the heavy, high-powered slug. On exiting, the round destroyed the COM system before it could send its emergency auto signal to whatever Caldarian support units were in the system. Jackson changed magazines and gave the signal to form a skirmish line and advance. The volume of fire increased as the team broke cover and advanced on the Caldarian position. Wicker and Larsen broke right to flank the Caldarian platoon while laying down several slasher rounds from their M2303 rifles. Jackson fired off short, three round bursts as he advanced, letting his targeting system evaluate threats and take them under fire accordingly. A Caldarian rose out of the darkness and Jackson's system swung to the threat axis and fired, stitching him in two rows across his chest and blowing him off the trail, the impact of the rounds making him twitch and gyrate like a puppet on a string.

Suddenly the firing ceased and an eerie silence fell, broken only by the soft gurgling sounds of the dead and dying. The stench of blood and excrement mingled with the acrid aroma of smoke and powder.

"Check," Jackson thought over the neural team net. Far off in the back of Jackson's mind an alarm was screaming at him—something's wrong here, that was way too easy. But for the moment, he pushed it aside.

"Six, clear."

"Five, clear."

"Three, clear."

"Two, clear."

"Four, clear."

"Eight, clear."

"Seven, clear."

Choi bent over one of the gurgling forms and fired once. The form twitched convulsively and lay still. "Chief, did you get the signal out?"

"Yes, Sir."

"Sir," Dyer's urgent whisper pulsated through the team's neural pathways, inducing a release of adrenaline and endorphins, instantly heightening the team's already bowstring tight senses. "You'd better take a look at this."

Jackson moved in a crouch over to where Dyer, weapon still in the ready position, knelt beside what was left of the Caldarian officer. "Boss, did you notice the insignia on their uniform? This isn't your run of the mill hunter-killer team, Sir."

Dyer reached one gloved hand down and turned what was left of the dead Caldarian over.

"I think he was the officer but there's no rank insignia on what's left. He must have been no more than a meter away when the claymores blew."

Jackson looked down at the patch over the left breast of the shredded uniform. A cold knot formed in the pit of his stomach as he recognized the unit designation, a black onyx stone superimposed over a burning planet. "That's impossible!" he breathed. "What's a Black Order platoon doing way out here in this backwater, shit-hole of an uninhabited planet? We just cut down an entire Black Order platoon." The firefight had lasted less than a minute.

Dyer tapped the patch with a gauntleted hand. "Sir, these are the folks responsible for Caldarian security and counter-intelligence. They're assassins and killers but they're full military.

"You and I both know what that means. You only make it into the Legion after two full duty tours. That means two full terran years of active, front line service. Which means the crème de la crème or some such shit.

"What's going on, Sir?" His question hung in the darkness and the team felt a sense of foreboding pressing in on them.

Heads swiveled in the dark to look at Jackson as comprehension dawned. With one hand Jackson reached down and picked up the ceremonial 'Darok' the officer had dropped when he had been hit.

"Legion discipline," he said.

"Yup, two explosive darts in the ear canal is a great incentive for line duty," Wicker responded.

"The coffee, I stayed in because of the coffee," Hearst breathed.

"Choi, give me one full spectrum sweep, all bands. Now!"

The team went silent, their eyes scanning the surrounding darkness, and prayed that their sensors would remain nominal. They didn't.

"Boss?" Dyer said.

"I know," Jackson replied, "we're not alone. They never travel alone. Where's the other team?"

As if in response to his question, he heard Choi's urgent voice over the team net. At the same time, each team member's passive sensors red-lined. "Sir, we got incoming traffic about five hundred meters out. The sensors just went off the board."

A red light suddenly began to blink in the bottom left hand corner of the team's tactical displays.

"Tactical breach!" several voices responded at once.

"They're moving through the cover above us, trying to flank us and they're moving fast," Choi said.

"Why didn't we pick them up until now?"

"I don't know Sir, but we have to move—NOW!"

Jackson checked the team ordinance display. "Chief?" The unspoken question hung in the darkness.

"We're down pretty fine, Sir. DeLuca and Wicker are down to 75 rounds and one slasher round each. The rest of us have less than 30 rounds."

"Redistribute ammo and let's un-ass. Doc, rear security. Chief, you and Choi take point. Let's move, people! Where's that goddamned extraction shuttle?"

"It's inbound," the Chief said.

Going up one, Jackson thought tightly. He switched over to the frigate's frequency and spoke. "Nightshade, Nightshade, this is Stalker. We are hot, repeat, we are hot, over."

"Roger Stalker, you are hot," shuttle pilot Ensign Marcie Chantella replied. "Hang in there, Stalker. ETA 12 mikes, repeat—12 mikes to extraction, over."

"Roger Nightshade, en-route now. We're running and be advised we have a Black Order platoon in pursuit."

Holy shit, Chantella thought to herself, something's wrong here! Where there's a Black Order ground unit, there's a Black Order flight unit as well. "Roger Stalker."

The frigate USS John Hancock was on station in a high polar orbit waiting for the encrypted transmission that would tell her to begin her pick-up run for the recon team. The frigates were fast, highly maneuverable, patrol craft. Captain Lin Zhao stood behind the con. Lines of worry etched the delicate lines of his face. They had been on station for six days. The Hancock had been at general quarters for the entire time, shifting out only to eat and change watch.

The bridge watch was listening to the traffic from the recon team on the surface of the planet. "Ms. Lewis, come to course two-six-seven, mark four-four. Make your speed sub-light 5. Get ready to retract pick-up shuttle and stand by star drive."

"Coming to course two-six-seven, mark four-four, engaging sub-light 5, stand by star drive, aye, Sir," Commander Lewis replied.

"Disengage chameleon mode on my mark: four, three, two, one, mark."

"Chameleon mode disengaged, Captain." Commander Debra Lewis was 28 years old, held a PHD in astral navigation and was generally conceded by her peers to be one of the best frigate drivers in the fleet. She also had feelings for Lieutenant Jackson but that fact was a carefully guarded secret—for the moment. The Confederacy found that women had a better aptitude for piloting than men did and most of the pilots in the fleet were women. Not only did they excel at flying but for some strange reason they seemed to add a quality of peace and confidence to the bridge—an aura, as captain Zhao had once observed. Right now, the aura was stressed. Everyone on the bridge had heard Jackson's terse comments about the platoon of "Blackies" on the planet surface.

The frigate edged out of her polar orbit and began the run to recover her shuttle and the recon team. "Mother Hen, Nightshade One is commencing her run, 56 kilometers out and closing, altitude 3,000 meters," the voice of Marcie Chantella said.

"Roger that. Nightshade, be advised..."

A shocking explosion ripped through the frigate's port nacelle and raked her port side. Decks 3 through 9 were immediately vented into the vacuum of space. Everything within those decks was decompressed and sucked out. Bodies imploded and then froze in grotesque forms as they floated in a sub-orbital cloud around the stricken frigate.

"Where did that come from?" Captain Zhao shouted.

"Sir, sensors show nothing at all out to maximum range but the residual halo signature is consistent with Caldarian main battle class particle weapons."

"What?" Zhao exclaimed. "That doesn't make sense!"

"Helm—course one-zero-five, mark four-two, full sensor sweep off the port quarter, full sub-light now!"

"One-zero-five, mark four-two, full sub, aye, Captain!" Lewis' hands flew over the NAV console. "Come on baby," she whispered, "come on." The frigate's nose clawed about in a hard turn, trying to find her unseen antagonist and bring her weapons to bear. She staggered and reeled as a second broadside tore into her. The frigate had no armor and her energy envelope had been off-line but now it was gone, destroyed in the initial attack by her unknown and unseen assailant. Built fast but built light, the frigates depended on their speed to move them out of harm's way if necessary, and on their sophisticated sensors to warn them well in advance of any threat. She was dying.

"All hands, this is the Captain. Abandon ship. Repeat, abandon ship. Initiate escape pod auto-countdown. All crew members, man your designated escape pods.

Lewis undid her battle harness, grabbed her survival pack and ran for her pod. Entering, she turned and locked out the auto eject system, turned on the pod's internal NAV system and set the NAV console to manual flight mode. She then put on her EVA helmet, locked it down, strapped herself into her seat and hit the eject bar only just in time. As the pod ejected, it tumbled on its axis as the frigate was hammered again. Four pods in front of her exploded from unseen fire, the closeness of the explosions making her pod cartwheel as it spun out of control toward the planet's surface. Lewis decided to let it tumble before she brought it back under control.

Just in case, she thought. Lieutenant Commander Debra Lewis was going to land 2,000 meters northwest of the Secondary LZ.

A fourth series of smashing blows hit the Hancock again amidships, gutting the bridge and blowing a 35-meter hole in her side. The bridge structure collapsed and a steel truss fell across the Captain, crushing his armored suit. But he didn't feel it. He was already dead, his decapitated head spinning and bouncing off the torn bulkhead as blood spurted from his torso to freeze and mingle with the viscera and other body parts on the destroyed bridge. The frigate corkscrewed end over end, out of control, picking up momentum as the gravitational forces of the planet tugged at her, her outer hull already starting to glow as she entered the atmosphere.

Stunned, Ensign Chantella sat rigid at the shuttle controls and listened in horror to the death throws of the Hancock and her crew. "Gone, blown away, and we don't even have a clue what or who did it," she whispered. Then discipline and training took over and she overrode the auto NAV system, savaging the controls, banking the shuttle down and around on its final approach to the extraction LZ.

"Stalker, Stalker, this is Nightshade, over."

"Nightshade, we have you on chameleon-track, two clicks out at our twelve o'clock, over," Jackson responded.

"Roger your twelve o'clock, authenticate."

"Authentication code sent, Nightshade."

"Confirm authentication code, shuttle in auto sequence now, elevation 50 meters, rate of descent 0.2 meters per second, confirm ground zero now, Stalker. Nightshade turning Chameleon mode off, shuttle door opening."

"Roger, Nightshade."

Jackson dove and rolled for cover as particle fire rippled into the tree he had been standing behind moments before. The team had been running and trying to disengage from whomever or whatever was following them but every time they thought they had evaded, particle fire would hit them. They couldn't see the source and whoever was shooting was completely cloaked.

"Wicker, Larsen, when I give the word, lay your last slasher rounds down the edge of the trail." The team could feel the disciplined calm flowing from Jackson's neural link. It steadied them as they moved, trying to break contact. "Chief, you and Dyer grab Choi and go for the shuttle. Once you're inside, cover us and we'll make our move."

Choi groaned unconsciously. He had taken a particle shot in the lower abdomen. His suit electronics had been overloaded from the hit and the dense beam had torn through a lung. "Nightshade, lay your phase cannon on the tree line along the bottom of the trail and set for auto engage, deflection sixty degrees."

"Roger Stalker, engaging now."

"OK Chief, NOW! Go, go, go!" Wicker and Larsen dumped their last slasher rounds down the trail line and there was a high pitched hum as the auto cannon from the shuttle began to see-saw back and forth, chewing up foliage and hopefully anything else that might be out there. Jackson, Wicker and Larson retreated, expending the last of their ammunition as they converged on the shuttle. As they clambered aboard, Chantella already had the shuttle engaged and was lifting off when a series of flashes and crashes hammered against the shuttle's hull plating.

"Particle rifle fire," Jackson breathed. But the shuttle was already gone, its terrain-hugging guidance system keeping it low and fast as it hedgehopped at Mach 3.

"Sir, the Hancock's gone."

"I know Ensign, I heard," Jackson replied gently. "Take us to the secondary insertion point."

"Sir?" Chantella exclaimed.

"So we can find out who the hell is shooting at us and who or what killed the Hancock and why this place is so important."

"Aye, Sir, engaging chameleon mode and initiating auto navigation for secondary LZ." It was only then that Chantella realized that Jackson's hands were shaking.

Five hundred and fifty kilometers above them, a shape slowly began to materialize. The lesser stars behind it twinkled briefly, then went out as the shape took on substance and etched itself against the background darkness. It had no color. It seemed to absorb the darkness, like light was being squeezed away from it. Sleek and deadly, the shape exuded lethality. It was the Sipedesis, a Viper Class Caldarian cruiser. On her darkened bridge, a voice spoke quietly to the other individuals gathered there. "Well done, Legate Dra. The Confederate frigate did not detect us. We were able to close the distance to one kilometric and engage them at point blank range."

"Consul, the shuttle escaped," the legate replied.

"As planned," the Consul responded. "Our recon team will find them and terminate the survivors. The Confederates are already on their way to their secondary insertion point, running swiftly into the net we have set for them. All we need is the last piece of the puzzle."

"And why Consul, has this isolated, dreary planet suddenly become so important to us and the Confederates?"

Va's eyes took on an obsidian cast and his voice held a subtle edge of menace when he spoke.

"Return to our baseline and continue our patrol. Unless I am totally mistaken, the Confederates will be sending a reaction force from their dwindling fleet to this...(What did you call it?)...dreary, isolated planet soon."

In the clearing, on the ground that the shuttle had recently departed from, fourteen figures materialized from the background of the surrounding forest. A shimmer, a flicker in the darkness on a hostile world, they took shape—dark, composite body-armor merging with the night, shadows within shadows. Their battle masks gave them a stark menacing appearance. A solitary patch was the only break in the totally black durilium armor, a black onyx stone superimposed on a burning planet. The tallest knelt and spoke quietly into his tactical COM. "Viper wing, position secure. Decoy team terminated, over."

Five hundred and fifty kilometers above them, a single word was coded and transmitted on the sub-space-encrypted frequency used only by the Black Order Legion.

Beyond the dark confines of a system designated only as Alpha-237, a flattened, cylindrical object began to execute a series of high-speed course changes on a pre-programmed route designed to allow it to egress the system undetected. It then turned to course one-seven-four-prime and accelerated to maximum star drive. It was a deep space slot buoy that had been automatically ejected from the dead frigate as soon as the NAV system had detected the auto eject sequence beginning on the escape pods. The slot buoy's navigational computer was continually updated live from the frigate's main NAV system so that, if condition "Styx" was ever reached, the buoy would have the frigate's last known coordinates locked in its computer. It was so nicknamed in a dark attempt at humor by the Confederate navy, after the river in Greek mythology that separated the land of the living from the land of the dead.

Course one-seven-four-prime was a dead run home to the Lexington in Battle Group Six, holding station in the Degus system, once the evasive course maneuvers were completed. The onboard navigational system charted its course and made corrections to flat-line for home. The moment it settled onto its base course, it began sending a single encrypted pulse transmission. It would do this for six hours and then onboard charges would detonate, the buoy having completed its specific mission.

The Hancock was dead. The Caldarians were coming. It had begun...

CHAPTER 2
CONFERENCE

*"War is cruelty. There's no use trying to reform it;
the crueler it is, the sooner it will be over."*

—William Tecumseh Sherman

Admiral David Greig, commanding officer of Confederate Battle Group Six on the Carrier USS Lexington, was always impressed at the complex choreography of a Battle Group traveling in formation. His day cabin, located one deck above the Lexington's battle bridge, had a panoramic view of the fleet. At the center of the group were the carriers that held the fighter wing and attack elements of the group. It was also the group tactical command center. The carrier's single purpose was to deliver a weighted, alpha strike against the enemy and allow the capital ships to close with the main elements of the enemy group. There were cruisers—fast, heavily armed and lethal in the extreme. Then there were the hundreds of destroyers, frigates and droid craft that carried out patrol and picket duty and acted as harassing forces in the enemies' rear and flanks. First contact usually meant detection by the picket craft, the destroyers and the frigates on long range sensors. And then, Greig thought as he smiled grimly to himself, the old axiom that a battle plan never survived the first contact with the enemy usually proved itself true.

"It sure has this far," he said out loud.

Greig had a reputation for having a temper. He was fair with his men but hell on wheels when it came to fighting. His standing orders were simple: attack, attack, attack. He had grown up on the deep space station Meridian, located in the Bersilus sector. His father had been a marine colonel attached to the First Marine Division on the frontier world of Vandara and had been killed in an ambush set by the planet's Uridian crystal-smuggling warlord. The Marines had been sent in to interdict the crystal smuggling. Greig was fourteen years old when his father was killed and he never forgot his father's parting words.

"Bullies are cowards, Son. The only thing they understand is force. They misconstrue compassion and restraint as weakness. Never run from a bully, Son," he had said. "Sooner or later you will have to decide to stand and fight. And when you decide to fight, there is only one way to fight and that's to win." His father had clutched him and whispered, "I love you, Son," and disappeared into the transport.

Greig had taken his father's advice to heart. The station where his mother taught Terran-English in one of the mid-grade schools was a hellhole with a population of fifteen thousand mostly transients, ninety-five percent thieves and cut throats, the other five percent, victims. Greig was small for his age and when it was known that his father was the marine colonel who had been killed on Vandara, he became a target. He was bullied mercilessly, punched, kicked, spit on, his possessions stolen and his clothing torn. He realized that his father's words were true. Instead of scaring him, it built a white-hot fire of rage inside him. He made his plans. He had been training in traditional Shotokan Japanese Karate since he was six and his father had begun training him in Hideyuki Ashihara, known as fighting karate, at eight.

He went to the old marine gunnery sergeant who was posted to the station and asked if he would teach him how to fight like his father. The old marine had looked at him with his hard, flat, black eyes and taken him into the gym and began to work with him. Greig's body became lean and hard and he moved with the lithe suppleness of a stalking panther. The bruises healed and he waited, biding his time.

One day, as he was leaving the holo theater, Greig was confronted by three teens who had made a habit of beating him and stealing whatever they felt like taking at the time.

There was a soft snick as the leader's switchblade opened. "Hey, you little piece of shit, what'd you bring us today? Did your whoring momma pack us some lunch, you little shit?"

Greig ran but he ran with a purpose. He darted down a passageway that was dimly lit and the three thugs followed him in. They had done this countless times before and usually caught up with him as he streaked for the passage behind the quarters where he and his mother lived. This time, he swung right and waited. The three teens raced along and turned the corner but stopped when they couldn't see Greig in front of them. Greig stepped out behind the three unsuspecting teens.

"Looking for me?" he asked softly. They turned toward him, startled, and he waded in. His first kick caught the rear thug in the groin and as he doubled over in pain, Greig brought his knee up to meet his face and smashed his nose. The teen dropped to the pavement unconscious, blood flowing from his broken nose. Greig then pivoted and blocked a wild punch from the second teen and landed two hard, heart punches that staggered the older boy, the extended knuckles of his index and middle fingers breaking the small, spoon-shaped bone of his solar plexus and lacerating his liver.

He turned toward the leader who was standing with a sardonic grin on his face. The leader swung his blade. "Just you and me, piss ant. You like steel? I'm gonna dice you and piss on the chunks," he taunted.

He moved in but Greig was ready. His months of practice with the marine platoon had shown him what came next. Greig waited and as the leader swung, he moved. He blocked the knife and grabbed the leader's wrist and arm as he came in. He pivoted, grasping the knife hand and with the leverage he had, broke the leader's arm at the elbow joint as he brought his other forearm across. The leader screamed in agony and fell to his knees. Greig stepped back. "Get up, tough guy," he said. The leader lunged to his feet and swung his good arm at Greig. Greig moved in and proceeded to beat him senseless. He broke his nose and pulped his lips to a bloody hash. With an open hand thrust, he broke a rib. As the leader lay bleeding on the ground, Greig bent down and whispered in his ear.

"Here are the rules, tough guy. You send anybody after me, I kill them and then I go hunting and I kill you with this." He picked up the leader's switchblade, closed the blade and laid it on his chest. He stood up and walked away. When he got home that night, Greig took down the Academy application cube his father had given him, put it on his desk and activated the timer. Three years later, when the Academy detected the pulse transmission from the application cube, he walked through the gates of the Confederate Naval Academy on Urilis-Prime.

He let his mind drift back in time, wondering how history would record this moment.

In 2091, Dr. William Dernelli came to work at the NRL to task the lagging research in star drive technology. In 2097, he unveiled his prototype star drive in a Lockheed Martin Delta cargo carrier. The canister type cargo platform was altered to house Dr. Dernelli's star drive system and first launch was scheduled for October 14, 2100. The flight lasted exactly twenty-three minutes. In that twenty-three minutes, Dr. Dernelli made history.

When he brought his star drive engines online, the astonished ground control stations watched as the Phoenix vanished off every tracking scope on the planet. The tracking station circling Mars and the one further out at Neptune station didn't even get a reading. It was as if the Phoenix had ceased to exist. One second she was on the scope, the next she was gone. Twenty-three minutes later, she reappeared in stationary orbit around the earth. The only difference was that she had been half way to Alpha Centauri and back again in that twenty-three minute segment of time.

As the Confederacy melded technologies, naval academies sprung up in various locations and armed forces traded technology and training facilities on a number of different worlds. But that changed forever in 2245.

A deep space research station on the edge of Confederate space suddenly detected the movement of a large formation of unknown vessels that materialized out of nowhere, closing the station at speed. The sensors detected a star drive signature of a type and variant unknown within the Confederacy. The station commander hailed them repeatedly with no response and decided to notify Confederate naval authorities as a precautionary measure.

The hair began to prickle on the back of his neck and his intuition told him that he and his station were in serious trouble. He was correct. But he never got to prove his premonition. A screening frigate on the outer starboard edge of the formation immediately broke position and closed the station. Seconds after the station commander began to transmit his sub-space message, the frigate opened fire.

Two research teams had spent six months on the surface conducting research. The station had no shields or weapons of any kind. All of its personnel were civilian.

The two teams of research biologists and paleontologists on the planet surface tried unsuccessfully to contact the station and figured that they would try again on the net that evening, a routine that had become part of their regular daily ritual for the last six months. What wasn't part of their ritual was the black, armored troop carrier with a platoon of black-clad soldiers that touched down at their camp and systematically and with surgical precision, slaughtered every single person on the planet surface. Before he died, one of the scientists noticed an insignia patch over the right breast of each soldier—a black onyx stone superimposed on a burning planet.

Greig put his hand on the Alumina-matrix view port. Even though the matrix was a meter and a half thick, his fingers still tingled as though needles were being driven into the tips from the security field surrounding the port. He could feel the tingling pain as it moved up his hand, following the nerve path to his brain. He knew that if it reached his brain, it would kill him. He enjoyed pushing the envelope of his tolerance.

The bastards, he thought as he pulled his hand away from the view port, those murdering bastards who commit sentient genocide on a planetary scale, whole civilizations blotted out, entire systems! The Pretharians and the mild-mannered Carans, who believed up until the last moment that they could reason with the Caldarians. And the look of utter hopeless terror and anguish in Ambassador Mira Siralis' eyes as she and the one hundred and twenty-three children inside the control bunker with her dissolved into a puddle of residual protein resin from the genetic blast that killed her planet.

Greig and his bridge crew had watched the transmission as they raced for the Veran system, powerless to intervene.

"Yes," he spoke softly, "I'm coming for you."

Greig came back to the present at the persistent chiming of his Command COM.

Commander Tom McGivens' face appeared on Greig's view screen. "Sir, Admiral Aiko and Admiral Chesterton have arrived from the Zuikaku and the Illustrious. Regent Kandor will be arriving shortly by shuttlecraft. Dr. Zhao and Commander Weir are already in the briefing room."

"Alright, Tom, I'll be down shortly. Tell the steward to bring the coffee and Myloen mead into the briefing room and ask Captain McMann to join us."

"Aye Sir," McGivens replied and signed off.

Greig passed his palm over a COM disk.

"Captain McMann?" he called.

"Here, Admiral," McMann replied at once.

"Captain, make a signal to all fleet units. Set the acquisition grid to active and charge all particle coils to one hundred and ten percent."

Greig paused for a moment to let that sink in and to see if McMann made a comment. There was none.

"I want to cut through those bastards' reactive plating and I want the re-absorption nodes set multi-band active. Anything that hits us, I want it re-directed right up their ass the moment the nodes go active and a detection pulse makes breach. No lag time, no safeties. They hit us, we don't run. We're going to make them pay for every parsec they try to push us back."

"Aye Sir," was all McMann said, and then the COM went dead.

Greig turned to the picture of his wife and spoke softly, "God help us all, Annie," and exited his day cabin. The marine guard came to attention and saluted as Greig exited and made his way to the lift station. He stepped into the holographic chamber that scanned his DNA and the blood code chip that all Confederate personnel had implanted after they passed boot.

Once cleared, he rode the short distance to the main briefing room beside the Combat Information Center, where he was greeted by a hard-eyed marine Gunny sergeant who gave him a salute and a curt, "Good morning, Admiral," as he passed into the briefing room.

"Ladies and Gentlemen, let's get started. I'm going to give you a short overview and then Dr. Zhao is going to brief us on a development that until today has been code black, and very few people within the command structure know of its existence. Its code name is 'Element'. The document brief each of you has in front of you is considered so sensitive that it was handled by courier instead of the secure FTL (faster than light) channel we usually use for passing highly sensitive traffic."

If Greig had only their partial attention before, he had their undivided attention now. He let his gaze scan the group. Only Commander Alex Weir's face bore no expression. His hard, seasoned eyes gazed back at Greig as if he had just asked if he would like to take a stroll around the Lexington's training deck.

"It is UCT (United Confederate Time) 247.0813, 12:20 inter-galactic time. Today we received a pulse transmission from the Hancock's slot buoy. It was code black, which means that the Hancock is dead and we don't know who or what killed her. She was operating covertly in support of a SEAL recon team in a system designated as Alpha-237, on a small M-class planet named Zilith. After Dr. Zhao brings us all up to speed on 'Element', Commander Weir will brief us on Mike Platoon, operating on Zilith."

Dr. Lucinda Zhao was a tall, handsome woman whose shoulders had a permanent hunch to them from too much time bent over test equipment in her laboratory on Urilis Prime. Her shoulder length black hair had no hint of gray and her deep green eyes held an intensity that usually left people with the impression that she was not a person to be taken lightly. It was an impression she cultivated.

Right now she looked somewhat wrinkled in the blue transition suit she had been given to wear while recovering from traveling in a class four, high speed courier capsule for the last 72 hours. The suit did nothing to hide her tight, athletic figure. She was 48 years old. Her husband had been killed when a geophysical research platform monitoring the fluctuations of a gas giant on the edge of the Rygelan system lost its reactor fusion pods.

"Thank you, Admiral Greig. Several years ago, Dr. Kai, directed by the Confederate Naval Research office based on Earth Prime, was given the responsibility of weapons research and development. At the time, we were asked to seek new technology and to use whatever measures necessary to buy or negotiate technology that we did not currently have within our inventory. You are all familiar with the new integrated Chameleon deck-plating that is now standard on all Confederate military vessels. What you are not familiar with is the fact that up until two years ago, our cloaking technology was nowhere near that advanced. That technology was acquired from the Botth.

"Within the Berilian System, there are three inhabited planets, all of which have a thriving inter-planetary trading agreement. As you all know, the Botth are new members of the Confederacy, just now on the brink of star travel. They are on the brink of star travel because we traded technologies. They received the patents on first-generation Dernelli star drive engines and we received design patents to their Chameleon cloaking technology, which their military has used for over one hundred and fifty years. As you are also aware, that technology does not produce a one hundred percent cloaked sensor wash."

"There is no true cloaking," Regent Kandor broke in. "Even the Caldarians don't have cloaking ability greater than eighty-seven percent."

"There is now," Dr. Zhao answered softly. "The Element provides true cloaking." She paused for a moment to allow that fact to sink into their consciousnesses.

As marine plants sway and are pulled by the current, Greig felt the dark undercurrents of emotion move and ripple toward Lucinda Zhao as she talked. He glanced sideways at McMann and wondered if he was having a hard time controlling his feelings for Lucinda. Urilian females had a unique empathic ability to arouse and control their male counterparts. He knew they were trained to contain and control their abilities but he also knew that under stress and duress, some of that ability "leaked out" as their intensity grew. He shuddered at the thought of a rogue Urilian female loose on the Lexington.

When she continued, there was a hard, brittle edge to her voice. "Dr. Winston Green discovered the 'element' while investigating the anomalous geophysical recordings received from an unmanned, deep space geophysical probe on a dark planet in an uncharted parsec beyond the furthest edges of Confederate space. The Confederate NRS had launched the probe in 2230 as a combined research/exploratory project, and it had been more or less forgotten in light of more pressing and immediate developments and concerns. As the probe continued on its course into the unknown expanse of the galaxy beyond Confederate space, its electronic brain dutifully performed the execution and recording of geophysical data that it routinely coded and transmitted once every 36 hours to the Confederate research facility on Urilis."

She paused for a moment and let her eyes scan the room.

"In a sweep of an unknown system designated as Alpha-237, with three M-class planets, a smaller, fourth planet was found whose magnetic poles were strangely shifted. The planets were officially designated as Vedra, Melkor, Zelon and Zilith, named for the Urilian's four mystical gods of war. It was Dr. Aolan Kai, a geophysicist from the Varanthian system, who designed the probe's sensitive suite of geophysical standoff survey software, enabling it to have a much narrower survey envelope.

"Zilith is a geologist's dream come true. It's a planet that is currently in geologic upheaval. Rings of active volcanoes spread across the surface of the planet from the northern pole to the south polar regions.

"It would have been overlooked except for the fact that the preliminary sweep indicated that there were huge formations of a highly conductive material called graphitic schist. Generally, minerals having a metallic luster such as pyrite, chalcopyrite and galena are good conductors. Graphite and graphitic shales and schists, pyrolusite, etc., are also good conductors. But it wasn't just any graphitic schist. It was here that the software designed by Dr. Kai hit pay dirt. The software was designed so that if any conductive material was detected that could possibly be host material for critical, metallurgical ore, the probe would automatically run the filtering parameters built into the software and narrow the search for specific material associated with the host formation. The concept behind the software was deceptively simple..."

"Meaning by association that if we find a certain type of ore within a certain type of host rock, the same pattern should repeat itself anywhere in the galaxy," Regent Kandor stated flatly.

"Exactly," Dr. Zhao said.

"On detecting the huge graphitic conductor deep below the surface of Zilith, the probe's electronic brain began running its narrowed sensor sweep of the planet. It altered course for a single orbital run around the planet before it was once again flung out into deep space to continue its long journey. Its sensors probed and recorded what the filtered sweep detected and then its navigational system fixed its position in relation to its overall mission and once again slung it toward deep space and darkness. Thirty-six hours later, the recorded logs were encoded and a single pulse transmission on a pre-set frequency was sent to Dr. Kai on Urilis. The probe continued on its way, totally unaware and unconcerned over the furor its findings caused when we down-linked the data."

She paused and Greig sensed she was striving to control herself. A barely perceptible shudder seemed to pass over her and when she continued, her voice held an edge of iron control.

"The graphitic host rock was of a type first found on a volcanic world discovered in the Pyrillis system. The host rock contained a type of metal ore called triplex magnetite. This iron ore was used to blend and manufacture a very strong metal used as hull plating in Confederate vessels. It was light and strong, could withstand tremendous battle damage, and could be used to design a type of reactive armor plating that was light years ahead of current technology."

"And?" Admiral Chesterton asked the question.

"We found the triplex magnetite. We also found the 'element'."

"When Doctor Green first reviewed the data, he was convinced that the unusual readings bore closer scrutiny. A research team was commissioned and some of the best geophysicists and drive coil engineers in the Confederacy were tasked with the specific mandate of determining what was causing the geomagnetic anomalies. The research vessel Terra, the most advanced and well-equipped research platform within the Confederacy, was commissioned as the mother ship, and would remain in stationary orbit to provide long term support, provisioning and backup for the field teams. It was more than just a utilitarian space platform. For Dr. Green and his research team, it was essentially home. It had been designed and built with the intention that, in all likelihood, it would be home for the team for a very long time and as a consequence, it was made to be as spacious and habitable as possible. It was as well equipped and provisioned as any planet-side research facility and fabrication lab within the Confederacy, and its power supply could remain online at full capacity for several decades. On minimal life support, it could support the team in stasis indefinitely.

"The primary mission was to determine if the deposit contained any peripheral ore deposits that could be used to give the Confederacy new technology. Eighteen months ago, when war broke out, we realized how far ahead of us the Caldarians were, technology-wise, and we notified Dr. Green on Zilith that this project now had priority. Enduring incredible hardships on this strange, dark planet that seemed to be in perpetual twilight, almost as if daylight was being sucked into the very heart of the planet, Dr. Green made an astonishing discovery.

"While surveying a narrow, rock-strewn canyon, they came upon a small volcanic vent. The vent led in and down from the base of the cliff, into the side of the canyon wall itself. The passageway wound down and bottomed out five hundred meters below the bottom elevation of the canyon floor, into a large underground cavern. They had come equipped to spend several days and decided to set up camp within the cavern itself. Although warm, the air was clean and seemed to be moving toward the surface. They set up their sensor grid, rigged the auto-defense perimeter and set the beacon locator, designed to be detectable from five kilometers underground, to enable the circling mother ship and the follow-on support team to find them without difficulty."

"Dr., excuse me for the interruption but can we cut to the chase here without all the geological minutia?" Admiral Akai asked.

Greig looked over at Admiral Akai. He knew the enormous stress they were all under and how difficult it was for a man like Chuichi Akai to remain and sit patiently. His squadron had been hammered by the Caldarians at the battle of the Hurlis Gate and he had withdrawn his battered forces through the Merlock Corridor. That he had been able to withdraw at all with any of his forces was a tribute to his tactical brilliance and his undying loyalty to his men. It was there that the Caldarians had bled and realized that they weren't going to gain a quick victory.

"Yes, the minutia is essential to your understanding," Lucinda Zhao replied softly. "You don't understand the danger yet and the dark chasm we are all hanging over, but you shall." The very softness of her voice sent a shiver of fear rippling across the room.

Admiral Akai rose and bowed and then sat down, and Lucinda continued.

"The floor of the canyon was actually the cupola of a huge batholith. Batholiths are magmatic intrusions of hot, molten magma that thrust up through the planet's crust from deep within the planet core, penetrating into the surrounding host rock. They have no bottom and may be dozens of miles wide and hundreds of miles long. In many mineral districts, there is a zonal arrangement of ore minerals that extend outward from the hot center of the intrusive itself. Basically, what this means is that hotter temperature minerals cool off closest to the center of the intrusive, while lower-temperature minerals cool off and form last on the outer periphery. The floor of the valley was, in reality, the eroded roof edge of the ancient magmatic intrusive.

"Spiraling up beneath the actual cupola was a thin vein of very dense ore that was older still than the intrusive itself. Millions of years before the geological epoch that formed the batholith, we believe a meteorite composed of the 'element' slammed into the host rock and plunged into the magmatic chamber deep within the planet's core. There its alien complexity responded to the tremendous heat it recognized, and the alien element elasticized within the geological matrix of the seething sea of magma struggling toward the surface. Spawned in an alien galaxy older than time itself, it had crossed a rift of time and distances so vast that it was immeasurable. Denser than any known substance and composed of a chemical matrix that fed and regenerated itself, it morphed and reconstructed itself within the magma chamber, absorbing and adapting until it had stabilized at twenty thousand degrees Celsius. An epoch later, a convulsion of the planet's crust lifted a thin vein from the swirling magma chamber in a spiraling pipe. The 'element', caught up in the rising magmatic intrusion, climbed twelve thousand miles. Boring and cutting inexorably through cold host rock to within eight hundred meters of the planet's surface, it cooled once again into dormancy, allowing it's elasticized matrix to fan out in stringer fissures within the central zone of the batholith's cupola, harder than death, strong in it's infinite patience. The combined action of time and erosion had exposed one of the veins in a lateral fan that was now exposed on the walls of the cavern.

"The deep Azurite hue of the substance exposed on the cavern walls drew Dr. Green and his team like a beacon but it wasn't until they began their testing and scanning that they began to realize that the substance within the igneous intrusive was not native to the planet of Zilith. Its chemical composition was unknown and when the research team finally managed to extract a sample and subject it to tests, it produced some startling results. The first surprise was that it had a crystalline lattice structure roughly similar to the Uridian crystals used in star drive power modules. It was also harder than any known metal and beyond any current metallurgical science the Confederates had. It was there however, that any similarities ceased.

"Dr. Green and his team of researchers took a sample of the material back on board the Terra and began the tedious and time consuming, but critical process of mapping the unknown substance's physical, chemical and energy characteristics. What they discovered sent a ripple of fear through them all. It gave off no energy transmissions of any detectable type within the known spectrum, and it regenerated itself and consumed all traces of residual waste at the molecular level. In other words, the strange element was self-sustaining."

"You mean," Regent Kandor broke in, "this element provides true cloaking ability?"

"Yes! But it is far more than cloaking technology. The substance code-named 'Element' provides true cloaking. It also has unique power capabilities. Ten kilograms can power a battle carrier and its particle weapons with no detectable power signature. There is no detectable waste and it regenerates internally."

"How do you know this for sure?" Kandor asked.

"Because we have Dr. Green's field reports and we've built a complete holographic model of a fleet class destroyer drive module," Lucinda said. "All we need is the actual Element power pack Green was bringing out."

Complete silence filled the room. Only the quiet hum of the holographic displays and security dampers could be heard. Each individual realized the implications of what Dr. Zhao had just said.

"But I thought we had no hard intelligence on this project!" Admiral Chesterton exclaimed.

"Our office, in conjunction with Admiral Tra on Urilis, has received routine slot buoy transmissions from Dr. Green's team every ten days since he first arrived on Zilith five years ago. What we don't have, are samples of the element," Lucinda responded. "That was coming out when Green disappeared."

McMann was watching Lucinda intently. He sensed, rather than saw the tensing of her muscles and how she collected herself before continuing. He wanted somehow, in some way, to reach out and touch her to let her know that this was all going to go away and that life was going to continue on just as it always had in the past. But his instincts and training told him that whatever transpired here, nothing would ever be the same again.

"When Dr. Green subjected the element to the narrow beam of a drive pre-coil laser, the extremely high temperature beam had a dramatic affect. The element, which had resisted every attempt to extract even a molecule, began to glow a deep, azure blue and to shape-shift, conforming to the small test container it had been placed in. Suddenly, a high frequency hum that hurt the ears emanated from the test sample, rising quickly in pitch until it was outside the aural range of everyone in the room. But the most intriguing surprise was what it did to the sensitive electronic equipment monitoring the element.

"The readings went off the scope. Tri-lithium-molecular detection scopes registered and flickered momentarily, and then settled back to nominal reading, even as the power monitors continued to climb beyond the highest known capabilities of any power generating device we own. It sucked power from the laser, and the limiting capacitors and diodes in the laser itself blew, and it automatically went into emergency shut down sequence. The element had resumed its conformal elasticity but the power monitors connected to the sample were still drawing power at a phenomenal rate—enough power by the indications to power a star drive. But there were no emissions, no evidence that the element was giving off any waste products and there was no power signature of any type emanating from the element. Green and his team powered every system down except the monitors and still the power readings climbed. It was self-generating. And then momentarily, in a nanosecond, every person in the room sensed a kaleidoscopic waterfall of emotion that surged and crashed through every mind and then vanished as quickly as it had begun, leaving each person with the impression that some tremendous, singular event had just taken place. It was as if the element morphed and blinked awake and then shut down again."

There was a sudden stunned silence in the room and Lucinda could feel their shock and fear as sudden understanding dawned. It filled her mind and her empathic receptors began to respond to the aural energy she was capturing.

"Yes," she whispered. "We believe it's sentient."

Greig felt his skin crawl in the dead silence that ensued.

CHAPTER 3
CONFINES

"Be convinced that to be happy means to be free
and that to be free means to be brave.
Therefore do not take lightly the perils of war."

—Thucydides

"We believe that something far more malignant than Caldarians has been discovered on Zilith. And if this 'Element' is as singularly unique as we think it is, it will shift the balance of power overnight. But the far more important question is what is it and what are its intentions, if it has any intentions at all and is not just some form of beacon? And we don't think it's just a beacon."

"Why?" Chesterton asked.

"Because Dr. Green's report says they all felt something, like a presence, a conscious malice that stirred and was immediately aware of them and then went silent."

"Our ships will..." Admiral Chesterton began but Greig cut him off.

"Our ships will never see it if we don't find out what happened to the Hancock and where Mike Platoon is," Admiral Greig broke in. "Commander?"

Commander Weir stood up, moved to the holographic control panel and held his right palm over the control disk. It displayed an image of a heavily forested planet. His thumb and index finger worked the frontal display and a dark landscape that was dominated by volcanic ridges and plateaus as far as the eye could see, came into focus.

"This is the planet Zilith, where Dr. Green found the substance code named 'element'. The Hancock's mission was to find Dr. Green or information that would lead to his recovery or location, and to recover any portion of the element they could and courier it back to Confederate lines. We had lots of electronic intelligence on the planet but nothing we could trust. We suspect that the Caldarians have somehow tapped into our security network and that we've been compromised.

"Dr. Green and his team of researchers realized the staggering strategic and tactical potential of this unknown substance. It could power starships almost indefinitely, make them undetectable and permit true, real-time cloaking ability. Moreover, the element could be utilized at the tactical level. Particle weapons would give off no energy signature of any type. Powered battle armor and recon suits would be virtually invisible to all detection technology known to be in either the Caldarian or Confederate inventories. In short, it would shift the balance of power to us overnight and give us overwhelming tactical and strategic superiority."

"Please explain," Admiral Aiko asked.

"Dr. Green had worked in Confederate intelligence doing political studies based on theoretical projections of power shifts within galactic governments, obtaining what is referred to as an orogenetic discovery.

"Orography is the branch of physical science dealing with the formation of mountains. Some orogenetic events such as volcanoes and earthquakes are so violent and quick in the context of geological time that they completely alter the landscape and remake the topography," Weir explained. "A political orogenetic event is a sudden and complete shift of power due to an unprecedented and sudden technological breakthrough. It would be like the ancient Britons suddenly acquiring particle cannon technology. The political and economic shift of power would be swift, violent and complete.

"Green realized the element was such a find. He was alarmed at his discovery and immediately dispatched a top-priority message to Admiral Madra Tra of the Confederate Research division stationed on Urilis-Prime."

"And this operation is starting to unravel and come apart at the seams?" Admiral Aiko responded.

"Yes Admiral, it is. The Confederacy is dying. We're being pressured relentlessly by the Caldarians. That's why we sent SEAL Team One, Earth-Prime in to recon. They were operating under total electronic silence. They were only to break silence when the mission requirements had been met and they called for extraction. If everything went as planned, and we are assuming it didn't, that should have happened at 14:00 galactic time, UCT 247.0810. That was three days ago."

"What were Green's operational orders from Admiral Tra?" Kandor asked.

"Admiral Tra's reply was succinct. Green was to continue the project with utmost haste.

"As I've already mentioned, we believe that in some way, the Caldarians breached our security and we've been compromised. We believe that, as Dr. Green and Dr. Wurst were exiting the system in a high-speed courier transport, they were captured.

"He and Dr. Wurst had agreed to have tricynic capsules surgically implanted in their dental plates before they left on this mission. They work instantly and painlessly. They would be dead in milliseconds."

Regent Kandor stirred but remained silent.

"And your interpretation of the data, Commander?" Admiral Greig asked.

"Sir, our interpretation of the data we have is that Green and his entire team are dead, and SEAL Team One has made contact with Caldarian ground units and is now on the run. Whether or not they acquired intelligence concerning the element is unknown at this time." He hesitated.

Greig raised an eyebrow in inquiry but remained silent, letting Weir collect his thoughts. Something has scared the shit out of him he thought, and that's saying something.

"We also believe," Weir continued flatly, "that the Caldarians are in possession of this substance code named 'element'."

Greig nodded slowly before speaking.

"I agree with that analysis, Commander. It also confirms every intelligence report we've been able to splice together over the last three months. Only now do we realize the critical nature of the situation. Something is killing our patrol and picket craft and leaving no trace. I would say not only do the Caldarians have knowledge of the element but also somehow, in some way, they have managed to capture enough of the substance to adapt it to their drive and weapons systems. But I also think that they only had enough for one drive and there is a new Caldarian cruiser class out there stalking our patrol vessels. Otherwise we wouldn't be sitting here having this briefing. Which leads me back to our primary brief—what happened to the Hancock and where is SEAL Team One?"

"But why have they just contented themselves with taking out the occasional picket vessel instead of penetrating to the center of the battle group and killing the command ships?" Chesterton asked. "Even a destroyer with full cloaking capability could close and kill any one of us at random."

"Because they only have a piece and they want the source," Greig said in a hard, flat voice. "And that's what makes Mike Platoon's success so vital."

"The present strategic situation is grim. The Caldarian fleet has pushed us back to within striking range of four prime home worlds: Earth Prime, Mylaris, Raius and Persilion. They've forced a salient into our sector and are being contained at present by the Sixth Battle Group, with the Myloen fleet guarding our left flank. But that won't last long if they've obtained the element. It's only a matter of time before their technology sweeps us away and leaves our home worlds, not to mention numerous protectorate allies, in the breach.

"As far as we know, the Confederate Expeditionary Force on Diadreas has been destroyed. We haven't had any communication with either the ground command or the flight units in support, for over a week. If we lose the construction yards and the deposits of Uridian crystal-bearing ore located there, the loss will be catastrophic. But that's not the most important reason Diadreas is so critical. It's also a strategic gateway to the commerce and traffic lanes of the four prime home worlds. Military and commercial traffic all pass through the Diadreas Gateway. Control of Diadreas means control of and access to those systems. And that makes it a very important piece of real estate.

"There are, or were five thousand troops engaged in holding the city against Caldarian ground forces. The size of the Caldarian ground force is unknown but we assume it's sizable. The 26th Marine Expeditionary Unit - Special Operations Capable (SOC) BLT (Battaliion Landing Team) has been dispatched along with a Mech company of Ramillion armor. Regular Confederate army units from Earth-Prime, Ramillion Mariness from Raius and a company of the Imperial Guards from Mylaris are engaged now. The center of the Confederate line is being held by II Brigade under Colonel Alexander Ridgeway," Commander Weir continued. "More units are being mobilized but it takes time."

"What assets do we have available that we can send to Zilith, Commander?" Admiral Chesterton asked.

"As we all know, our assets are spread thin. We're going to have to strip our picket and patrol lines in order to send a reasonable force to help Lieutenant Jackson and his recon team and it has to be at least a three-ship patrol. We can't risk sending only one. If it doesn't get through, we would end up jeopardizing the whole operation, and right now recovery of the element is the key issue. Whatever else happens here and on Diadreas is secondary. We need the element, or all the losses we've suffered so far will be nothing compared to the slaughter that will follow. This has to be done as quickly as possible, so again the question is, what resources do we have that can get to system Alpha-237 in the least amount of time?"

Commander Weir tapped his console and paused before he spoke. "The frigate Shirayuki and the destroyers Hunt and Haida are working a deep end surveillance LP behind the Caldarian's right flank. From their position to system Alpha-237, it's a 30 hour run at flank speed and about the same to get back to the Sixth, but that would mean trying to pass through the main Caldarian battle fleet in a direct run."

"And the odds of them getting across the frontier in a flat run?" Greig asked.

"They'd never make it." McMann stated the obvious. "They'd have to circle too wide to avoid detection to get back and by then it would be too late."

Regent Kandor raised a dark eyebrow in silent query.

"We slipped them out there to gather intelligence and to sit dark and quiet in the hopes of taking out one of their command ships," Greig answered the unspoken question. "And then to get the hell out and hopefully draw off enough Caldarian fleet units for us to make our move against the main elements sitting in front of us."

"Those destroyers are the mainstay of the fleet. We sure as hell can't afford to lose any more of them," Weir commented quietly.

"And we sure as hell can't afford not to send them, Commander." He looked across the briefing room table into Weir's eyes. "I know what you're thinking but they are expendable. I don't like it any more than you do but we have no choice.

"We all know the risks," he continued quietly. "We do everything we can to reduce the risks and lessen the odds but when a crew goes into harm's way, we take casualties. And if we don't do this, if we acquiesce, it will mean far more casualties later down the road. We're on the cusp. We have to find out what happened to Green and if Mike platoon made contact. The door is open now; it won't be for much longer."

There was silence around the table.

Greig sighed. He turned to Aden McMann, Captain of the Lexington. Greig had overall command of the battle group but McMann was the acting skipper of the Lexington, and although Greig commanded the group, McMann still fought his own ship.

"Mitch, what do you think of our current disposition and of the deployment of the Caldarian fleet flexing their muscles just in front of us?"

"Six days, twelve at the most, and they're gonna hit us. And when they do, they're going to be moving in to knife cutting range. I'd bet on it. The little skirmishes and exchanges we've had so far are nothing." The little exchange McMann was referring to had cost them two battle cruisers and three frigates, vessels they could ill afford to loose.

Regent Kandor snorted before speaking. "Yes. Well, if we have too many more of these little exchanges as you call them, Captain, we'll have the quartermaster pipe 'ship's mess down', and bring out the mead!"

They all laughed at the Myloen's referral to their traditional shipboard drink but the lingering tension in the room rippled and snapped like swirling, dark lightning.

"Regent," Greig said, "how you people can drink that black toxic waste is beyond my capacity to comprehend!"

"As you say, Admiral, comprehension is everything. Besides, we Myloens feel it acts as a rough reminder that we are distinctively, shall we say, eclectic in what our military forces prefer to drink before battle," Kandor replied with a tight lipped smile of his own.

Greig smiled back and then looked across at McMann. Greig and McMann went back 28 years to their days together at the Combined Confederate Naval Academy on Osirion, a deep ocean, M-class planet in the Coralus system ideally suited for fleet academies and deep ocean research. Aden McMann was a beefy man with a shock of red hair that never seemed to comb straight no matter what he did. He had a superb intellect and his grasp of space warfare and tactics had marked his career from the beginning. At times, he seemed to disconnect himself from the bridge of the Lexington and view the entire tactical picture as if, in his mind, he could see a three-dimensional picture of the battlefield and anticipate what the Caldarians would do next. His tactical genius had gotten him the affectionate nickname 'the witch' in the academy and he was known as 'Mitch' to his friends in an off-hand reference to his nickname.

His cold, blue eyes seemed to take on a hard gleam whenever his back was up against the wall. Greig knew enough about his friend to discern that despite the bravado, Captain Aden McMann was a man to ride the river with, and he couldn't think of a better man to be conning the Lexington when the Caldarians came for them.

"No bullshit, Mitch, your gut on this one." Greig held the other man's eyes and saw the determined gleam. McMann scrubbed the knuckles of his right hand across his forehead and looked at Greig.

"Admiral, with all due respect, you won't need to worry about deploying the fleet because there simply won't be a fleet to deploy. If they hit us like I think they will, the Sixth Fleet will cease to exist as an effective fighting force. I estimate losses as high as eighty-five percent in their first strike and almost one hundred percent lethality for all our capital ships. All that will be left are a few outlying picket vessels on the fringe that, if they're smart, will head for the far end of the galaxy. They'll nova the center first and then clean up the stragglers later," he finished softly.

"Right—we have to push them then, make them think we're coming for them. We have to make sure their eyes are focused on us here and with the Seventh Fleet pushing their right flank in the Rylius sector. Cut the orders for the Shirayuki, Hunt and Haida. They are to munition and leave at 18:00 hours today—full Chameleon mode, maximum dispersion. We're going to move the fleet, not much, just enough muscle to get the Caldarian's attention so those cans and that frigate can hopefully slip away undetected. Have three separate courses laid across so they stagger their approach to Zilith from different sectors." Greig looked around the table. "All right then, there it is. Good luck and good hunting."

Aboard the frigate Shirayuki and the destroyers USS Hunt and HMCS Haida, three separate sets of standing orders were received and decoded in what was still called the radio room. Confirmation codes were encrypted and locked in on the sub-space frequency and sent to Admiral Greig in CIC on the Lexington, and helm orders were given.

Even as they were given, electronically powered doors slid open, revealing internal weapons bays. The small, cylindrical-shaped craft inside moved toward the open doors in each ship. On the bridge of each ship, a program was downloaded into the computer brains of the small craft. Three commands were activated and the strange craft leaped out of the bays. The doors closed and the ships came about. Once they settled on their new base course, they went to one hundred and ten percent on their single coil star drives, their destination a system known only as Alpha-237.

The strangely shaped craft accelerated well away from the ships that had spewed them out and then settled into the position each ship had been maintaining in the patrol grid only moments before. They were LEMOSS, Long-Endurance Mobile Spaceship Simulators. Each 'Mossie' would generate the electronic signature of a standard Confederate frigate. On Caldarian sensors, they would appear to be frigates patrolling in a standard overlapping patrol pattern. And unless the Caldarians closed to track them visually, they shouldn't detect that there had been a change and that the patrol craft were gone. At least that was the theory.

Back on board the Lexington, Dr. Lucinda Zhao walked along the corridor beside Aden McMann. They were silent. They did not speak until they reached the elevator but the intensity between them could be felt like heat waves shimmering in the sun. Each was acutely aware of the other's presence.

"Is it as bad as I think it is, Mitch?" Lucinda asked.

McMann took his time to carefully form his reply before he spoke. "Yes, it is. I think you should take the first available courier back to Urilis and get off the Lexington while you can. Once the Caldarian battle fleet completes the circle, you won't be able to get out."

Lucinda's temper flared but she controlled it. Ever since university, she had had to fight the urge to lash out and attack anyone who trespassed into what she considered her space.

"No, I'm staying. Before this is over, and if that SEAL team manages to get back to Confederate lines with the Element, you're going to need my help. I'm the only one with any hands on experience with this thing and if, as you say, the Caldarians come a-shooting, there won't be time to bullshit around with a bunch of Confederate techno-wienies pissing away valuable time. I'm staying."

McMann looked at her in silence, his eyes hard and cold. She shivered and hoped he didn't notice.

McMann reached past her shoulder and hit the Executive COM switch on the elevator overhead display. "Lieutenant Gonzales?"

"Gonzales here, Captain."

"Lieutenant, will you meet me at the aft number three turbo lift with the watch security detail please?"

"Aye, Sir."

"You will then escort Dr. Zhao to the transport lock on deck 12 and ensure that she is on the next courier bird off the Lexington to the naval station on Urilis."

"Aye, Sir," Lieutenant Marie Gonzales replied again.

Lucinda's lips were white and stretched in a thin line, her fists clenched at her sides as rage built up inside her.

"One more thing, Lieutenant."

"Sir?"

"You will use whatever means necessary, Lieutenant, to ensure Dr. Zhao's safe and expeditious departure from the Lex—even if it means packing her in a Uridian containment pod. You will then report to the duty officer and inform him that Dr. Zhao has left the ship and that her belongings are to be properly collected and itemized for transport on the next available follow-on courier bird. Dr. Zhao is not, repeat, not to go to her quarters under any circumstance. Is that clear?"

"Aye, Sir," Gonzales replied one last time but this time with a detectable note of incredulity in her voice.

Lucinda rounded on McMann. "God damn you, Mitch, you can't do this!"

"Dr. Zhao, you are a civilian onboard a capital ship of the Confederate Navy about to be engaged by elements of the Caldarian fleet. By order of the Secretary of the Navy, no civilian shall be retained aboard a Navy vessel that is in a war zone pending combat operations." In a gentler voice he added, "You're going home, Lu."

At that moment the elevator halted and the doors hissed open. Lieutenant Gonzales and two Marine privates were waiting in the hallway.

Lucinda eyed McMann, her dark eyes like slate, and slowly nodded. "I'll be back, Captain. Please tell SEAL Team One to be careful with the Element."

McMann watched her as she stalked down the corridor, her back stiff with anger, flanked by Lieutenant Gonzales and the marine security detail.

☙❧

Black Stealth

A black-gloved hand reached out and made a minute adjustment to an instrument and then retreated back to its stationary position, hovering over a palm activated control disk.

A dark clad figure standing behind the six seated legionnaires watched the displays and monitors.

"Event signal from the Lexington. A courier capsule has just been retrieved and is docking now," a legionnaire at the port center console said.

"Patience!" Legate Burcil Naylis exclaimed. "Good things come to those who wait. Let us see what develops and who has been delivered. It must be extremely urgent, to send someone halfway across the galaxy in an unescorted courier capsule," he mused aloud. "Something tells me this has something to do with our efforts in system Alpha-237 as the Confederates name it. Let's wait and see."

Time seemed to stand still and narrow down to the darkened control room and the six surveillance monitors collecting and collating the endless stream of electronic emissions from the Confederate fleet.

"Murlaris, what is the name of this, this Confederate hulk we are hiding in?" Legate Naylis asked.

"It is the HMS Sussex, Legate, a fleet class battle cruiser. According to the data stream we captured, it was commissioned from the Earth European coalition." Naylis typed in a command and a data stream of captured tactical information scrolled down the screen.

"It was finally killed by the Drudaris legate after severely damaging the lead cruiser in our point element, the Hursparian. We tried to recover her but her reactor went critical and we lost her." He hesitated a moment before continuing. "We lost eighteen hundred assault troops from the 8th Legion, Legate, when she novaed."

"The Confederate forces initially acting as a blocking force in front of us were a composite force, hastily assembled. Did you take the time to run a battle analysis of the action, Legionnaire Murlaris?"

"Yes, Legate!"

"And what were your conclusions on that analysis?"

"Legate, my initial analysis indicates that the Confederate vessels we engaged acted randomly and without coordination, as if the flotilla commander was unfamiliar with his command structure. This allowed us to split their center and envelop the lead vessels, Sir."

"Very good, your tactical perception is improving. However, even as uncoordinated and blundering as the Confederates were, they still managed to kill the Hursparian and stop our advance. What conclusion can we draw from this?" He let the question hang in the air and gazed at the other legionnaires manning the monitors.

"That the Confederates are learning to adapt," a legionnaire on the outside bank of monitors spoke without turning his head.

Naylis nodded. He waved his hand in a gesture indicating the huge debris field. "History and time will tell. Space debris does not get buried, nor does it sink to the bottom of an ocean to rust and be forgotten. It is an eternal memory of each battle, each death and each final ending. There are no victors, only blasted hulls and frozen, twisted bodies cast forever adrift in a vast cosmic graveyard, a story for future generations to read or space historians to ponder. This battle raged and moved across eight parsecs of space for three days until the Confederates withdrew deeper into their shrinking territory, leaving their dead and broken vessels behind.

"There are thousands of bodies floating amidst the debris. And if you haven't noticed, many of them are Caldarian.

"This Sussex died a hard death. We were trying to kill their carriers before they could launch their strike craft. In that respect we failed and the Sussex succeeded. The Sussex came under sustained and accurate particle cannon fire before she could bring her own weapons to bear, yet still she continued to close the distance. Her shields weakened and her hull plating buckled and collapsed as her dispersal system overloaded. Finally, she was able to bring her weapons to bear and returned fire to the Hursparian. Pieces of hull plating buckled and disintegrated off both vessels as they tore at each other's throats at point blank range. One by one, the Sussex's systems went down and her cannons grew silent. The wounded Hursparian drifted off and the Drudaris closed to within one kilometric and fired two full broadsides into the already dead Sussex. The Hursparian wouldn't die for another four hours until her plasma conduits ruptured and she novaed from hits sustained from the Sussex.

"I would be very careful to remind you that these Confederates are not to be taken lightly. If we underestimate them, they will tear our throats out as quickly as we would theirs. Let that lesson sink in," he finished.

"We have no drive capabilities, we are dead the moment the Confederates detect our presence but we will kill as many of them as we can before we die. We have a mission to complete and I intend to see that every bit of data that radiates from the Confederate fleet is sent to High Admiral Corack-Va-Morlaris on the Shimmering Wind."

A frequency monitor on one of the consoles began to display a sinusoidal waterfall of colors as the complex traffic began to scroll across the screen. Legate Burcil Naylis leaned in closer to watch.

"Legate, high stream particle traffic on the Confederate tactical link has just been encrypted and sent to picket ships on the Confederate left flank," the legionnaire said. He hesitated. "The traffic is directed to the three Confederate vessels they inserted as a deep end listening station four days ago."

"So the fox moves from cover at last," Naylis whispered.

✌︎

Diadreas

The flash and ripping sound of heavy particle cannon fire could be seen and heard from the CP where Colonel Lionel Orson and the brigade Executive

Officer, Lieutenant Colonel Jim Marlow stood watching. In the darkness under the overcast sky, the whirring sound cut through their exhaustion and made Marlow wince. Colonel Orson had been the acting II Brigade commander since General John Simms had been killed when a Caldarian darter drone had found the brigade TAC, or Tactical Command Post. They were holding the center of the entire Confederate line. They had arrived on Diadreas and set up a defensive perimeter eight kilometers from Dias-Ta, the jeweled city of Diadreas, on the high ground overlooking the Artesian Highlands—the location intelligence had said the Caldarians would attempt to establish their airhead on.

"They'll be coming again soon, Colonel," Major Jeppor Rolark, his Ramillion liaison officer said wearily from his guard position on the left flank of the CP. He lifted a grimed gauntlet, unlatched the faceplate on his battle mask and spat, the oily spittle making a dark smudge on the sandy soil.

Orson grunted and looked at Rolark. His battle armor was filthy and stained with fusion residue from firing his particle rifle, and the ceramic plate armor on his breast had a small concave depression where a Caldarian particle round had glanced off.

"I wish we had a few more of your people here right now, Major, but I'm sure they have problems of their own on our right flank."

Rolark grinned and Orson could see his teeth, permanently stained from that god-awful Korsk bark they chewed, and then slapped his faceplate down.

"They could have wiped the planet clean but they need it intact and all the sprawling infrastructure here," Marlow said. "Their navy could have turned the whole fucking planet into a cinder block but they can't hold the ground. That's why they had to send in their legion."

"Yup, that's what we're here for, along with the other five thousand troops in the CEF. At least that's what we started with ten days ago," Orson added. "God knows how many are left now. We're spread way too damn thin trying to defend from an estimated invasion force of... What was that estimate G2 gave us?"

"Twenty thousand Caldarians, Colonel," Marlow answered wearily. "Where in the hell does G2 get their goddamned intelligence from, is what I'd like to know. We could probably double that number and it still wouldn't be anywhere near accurate."

"And Dias-Ta is their primary objective. If the city falls, then their airhead is intact and they've split the CEF ground forces. Then they can envelop our flanks and bag whatever is left of us when it's all over," Orson said.

"Dias-Ta," the colonel smiled grimly as he said the name of the city they were defending. "It means brilliance or brightness."

"Kind of a contradiction when you look at all the filth and squalor once you get past the upper towers and down to the sub levels where all the work is done, Colonel," Marlow replied sourly.

"Our perimeter is just about gone. Not much left when you figure that when we deployed we were a complete heavy mechanized brigade," Orson said as he gazed out at the vast wasteland of destruction.

"Three hundred and fifty M-240 main battle pods—gone. At least we think they're gone. Once they burrowed into the ground, hull down and turned on their Chameleon generators, it was a bitch to tell where they were, even with our acquisition grid on. And now the grid's gone."

"Sir, some units are down to one spare power pack for their assault rifles, and main battle armor power across the grid is at twenty-four percent. And you know what happens when the suits start to shed load to conserve power. The first thing that goes is the electronics, then the manipulators, and after that, well all you have left are your balls and guts."

There was a whispering snicker as Rolark chuckled behind his battle mask.

It irked Orson that they had to defend. It meant they could only 'react' while the Caldarians were free to maneuver around them. At least for now, he thought. And then the assault had begun. First came the phase cannon bombardment. How anything could survive such an assault never ceased to amaze the Colonel. Then the long-range sensors, what were left of them, detected multiple inbound bogies—hundreds of them—and he knew they were infantry space fighting vehicles, each carrying two full platoons of Caldarian assault troops. The Scorpion crews and the multi-phased Saber gun crews had accounted for dozens and they kept dropping off the sensor arrays but it was like trying to stop the tide. There were just too many of them.

Then the ground assault began. Orson was used to combat. But this was like nothing he had ever experienced in twenty-five years of front-line service. It chewed up men and material at a staggering rate. Three times they had held the line. It had bent, flexed and Orson had moved his mobile reserve to plug the gaps in a dozen places. No subtle probing attacks, feeling out the defenses. The Caldarians had hit them in force. They wanted Dias-Ta. They had two M-240's left on the right flank where the Caldarians had tried to break the line in their last assault. They had no heavy phase cannons left. The companies were down to the last power packs for their assault rifles. The dead lay in heaps in front of the forward positions, their broken and smashed battle armor twitching as the electronics sought direction from the broken bodies within. Some of the men had needed to scrounge for discarded weapons amongst the dead. Some were using conventional cartridge weapons.

But it was over. Their reserves were gone, power packs depleted and some companies were down to only 30 effectives.

"Colonel, Third Battalion's Bravo company's forward LP detects movement to their front, about fifteen hundred meters out, all along the line. Here they come again, Sir, and I don't think we can hold them this time."

A serpentine coil of red light began to flex on the command display of

Orson's battle helmet. Caldarians, lots of Caldarians, boiling out of the creeping ground mist and surging forward.

The colonel slapped the arming switch on his particle rifle and watched the blue arming diode go active. The pack was down to thirty-four percent nominal. He looked down at the broken body of Sub Regent Lyran Mithran, his Myloen liaison officer. So young, he thought bitterly. Like my son. A swelling rage rose within him and he felt a savage elation at the prospect of killing more Caldarians.

"Alright you sons o' bitches, come and take us."

Orson swung himself out of the dugout and strode toward the forward fighting positions, stopping to fire his rifle at the relentless wave of black-clad legionnaires, his huge battle-armored shoulders shaking at the crash and recoil of the heavy weapon every time he fired. He was totally oblivious to the crash and roar of battle, shouting orders, cursing vehemently at the Caldarians and giving encouragement.

He felt an iron fist grab him by the back handle of his load bearing harness and in the next instant he was thrown to the ground. A faceplate clunked on his and he could see the sour, angry eyes of Sergeant Major Ord Lapenza staring accusingly at him.

"Goddamn it, Colonel, when're you ever gonna listen to me? I told you already we can't afford to lose you. You're the only goddamned senior officer we got left in this whole fucked-up brigade and I'm gettin' almighty tired of dragging your sorry old ass out of every cowboy goat screw you piss yourself into."

Orson had to grin. Sergeant Major Ord Lapenza still treated him like a green shavetail fresh out of officer training. They had been serving together for twenty-two years, Ord refusing a battlefield commission to stay with the man who had saved his fire team on Orlaris-One.

Orson rolled away and they both fired and rolled and then fired again as they fell back to the command post.

"One of these days, Sergeant Major, you will learn to address me in proper military fashion. It's Colonel Orson, Sir; not Goddamn it, Colonel," he finished as they both dove into the CP.

Ord shook his head as he fired.

"Colonel, we have breach," Major Marlow said, his voice taut with tension.

"OK Jim, tell them to withdraw to phase line yellow, all units! It will tighten up our perimeter and shorten our communications envelope. With the Caldarians jamming as hard as they are, the only functioning net we have is battalion. God knows what's going on in the other sectors.

He reached up and took the tattered battalion guidon off the antenna nipple of the dead command track, folded it with an armored hand and put it into a storage compartment on his battle suit.

"Another day, Colonel," Marlow said quietly.

"Sir, the last traffic we received from ComSpac was that the 26 MEU (SOC), along with two companies of heavy Ramillion armor, was enroute with units of the Sixth Battle Group."

"Right! Time to un-ass and wait for the marines but God, it's gonna be hard to keep those Jarrheads from getting their heads all 'swolled' up' on this one."

Marlow grinned wearily. "Your eloquence with the English language concerning our esteemed comrades in arms leaves me speechless, Colonel, but I have to admit it will be damn good to see 'the few and the proud' coming up on horizon breach."

"Oh come the bitter night winds stalk

To whom the blade shall find

To arms, to arms, the blood blade calls..."

The colonel broke off. "So said Raos-Mau-Mylran, the Ramillion battalion commander, before the Battle of a Thousand Tears."

"Well spoken, Sir, but I hope our end is somewhat different than theirs."

CHAPTER 4
INTELLIGENCE

"Now, I recall the Recon Marines' ragged, filthy,
cammie-shirted young men in green paint who move
silent like the fog with deadly purpose in their eyes.
Swift, Silent, Deadly. I smile."

—GYSGT Correll, USMC,—Recon Marine

Zilith, 19:00 hours—UCT 247.0813

Larsen, the team medic, bent over the unconscious form of Jeff Choi. Choi's URK suit had been torn and the surrounding material charred and melted where particle fire had hit him low down in the abdomen. The high frequency particle beam had cut upward, ripping his stomach and cutting his right lung in half with the surgical precision of a light scalpel, before burning through his back.

"How is he?" Jackson asked.

Larsen looked up and shook his head.

"He's dying, Sir. I'm amazed that he's still alive. He's lost so much blood that I doubt if he has the strength left even to open his eyes. Even if we had him on board the Hopkins, there's nothing they could do to save him."

Choi shuddered once in his coma, let out a gurgling sigh and lay still. Larsen put a hand to his neck and shook his head. "He's gone, Sir."

Larsen looked up at Jackson. "What's even more amazing is that his suit didn't deflect the beam. Look here." Larsen reached down and pulled the charred edge of Choi's suit tight and brushed his fingers over the bottom part of the tear. Minute fragments of re-crystallized ceramic particulate scattered in a small cloud from his touch. "Here's the initial point of contact. The beam cut up and across from here."

Jackson bent over to stare at where Larsen was pointing. "What the hell?" There was a perfect circle about a millimeter in diameter that looked like it had been burnt through with a magnifying glass.

"Ah huh, deflection angle of about fifteen degrees. There's no way there should have been a burn through at that angle for that duration. Here's the readout from Choi's monitor. Initial contact, 0.04 seconds, nominal hold-over. He took a glancing blow that should have easily been shunted and yet it bored through and cut his lung in half as if he'd been naked."

"Something new we've never seen before. This has got to be called in. Whatever they have, if it's been deployed to their line units, we're in deep shit," Jackson said. He started to turn away but Larsen put a blood-smeared hand on his arm to restrain him.

"One more thing, Sir," he said quietly. "I've run a full contact diagnostic from each suit and from what we have left of Choi's. There's no residual energy signature."

The chief suddenly looked up from where he was working on the suits. "That's not possible. That should have registered on the suits' passive detection grids and there should have been a log of the beam's frequency."

"First I have to talk to the Ensign and then we'll go over what we know so far," Jackson said in response.

The interior of the pick-up shuttle looked like a butcher shop. The team still had their battle suits on and there was mud and blood splattered everywhere. The smell of RDX and gunpowder was thick and pungent inside the confines of the shuttle's crew compartment. Jackson made his way to the hatch leading to the cockpit and pressed the security release bar that scanned his palm before opening.

The hatch opened and Jackson stepped inside, the hatch sealing behind him. Ensign Chantella sat in the left-hand seat plying her hands over the NAV controls, so involved in flying that she did not at first notice that Jackson had entered the darkened cockpit. Her face was backlit by the soft glow of the instruments and the Heads-Up Display on the transparent Alumina-Matrix window.

Jackson sat down in the right-hand seat and watched the landscape below him. The sun had sunk into the cloud wrack as it set to the northwest. "What an unbelievable place," he spoke as he watched the storm clouds that moiled and seethed in a solid line across their path.

"Sir, see that huge line of volcanic vents and rifts?"

Jackson nodded. "It looks like festering wounds that won't heal."

"In his reports, Dr. Green briefed us about the night creatures that stalk the forests of this planet. He spent several years on the surface and warned against any movement during the night hours. And Zilith has a longer night cycle than is normal because of the axis tilt."

Jackson nodded slowly in confirmation. "That's why we brought the lights, Ensign but we're going to have to chance it with conventional weapons until we've neutralized the Caldarian ground team or we've recovered the Element and are on the extraction run. We can't risk radiating a power signature until that's complete. So we go in with what we have.

"As if trying to evade Caldarian legs wasn't bad enough, we have to worry about the local fauna having us for dinner," Jackson mused.

"Where are we, Ensign?" he asked.

"Sir, we've just passed the half-way NAV mark and are coming up on the alternate LZ from the southwest; ETA 45 minutes at current speed; all systems are nominal; nothing on the scopes and no hits from any known sensor types."

Jackson swung the seat around and called up the three-dimensional holographic display of the terrain on the navigational HUD. He set the NAV visual eyepiece on his head and let his eyes scan the area surrounding the LZ, the display automatically tracking where his eyes were looking. He moved the palm of his hand over the terrain contouring control and studied the landing zone.

"There's too much spillover from all the volcanic activity."

"Adjusting magnetic discriminators and setting the geothermal filters to seventy-five percent nominal," Chantella responded.

"The terrain is too dark. Set the night mask to override mode and let's see what that does for us."

Chantella's hands made the adjustments and the ground leaped out in sharply defined features.

They both sucked in their breath in wonder at the scene before them.

"I've never seen anything like this," Jackson said. "Look at those canyons and coulees. They lead off in hundreds of directions. It would be suicide to try and wander around through that broken country. Moving through that terrain will take weeks and we've only got hours."

Jackson hit his COM switch. "Chief, can you come in here? I need you to look at this."

"Aye, Sir." The hatchway hissed open and Chief Miller moved up behind Jackson as the hatch closed behind him.

"We have the coordinates of Green's base camp but unless we can find a place above the lava field, we're pooched."

The chief stood silently for a moment, watching the terrain unfold below him. "Dr. Green's camp should be at the base of the plateau, along the edge of the lava field. The edge of the lava field is covered in talus and debris from the plateau above, and the forest cover washes up against the cliff face all along the lava field because the prevailing winds here are southerly. We need to find a place on top of the plateau and work our way down, Sir."

Jackson watched the NAV plot on the display and pointed with his finger.

"Right there to the northeast of the LZ there's a lower, bowl-like depression in the display. It has to be a clearing that we can use for the insertion."

His fingers brushed over the image and followed a long depression in the display. Chantella watched his long, aristocratic fingers trace the edge of the holo-plate, noticing how deceptively sanguine his movements were and wondered if he had ever played the piano.

Poise and practice, she told herself and shivered inwardly. And if even a tenth of the stories I've heard about him are true, then he's a stone killer.

Jackson's eyes searched along the course they were currently on and settled on a narrow canyon fissure coming up over the horizon. He moved his cursor over the spot and transferred the coordinates to the main navigational computer.

"There, Ms. Chantella. I want you to swing us around to 45 degrees true and bring the shuttle down as low as you can take her. See that canyon opening on the right, coming up on the horizon?"

"Yes, Sir."

"Slow down as you approach and swing into it, tuck us in as close as you can to the canyon wall and put us in hover. I'm going back to see how the team is doing and make some plans. When you're in 'hover and hide' mode, come back and we'll take it from there."

"Aye, Sir."

Jackson unbuckled his flight harness from the NAV seat and re-entered the crew compartment. All eyes shifted to him when the door hissed open and he and Miller stepped in.

"OK, here's the game plan. Chief, I want a full suit check run and a scrub down. Make sure all suits have a full charge and run a full system diagnostic on each sensor array and the cloaking electronics. Make sure they're all fully functional."

The team was already methodically stripping and cleaning their personal weapons and proceeded to scrub down their suits to insure optimal cloaking when worn.

"Next, I want ideas and comments. Anything you might think of that might explain what the hell is going on here. I don't care how off the wall you might think it is. Our orders were to find Dr. Green or what happened to him and to recover parts of a black project he and his team were working on for ComSpac.

"So to start the ball rolling, I'm going to throw out a thought, something that just doesn't sit right. We just took out what appears to be a full Black Order hunter-killer team. What I want to know is why it was so easy? You and I both know that Blackies die hard, especially a Blackie hunter team. This was just too easy."

"They weren't Legion."

Everyone turned to look at Jamie Wicker. He was a medium-built, sandy-haired youngster from Murilia, in the Medesa System, who had been born in Victoria, British Columbia, in what had once been called Canada. His parents were marine biologists doing Cetacean research in the Murilian Sea. Since Earth had become a member of the Confederacy, old nationality regulations restricting enlistment had been superseded by enlistment standards, allowing anyone from each home world to enlist in the service branch of their choice. Wicker had initially been a member of the Canadian Airborne Regiment but had transferred to the teams when the opportunity for inter-service specialization arose.

"They weren't Black Order Legionnaires," he repeated. "Before the other platoon showed up on our sensors and we had to run, I checked each body. There were no brands in the right armpits."

"We don't have a lot of Intel on the Legion but we do know that when they graduate, each legionnaire receives a digital implant and a brand in their right armpit, declaring their allegiance to the Legion and to ID them."

"Sort of like how we get an ID chip implant when we graduate."

"Exactly," Wicker said. "These boys didn't have a brand but I'm betting the second team that hit us sure as hell was the real deal."

"Which means," Larsen added, "that they knew who we were and where we would be all along."

The hatchway to the cockpit hissed and Ensign Chantella entered the compartment.

"We're in 'hover and hide' in a small canyon about 20 minutes flying time southwest of the secondary LZ," she said. "Sir, just before I switched on Chameleon mode I got several returns on the passive array, multiple in-bound bogies scattered across a sixty degree section of the sky."

"Any signatures?" Jackson asked.

"Yes Sir. Standard Confederate distress beacons on the guard channel. Only we're too far out for any patrol craft or recovery birds to be out this far. I'd say they were escape pods from the Hancock, about twenty all together, spread out over roughly fifteen hundred kilometers of sky.

"That would be only about a quarter of the crew, depending on which pods got free and how much time they had, but from what I saw, whatever hit them moved in close and hammered them at knife cutting range. When I projected the inbound course on a few of the closer ones, I estimate that they put down pretty close to our current location, Sir."

She hesitated a moment. "And there was something else."

The team watched her, waiting. "Just before we went nominal across the board, I got a twitch on an unknown. I'm not sure. It was erratic and the acquisition envelope was extremely narrow. I tried to filter it out of the background but it was gone before I could narrow the filters enough to account for all the background clutter, so it might have been nothing more than all this volcanic activity distorting the arrays. But for a moment, it looked like a faint electromagnetic signature from a power source."

"So what you're telling me is that it was all the geothermal interference?" Jackson asked.

"No, it was too consistent. It had to be sentient-made," Chantella replied.

Jackson took in a breath. "OK, we have possible escape pods on the ground from the Hancock and a possible bogie on the ground...where exactly, Ensign?"

"Approximately fifteen hundred meters due east of the secondary LZ, Sir."

Hearst spoke up, the anger in her voice betraying her temper. She had a short fuse. "They weren't looking for us, they were pushing us. All along they knew where we were and how we would react. They let us detect them and when we started to run, they cloaked. And we all know that no cloaking technology is that good, that close. But these guys totally disappeared off our sensors and instead of flanking and killing us, they let us run. Why?"

"Fox to the hounds, Doc," Chief Miller said. "They aren't trying to catch us, they're driving us. They know something we don't, a piece of the puzzle that we don't have. And my gut tells me it has to do with whatever it is Green and his team found here."

Michelle Hearst wasn't called Doc because of her medical abilities— she was called Doc because of her surgical ability with a particle rifle. Everyone who joined the teams had to shoot the standard Navy qualification course using a number of current and non-current weapons before they picked their weapon of choice. 'Doc' Hearst qualified as Expert on the qualifying range but when the old Gunnery Sergeant brought out the particle weapons and Hearst hefted one for the first time, she fell in love. When she saw what a particle weapon would do to a target, she knew she had found her calling.

"Oh yeah, I want one of these babies!" she chortled in glee.

Like a hound sensing its quarry, the master gunner looked up at Hearst with sudden interest, his flat, black eyes betraying nothing as he watched her gently caress the weapon. A natural, he thought.

"It's frequency agile too! I'll bet it'll cut through base ceramic armor with a deflection angle of forty degrees."

"It'll cut through 1.2 centimeters of ceramic frontal armor with a deflection pattern of thirty-eight degrees, twelve minutes with a sustained lay of 0.5 seconds," the old master gunner stated flatly, grinning at Hearst.

"The answer to that statement," Jackson said, "is yes. The briefing we received before we left bears that out. The team we took out was bait to draw us in, show ourselves and make us run. So far, all the cards have fallen to whoever is chasing us. We have to take the initiative away from them and make them react to us or we aren't going to get off this planet alive. If this were just your basic firefight, we'd all be dead. What does that tell you?"

"They can't hit shit?" Doc asked. The team laughed.

Jackson continued and the team sensed the subtle change in his voice. "OK, so we have to take the fight to them, make them react to us. That starts now. From the briefing we received from INTEL, we know that Green was on his way back to Confederate lines. In the main message communication that Green routinely sent in his reports, we found a sub-carrier pulse bead, piggybacked to the main carrier frequency. We missed it for months until a signal technician on the Lexington ran a variable frequency diagnostic scan on the original messages."

"And?" Wicker asked.

"And," Jackson continued, "it proves that Green was a very careful man. I've never seen his bio-chip but somewhere he must have had military training, even been a spook for awhile before he returned to physics. Anyway, what Confederate intelligence found was the co-ordinates of his last camp, which is roughly two kilometers west of the secondary LZ and the real objective of our mission."

"Then why the hell did we insert on the other side of the planet?" Larsen asked.

"Because Confederate military intelligence feared exactly what Green anticipated and planned for. They feared that the Caldarians would in time, breach our security and find out about Green and his project, and they didn't want us to insert and draw the Caldarians down to the main objective. They wanted us to insert a long way from the target and set up a shuttle rendezvous first. If we got to the shuttle clean, we were to proceed to the secondary LZ. If we didn't, then they would still have the location and the Caldarians wouldn't, which means we would still be one step ahead of them."

"Yeah, and we'd be dead too," Doc said.

"But the REMF's don't give a shit if we end up dead because we're expendable, is that it?" She asked, her voice tight with anger.

Jackson turned to look directly at her. "Captain Ortello apprised us all of that risk before we left, and we all know the hazards from working these missions before. It comes with the territory. We all know that, from the moment we walk across the grinder."

"I know that, we all know that, but it doesn't make it any easier each time we do it Sir, knowing that somebody up the line thinks we're expendable. If I could have five minutes, just five minutes with the REMF motherfucker who cut our orders..."

Jackson held up his hand and Hearst checked herself. "It's OK, Doc. I understand what you're saying...but you can hold my BDU's while I do it."

Hearst's mouth fell open in surprise and the team whooped with laughter at her momentary consternation.

In the fourteen months that Hearst had been with Mike Platoon, they had never seen her perturbed or shaken. The Ice Queen, they called her. As cold to kill as she was to sit and be stalked by the scum who inhabited the border bars and brothels of Kaldara-4, a hard, dangerous border planet that attracted scum from across the galaxy, who went there for the whoring and the drug traffic. They all knew the stories, even though she hadn't spoken a word when she had returned from a three-week leave she had suddenly requested.

As Jackson watched Hearst, his mind drifted back to the incident involving her and another female SEAL from Mylaris. Nothing was ever said but the Navy board of investigation and Commander Ortello had apprised Jackson of the incident shortly thereafter.

She and another female SEAL had gone to find the three men who had raped and murdered LPO Patricia Langley from SEAL Team 8, Mylaris-Prime, the first off-world team to join the SEALs. Hearst and LPO Langley had completed SEAL basic training together at the Strand on Mylaris Prime.

The two SEALs had dressed to fit the part, Hearst's tight, compact figure turning heads in every bar and sodden Tylarian wine shop in the port city. It was four days before they found the three they were looking for, with four of their friends in a nightclub in one of the worst, rat-infested dives in the city.

The leader was pushing fifty. His filthy flight suit sagged over his paunch and stank like vomit and stale beer.

"Well, what do we have here, little darlin'?" he purred as he came up behind Hearst and her companion. His breath stank like rotten teeth and cheap bootleg whiskey but his eyes were stone, cold sober; mean, cruel eyes that lived to hurt and torture from behind closed doors.

"Piss off, you slobbering piece of Gandarian Dak shit," Hearst said as she turned toward him. She knew exactly what she was going to do but she wanted him to know what was coming and who it was coming from. His eyes widened in shock but his rage shook him like a wind. The bar grew silent and his friends moved in, forming a tight half-circle around the two women. Bullying Tylarian merchants and terrifying the local women was his long suit. He had no idea what he faced and didn't realize that death was only a heartbeat away.

Hearst's fellow SEAL clutched what looked like a typical evening purse in both her hands at chest height. Inside the purse was a multi-barreled device that contained a small, electronic scanner that catalogued heart frequency. It could track and isolate up to eight thoracic signatures at a time. It was only effective at very close range and once the triggering device was activated, it had to be re-loaded. Once the dispenser was activated, the sub-sonic rounds were deployed and tracked in on the individual signatures it had been programmed to seek. It was deadly out to 30 meters. At four meters, it was one hundred percent lethal. The leader's four friends had been iden-tified and their thoracic signatures scanned and logged into the device's small computer brain. Those four signatures were then, in turn, programmed sin-gly into the guidance system of one thoracic dart. All that remained to do was simply press the button.

The men moved in and then Hearst and her fellow SEAL moved. There was a blur of motion and the hand that the leader had drawn back to strike Hearst with, was hanging uselessly at his side and his crotch was dripping large gobs of dark, arterial blood. In the same moment, Hearst's companion pressed the button on her thoracic dart gun and the purse disintegrated as the rounds deployed and streaked toward their targets. There were five dead men lying on the ground, four of them had a hole the size of a fist in the middle of their chest, directly in front of their heart—blank eyes wide, no time for any emotion but death to register. The fifth's throat was cut from ear to ear as surgically as if it had been done with a surgeon's light scalpel. Hearst's companion sheathed the double bladed Berillion dueling blade she kept in a sheath between her shoulder blades.

Only the leader and his number one were still alive...barely. The leader was clutching his genitals, staring in disbelief at the blood, his blood, stain-ing the filthy, tiled floor of the bar. His number one was slumped against the wall sobbing, vainly trying to hold his intestines in place while bloody coils dribbled out onto the floor between his fingers. The leader was moaning in a soft, crying voice while he watched his body bleed out. Hearst bent over him and touched his throat with the small blade she had already used to de-man him.

"Do you know who I am?" she asked softly, looking directly into his eyes. Terrified, the leader shook his head, shock and loss of blood beginning to set in. "I'm Weapons Specialist Michelle Hearst, Mike Platoon, SEAL Team One, Earth-prime." His eyes widened in horror. He knew then what was coming.

"Perhaps you remember a friend of ours," she said in that dead, soft voice, "Leading Petty Officer Patricia Langley. The blonde one, remember? The one you and your boys raped and then murdered?" The leader trembled feebly, darkness beginning to cascade in upon him. The knife in Hearst's hand flicked once, and the darkness was complete.

Hearst had fought with them and drank with them. She had mourned their losses and rejoiced with the team members when the little moments of life and laughter happened that drew them closer together than any family she had ever in her life known. And in so-doing, she became a part of that bonded family only combat closeness can meld.

Jackson brought his mind back to the present and continued.

"We have the grid co-ordinates of the last field camp where Green spent his last two years. They are two kilometers west of the secondary LZ, in that broken lava debris field at the bottom of the plateau we are approaching. Eight clicks northeast of the LZ, there's a small clearing. Not much but enough to get us on the ground. Once we're on the ground, we head for these co-ordinates." He spread the topo map on the crew table and pointed to a small crosshair he had drawn with a grease pencil at the base of the cliff indicating the location of Green's camp.

"That's where we're going," he said.

Larsen broke in. "Lieutenant, you see all these tight, squiggly lines running from the top of that plateau down into that valley?"

"Yes," Jackson said, knowing what was coming next.

"And do you know what each one of those tight squiggly lines represent, Boss?"

"Yes!" Jackson said again, a grin beginning to form at the corner of his mouth. He and Larsen always played this little 'ten questions' game before going down range.

"Each line represents a ten meter contour interval. That means that by the way they're all scrunched in tight like that, there must be a five hundred-meter difference in elevation between the top and bottom. Are we actually going to climb down that, Sir?"

"That's the plan, yes," Jackson replied.

"Damn Sir, we ain't no line leg unit, we're a little more technical than that."

"Which means," Jackson drawled casually, "that you have trouble chewing gum and putting one foot in front of the other, doesn't it, Seaman Larsen?"

Once again the team laughed at the timeworn verbal sparring between the two men.

Abruptly, Jackson shifted gears. "Ensign, I want you to take us back out and swing us in as close as you can pitch this bird to the ground. I want you to follow standard insertion procedure to the secondary LZ, just as if we were going to do a standard drop. Then I want you to haul out and cross directly over that clearing before jumping to an orbital track. I want you topside so that you can get out if necessary and warn Confederate command that we're dead and the package has not been recovered. Also, I want a priority black pulse bead coded and sent as soon as you're in orbit, requesting back-up ASAP, this position. I have a feeling that if we don't find whatever it is Green left here, the Confederacy is screwed."

"Sir, whatever killed the Hancock is still up there."

"I know. Switch to full Chameleon mode, set yourself in a low north polar orbit, shut down all non-essentials and wait for our signal. It will only be one of two orders. Flat-line it for Confederate lines or come a-runnin' to pick us up. Either way, you're gonna be pushing this piece of re-worked Ramillion scrap iron to the limit."

Chantella smiled. "Aye, Sir."

"OK, people, weapons check in ten. Let's move."

For one brief moment, his mind flared and opened like a portal into another world to allow a single thought to intrude into what he was about to do. Debra Lewis. And then just as quickly, the portal snapped shut and he was Lieutenant Thomas Daniel Jackson, Mike Platoon's Wheel, SEAL Team One, Earth-prime once again.

CHAPTER 5
INTO THE DARKNESS

*"Tactics is the art of using troops in battle;
strategy is the art of using battles to win the war."*

—Karl Von Clausewitz

The shuttle was in hover and hide mode, tucked beneath the overhang of a canyon wall south west of the secondary LZ. Ensign Chantella was in the cockpit monitoring her passive sensors and checking for any movement outside. It was deep night. The only illumination was the soft glow given off by her control console. She adjusted the console illumination so that the monitors and controls were only just readable, and all her attention was focused on watching and listening. Chantella was uneasy; she felt or sensed something in the darkness drawing near and she wanted to move or turn on the shuttle's exterior lights. The powerful flood lamps could illuminate a surrounding area of five hundred meters like daylight. She wanted daylight now. She wished she could open the hatchway to the crew compartment and at least see someone. Being isolated in the darkened cockpit kicked her fear and imagination into overdrive. Chantella tried to bring her mind back to the job and let discipline and training override her fear. But cut off and alone, it was a loosing battle.

The table in the shuttle's crew compartment was covered with a soft felt blanket. The team was cleaning their personal weapons. Chief Miller checked the electronics on the last suit and laid it on the seat beside the weapons locker.

"Suit checks are complete and green across the board, Sir. I've tweaked the filtering passband a bit, to narrow it down some, so the isolation will be sharper. There're so many small, unknown biologics running around here that it was confusing the hell out of the detection circuits. We've had enough problems with the suits that we don't want to be drawing any Caldarians in the area because the filtering passband is too wide and somebody gets a little antsy and starts shooting at the local fauna.

"And I've set the survival override on auto so that if we do get compromised, we won't have to stop what we're doing to activate the survival node, even though we usually patrol with it in standby."

Larsen snapped the fire control module on his MP-225-N into its lock position and snorted. "You mean when we're unconscious or bleeding out from a suit breach, they'll still manage to find our bodies?"

"Yeah. Well, I'm just glad our field suits aren't as bulky as the battle suits the line grunts wear," Hearst spoke up. "Those things weigh over two hundred kilograms with all that articulated rib armor and ceramic plating. And besides, ours feel sooo silky smooth as the tubing sucks all that moisture away. And think of what a bad hair day you'd have if the nuclear power modules packed it in. We'd have to patrol like in the old days with, oh my God, just guns and gear!" She put her hands on her hips and swung them in a slow gyration, winking at Dyer.

Dyer blushed and concentrated on cleaning the slide on his Tango 251. He was 23 years old and had had a crush on Hearst ever since she had outshot him on the tactical range three days in a row the first week she arrived on the team. The team kidded him unmercifully, since he was the recognized expert when it came to long-range shooting. He suspected that Hearst, in her intuitive way, sensed how he felt toward her and it made him feel even more awkward.

"Just be damn glad that the ceramic absorption disks and the electronics keep your ass safe when you're humping it, Doc," he growled.

Hearst blew him a kiss and winked again.

"OK," Jackson said. "Think! Every Special OP unit in the galaxy practices some type of small unit tactics. What makes us special? Our training! Let's get down to basics, forget all the high tech stuff we use and think for a moment. What's basic to our profession?"

"The ABCs of warfare," Chief Miller replied, "shoot, maneuver and communicate."

"Correct," Jackson said. "Similarly, every small combat arms unit worth its salt has developed a discipline comprised of several standard operating procedures and battle drills. But what makes us different when you distill it all to its fundamental points? What makes us unique?"

The team watched him in silence, waiting.

"We're the best at what we do?" DeLuca asked, quietly and immediately sensing that he had answered incorrectly.

"Good PR answer straight from the book," Jackson shot back, "but it's canned bullshit. Wicker transferred from the para's, DeLuca bailed from a mech platoon marine and Dyer, God help us all, lowered himself to our level by coming over from a Marine recon team, which he reminds us of every hour on the hour, 24/7."

"Semper Fi," Dyer said in response.

"Think deeper. You all know why, even though it's buried someplace deep inside. No other Spec. Op. force in the Confederacy receives the warrior protocol scan that we do. When they find the trait, we're flagged. That's one reason we pull long range. It's not an implant or an artificially enhanced strand of DNA to fuck up when somebody dumps a tactical nano stream in theatre; it's us. We are what we are by nature. That's why we go through five psych evaluation levels before we even start the actual training. And that's what gives us the edge.

"So we need to do the unexpected, something they won't anticipate. First, I'm going to get the Ensign, because she's going to be the one making the drop and she needs to be here."

Jackson stood and moved to the hatch but before he opened it, he turned the regular interior lights in the cabin off and switched on the nighttime infrared. The cabin was bathed in a soft red glow that made the faces of the battle weary SEALS look like dark images from hell. He didn't want to destroy Ensign Chantella's night vision. The pupils will dilate and open wider as light recedes. In total dark, the pupils are fully dilated and sudden exposure to bright light can damage the retina. It also takes a long time for the eyes to adjust again to the surrounding darkness and Jackson didn't want their shuttle pilot to lose her already night-adjusted vision. He opened the hatch and Ensign Chantella turned toward him. The look on her face stopped him cold. A dark dread crept over his heart.

"What is it?"

"Sir, there's something stalking us and it's not the Caldarians."

"Did the sensors pick anything up?"

"No, Sir, we've got no active systems online and we're in passive mode only."

"Then how do you know, Ensign?" The rest of the team stood in the darkened doorway, watching and listening.

"I can't say for sure. It's—it's just a feeling I get when I know someone's watching me. It's the kind of feeling I used to get when my parents would leave me at home while they delivered produce to the portal outpost on Selinas. Most times they would spend the night, in which case I had to stay home and look after the hydroponic beds. They were located in outlying solar greenhouses about a hundred meters from the main house but still within the compound walls. I didn't mind it so much during the daytime, it was quiet and peaceful, but after sunset, the Lemoks would come out and stalk the fence line. They would snarl and hiss, trying to break in, but the fence and force field around the compound would keep them out. In the early days, we lost quite a number of colonists.

The Lemoks realized that humans were relatively easy prey as compared to the other indigenous wildlife on Selinas and it was never safe to go out unarmed or alone, especially at night. They hunt in pairs, a male and female together; usually the female would stalk while the male waited in a pre-determined spot. They were exceptionally quick and intelligent. It didn't take them long, once the force field was set up and in place, to figure out that they shouldn't attempt to breach it. So they would prowl around the gates and roadways hoping to catch an unwary or tired colonist.

Then the tourists discovered that Selinas was a great getaway place and all of a sudden there were inter-planetary resorts springing up everywhere. And well, you know what tourists are like, Sir."

Jackson smiled to himself. He knew that Chantella's family had been one of the first families to colonize Selinas in the Taurus quadrant. It was a small colony. Selinas itself was much like Zilith except it did not have all the volcanic activity.

"Yes, I guess I do. All smiles, no brains. Let me guess, you started to lose tourists at an alarming rate, right?"

"Yes Sir. We barely had the resources to protect our small colony, let alone dozens of isolated resort facilities. But I always knew when Lemoks were watching and stalking the compound. It was an acquired survival skill. I could feel it. Just like I do now, Sir," she added quietly.

Jackson looked at her and nodded his head. "OK Ensign, you've convinced me. From the information we received from the reports Dr. Green sent about this place, we know there's a large, ugly predator out there. We spent seven nights on the ground and didn't detect anything during the daytime or night hours but that doesn't necessarily mean they weren't there or weren't watching us. Maybe they were just gauging us, which means, if they're as smart as Green said they were in his reports, we need to be extra careful after we make our drop."

Jackson turned back into the crew compartment, gesturing to Chantella to follow him.

"Right now, we're twenty minutes south of the secondary LZ. Three kilometers northeast of the LZ, on the top of the plateau, there's a small clearing. We don't know where the real Blackie platoon is but I have a feeling they're going to be close. So here's the plan.

"Ensign, when we leave here, make for the LZ and follow the drill like it was just another routine drop. Then head for that little clearing. We have the LAP (Low altitude parachute) packs on board. That's how we're going in."

"Tell me I didn't just hear what I think you said, Sir?" Dyer asked.

Jackson smiled. "You bet Mike, that's how we're going in. We're all jump qualified on the system. You know that to stay current, we're all required to do jump re-qualifications on Mylaris Prime every six months, and the Low Altitude system is one of the required jumps and we all re-qualified two months ago."

"Sir, that equipment is over two hundred years old!" Dyer said in alarm.

"The technique is. The equipment is new issue."

"Why can't we use the shuttle's insertion pods and engage Chameleon mode?" Larsen asked.

"Oh, the insert pods are going in and Chameleon mode will be engaged; it's just that we won't be in them," Jackson replied.

The team stared at him in confused silence, thinking that their lieutenant had finally gone over the edge. Jackson smiled at the looks on their faces.

"That's exactly what the Caldarians expect us to do. We've been over the river and through the woods with them in the past, and we all know to a certain extent how the other side operates. We've been matching technology against technology, playing the same old techno-swap game with them. We're going to change that, or at least hopefully throw them off long enough to do what we have to do. The game is always insert, evade contact and withdraw without being compromised. If contact is made, we normally disengage and get out.

"I've already gone over the plan with Ensign Chantella. The shuttle's NAV computer will give us a precise jump run. As soon as she dumps us, she heads upstairs. You know the drill. We'll be going out at exactly ninety-three meters using a cluster canopy chute made of clear, Alusilk fiber that is invisible to sensors and the high band detection arrays the Caldarians normally use when they're in the field. As of right now we're tactical, total quiet and I want a passive grid.

"Any questions so far?"

"What do we take for gear?" Hearst asked.

"Standard battle suit configuration and everything powered down except the suit's heat dissipation system. We'll use the neural team net and keep the tactical link in the helmets on standby. And everyone hydrates. Drink as much as you can and then drink some more. Empty your waste recycle conduits and if you can..."

Jackson waited as the team shouted the time honored chant. "Evacuate the bowels before proceeding on patrol to ensure waste recycling systems are at optimum performance," they all chanted in glee.

"Right, so your waste packs are empty," he finished. Make sure your kill sheet is filled out and that Ensign Chantella has a copy in the shuttle's databanks before we deploy. We patrol in ranger file. Chief, you have the point and Wicker, you take the slack position. Doc, you have rear security. I know all our weapons have Chameleon overlays but I want you to tape up anyway to break up the outline. Two days of TERATS (technically enhanced rations)each, a basic load and one P-350 collapsible particle rifle each. But make sure the power supply is in its shielded case. We don't want anything to radiate.

And take one extra power supply each for the 'urks'." Urks was team-techno slang for the I.R.C.S.P., which stood for Infra-Red-Cloaking-Suit-Passive made by the Bristol Dynamics Corporation. When the suits were first issued, a Machinist Mate 1st at Fire Base Three on the planet Delphia, immediately coined the acronym 'Urks' when he saw the similarity between the suit's capabilities and a small burrowing leech called an URK, native to Delphia's swamps. It was difficult to see because of its ability to blend with its surroundings and they seemed able to work their way under the most tightly wrapped garment.

"Why an extra power supply for the suit, boss? One will do us for a month," Wicker said.

"Because we're going to arrange a little surprise for our Caldarian friends, should they decide to make an appearance," Jackson said.

"Ensign, what do you have in the stores locker as far as service and maintenance material?"

"Not much. The shuttles get checked out once a week and the Hancock's service jocks were fanatical about doing system and diagnostic checks every day, especially on the Tac-birds we use for chauffeuring folks such as you on your picnic outings." Chantella grinned tightly.

"You usually carry a few containers of Chameleon hull coating, do you not, the elastic acrylic you use to repair any chips or cracks you get on the hull grid until you can get it into the fusion bay?"

"O—K," Chantella replied, not sure where Jackson was going with this, confusion apparent in her voice.

"Good. Chief, I want you to take six personal hydration packs and open the seams. Put a thermite grenade in each one and then reseal them. Then fill the packs with the Chameleon elastic coating. What's the base color, Ensign?"

"Standard navy space black, Sir."

"Do you have anything brighter?"

"No, Sir. Wait a second..." Chantella opened the crew emergency locker and rummaged for a moment before emerging. "But I have this," she held up her hands, "five packets of red, sensor reflecting space dye. Will that help?"

Jackson grinned. "Ms. Chantella, remind me when we get back to the Lex that I owe you a six of Mularrian beer!"

Chantella laughed. "Right, I'll hold you to that one, Sir!" Every EVA suit, along with its emergency locator beacon, carried a small package of marker powder that could be expelled by a compressed air charge. When dispensed, the dye would form a dense, red cloud of radar and sensor reflective material that would maintain orbit around the suit long after the person's air had been used up and the emergency locator had run out of power.

It had proven to be an extremely useful way of locating personnel who had been cast adrift. Sometimes they were even lucky enough to get to them before they ran out of air. But it was generally considered far better to be found dead than to be left to float alone in space without proper burial, tending to minimize the inherent agoraphobic concerns of people who made their living in the dark emptiness between star systems.

The team was watching him as if he had lost his mind. Suddenly the chief laughed as he realized what Jackson was going to do. "How do we locate a squad of Blackies who are using suits with Element cloaking capabilities?" he asked rhetorically.

"The thermite grenades won't do much to stop the Caldarians but they will heat the epoxy to its maximum elasticity! And of course, the marker dye will make them stand out like Castillian whores at a Foloan graduation! Remind me never to play poker with you, Lieutenant!"

"Aces and eight's, Chief!" Jackson answered, "the dead man's hand. Let's hope it's dead Caldarians. OK, get the gear and rucks ready. "Does everybody have the "E and E" (escape and evade) routes downloaded into your suits' TAC COMS (tactical computers)?" One by one they nodded. "It's just coming twenty-three hundred local. We take our Zirlaxin and everyone power sleeps for three hours. Ensign, standard watch. Wake us at zero two hundred. If you detect anything at all on the grid outside, I want you to wake me immediately."

"Aye, Sir."

The team stared at Jackson, waiting, smiles spreading across each face in expectation.

Jackson groaned but he couldn't keep his own smile from showing. "Do you assholes have to do this before each and every patrol?"

Six heads nodded in answer.

"SEAL axiom taken from 'The Myloen Principles of Recon Patrolling, Myloen SEAL Team Four'," Jackson recited. "Where the fuck are we?"

"Who the fuck knows!" the team chanted back.

"Why the fuck are we are?"

"Who the fuck knows!"

"Who sent us here?" Jackson asked last of all.

"The Rear Echelon Mother Fuckersssssssssss," the team shouted back gleefully.

The team quieted down and the realization of where they were hit them like a fist.

"We're a long way from nowhere with our shit hanging way out in the wind, Sir," the Chief spoke softly.

"I know Chief, let's cammy up and see if we can get some rest."

Everything was quiet. The team was sleeping. Chantella could tell from their breathing that they were in deep, body restoring sleep and that they would wake up as if they had had twelve solid hours of undisturbed rest. She had left the hatch open and was once again focusing all her attention on watching and listening. Her sense of unease and of stalking evil had returned, stronger than before. Planning and talking with Jackson and the team had temporarily made her forget but now, with the silence and sleeping team, it had returned—only it was stronger, more tangible.

The rain that had been falling had stopped and a creeping ground mist began to ooze out of the ground and climb up along the steep canyon walls. It was getting harder to see anything on the external monitors and it frightened her that she felt so exposed. She reached out and touched the interior walls of the shuttle, its dyrillium armor plating assuring her that nothing could get to her. She was very glad that her assigned task did not require her to leave the shuttle.

"Let's get this done and get topside where it's safe. Let these mud movers do their thing and get back in nice, clean, safe space," she whispered to herself. She gazed out the windscreen, trying to make her eyes pierce the fog and mist that was shrinking her visibility. Her mouth was dry. Her eyes moved continuously from the monitors to the windscreen and back to the monitors.

Chantella thought of her grandmother and the tales she had told them of her youth growing up in Sibiu, in Central Romania. Her grandfather had been a chemical engineer working in the Ploesti oil fields. New technology had opened up new reserves of crude oil that before had been too deep and hard to extract. Her grandmother, Andreea Chirila, had died at the age of one hundred and fifty-two years. When she was ninety-three, she had asked for and been granted permission by the governing council on Earth, to join her children on Selinas. Marcie's father was a botanist with a tenured position at Bucharest University. In an effort to adapt to the changing cosmopolitan nature of the new global political environment, he had legally changed their name to Chantella. Her grandmother, a family icon and doctor of linguistics, had been grieved at the changing of a family name that went back to the thirteenth century.

In the colony on Selinas, her grandmother had quickly taken over the general household duties, insisting that since her son was determined to forget the family name, she would pass along to her grandchildren their family history.

And so in the evenings, after the ponds were tended and the research data logged and transmitted to the Botanical Institute for Off-World Studies on Earth, she would sit the family down and tell them tales of the old country and the old ways. Of a time before space travel and Caldarians and an age that tended to look with skepticism on things that could not be collated, quantified or measured by empirical principals, of things that moved in the dark and groped for blood.

She would insist on turning the lights down and setting a fire in the large, central fireplace in the open area of the main living quarters, even though her son frowned on such a waste of resources and effort. And the children would shudder, glancing sidelong at one another, reading the fear in each other's eyes.

Marcie remembered the stories well. Her mind was thinking of them now. She watched the view screens as the fog swirled higher. She was watching the aft screen when a shadow materialized out of the mist on the edge of the aft camera's search envelope. She tensed. Her hands worked the camera controls, zooming in and using the filters to bring definition to the apparition but it was gone.

"Come on, come on!" She swung her head around, searching the other screens. A whisper of movement on the starboard monitor caught the corner of her eye but when she turned to look there was nothing there, only a swirling darkness of fog. She turned to the hatch and hesitated. Jackson had said to wake him if she saw or detected anything but she did not want him to think less of her. In all her years growing up in the colony and at the naval academy she had striven to prove to herself that she was free of the fear and nightmares that she told herself only existed in the fables and legends of her grandmother.

"Lieutenant?" she called softly through the hatch. "Lieutenant Jackson?"

Jackson stirred and his eyes opened a slit as he got his bearings and in one swift movement, came to his feet. His right hand held a particle pistol. She noticed that the safety was off and the power setting was at maximum.

"What is it?" he whispered. "What time is it?"

"I'm sorry, Sir. You've only been asleep for about ninety minutes but you said to wake you if there was anything on the displays."

"It's OK, what have you got?"

Chantella pointed to the aft monitor and sat down in the right hand seat. "A few moments ago, something moved into the aft camera's lens range. It was just on the edge and I tried to clear it up but when I looked again it was gone. Then a second ago, there was movement on the starboard screen but again nothing when I tried to clear it up. Sorry Sir, it's just too dark and there's too much fog. Even the high res. settings couldn't clear it up. That's when I decided to wake you, Sir."

Jackson stared at the screens and then looked out the windshield. Nothing. At that moment, a high-pitched wail rose and echoed off the closeness of the canyon walls. It sounded muted coming through the shuttle's hull but Jackson felt his skin crawl and was glad they were inside. The team was instantly awake and on their feet, weapons clutched in their hands.

"What the hell was that?" Hearst said, her voice quavering a little from being awakened suddenly from a deep sleep by such a noise.

"Rewind the tape, Ensign. Let's see what it shows. The team crowded the cockpit. The tape rewound and Chantella hit the play button.

"There! Freeze it! Back it up." The team stared at the grainy image on the monitor display. A huge form, roughly eight feet tall, was centered in the view screen off the port nacelle. It had a huge head but it was the eyes that held their undivided attention. They glowed with a deep, inner, yellow light and then seemed to shutter closed and the image faded back into the surrounding darkness.

"Sweet mother of God, what is that?" Wicker asked.

"Ensign, magnify and enhance, set filtering to remove background darkness and add ambient lighting. Project composite for primate stature and build from Dr. Green's database," Jackson said.

There was a pause as Chantella entered the construct information into the program and then ran her fingers over the holographic display control. A three dimensional shape began to form on the small holo-grid platform. Chantella sucked in a breath as she stared white faced at the image rotating on the platform. Large canines could be seen in a jaw that seeped dark ooze. But it was the object the creature was clutching in its left hand that left them speechless. It was a severed arm. On the third finger was a ring. The enhanced computer imaging made the bright gold and inset purple Rydlium stone stand out in stark contrast to the rest of the image.

"A Confederate signet ring from the naval academy on Hadar," Chantella choked as the bile rose in her stomach. "There was only one Hadarian on the Hancock. Ensign Racella Hurlis. Her battle station was the tactical plot in engineering. She would have had her battle suit on and buttoned up for battle stations. Her escape pod is only a few meters from her station. She was probably one of the only ones to get out of engineering alive. Poor Race, it would have been her twenty-fourth birthday tomorrow. She was eight months out of the academy and we were going to give her a special cake made from some of the special Hadarian sweet grain we had brought on board before we left Group Six," Chantella said.

At that moment, the shuttle moved and shifted. It settled back down onto its holding struts but immediately rose again as some powerful force below tried to tip it over. The team stared in horror at the deck, thinking of the incredible force needed to even move the shuttle, let alone lift it. A scraping, grinding sound from the entrance hatch turned their heads.

"It's trying to get in," Hearst said. They watched. Unbelievably, the locking handle flexed upward, straining against the lock bolts holding it shut. The floor groaned as something once again pushed it upwards.

Breaking the spell that seemed to have rooted them in place, Jackson hit the external floodlight control, pushing the darkness back and bathing the area surrounding the shuttle in brilliant white light. The sound of anguished screams came through the hull. Something slammed into the shuttle's starboard side. The external cameras showed several huge forms that seemed to glide away into the darkness on the edge of the lights. One of the forms stopped on the edge and turned to face the camera. It was the one holding the severed arm. Its mouth opened in a soundless snarl and it hurled the arm at the camera lens. The yellow eyes seemed to wink once and then slowly fade as if a curtain were being drawn over the retinas.

"Suit up!" Jackson said. "Ensign, lift off! Get us out of this canyon and airborne now."

The team needed no further urging. They scrambled to put their gear on. Ensign Chantella strapped into the pilot's seat and brought the main engines online. Her computerized dash came alive with a waterfall of displays and readings telling her that all systems were good and that she could engage. She extinguished the exterior lights, brought the shuttle to a hover and applied thrust, moving out of the canyon and turning to a heading of one-five-zero. She increased power and set the terrain mapping and acquisition guidance system on auto, allowing the shuttle to fly itself. She set the system on a five-meter 'zero contact' envelope. That was playing it razor sharp, she knew, but she wanted to keep it as low as possible until the drop point in case anything or anyone was watching.

Five minutes from the secondary LZ, Chantella climbed to one thousand meters. As she eased over the LZ, she entered a code on the control console and deployed the insertion capsules, making sure their chameleon systems were turned on and working. Six standard Confederate special operation insertion capsules, their onboard NAV systems monitoring the ground below, spread out in a staggered formation and dropped toward the ground. Chantella pushed the nose of the shuttle forward and headed back down to nape-of-the-earth flying.

They had put on their battle gear and strapped on the low altitude chute deployment packs, each person checking the one in front of them to make sure harnesses were tight and properly fastened. Jackson and his team sat in their jump positions and watched the bulkhead clock counting down to their jump point.

At the five-minute mark, a red light blinked on and an electronic female voice spoke over the internal COM system announcing, "Warning, five minutes to release point." The crew hatch hissed open, revealing a gaping black hole, and the team stood up. One last time, Jackson and the Chief checked each static line fastened to the overhead cargo stays used to deploy the chutes, to ensure that they were fastened properly.

"Warning, two minutes to release point," the voice intoned.

"Jump point nominal, speed 70 knots indicated airspeed," Miller read off his HUD display, feeling his stomach lurch as the shuttle canted.

"Manual override on my mark. Three, two, one, mark! I have the controls, coming 100 meters now," Chantella said tightly. The shuttle pitched forward.

DeLuca winced and watched his tactical display. He hated this archaic insertion equipment and wished they were inserting with the pods.

"OK, here we go, coming one hundred and thirty meters, deck plate active 'G'." The team felt the compression of the gravitational force holding them to the deck. "Diving now." The shuttle pitched down steeply, creating a negative g-force.

"Release point on my mark, three, two, one, release!" Chantella spoke over the intercom.

There was a quiet hint of movement as the team exited the shuttle and then the hatch door shut and she eased the throttles open, gaining speed. She had already programmed the NAV system for its orbital track and as soon as the shuttle's computer monitoring system told her the hatch was closed, she immediately jumped to orbit.

The team fell for three seconds to fifty meters and there was a tug on their chute harnesses three times as each chute deployed. The next moment they were on the ground, collapsing the air from the chutes and reeling them in.

The wind-whipped rain lashed at them as they struggled with their chutes. Larson and Wicker were down first. They immediately un-slung their weapons and knelt, their eyes searching the darkness as they checked left, right and up, the muzzles of their MP-225-N's auto-tracking, searching for threats while the rest of the team secured their chutes.

The team crouched on the LZ listening for sounds that would indicate that their insertion had been compromised. They watched their passive arrays; nothing! The only sound was the night sound of wind moving through the trees and the steady hissing beat of the rain.

Jackson watched his display. His mind echoed the commands for Chief Miller and Hearst, Miller to take point and Hearst to act as rear security. They quickly moved off the LZ and into the thick brush on the southwest edge of the small clearing, where they drew up to check their systems and take up their patrol positions. Every system on their suits was powered down except for the heat dispersal systems and the battle helmets' tactical passive displays. Jackson had considered going without the helmets but after the incident with the unknown creatures in the canyon, he didn't want to be creeping around in the dark with things like that stalking the team.

"OK, Chief," he thought quietly over the team's neural net. "Twenty minutes and then we rotate out. Larsen, you're next. I want everyone sharp and spaced out at three-meter intervals. Any movement whatsoever, we go to ground. We don't engage unless we have no other choice. It's 02:30 right now. Sunrise is at 05:27. That gives us about three hours of darkness before BMNT (beginning of the morning nautical twilight), then we find a place to cover until we assess the situation, rest and move out again. I want to be on that base camp by tomorrow nightfall. That gives us about sixteen hours to cover eight kilometers and to make our descent down the face of the plateau."

The team moved out, Miller on point and Wicker three meters behind him. One moment there were six figures crouched on the edge of the small clearing and the next, only the wind and slashing rain marked their passing. They seemed to vanish into the forest. A moment later, two dark shadows detached themselves from the surrounding deeper, night shadows and silently vanished into the thick cover to the right of the team.

CHAPTER 6
CONTACT

"Hard pressed on my right, my center is yielding.
Impossible to maneuver.
Situation excellent. I am attacking."

—Ferdinand Foch at the Battle of the Marne

On the darkened battle bridge of the destroyer Haida, a green COM light blinked and an electronics warfare technician punched a button to decode the transmission on the tactical circuit from the Hunt. They were keeping station at ten thousand kilometer intervals, running flat out as fast as their star drives could push them, Chameleon mode fully engaged as they raced for Zilith. The Haida had the starboard trail position and the Hunt had overall tactical command but each had individual orders to proceed to Zilith separately should they be detected and attacked. At a given navigational waypoint they would split up, if a distance of ten thousand kilometers could be called close, and approach Zilith from separate courses to rendezvous afterwards at a pre-selected point, and then proceed at flank speed to Battle Group Six, holding station in the Degus system. Whoever made contact with the recon team first was to confirm if the 'package' as it was euphemistically referred to, had been recovered and pick up whoever was left of the recon team and, if at all possible, any survivors from the Hancock. The other vessels were to run interference and act as a blocking force for the ship that had the package and the recon team. They all knew what that meant in terms of survival for the blocking ships.

"Skipper? We have an incoming transmission from Captain Middleton on the Hunt, Sir."

"Thank you, Mr. Petrie. I'll take it in my ready room. XO, you have the bridge."

"Aye, Sir," they responded.

The door to Commander Nolan's ready room hissed open and then closed. He flicked the tactical display on and the display split to show Captain Middleton of the Hunt and Captain Adachi of the Shirayuki.

"Good morning Gentlemen! In exactly 15 minutes we will reach waypoint 'green' and separate. I know Admiral Greig briefed us on the Lexington before we left. You have also read the report concerning the 'package' that was hand-delivered to you but I want to stress again the critical nature of our mission. Let's get this done and get out of here as quickly and quietly as we can. We'll worry about kicking ass once we're back and the package has been delivered. No transmission until one of us recovers the package and we rendezvous at the egress waypoint. Any questions?"

"At this speed, we can't approach undetected. We don't know how far out the Caldarians will be patrolling or what they will have waiting for us, and if they have a ship out far enough they'll pick us up. We'll get well within their search envelope but if we don't slow down soon, we might show our cards sooner than we want to," Captain Adachi said.

"I agree. That's why Admiral Greig gave us the flexibility to adapt and change on the fly if we need to. Once we hit green I want you to slow down, go to battle stations and then proceed to your ingress route as you feel the situation dictates."

"Thank you, Sir."

"Any other questions?" Middleton held each man's eye for a moment. "Right then, good luck and good hunting."

The COM link went dead and Nolan returned to the bridge.

"Status, XO?" he asked of his executive officer, Leftenant Jason Crichton.

"We're three minutes and counting to waypoint green, Skipper," Crichton replied.

"Sound general quarters."

A piercing PING reverberated throughout the ship, sounding the call to general quarters, and the internal auto-com system announced, "Action Stations! Action Stations! This is not a drill!"

Men and women raced for their stations and donned their armored battle suits. On every deck and in every compartment, status boards confirmed stations manned and ready.

"Skipper, we have a green board across the screen, all stations and sections manned and ready. Time to new course, fifteen seconds and counting, Sir," the XO said.

Nolan turned to the helmsman and spoke, the bulkhead battle clock ticking down the last few seconds. "Now, Ms. Gabriel!"

"Sir, waypoint green engaged, slowing to one quarter star drive," Karen Gabriel replied.

"Skipper, we've lost the Hunt and the Shirayuki on the sensor grid, Sir, all systems nominal, nothing out as far as we can see."

"OK Helm, move us in."

⁊·≋

The Sipedesis

The Sipedesis had moved outside system Alpha-237 and was patrolling in a long, S-shaped curve that brought her around and back in an overlapping envelope of cover, around the four planets within the system. Her attack shuttle was on the ground in support of the Black Order Platoon on Zilith and her dismounted troops were in pursuit of Jackson and his team.

"Our long-range passive array has detected three unknowns approaching the system at high speed. They were there and then they disappeared off our monitors entirely. We were unable to identify the signatures before they disappeared," the electronic warfare technician said.

"The Confederates responded quicker than I thought they would," Consul Dedra-Va remarked. "Move us back in toward the target planet and begin our search on the enhanced array. We won't have long to wait. We have the advantage of knowing they are coming and with our upgraded sensors we should be able to locate them and move in close enough to kill them. And they can't see us."

"Yes Consul," the captain of the Sipedesis, Legate Dra responded.

"Legate, we have three cloaked vessels moving in toward the target planet. The signatures are faint and fade in and out but they're definitely there. We're still too far away to give them a positive ID," the systems technician said.

"Where are they?" Dra asked.

"They are approaching from different directions. Two are approaching from either pole and the vessel farthest out is coming in over the planet's southern hemisphere, moving north."

"Adjust our course to intercept the closest vessel and close the distance."

"Yes, Legate."

Like a stalking Koralis spider, the Sipedesis began to close with the Shirayuki, which was crossing Zilith's north polar axis. They were both moving across the planet toward the southern hemisphere.

"Ten thousand kilometrics. Five thousand. Sir, the vessel has been identified as a Confederate Fubuki class patrol frigate, standard star drive plant configuration," the technician said.

"Bring us directly alongside her port side and parallel her course at a distance of one thousand metrics. I want to kill her with a single broadside so there's no time for anyone to get to the escape pods," Dra said.

"One thousand kilometrics."

The Sipedesis approached from the stern and slowly drew abreast of the Shirayuki.

"Five hundred kilometrics. Legate, the Confederate vessel is visible. We can see her outline through her cloaking.

"One hundred kilometrics."

Ten round doors on the starboard side of the Sipedesis' hull rotated open, revealing ten particle cannons trained on the unsuspecting frigate.

"Fifty kilometrics, twenty-five, fifteen, drawing abreast now, holding station one thousand metrics off her port nacelle," the helmsman said.

The Shirayuki's hull plating could be seen as it faded and seemed to shimmer in and out of focus at close quarters.

"Helm, as soon as we fire, come about to two-seven-zero, mark four-three and go to full sub light, and set a course for the Confederate vessel approaching the northern hemisphere. We'll deal with the vessel approaching from the south polar axis last."

"Yes, Legate."

"Fire!"

Ten particle cannons designed to engage and destroy enemy battleships at ranges in excess of five hundred kilometers literally vaporized the Shirayuki. At this close range the ten cannons discharging in unison looked like a single eight hundred-meter long bar of brilliant, yellow lightning. It was over in a heartbeat—the searing cannon fire, the silent impact and the initial ball of white fire that vanished almost instantly as the atmosphere within the frigate's hull was consumed and then extinguished by the vacuum of space.

"This is like shooting Varks in a tub," Legate Dra said.

Like a lethal, black cloud the Sipedesis slipped away, heading toward her next victim, the destroyer Haida, moving toward her from the south.

From her hover and hide position in the Hancock's attack shuttle, Ensign Chantella watched her sensor arrays. She had technically disobeyed Jackson's command to hover and hide over the planet's northern pole. She had detected a wide corridor of geothermal activity close to the secondary LZ and had put the shuttle as low and deep within the disturbed ionospheric clutter as she could drive it and had shut down every non-critical system and engaged the shuttle's Chameleon mode. An approaching vessel would have to practically run her over to detect her. She shuddered involuntarily. If she had gone polar, she'd be dead. She couldn't see the Confederate ships but she could track them. She had seen the blinding flash of particle cannon fire and her sensors told her that the halo signature was that of a main Caldarian capital ship. That scared and puzzled her. What surprised her even more was that, once the unknown vessel ceased firing, her sensors went nominal when she should have been able to detect a residual weapons signature. There was nothing. It was like a window had momentarily opened in space from which an intense shaft of light had leaped through and then snapped shut without a trace. She ran a full diagnostic of her sensor arrays, both passive and active, and everything was green. An icy ball formed in the pit of her stomach.

What the hell is a Caldarian capital ship doing way the hell out here she thought? And then she had watched as the Confederate frigate blew up and disintegrated before her disbelieving eyes.

"Bastard!" she breathed.

⨳

The Haida

Hers weren't the only pair of eyes to witness the destruction of the Shirayuki. On the Haida, the bridge crew watching the viewing screen saw the flash of particle fire and their sensors also detected the halo signature.

"Caldarian battle class," the tactical officer said, his voice taut with disbelief and anger.

"What?" But Nolan had no time to ponder riddles at the moment. He had a ship to fight.

"Helm! Bring us about, course three-five-five, mark two-one. Weaps, snapshot, open outer doors on the MOSS unit and spool her up. Helm, on my mark I want you to launch and bring us about to zero-four-five, mark seven-nine and go to flank sub light! We're gonna rake this son of a bitch and make him bleed.

"Open outer doors on tubes one, three and five. This is gonna be quick. We're only going to get a glimpse when he engages but I want him dialed in. As soon as we shoot I want you to move us in, not away, to an intercept course with an estimated track turning toward us. He'll be coming in hot once he realizes he's been duped and I want the bastard in my crosshairs."

"Outer doors open on tubes one, three and five, safeties removed. This one's going to be close, Skipper. Those mark 215's have a fusion density of 58 each," Weapons Officer Sub Lieutenant Jack Stacy said.

"I know. Steady, steady, on my mark, three, two, one, launch! Helm, come to zero-four-five, mark seven-nine, full sub-light."

"Zero-four-five, mark seven-nine, full sub-light. Aye, Sir!"

The MOSS unit leapt from its launch tube and immediately accelerated ahead of the Haida and then slowed. Its computer brain began to transmit a Confederate destroyer power signature and it engaged its Chameleon cloak, almost. The signature generated was distorted just enough to give the Caldarian sensors a twitch to draw them in.

The Haida immediately heeled over and went to full sub-light.

⨳

The Sipedesis

The Sipedesis watched the oncoming vessel. It began to swing closer, its weapon bays open, cannons tracking the destroyer from the signal being fed to them from the fire control system.

"Here she comes!" Legate Dra said. "Helm, bring us in to one thousand metrics again and we'll fire as we draw along her port side. Close, closer..."

The two craft closed and the Sipedesis drew abreast of what she thought was the Confederate destroyer.

"Legate!" The electronics weapons officer on the bridge of the Sipedesis cried out a warning but it was too late. Once more, ten particle cannons lanced out in a single bar of light and sliced...nothing. The MOSS unit was obliterated before the Sipedesis realized what had happened.

"It's a decoy!" the weapons officer cried.

"Helm, bring us about. Estimate decoy's course to point of origin and swing us in. Now! Give me a full sweep on the forward array."

"Aye, Commander."

⁂

The Haida

"I've got her! I've got a bearing on the point of origin!" Sub Lieutenant Jack Stacy shouted.

"Project course and lock it in. Firing order: one, three and five. Fire!"

"Tubes one, three and five fired, Sir!"

"Helm, bring us about, course two-three-five, prepare aft tubes."

"Sir, we've just been painted at close range by an unknown type of Caldarian sensor array. Bearing one-eight-zero, mark three-eight. It's a Caldarian ship of the line! Sir, we can see her. The detonation must have damaged her cloaking grid. She's visible." They watched in horrified fascination as the lethal form of the Sipedesis swung in to kill them. "Sweet mother of God, what is that thing? It's not a line ship; it's some kind of cruiser we've never seen before. But that doesn't make sense according to..." He broke off as he watched the shimmering image of the Sipedesis swing about. "Watch out! Here she comes!"

"New course: one-three-five, mark two-nine, open weapon doors, prepare to engage port cannons," Nolan said. Stacy wondered how Nolan could remain so calm in the midst of the rush and crash of battle, even if it was silent.

"Prepare for incoming fire!"

⁂

The Sipedesis

"I see you now," breathed Legate Dra on the Sipedesis' bridge. "Fire!"

⁂

The Haida

This time, there was no mistaking the impact. The Haida heeled over and staggered under the tremendous blows. Karen Gabriel cried out as her safety harness compressed and snapped back, her right shoulder dislocating from the shock. But the Haida wasn't caught cold like the Hancock. She was moving at full sub light and her hull-damping field was engaged. Most of the fire was re-directed and absorbed. As she passed the Caldarian vessel, her own cannon fired but did no visible damage. The Sipedesis fired again. The Haida's protective energy envelope shimmered, bulged and then collapsed as it shut down.

"Sir, a seeker pulse penetrated, we have a hull breach and venting atmospherics in engineering aft of the port nacelle and bulkhead fires on decks three and seven. Damage control teams are moving to contain the blazes. Particle cannons are off-line but we still have long-lance acquisition and the tubes are active, Sir." Stacey paused. "No response from engineering, Sir."

"Control vent on decks three and seven. Ms. Gabriel, you have emergency override, bear away."

The bridge crew looked up. They knew a controlled vent on decks three and seven would extinguish the fires. They also knew that it would kill anyone left alive whose battle armor had been compromised.

Karen Gabriel clenched her teeth. "Aye, Sir, bearing now. Sir, we're stern on and bearing away."

"Tubes one, two and three are unmasked, safeties removed," Stacey said.

Karen Gabriel grunted at the thought of a compromised battle suit. As if anybody in their right mind would think of going into battle without their armor on, she thought. All it took was one small piece of random particle shrapnel to breach the hull, especially in engineering or the bridge and everyone would be flopped over, slowly asphyxiating and unable to fight a ship that was otherwise totally intact and undamaged.

The Haida was dying. She was no match for a Caldarian cruiser.

The Sipedesis came about to deliver the deathblow. Nolan still had steerageway. At the helm, Ensign Gabriel was cradling her right arm and cursing in a steady, hard monotone through her pain.

"Helm, bring us about, collision course, head straight for her."

"Collision course laid in. Aye, Sir!" Gabriel grated through clenched teeth.

Once again the Haida swung about, this time her head coming around inexorably like a wounded badger, her intentions obvious.

As Lieutenant Stacy stood listening to the old man, a holographic image of a Confederate destroyer lit up his tactical display. He blinked. For a moment, he couldn't believe what he was seeing.

"Skipper, there's a vessel closing our position at flank speed. It's the Hunt, Sir, she's powering weapons."

❧❧

The Sipedesis

"Legate, the Confederate vessel is coming about. Sir, she's set a collision course and the other Confederate vessel is approaching off our port beam. She's arming weapons!" the legionnaire manning the tactical console cried out.

"Legate Dra, we will withdraw. We will finish the Confederates once we have repaired the cloaking grid on the hull," the Consul said. "Move us out of the system to do our repairs, then we will come back to kill. This time, there will be no creeping. We will engage the remaining Confederate vessels and destroy them. They are no match for us."

"Consul, I think..."

"Leave the thinking to me and do as you are commanded or I'll have you in the acid tank before you can blink," the Consul shouted!

"Helm, disengage! Bring us about and engage star drive. Set course for grid R-four-three-three, mark four-seven," Dra said tightly.

"Aye, Commander!"

❧❧

The Haida

Nolan watched the Caldarian cruiser swing about and in one fluid movement of casual, lethal grace, engage her star drive. She was gone, with only a lingering shadow of darkness in front of the stars to mark her exit. He shuddered. He had never seen anything that looked so evil and menacing.

"We delivered a full spread of fusion torpedoes, mark 215's, and all we did was scratch her hull plating," he said to the bridge in general.

"Sir, signal from the Hunt."

"Put it up, Leftenant."

A moment later, Captain Middleton's face appeared on the view screen. "Your status, Commander?" he asked.

"Sir, we have fourteen dead and five missing. The fires on decks three and seven are out and the star drive is off line. We have emergency steerageway but that's all, Sir. There's no estimate from engineering whether we will be able to repair the drive system or get our weapons back on line. Initial sensor lock evaluated that vessel as a Caldarian ship of the line but when her cloaking went off-line we discovered that it was a cruiser class that we've never seen before. We hit her with a full spread of mark 215's and it didn't even slow her down. She'll be back. I think she only withdrew to make repairs to her hull cloaking."

"I agree. Make a list of what you need and I'll send over what I can with a damage control party to give you a hand. We'll proceed to Zilith and see if we can raise the recon team." He paused and then continued quietly. "Well done Mark. I'd get your weapons systems back online first though, Commander. Do you have enough people to fight your ship?"

Nolan smiled tightly. "Sir, I'd fight this ship alone if I had to. We're still in the ball game."

Middleton raised an armored gauntlet to his helmet in salute. "Take care, Mark!" And with that, the COM link was broken.

~∞~

Zilith, 247.0813 23:20 galactic

Commander Debra Lewis felt her stomach heave as the escape pod corkscrewed and spun on its axis. Five of the pods in front of her had been obliterated almost immediately on being ejected from the stricken Hancock and the rest had spread out in a long desperate curve toward the planet's surface. Several more had been destroyed by whatever was up there but there were too many pods and they were already entering the planet's upper atmosphere. And for a moment, just a moment, a huge form had been outlined as it breached the first tendrils of the upper atmosphere in its haste to kill the pods. No cloaking technology could hide the heat glow of a ship that was entering the atmosphere too steeply and too quickly as the hull plating began to heat up. It was only there for a moment and then its trajectory flattened out and began to rise as the ship retreated back to the safety and darkness of space.

Lewis hit the auto stabilization control and the pod began to correct its tumbling and careening. First it corrected the left-right skew and then it slowly brought the ship under control as it rotated on its axis until it was descending more or less in a stable, bow down position. Next, she slowed the pod and flattened out the trajectory so that she wasn't descending at such a steep angle. The pods had very limited maneuvering capabilities and Lewis had to decide fast, while she still had a chance, if it was within the pod's descent envelope to put it down near the secondary LZ.

She searched the NAV bank in front of her and called up the last known position of the team on the ground. She then laid a holographic overlay of the terrain surrounding that point out to 3500 kilometers. And lastly, she overlaid the last detectable sensor sweep she had of the Shuttle's pick-up co-ordinates when it had momentarily de-cloaked to pick up the recon team. A single pale, yellow line stretched across the display from the pick-up point, streaking to a point about eight hundred kilometers to the northeast, where it vanished.

"There!" she said. "Right there! You turned your cloaking back on and I'll bet a bottle of Ramillion green wine that you headed for that broken lava field to the east of your base course. Lots of cover, lots of places to hole up and hide from whatever is chasing you, yet close enough to get to the LZ.

Jack, oh Jack, you are a clever boy," she breathed.

She had met Lieutenant Jackson for the first time while on shore leave on the resort planet Endarion. She had on a deep blue evening dress made of a special fabric called sileam, a fabric from the seamstresses' guild on Capartha. Once a garment was put on, the fabric morphed and shaped itself to the specific contours of the wearer's body. Her body attracted a lot of attention. She had watched Jackson come into the night club. Something inside her had made her legs feel like rubber and she felt his lethal aura and noted the way he studied the room and it's occupants before moving. When he had come to the bar she noted with a quickened pulse that his gaze flicked over her once and then ignored her. Miffed, she had taken it as a personal challenge to break the ice. When she did, surprisingly, the connection was mutual and intense and she began calling him Jack and the name stuck. It was their little way of sharing a rare moment of intimacy while on duty.

She searched for some kind of terrain feature, anything but the jagged lava fields and dense forest cover to drop the pod into. Above the lava field, rising out of the mist of the surrounding forest, was a vast plateau of relatively flat ground. It was thickly forested but it was better than putting down in the middle of that wasteland of twisted, alien rock. She moved her hand over the pod's limited navigation console and entered the co-ordinates for the edge of the plateau that rose above the northeastern edge of the lava fields, as close to the secondary LZ as she thought she could reach on the pod's dwindling fuel supply. The pod came about one last time to turn to the final approach course Lewis had just entered. It shuddered and bucked as it passed through fifty thousand meters and the upper winds tore at it. Lewis' flight harness went taut as it compensated for the forces raging outside. As more air was sensed moving across the pod's hull, small winglets deployed, giving it a certain amount of glide so it didn't drop like a rock once the onboard fuel was expended. Lewis let the pod decelerate. At twenty-five thousand meters, she slowed her rate of descent once more and hit a bar located just below the center section of the pod's dash. An old fashioned joystick control column rose and locked into its manual flight position.

"OK Lewis, let's see if you can still do it the old fashioned way," she said to herself. Lacking rudder controls, all she could do was help the pod glide itself onto the ground.

The interior lights flickered and dimmed as the last of the pod's fuel was consumed and it switched to its electrical only system. The shuttle fell. Lewis tried to maneuver the pod but it was no good. It wasn't designed for sustained flight, just to get a person on the ground in more or less one piece. Lewis hoped the operative was 'one'. A gust of wind tore at the pod and it slewed off course, sliding to the right and descending rapidly. The right winglet brushed the upper reaches of the forest canopy and it tore off. Almost like tentacles reaching to pluck prey out of the sky, the forest reached for the shuttle and sucked it down into its dark embrace. The shuttle ripped into the trees, shearing off branches, limbs and sections of hull plating as it slowed. A high density, internal air bag deployed, cushioning Lewis as the pod slammed into the ground and tumbled a hundred meters before coming to a halt against the base of a huge Rhodendis. Lewis gasped, trying to slow her breathing and gain control.

"OK, OK," she gasped, "I'm OK. I'm on the ground."

She was hanging sideways in her harness. She struggled, trying to brace herself to release enough tension on the harness to allow her to hit the quick release snap. Lewis struggled for several moments before she was able to gain enough by holding one boot against the pod's dash and her left arm on the hatch. The harness gave and she plopped down onto the air bag which deflated when it detected her weight. She was panting and out of breath and had to rest before untangling herself from the now deflated air bag that sagged around her like a punctured inner tube.

"God damn it!" Lewis cried. She found the large release strap and yanked on it hard. The hiss and pop of CO_2 gas was heard as the seams on the bag split from the small seam charges, leaving her head and shoulders exposed. She wriggled out of the bag and kicked it in her frustration. She came to her feet and began to push her way to the survival locker. She still had her ship board battle suit on and it was getting hot.

Lewis found the locker and put her palm on the scanner to release the locking mechanism. Each locker contained a standard navy issue particle rifle and a power source.

She swore. "Come on~n~n!" she cried.

The security scanner chimed, acknowledging that she was indeed Commander Debra Lewis, helmsman of the Confederate Frigate John Hancock, and she opened the locker. She pulled out her survival suit and put it on the floor beside her. Next, she took out the pack and checked its contents. Five days of TECRATS's, three liters of water, a small molecular water collector and a standard navy long endurance, high illumination headlamp. The thermal cloak was missing.

"That's just fucking great," she growled. "No power source and no fucking thermal cloak. Why didn't I get it replaced when I took it to supply?" she muttered. "They couldn't build a separate power pack and cloak; no, they have to combine it all so if one goes south they're both useless.

"God damn BUSOP assholes! Why the hell couldn't somebody, just one fucking time, design something that makes sense?"

She stripped out of her battle suit and began the process of putting her survival suit on. She shivered. After the warmth of her EVA suit, the cool, damp air was a shock to her exposed skin. She attached the sensors, pulled on the fleece underlay and wriggled into her survival URK. It was a modified suit that had no armor or sensors and was designed solely to keep a person covered.

She strapped on her boots, hefted and put her body pack on and cinched the hip belt and shoulder straps. She picked up the particle rifle, took the power supply out of its shielded container and snapped and locked it into place. She hit the arm switch and the power supply began to hum and a blue diode display chip informed her that the weapon was armed and the safety was on. Lastly, she snapped her portable NAV pack into its wrist holster on her left arm and reached for the hatch release bar, pressing the arming mechanism that blew out the external latch bolts, allowing the hatch to drop free. A cool night wind rustled the edges of the deflated air bag and a gust of wind blew droplets of rain into the interior of the shattered pod. It was utterly dark.

Suddenly Lewis felt afraid. The realization that she was on a hostile, uninhabited world with no hope of rescue struck her like a blow. She had to steady herself on the edge of the pod.

"In for a penny, in for a pound," she whispered to herself. "The survival gurus say 'stay with your pod, it's your best chance for survival.' But we're on the backside of the galaxy and there's no way in hell there'll be a CSAR (combat search and rescue) out this far. What do I do? Think dammit! No choice girl. 'God helps those who help themselves' or some such axiom. We have to head for SEAL Team One and the attack shuttle. It's our only hope.

"Once again, into the breach, dear friends."

Straightening her shoulders, Lewis turned on her NAV system and typed a command. A small, dark red circle appeared on the display grid two kilometers to the northeast. She set her waypoint, locked the console on continuous update mode and gripped the stock of her particle rifle. She tried to recall the briefing they had received on the dangerous wildlife that stalked this planet by night. She wished she had paid more attention to that briefing but no one ever dreamt the Hancock would be destroyed. They weren't ground grunts, they were navy, she remembered thinking at the time.

Well, I sure as hell am now, she thought.

With one last forlorn look at the interior of her escape pod, she plunged into the forest.

CHAPTER 7
GRID R-433, OUTSIDE
OF SYSTEM ALPHA-237

"For time means tucker, and tramp you must,
where the scrubs and plains are wide,
with seldom a track that a man can trust,
or a mountain peak to guide..."

—Henry Lawson—Australian Poet—1867—1922

The Sipedesis decelerated to sub-light and compensators in the bow detected a slight course variance and adjusted to match what the helmsman had initially laid in. She slowed and came to a full stop at Grid R-four-three-three.

"The hull cloaking network was damaged in section 132-C on the forward edge along the port side and in section 43-S. There's an overlapping piece of 'T' section just above deck three in the bow that was damaged as well. We were running straight in when the Confederate torpedoes detonated," the Electronic Warfare Principal, Cran Narisin said. "The damage is minor and will not take long to repair but we will first have to strip away the reactive plating to get to the cloaking grid and then reinstall new plating. We have the material on board. The damaged piece at section 132-C is the control node for the port side, which is why we were momentarily visible. If the torpedo detonation had damaged any other section, the grid compensators would have re-routed the cloaking field and maintained the cloak."

"How long to complete the repairs?" Legate Dra asked.

"At least fourteen hours, Legate. The port section will be easy. All we have to do is unlatch the damping lock on that section, fix the underlying grid and bond the new plating in place. The bow section will be more complicated since it runs along the dorsal line from fore to aft and it also includes a piece of the next aft plate. That piece will have to be replaced as well, and the seam along the dorsal line will have to be re-matrixed. That is what will take the time. If that is not done correctly, the next hit could peel the hull open down the dorsal line. It was a very lucky shot on the Confederates' part."

"Begin repairs at once," Dra grunted. "Helm, standard orders, full battle watch. Power down all sensors to stand-by mode and set the passive arrays for multi-mode. We don't want to get caught out here while making repairs. With the hull open, we will be defenseless and unable to maneuver. Deploy robotic defense drones and set for an elliptical overlap pattern of five thousand kilometrics. That will give us sufficient warning should any Confederate vessels approach."

The weapons bay doors on both sides of the cruiser opened, and seven defensive drones sped away to take up their programmed positions, each in a mini orbit around the Sipedesis. The drones each carried four ion torpedoes and one frigate-size particle cannon.

Twelve Caldarian crewmen exited the cruiser and headed for the damaged hull sections, while twenty more broke out the spare sections from the storage bay and prepared to move them to the outside. The bow section of plating was proving difficult. Closer examination revealed that the adjoining plates had buckled and warped from the intense heat of the detonation. This slowed down the repairs and created frustration and anxiety in the crew members doing the work, knowing that every minute it took increased their risk that someone might stumble upon them in their vulnerable state. The warped sections had to be cut out and new sections heated with a hull arcing laser. The portable fusing press was rolled into position and then programmed to gradually heat and press the new sections into place. This took time and the men began to feel the effects of fatigue.

"Proctor Lyrisian, shift out the duty teams and relieve them with fresh crewmen. I don't want anyone hurt, nor do I want to have one of the new hull sections drift off while no one is watching. Put fresh men on the job. Maximum two hours and they shift out for food and rest."

"Yes, Legate," Prast Lyrisian, the damage control proctor in charge, replied.

"Ready on the bolt release!" the number two proctor spoke. "Clear, check!" Six throat clicks indicated that the men were clear and the section was ready to be released.

"On my mark...three, two, one, release!" There was no sound, but the gases vented from the bolt releases condensed and froze as they cut through the seam locks. The damaged hull section rose and began to drift slowly away, exposing the network of cloaking coils and armored optical cables. The damaged and burnt control node was a massive block of melted crystal. It was carefully detached, the new node set in place, and the cloaking network was reattached.

"Anti-gravity couplers are online and stable. Depressurize the bay and float the first section out," Lyrisian said. Through the cargo hatch the new section floated, six crewmen guiding it into place. It was gently lowered and the hull arcing laser pulsed.

"Careful, careful," he cried out, "the hull plating is triple-layered Dihedrix steel. Look for the thermal etching. That will tell us whose house made the plate."

"And who will end up in the acid tanks because the grid failed," one of the crewmen added.

"That is as it should be." Va spoke impassively from where he stood watching the work. His voice held not the slightest trace of emotion but the Caldarian crewmen shuddered involuntarily.

"Caldarian trade families reach back to the time of fire. It is a source of pride to be able to trace your trade to the time when Caldara was a savage land and our fathers lived by the blade." Va took a step closer and pointed to a barely discernable smudge on the section of hull plating they were maneuvering. "Look there, what do you see?" The two crewmen bent over to see what Va was pointing at. The snapping sound of canines lowering and grinding was clearly audible over the COM link.

"Yes, it is as you see—a Duralis stone, the sign of the Imperial Shadow, the forefathers of the makers of the killing blade of the Emperor, the ones who taught us to kill under the cold light of our inner moon, Irana. Only thrice in two thousand years have the dark ones come forward with a new blade for the Emperor. Always it is a time of tempering and destiny, and would you not agree that killing is best tasted under its cold gleam, Proctor?" Va asked, turning toward Lyrisian and watching him from behind his gold-visored faceplate.

Lyrisian slowly stood to his full height and stared back at Va. There was a brittle edge to his voice. "As you well know Legate, the time of killing was the forging of our destiny. It made us as hard as the alloy in this plating, and the time to kill is upon us once again."

"And what will it shape for us, Proctor Lyrisian?"

Before he could answer, a piece of the damaged bow section broke off, catching two crewmen across the chest and shearing them in half. The severed portions drifted apart, while the upper torsos were restrained by their safety harnesses.

"We need to recover the bodies," Lyrisian stated tightly.

Two crewmen were in the process of detaching their tethers when a cold, emotionless voice stopped them and held them motionless in place.

"No!" Consul Dedra-Va said. "They're dead. Leave them be. They are unimportant. The mission is everything! They are nothing. Continue with the repairs. I will have two crewmembers sent out to replace them. Continue with the repairs!"

The other crewmembers immediately turned to comply but Lyrisian momentarily forgot who he was speaking to and his anger overrode his discipline. "We have to recover their bodies!" he grated, his voice tight with anger.

In one swift movement, Va drew his darter, raised it to Lyrisian's helmet and pulled the triggering device twice. Lyrisian's visor exploded and a millisecond later the explosive contacts on the darts penetrated his head and detonated. His visor burst into a hundred glittering shards that glistened wetly in the harsh glare of the arc lamps, and his body somersaulted backwards from the force of the impacting rounds. Va detached the restraining clip on Lyrisian's harness and watched as his lifeless body cart wheeled in slow motion, drifting away from the ship. Va chambered another explosive dart into the dispensing chamber but did not re-holster his weapon. He turned to the other legionnaires who had watched the entire episode.

In a calm voice he said, "Now we will continue with the repairs. Are there any questions?" There were none. "Good, then carry on." He drifted to the docking bay and re-entered the ship.

"Legate Dra, please assign four more men to help with the hull repairs, two to replace the ones who decided to leave us and two for extra hands. Proctor Mydris Hurlion, are you monitoring this frequency?"

"Yes Consul," Hurlion replied.

"Good, you are now Proctor One of the starboard weapons order. Congratulations. What is your house sign, Proctor Hurlion?"

"A stooping black falcon, Consul, from the mountains of Versellus."

"Ah! A most appropriate family sign for your newly acquired position. Well Proctor Hurlion of the house of Black Falcons, I trust you will fare better than the late Proctor Lyrisian. We must sit some day, when we are not as pressed for time as we are now, and you shall speak to me of this falcon that hunts by moonlight in the great vales of Versellus. For now, there is work to be done—to your station. Captain Dra, will you please meet me in my quarters?"

"Yes, Legate," Dra responded.

Mydris Hurlion wet his lips with his tongue. He glanced at the other crewmembers standing 'to' at their battle stations in full armor. To be singled out by Consul Va left a raw feeling of dread in his stomach.

We fear them almost as much as the Confederates do, he thought as he glanced at the men standing at their stations. He caught the cold glitter of fear in their eyes. He knew what they were thinking. To be so singled out meant that he was a marked man. His life now hung in the balance. Even among the regular Caldarian military, members of the Black Order Legion were a mystery, cloaked in fear and shadow. But the whispered stories about Consul Dedra-Va set him on a different plane.

Va strode to his day cabin and connected his security implant to the locking network. As his door hissed shut behind him he paused and gazed around his sparse quarters. His eyes stopped on the blood blade that was sitting in a crystal case on his desk. There were dark stains along the blood channel and the hard Lucidian grip was scored where a war axe had glanced off it. Va closed his inner eyelids and allowed his mind to drift back. The bulkhead disappeared and the stench of viscera mingled with shit and blood filled his nostrils.

Va was larger than most Caldarians, his dark, deep-set eyes would kindle and go slate black when he was angry. He held his emotions in tight check and kept his thoughts to himself. He had proven himself in the only place that really mattered to a Caldarian—the battlefield. His family sign was the Koralis spider, a predator in the dark forests of the northern sub-continent of Caldara that only hunted and killed other spiders.

"You are being sent to the Solaris system for outpost duty," Seth Var, the Legion overlord told him.

Va stood at attention, his eyes staring past the overlord.

"The planet has a number of pre-industrial societies who are working the Uridian crystal mines for us. It is part of our payback for allowing us access to their planet."

"You mean we take what we want," Va asked quietly.

The overlord let out a gurgling sound deep in his throat.

"No, we let them live long enough to extract the ore before we kill them," he stated flatly. "You have eighteen months of duty, Centurion Va, and it is hoped that one with your noted rapacity will be able to complete the pacification cycle and come home, whereupon the Council will recognize your skill in diplomacy and bestow on you the title Legate of the Twelfth Legion. Do what is necessary to keep your troops in line but do not fail me, Centurion Va."

Va walked across the compound to the communications building, the rain and mud splashing up and across his battle armor. The retinal scanner flashed briefly and the locking mechanism opened.

"As you were, as you were," he said to the three technicians who had begun to come to their feet. "Perimeter report?"

"Centurion, the perimeter is clear out to the 1,500 metric mark, the force field is active and we have no traffic to report from the 12th Escadrille holding station in the Trident quadrant. These savage, unwashed pigs are too dull and stupid to realize what we have been doing to their planet in the seventeen moon cycles we've been here."

"I think Calis, that your brain has become slow and fogged...perhaps by these large-titted Solarian females who come here every night with their spiced oils and liniments to help you, 'What shall we call it?', maintain your focus."

There was a deep throaty growl of agreement from the other two legionnaires.

"Ah Centurion, I think our technical friend is perhaps thinking with his overly short phallus that he likes to brag about," Vandok shot back.

Va frowned in mock severity. He knew well enough what went on during the night watch. "I think the three of you should report to Proctor Ilarion at the lift pad by 1800 in full patrol armor.

We will be gone for several days and maybe in that time you will remember what it is to be legionnaires. I have a feeling these unwashed pigs as you call them are not as dull as you think they are. The idiots in the Pacification Cohort seem to think everything is under control but I think they are too blind to see. Keep your blood blades close."

The three came to rigid attention, their right hands making fists over their left breasts. "Duty first, death second," Prastin intoned.

Va smiled a tight, sardonic smile and walked out.

And then, in one night, the primitive inhabitants of the planet changed his life forever. What the Caldarians considered dull-witted and uncouth savages proved to be anything but. They waited for a night of darkness and heavy rain to ensure that the particle assault rifles the Caldarians carried would be next to useless.

"So who will it be tonight, Solinas?" Suror teased. "I know how much you especially love Vandok, the one with the glittering eyes."

"Leave her alone, Suror," the oldest of the three whispered. "I don't care who you take. I want Calis. I have something to give him that I have been waiting a long time for."

"Fourteen turns of the moon. Fourteen long turns we have waited, Chana, and tonight in this rain, when their weapons will be useless, we will strike. But first a little honey in the pot and then I will let him know how I hate him," Solinas hissed. "It has been three days since we were last here. They won't even scan us." The other two women laughed.

"All their bright, off-world talking walls won't help them," Solinas whispered.

"They are called scanners," Suror corrected. "Walls do not talk. Even you should know that after fourteen months."

"I know that they butchered my life mate and our three children and made me watch," Solinas replied. Her voice couldn't hide the choking rage inside her. She allowed her fingers to caress the object she had hidden deep inside her garments.

"We have company," Calis declared when he heard the airlock hiss open. The three legionnaires stood up to greet the Solarian women. Over the last fourteen months they had each selected a favorite.

"Leave the food until later," Prastin said huskily as he took Suror in his arms.

The interior of the COM center was dark. The sounds of people on the brink of sexual release could be heard spilling out from a number of recessed alcoves behind the monitoring stations.

The women had taken their designated target, allowing him to penetrate, prolonging their orgasmic passion to ensure that the victims were satiated to that state of sexual release that relaxed the body and set the mind in a contented, unguarded stupor.

Solinas pulled Vandok closer and her breath filled his mind with desire. She was enjoying this moment. She hated the Caldarians with a deep, cold hatred. As she caressed him and pulled him deeper, her right hand reached out and closed on the hilt of her dagger. With her left hand she gently stroked his head and let her lips trace the outline of his right ear, turning his head so that his left ear was clear.

"Vandok, do you know what you are?" she whispered. Vandok's head rose slightly at the gentle caress of her hand. Suddenly she took a handful of his hair and yanked back. "You are Kalosh Var," she hissed savagely in his ear, and thrust the needle dagger as hard as she could drive it, into his left ear canal. There was a momentary last thrust as his body convulsed in death, a small trickle of blood seeping from his left ear. She thrust his body off her and kicked it savagely in the head, feeling the nose cartilage crunch and break with the impact of her heel. She spat on him. "I hope the whore whose breasts suckled you has many years left to think of how you died at my hands, you pig bastard."

Naked, she raced to the control panel. She had watched Vandok work the numeric touch pads countless times and had long ago memorized the sequence that deactivated the electronic perimeter alarms and dropped the security grid. Once that was done, it wouldn't matter. The clubs and axes would destroy the equipment.

There was a swish of movement behind her and she whirled, fist up, dagger in hand, but it was Chana and Suror.

"Is it finished?" Chana asked. There were no words. Their eyes met and communicated the message that only vengeance can display. The outer door opened and there was a rush of painted, savage bodies in the dark, swirling toward the barracks and other buildings. One of the bodies stopped, reached over his back to the pack he carried and removed three war axes, which he tossed, one at a time, to Solinas who caught each one with the deft ease of a practiced warrior. The painted figure glanced once into the room, smiled a tight, grim smile and melted into the darkness to join his companions, leaving Solinas and her companions to systematically destroy every piece of equipment inside the COM center.

"Red Base, Talon Lead, over," Va called over the command circuit.

"You stupid, lecherous bastards," he cursed. "When I get back to base, I'll personally peel your skin off and throw your worthless carcasses into the acid tank."

He turned to his cohort proctors, gathered around him. "Something is wrong. That's the sixth check-in they've missed and even if they couldn't call, the auto-transmit should have sent the response. We're two day's hard march away and have only the patrol shuttle. The lift vehicles were cycled back to Red Base and are assumed casualties.

"Proctor Hurvada, take the shuttle and go to an orbital track. Send an emergency flash message to the 12th Escadrille and tell them we need the 12th Reaction Force immediately. Then I want you to head for Red Base and try to raise the garrison and see if you can see anything. You're thirty cyclets flying time from Red Base. I want you to call me every five cyclets and don't do anything rash. Make your assessment and then proceed back here at once."

"Yes, Centurion," Hurvada replied. He moved off, buckling his flight helmet as he ran for his shuttle.

"All Quadra, lock down. First Quadra take the point, battle formation. Second Quadra, take the left flank. Proctor Larst, I want you and Third Quadra on the right and Proctor Arist, you take Fourth Quadra as rear security. Move out! Keep it tight and watch your sensor readouts. I have a feeling those gutless fools in the Pacification Cohort are about to learn a rude lesson about unwashed pigs."

"Talon Lead, Red Shuttle, over."

"Talon Lead."

"Talon Lead, Red Shuttle. Orbit stat, SITREP sent to 12th Escadrille. Be advised that 12th Legion Reaction Force is enroute. ETA three dayras, over."

"This is Talon Lead. Red Shuttle, make your run and advise. You are weapons free. Repeat, you are weapons free."

"Talon Lead, Red Shuttle. I copy, weapons free, out."

Hurvada was no fool. He was a seasoned veteran of many battles and thought he understood the nature of the situation he faced. He headed for the deck and tree-hopped toward the compound at 400 knots indicated air speed.

"Talon Lead, Red Shuttle, over."

"Talon Lead."

"Talon Lead, Red Shuttle. I am at the five cyclet waypoint and have the compound in sight. Coming 500 metrics, 200 knots—flaring now. I have targets in sight. Centurion, the COM center is burning. There are several hundred Sols in front of the main compound building. They have not dispersed. I am breaking to commence my run along the main road approaching the outer perimeter wire."

Solaris stood with the others in front of the compound building, watching the shuttle make its pass. "Come on, come on," she whispered.

Hurvada removed the safety on his particle cannon. "You vermin. I'm going to stick my particle cannon right up your asses and watch your bodies vaporize as your body fluids boil away. That's it, stay right there, here it comes, wait for it."

"Talon Lead, Red Shuttle, over."

"Talon Lead."

"Talon Lead, Red Shuttle. Passing the fifteen hundred metric marker, particle cannon is active and tracking. Splash on my mark. Going active..."

The hand was filthy. Caldarian blood was caked and crusted over the skin, and the fingernails were dark.

"Steady, Solak, steady. Wait for my word. We don't want our Caldarian masters to be disappointed in their unskilled students," Arren spoke.

"Master diode armed and active, tracking grid is in passive mode. Target is hard lock, waiting to go active for particle discharge," Solak repeated.

"Here comes our little sparrow now, exactly as they said he would." His hand tightened on Solak's shoulder as they watched the shuttle grow large in the digital sight of the Black Viper anti-air cannon.

"Now," Arren breathed.

Solak depressed the arming trigger and the Caldarian sensor array instantly went active, illuminating the shuttle. In the next instant he pulled the arming nipple on the control yoke.

As Hurvada passed the outer perimeter wire at the fifteen hundred metrics range, his threat receiver suddenly went off the board. It took his unbelieving senses just half a second to realize he was dead and that he had been hustled. Two Caldarian Black Viper anti-air cannons were locked on his shuttle. He fire-walled the throttle, rolled out hard to starboard and headed for the deck, knowing it was no good. The shuttle leaped forward, clawing around. A millisecond later, two beams of superheated particle fire blotted the shuttle out of the sky. It cart wheeled and tumbled on its axis, impacting with a thundering explosion as its onboard particle munitions fireballed into the sky several hundred metrics from the compound.

There was a short pause before Va and the entire cohort heard Hurvada's scream and then static.

The warriors on the ground shouted and shook their weapons at the sky. Arren and Solak roared and jumped up and down as the shuttle died.

"Red Shuttle, Talon Lead, over." Va knew it was no good and they were in deep, serious trouble. This was no mere local tribal uprising.

"All units, form on the front echelon and advance to grid Delta-234. There is a small hill there and we'll stop to assess the situation and rest. Acknowledge!"

Nine encoded chirps told him that his message had been received and passed on to each section member.

"Full cloaking, and set suit sensors to multi-scan, full battle mode. They will be coming for us as soon as it grows dark. Set your rifles on maximum dispersion. Section eight, you have the point. Move out." They moved out warily.

On one point, Va was wrong. The Solarians didn't wait until night to hit them. They hit them in broad daylight, as their patrol line was strung out traversing around the southwestern end of a small, boggy swamp where the forest came down in thick clumps and the trail bottlenecked at the soggy shoreline. They moved cautiously, one section at a time, providing over watch for each section as it made the traverse. The suits cloaked whatever was underneath them. Once the outer layer of the suits were soiled or contaminated, it took time for the Chameleon circuits to adapt to the interference caused by the contamination—enough time for the Solarian warriors to locate them. The number of contacts overloaded their suit sensors. They couldn't track them all and they couldn't see anything to shoot at. They felt, more than saw the warriors following them. Suddenly, seventy warriors broke cover from three sides and swarmed toward the Caldarians. Racing twenty meters in front of the warriors were half a dozen large hunting hounds whose olfactory acuity led them straight to the cloaked Caldarians.

"All quadra—engage! Kill the hounds first. Get the dogs!" Va said over the TAC net. Phase fire rippled out and snapped and hissed as it cut flesh. All but two of the hounds were hit and thirty warriors went down in a heap but the others continued to follow the remaining two dogs and, attracted to the bright light of the particle rifles, zeroed in on the cloaked Caldarians and moved relentlessly forward.

Their backs to the water, their attention on the approaching warriors, they never saw the sixty heads rise slowly from the black water behind them. Sixty arms rose out of the water and uncovered their war slings from their oiled coverings. A whirring sound filled the air and sixty small, leather, lead-weighted pouches whistled toward the cloaked Caldarians. On impact, the pouches broke, splattering whatever they hit with a greasy, red ink. Twenty found Caldarian troopers, their outline clearly defined under the ink. Once more the slings whirled and sixty pouches found thirty-four more Caldarian legionnaires. Sixty heads sunk back beneath the water, breathing tubes clamped in their mouths. The Caldarians who had been hit felt the impact of the missiles and at first, didn't realize the significance of what had just happened. However, when one legionnaire toppled over, the shaft of a six-foot war lance protruding from his chest, they understood. They were visible.

With a roar, three hundred painted warriors wielding war axes and curved war knives rushed out of the trees and thick brush toward the Caldarian position. Particle fire rippled and flashed at the onrushing wave but there were too many of them. Suddenly, from behind the Caldarian position, from the lake, sixty warriors who had waited in submerged ambush rushed into the fight, axes twirling and glinting in the bright sun.

But this was no rival tribe feuding over women and crops. It was a cohort of Black Order Legionnaires.

"Kuta nosh!" Va roared. In one smooth, rippling motion the legion flanks pivoted and anchored, the front column going to one knee. The rippling particle fire looked like a solid bar of killing gold as it cut Solarian flesh. The Solarians closed relentlessly.

"Get ready. Steady. Now!" Va cried out. With a roar, the kneeling legionnaires dropped their particle weapons, drew their blood blades and surged forward to meet the swarming Solarians while the rear ranks laid down suppressing fire. Va ran forward and fired point blank into the chest of a huge warrior and then his particle pistol was knocked out of his hand. He drew out his blood blade and parried a blow from a garishly painted warrior and drove the tip of the blade into the warrior's stomach, twisting the blade from side to side and then wrenching it upward as the warrior's eyes glazed over and he fell to the ground. And then the world dissolved in a fog of killing. Va felt a stunning blow to his blade and pivoted, only to see a war axe coming around to smash his face. In the next instant he was thrown to the side and the warrior's face disintegrated as five explosive darts tore his head apart.

The charging Solarians wavered, then broke and fled back into the cover of the surrounding forest. One hundred and twenty-six dead Solarians lay on the ground.

Va's chest was heaving as he desperately gulped air. His battle suit was covered with blood and bits of gore and grey brain tissue. He glanced around. The legionnaire who had saved his life was dead; a war axe had split his head in half.

"Quadra form on my NAV mark now," Va commanded. "When I give the word, we will move to our objective. It is only fifteen hundred metrics ahead." Slowly the legionnaires swung and pivoted, closing ranks on Va as their training and discipline took over. Disciplined phase fire kept reaching out, cutting down warriors by the dozens. But the legionnaires had suffered. There were only forty-eight left of the original ninety. Va himself held the rear as they moved toward the hilltop. The Solarians kept their distance, having drawn out of range of the particle rifles.

"They've drawn off," Proctor Larst said.

"For the moment," Va replied. "They'll be back. You can take my word for it." He slapped Larst on the shoulder before moving down the line.

Every once in awhile, a group would rush in and sling pouches at the advancing legionnaires until at last, every legionnaire was marked with red ink. It had cost the Solarians over three hundred warriors but fresh forces arriving to join the battle had already replaced those who had fallen. It was slow going. Finally, weary and fatigued, the remaining thirty-nine legionnaires reached the hilltop. Va moved amongst them ceaselessly, ordering the night perimeter to be set and to break out the rations. They had no way of hiding from the warriors who encircled them. All they could do was hope to hold them off until relief arrived.

"Go easy with the water," Va said. "In the morning we will set out the water reclamation cells but until then, drink sparingly." He moved from position to position, encouraging, giving a suggestion. At last, the sun went down and all was still. The land seemed to be waiting. Hundreds of fires flared up around the hilltop. Their night vision optics flared, compensated, flared and then closed, trying to compensate for the hundreds of multiple images that shimmered green and ghostly in the lenses. They tried setting the filters to isolate body thermals but there was too much distortion. They finally had to turn the systems off and rely on normal vision, exactly as the Solarians had intended.

Movement teased them. Warriors would rush the hilltop and drop. Particle fire would reach out. Some would hit and the snapping sound of searing flesh would be heard. But each time the warriors rushed, they dropped closer to the battered group of weary legionnaires.

"Fire order, conserve your fire. Mark your target and set your power modules for timed relay. Give me a count." All along the line came the collective response—power modules below twenty-three percent.

There was a keening in the night that wasn't the wind. It rose in pitch and seemed to fill the little hollow they were holding.

Va looked about him. "Draw your blood blades!" All along the line, there was a whisper of steel as thirty-six legionnaires once again drew their close combat weapons. "Watch the left flank, it's closest to the scrub brush along the bottom of the hill. They've come for us the last three times from that point."

A legionnaire beside him unlatched his battle mask and threw it to the ground. "Masks dead, Centurion. And I want to smell the wind again before I die." His right side was seeping blood from a lance wound and there were no more MED packs of sealant left." There was a soft click as he lowered his canines.

"A drink of Durillian mead would do just fine now, Centurion, don't you think?" Va grinned in the darkness. Without taking his eyes off the dark terrain to his front, Va unlatched a small cargo container on his battle suit and tossed the small flask of mead to Duris Val-Seedra. Seedra caught it and took a sip of the strong, sweet liquor and coughed as a thin line of frothy blood seeped from his mouth.

"You are a pig and a whore's dark hole, Seedra but I hope you can still see well enough to squeeze the arming nipple on your weapon when they come for us."

Seedra grinned. It wasn't until morning that Va saw how well he had done before a war axe had torn his chest open.

For two days they held them off. Power packs were depleted, the wounded lay untended in the midst of the small circle on the top of the hill. There were fourteen Black Order Legionnaires left when they heard a ripping thunder approaching from the northeast. It was a flight of attack shuttles from the cruiser, Brudaris.

For that action, Va had received his sixth honor braid.

His tightly woven honor braid, tucked beneath his battle helmet, protruded from the edge of his black uniform collar. He reached up with his right hand and put it back in its proper place. Three knots were the norm for a consular command from a war-hardened race. Five were considered exceptional. His braid had six. Seth Var, the overlord of the entire Black Order Legion, had tied the last knot himself. As he had bent to Va's ear, he whispered, "Congratulations, Consul. I would trade my house sign to have accomplished such a feat."

Slowly the swirl of battle faded and Va's inner eyelids opened.

He turned at the sound of the door opening to see Legate Maran Dra standing at battle rest before the desk.

"Consul," Dra said in greeting. His black eyes gave no hint of emotion or sign, as to what he thought of what had just taken place.

Va turned and moved to the center console. "Estimated time to complete repairs?" he asked flatly.

"Your morale-boosting efforts have been successful, Consul. We should be ready to move in nine hours. The cloaking system is back on-line and electronics is running a full system diagnostic now."

Va didn't respond to the mention of his actions outside. "I will remind you, Captain, that what is at stake here is higher than the lives of a few crewmen who did not see the necessity of haste. If the Confederates recover the Element, the balance of power will shift and that will prove catastrophic for the Caldarian people."

"I will remember to inform the deceased's families of that fact, Consul, when I have to explain to them why there will be a break in the line of the dead in their family plots."

Va's face went dark and his eyes glinted but he maintained his calm. Only his eyes showed a shadow of the dark menace behind his carefully worded response. "All in due time, Captain. You will understand that clearer once we regroup with our fleet but in the meantime, we must complete our mission. Has our team on the ground been contacted?"

"Yes Consul. We have informed them that we will be delayed for several cycles and that we have been in contact with Confederate vessels within the system. They are in the process of executing phase two of the operation as we speak. Once they have eliminated the Confederate ground force and recovered the Element, they will call for extraction."

"Excellent!" Va said. He came around the corner of the console and stood directly in front of Captain Dra. "We will succeed, Captain Dra, or we will die trying. That is non-negotiable."

Dra didn't flinch. He held the consul's eyes, feeling the tense hostility inside Va, knowing that he was standing on dangerous ground. "As you said, Consul, all in due time." And with that, he turned and left the cabin.

CHAPTER 8
MIDNIGHT BLACK

"A piece of paper makes you an officer;
a radio makes you a commander."

—General Omar N. Bradley

"Chief?" Jackson's thought called softly over the neural link. "You OK?"

The wind and rain tore at Miller's helmet, the night vision faceplate and Heads Up Display making the forest glow in a way that reminded him of a graveyard at night. His eyes scanned the surrounding brush, trying to penetrate the darkness, constantly moving from his front to each side, up into the overhanging branches and down to the ground in front of him again.

"This wind and rain is degrading our helmet electronics." Miller was down on one knee, the butt of his MP-225-N tucked into his right armpit, his right hand firmly holding the rifle's pistol grip and his index finger taking up the slack on the trigger. He held the fore stock with his left hand, his arm straight, pointing along the barrel with his left index finger. "They keep trying to compensate and the systems get overloaded. I've got my audio and night enhancement filters set on auto-override and they keep snapping wide open one moment and then going nominal the next. Anything out there can get a hell of a lot closer than we want them to before we know they're out there. And with everything shut down except our night vision optics, that's going to be damn close, Sir." His eyes never stopped moving even as he talked. "Our patrol line is tighter than usual but that can't be helped in all this thick cover. We can take one step and be face to face with a Caldarian point element or worse, and things could get ugly real quick."

"I know, Chief. I've allowed extra time for slugging and detouring but it's still going to be a bitch to reach the edge of the plateau before dawn and at least another six hours after that to make the descent to the plain below."

The chief stood up and cautiously began moving forward again.

Jackson looked at the dark image of Jamie Wicker, his big M-363G machine gun held in the trail position. He was just visible about three meters behind the Chief. Jackson called up his team armament readout and saw that Wicker had loaded the feed drum with a multi-dispensing array of munitions. The safety was off. Good move, he thought.

Wicker, as the slack man in the line, followed Miller. His role was to provide suppressing fire if Miller walked them into an ambush or made contact. It was at that point that the team had to decide in a hurry if they should break contact or try to outflank the ambush team and take them under fire. He was far enough behind Miller not to draw attention to or distract him, but close enough to support him if the Chief made contact.

"Damn mud," Wicker muttered, feeling it suck at his boots, knowing that if he had to move in a hurry, it would slow him down. He shifted his weight and moved his feet, trying to gain a better purchase with the soles of his boots but all he accomplished was to sink a little deeper in the dark, foul smelling ooze. Slowly moving his left thumb, he felt the selector switch on the stock and unconsciously wiped the rain away with his gauntleted hand. He checked the arming mode on the diterium grenades and glanced at the arming diode that glittered a dull blue dot of menace. A small trickle of cold moisture made its way down his neck, making him shiver despite his suit's heating grid. He desperately wanted to scratch it but knew he couldn't reach it without taking his hands off his weapon. He wondered what it would feel like to have a 'blue' detonate unexpectedly, and then wished he hadn't.

As if reading his thoughts, Jackson spoke. "Wicker, make sure those blues are in passive. We don't want an incident like what happened on the Gonzales three months ago. Those grenades are frequency sensitive and no one realized that the activating frequency was a sub-carrier that's used on standard Confederate docking nodes."

"Sir, they've changed the carrier frequencies on all Confederate docking nodes since then and they've narrowed the passband skirts on the arming circuits on the grenades so that they attenuate a larger harmonic range. That's why they narrowed the frequency acquisition envelope; it can't happen again, Sir."

"Well, when those grenades blew, they took out the attack shuttle and SEAL Team Five, Earth Prime, and twenty-eight of the Gonzales' crew, not to mention that the Gonzales had to be towed to space dock for repairs," Dyer added.

Jackson nodded and noticed that his command display indicated that it was time to log a suit STAT report.

"Give me a suit check," Jackson's thought echoed.

"My outer layer is soaked but the heating coils are coping...for the moment," DeLuca said, the others coming back with similar reports.

"OK, I want everyone to set their suits on auto and let them do what they were designed to do. I don't want anybody going hypothermic. I need everybody focused and alert. And keep your eyes on your power monitors."

The team was tense, every sense concentrating on watching and listening. All was dark and the only sound was the wind sighing in the upper branches of the forest canopy, but the team's unease and nervousness grew, the further they went. It wasn't Caldarians that worried them anymore but the memory of the creatures that had attacked the shuttle in the narrow box canyon.

By unspoken command, the team halted, each member going to ground, one knee up, one knee down and training their weapons out at the threatening darkness. Each member of the team sensed a gradual feeling of evil drawing close.

"We're moving quiet, Sir. Even in this mud, I can't detect any sound at all from the rear." Hearst was acting as rear security. She would pause and wait to listen for any sign of movement approaching from the rear, watching her passive arrays, and then move forward in a guard position to catch up with the team. The last time she paused and waited and lost sight of the rest of the team, it scared her in a way that she had never felt before. Even now she couldn't shake the feeling that something was out there, stalking her. Shit, she thought, I'm the Ice Queen. I've done this a hundred times. What's wrong with me?

The darkness pressed in on her and the hair at the nape of her neck prickled. It was just as she was about to move forward that a blackness deeper than the forest dark glided across her peripheral vision and moved into her twelve o'clock. It melted into the darkness on her left. The only thing that kept her from dropping her weapon and bolting forward was her training and discipline. Instead, she inched forward, forcing herself to move slowly and carefully. The shadowy form of Dyer materialized out of the darkness, taking shape in her display.

"Sir," she said, "I saw something just before I moved to catch up. It was just a shadow but it was definitely there, and it vanished into the trees and brush on our left flank. And whatever it is, it's not Caldarian."

"How do you know?" Jackson asked.

"We all know how the legion patrols and uses an ambush site. If they had been Caldarian, the first warning we would have had would have been incoming fire. And one other thing just doesn't fit the mold, Sir."

"What's that, Doc?"

"I could feel it, Sir." Every helmet turned to look at her in the darkness. She couldn't see their eyes but she was sure they all registered the same fear that she felt, assailing them, drawing near in the darkness.

"I felt it too," DeLuca said. "Something is out there keeping pace with us."

"Anyone else sense anything?" Jackson asked.

Six helmeted heads nodded in affirmation. Jackson checked their location and the time. "Dawn is three hours off yet but I think we better find a hole, hunker down and wait for daylight before we attempt the descent off this plateau. DeLuca, you take the point. The first spot that looks good, we stop and wait till dawn. Doc, you OK on rear security or you want me to spell you?"

"I'm OK, Sir. I just needed to check to see if you guys felt the same thing."

"Well, Doc," Larsen drawled, "I don't know about the rest of these mud-flapping ground pounders but if you can help me unpucker my ass from this stump I'm sitting on, we can move out." The team chuckled quietly and then DeLuca took point, and one by one the other members moved out, Hearst taking up rear security once more.

Twenty minutes later, DeLuca raised his fist in the air and crouched down on one knee. Jackson moved up and DeLuca motioned to his right.

"There," his mind whispered across the TAC net. "That huge Rhodendis with the low hanging branches, the secondary growth is thick and at the base there's a small area large enough for all of us to hole up in. The upper branches will give us some cover from the wind and rain, as well."

"OK," Jackson nodded. "Let's pass it and go about another two hundred meters, then I want you to stop and we're going to reverse order and fish-hook back. Doc, once we stop, you've got the point, so move us in nice and slow."

"Do you hear that?" Larsen asked. He checked the waypoint on his NAV. "We're within five hundred meters of the edge of the plateau. That wind's coming up the slope and over the top of the plateau and I'd estimate it must be gusting to 100 kilometers an hour." The sound was like an endless wave coming in on the long, flat shoreline of some vast, lonely beach. He shivered.

They moved past their RON and then DeLuca, on point, slowed their pace down. It took them another ten minutes to move the entire team past and then he went down on one knee and checked in.

"Point."

Each team member checked in and then Jackson said, "rotate" and the team began their sweep back to their hide position with Hearst on point.

"Four clear," Hearst said as she went to one knee beneath the Rhodendis. "I have no passband emissions; all sensors are nominal, shutting down now."

Cautiously, the rest of the team moved into the small clearing until there were seven weapons and seven pairs of eyes watching the surrounding area. Jackson reached up and touched Larsen on the shoulder and he in turn, reached out with his left hand and touched Dyer. There were no words spoken. They knew the drill. They put their weapons down within easy reach, unlatched their battle masks and lifted the faceplates up without taking their helmets off. There was the faint hiss of air equalizing. They each opened a front latch on their packs and took out a meal ration. They ate in total silence. The other team members never took their eyes off of their area of responsibility or glanced at Larsen and Dyer. Once they were finished eating they closed their battle masks, took up their weapons and took their positions while two other team members repeated the same drill. In twenty minutes, they had all eaten and hydrated.

"OK," Jackson said. "Right now we rest. Three of us will rest for an hour and twenty, and then the others shift out and we watch. Chief, I want you, DeLuca and Hearst to take the first watch so that you can rest last. I want all three of you as fresh as possible when we move out. I need you on point and rear security. Sleep if you can but we don't gear down. We sleep suited.

"I don't want anyone fatigued. We've still got a long way to go and we all need to stay focused. You lose focus and someone ends up dead, it's that simple. We've all taken the sleep training, so I want to see everyone's biomonitor logging at least ninety minutes of stage five sleep."

Jackson and the others not on watch lay down, weapons clasped in their hands and were asleep within moments. The night moved on. Alien stars slowly moved in their intricate dance overhead and the planet turned slowly towards the dawn. The wind whipped the upper branches while three pairs of eyes watched, senses alert, for the slightest sound or movement.

A pair of yellow eyes watched the seven life forms from a hidden position a mere fifteen meters away. Tapetum structures in its eyes reflected light that was not absorbed by the retina back to the photoreceptors, providing better vision in twilight, making them shine in the dark, and allowing it to see in conditions that most sentient beings would consider the total absence of light.

It sniffed the wind, recognizing the peculiar odor of flesh it had fed on in the past. Its salivary glands began to run and its stomach responded to the need for nourishment. It remembered how easy they were to catch and how soft the flesh was in comparison to its usual diet. It had gorged for several hours on one of the aliens it had found sheltering beside a large oval-shaped object. It had tried to escape, tried to climb into the object but died quickly from a blow to the skull.

The creature had approached to within two meters of Doc Hearst and had been ready to snatch her when she suddenly whirled and began to move toward the others. It planned to feast again before the white face climbed into the sky and it had to seek shelter from its burning, hateful presence. There were three of the creatures in a rough triangle around the aliens. They had been trailing the team, keeping abreast of them in the heavy cover since the start of the hunt. It bent its thought for the others and slowly they crept closer, seeking an opportunity to attack.

The muscles along its back rippled as it moved silently forward, its massive five hundred pound bulk gliding with no apparent noise. Something deep inside its brain instinctively warned that these aliens were not the simple prey the others had been and it was cautious now. They were wary and moved with a smooth precision. Three times it had begun to approach closer, to kill the trailing creature at the rear but each time it had to break off because it sensed that somehow they knew it was there. But now they were stopped. It had already identified its target and only waited for the alien to relax its guard slightly. It tensed, preparing to strike. Contracting the digital flexor muscles in its forearm, five six-inch long claws extended on each hand, the flexor tendon under the claw pulling taut.

"Chief?" DeLuca whispered over the net, his fear sending a neural signal to the team's neural nodes.

"I know. I feel it too. Whatever the hell it is—it's close, very, very close. Doc, you copy?"

"Affirmative."

The chief reached one hand down and touched Jackson on the shoulder. In one smooth movement he was awake and on his knees beside the chief. He gently touched Dyer and the danger signal went to the other sleeping forms. In the dark, with their battle helmets on, they looked like insects.

"Our optics are nominal and with the suits' sensors powered down I can't say for sure but I'd bet hard Sythian gold that there's something out there and it's damn close," the chief said.

"Caldarian?" Jackson asked.

"No, Sir. If they were Caldarian, we'd already be dead. No, this is different. The only indication we have that something is out there is the presence that we feel."

"Chief, go active. Give me one full multi-band sweep. People, when I give the word hit your lights. Visors down, optics on auto." All seven of them were kneeling, weapons at the ready. DeLuca could feel his right knee slowly sinking into the muddy ground as he applied pressure with the toe of his boot, tensing for what he sensed was about to happen.

There was the tiniest whisper of sound above the background night sounds of wind and trees rustling, like soft silk brushing nylon, and three forms could be seen advancing swiftly on the team's position.

At that moment, the chief cried out a warning. "Contact! Shit! Three tangos inbound, nominal distance!" He swung his weapon to bear on the closest contact.

"Now!" Jackson shouted and instantly the darkness turned into brilliant daylight as the powerful helmet lights turned on. There they were, fifteen meters away and closing, three huge forms. Light glittered off the overlapping folds of their scale-like skin that formed interlocking plates of calcified armor, harder than diamonds.

A sharp rippling bark of automatic weapons on full auto tore through the night.

The deeper cough of the big 363 echoed above it all as Wicker engaged the moving forms. Too close, he thought. Six meters, five, four...

The rounds glanced and careened harmlessly off the creature's tough, protective hide. Wicker watched incredulously as he walked his rounds up and over and back again across the closest and largest of the creatures. It didn't even slow down as it tried to open its eyes and find the source of irritation. One meter...

It must be the leader, he thought. Wicker pivoted and spun, bringing the barrel of his weapon up. Too late! The huge alpha leader crashed through the group. Wicker was thrown to the ground. The huge creature extended an arm and five razor-sharp claws hooked Wicker just below his helmet where the Ramillion ring armor joined the main body of his suit, tearing downwards. For a moment it lifted Wicker like a rag doll and then dropped him, vanishing into the surrounding brush with hardly a whisper of sound.

The team knelt or stood in stunned silence, waiting for a second assault. But it never came.

It was the lights that saved them. Lacking the heavy weapons necessary to penetrate the creatures' skin and unable to bring their particle weapons to bear, the powerful illumination from the xenon lights had turned the creatures aside and stopped the attack. The xenon lights timed out and the darkness swirled back in while their night optics adjusted.

"Sweet mother of God, what were those things?" Dyer spoke. All thought or worry about Caldarian ambush teams was momentarily forgotten. "We hit them, should have shredded them, and it didn't even slow them down." The soft, gurgling sound of someone bleeding out made each of them frantically turn to see who it was.

"Give me a count." There were only six acknowledgements. Jackson looked around. "Wicker, confirm?" He spoke but he already knew. He saw a form on the ground and bent down to Jamie Wicker's side. The 363 was still clutched in his hands, the barrel twisted and bent like a horseshoe. The team stared unbelievingly at Wicker, then at the twisted barrel made of the same steel used in ship plating. Wicker's URK suit was torn and ripped and his chest cavity was completely eviscerated.

"He's dead," Jackson spoke softly. "Take his bio-chip. We'll deliver it to his parents on Murilia when we get back. Make sure the auto distress beacon is off. We don't want the Caldarians triangulating on the signal. Let's go.

We'll recover his body later."

"Dyer, switch out to your Tango five-one. Put the can on. Do you still have your TAC load up?"

"Yes, Sir, I've got 200 grain, Urillium cored hard points in a ten clip and four more on board, as well as my standard load."

"You think you can take one of those things down with your current load?"

"Yes, Sir, I think so. We all read Green's brief. He said they were hard to kill, not impossible. It's harder because this is their turf and they're as quiet as an open grave. We all saw how close they can get but give me just a glimpse in the trees and I'll tap 'em."

"OK, I want you behind the chief when we move out. I don't want those things getting that close again. When we get to that bend we can see, where the trail switches back, I want you to switch out with Larsen so that you can cover Doc as she moves off of rear security. Anything moves or shows, kill it—no questions. Chief, I want you to turn your suit sensors on and set for multi sweep, low power. That should give us some warning and if there are Caldarians around, we'll just have to risk it. We've been lucky up until this point but if those things come back in any number, we're dog meat. Move out. Chief, you take the point. Let's go."

The chief hadn't moved ten meters before he spoke over the team net and the tension in his voice told the rest of them all they needed to know before he spoke.

"Sir, I have multiple tangos (targets) at our twelve o'clock. At least ten thermal signatures, unknown and un-catalogued species! They aren't moving fast but they are staying with us. They're between us and the plateau ledge!"

"Shit!" Jackson exclaimed.

"Sunrise in 020 minutes." Jackson tapped his wrist NAV and studied the terrain.

"Chief, about one hundred meters south of us there's another ledge that follows a narrow ravine that looks like it would move us down in the general direction we need to take. Let's hope the SAT files the survey drone compiled are accurate and see what happens. Look sharp, people!"

The chief moved out, the team following. No one wanted to think about what would happen if the creatures caught up with them while they were on the move. The wind picked up and the horizon to the southeast began to glow a deep, crimson pink.

"Come on, sun!" Larsen breathed. The chief stopped abruptly and knelt down at the edge of the plateau. The other members gathered around, eyes searching the thick brush around them. Slowly, the deep dark receded back into the trees as the sun came up, light beginning to spill over the eastern rim of the world. From their vantage point above the lava fields, they could see glowing vents and fissures that seemed to wink and recede as the light grew stronger.

"Sir, they're moving off. Sensors are going green across the board." They all gazed over the edge and down the narrow trail they had to take. It was steep and strewn with debris and talus that had spilled over from the plateau above and washed down and over the trail in numerous spots.

"OK Chief, shut your sensors off. DeLuca, switch out with the Chief and let's get this done. It's about five hundred meters down in elevation but it's further than that because of the slope. The LZ is just to the east of us, once we get to the bottom. We'll decide how to proceed from there."

"I don't like the feel of this, Boss. We're too exposed. They hit us here and we're screwed, big time," Doc said. "See the way the wall is sheer and the trail turns about eighty meters down?"

"What about it?"

"That's the critical point. Someone will have to get around the corner and set up point security so the rest of us can get around. The face all along this plateau is honeycombed with openings and broken clefts from all the geothermal activity. Who knows what could be lurking inside those openings and we have to pass each one of them on the way down. There must be dozens of them."

"A comfort you are Doc, a real comfort you are," Jackson said, turning to look at Hearst. He heard the soft chuckle from Hearst and snorts from the other team members as they listened to the conversation. "Larsen and I will act as point security. The rest of you cover us until we get around the corner, and then follow us down and around one at a time. Dyer, I want you to come second last. Stop at the ledge about fifty meters up to cover Doc while she makes her way down to the bend. You should have a clean shot at anything that shows from above."

"We have horizon breach, full corona, wind velocity is sixty-four kilometers per hour and rising," DeLuca said.

With Jackson on point and Larsen five meters behind, they moved down the narrow trail to the switchback, fully illuminated by the rising sun, buffeted by the rising wind. Jackson edged around the corner, hugging the outside edge, close to the drop off. He checked his display. "The canopy extends about a hundred meters from the forest floor. That means it's about Three hundred and forty-four meters to the bottom from here. Dyer, take the rear and cover DeLuca and Doc as they move down. Anything so much as twitches, kill it."

Nobody was left alone, there were always two together. Jackson gave the signal and the team continued down, their calf muscles aching from the tension of moving downhill. Dyer came last, watching the rear, the big Tango

51 in his hands.

"Look at these openings," DeLuca said, covering Doc as she passed a large, fissured crack. "They look like a line of dead eyes watching us. I wonder how far in they go back and where those creatures are."

There was a peal of thunder and they all glanced at the sky. "Sir, the temperature is falling again," DeLuca spoke. "There's another system moving in from the southeast, overtaking the sun, and it's going to get very wet very fast."

Dyer turned to look up at the sky and then spoke. "That's because of Zilith's position in the system and its geological make-up. It has a very short day, as far as cycles go. Storms are a daily occurrence here. They sweep up from the southeast and hammer this cliff face and the plateau. Look," he pointed away and down. "You can see the front approaching us. This isn't going to be a good place to be in another hour."

"A savage place," Hearst said softly. "Even the grazing population is tough. And those creatures that attacked us last night are at the top of the food chain."

"That's another thing," DeLuca said. "Those creatures that attacked us and killed Jamie knew we were there but they waited. With our sensors off and on their turf, they could have attacked us as we were moving but they didn't."

Jackson turned to look at DeLuca. "They were watching us," he stated. "They must have picked us up and trailed us shortly after we inserted but my take is that they were studying us. They've never seen a recon team before. They had only encountered Green's field personnel, and they sensed that we were different."

"They were herding us," Hearst said. Her voice was stony with dread. "Which means they waited until we were where they wanted us, almost at the cliff edge with no place to run. We didn't have our sensors on and we can't use our particle rifles until we've either recovered the package or at least found out what happened to it. We can't risk the chance of being detected by the Legion ground force that attacked us at the pick-up point."

"These creatures are nocturnal and spend the daylight hours in the caves and rock enclosures that are everywhere. That would explain to a certain extent why we didn't see them when we were on the ground before we made contact with the Caldarian legs," Dyer explained.

"Their eyes are multi-lidded," Dyer continued. "The retinal muscles surrounding the eye open and shut in tiny slits or open wide to allow any ambient light to reach the photoreceptors. That's why they seemed to just fade out when we had them on the shuttle's view screen."

"Which means if we don't get off this trail and into some cover with our sensors on, we're dead," Jackson said. "They've made their recon and decided we're worth the effort and they can take us. They were testing us last night. There were only three of them. We all saw how many of them there were just before the sun came up and we headed down." Each team member stared at the dark openings in the cliff face.

"They're waiting until dark to hit us again," DeLuca said. "We need to get off this trail."

Jackson signaled the chief to take point and Dyer to move up behind him. He checked the waypoint on his wrist NAV.

"Three hundred and thirty-four meters to the bottom. Let's go!

Miller moved out and the team followed. Slowly the top of the plateau receded and the thick forest cover at the base of the plateau came into sharp focus. A hundred meters from the base Jackson called a halt and the team formed a defensive perimeter. They felt exposed and wanted to get down and into the trees. They almost wished for darkness and its protective covering until they realized what the night would bring if they failed to find better shelter than they had the previous night. The wind whipped at them and large droplets of rain began to splatter the ground.

Hearst looked up to the crest of the ridgeline, now far above them. She let her eyes search the trail and the brush on each side as she followed it down. She spoke a word and her HUD magnified the image. Suddenly she tensed. A flicker of dark movement, a shadow gliding across the trail and into the denser cover to the left of the trail about four hundred meters above her attracted her attention. The rain began to fall faster. At the same moment, the chief cried out a warning.

"Sir, I have movement at our six o'clock—multiple unknowns moving in toward us."

There was a piercing scream from above them that made the blood run cold in their veins. It was answered to their dismay, from the thick cover below them and about two hundred meters east of their position.

"I thought they couldn't come out in the daylight!" Larsen swung his weapon in the direction of the scream from below. "If I ever get off this goddamn planet, I'm gonna go and buy myself a farm in Iowa where the highest point of land will be my dick when I'm banging my old lady," he growled.

"Won't be very high," Doc retorted. They laughed.

"Fuck you, Doc."

"Sir," Hearst exclaimed, "we have to get off this trail! See those red streaks staining the exposed surfaces of the rock outcrops?"

"More good news, Doc?" Jackson enquired.

"Those are iron sulfide stains," she said, her voice tight with tension. "The only way iron sulfide can stain rocks like that is in a washout. This narrow ravine we're in is going to be running wall to wall with water about thirty seconds after that approaching storm hits. And it's gonna be moving like a Serillian slave tramper dodging a Confederate interdiction frigate." As if in answer, lightning walked across the sky and a crash of thunder rolled across the plain.

"Chief, take us down." They began to move down. Once again, they felt and sensed approaching evil. The rain was falling faster now, making the ground slick. Their muscles ached. Glancing back, they could see forms gliding in and out of sight. The creatures were getting bolder. Dyer dropped back, lay down in the prone position and flipped the cover off his scope.

"Careless, careless, careless," he whispered to himself. His trigger finger gently took up slack and he waited. A flicker of movement and still he waited. He ranged on the phantom shadow. "Four hundred and thirteen ought three-three meters. A woosie shot. My blind grandmother could make this shot any day of the week and twice on Sundays."

The team moved further down the slope. Again movement but this time the big .50 spoke and four hundred and thirteen meters up range a creature's skull exploded as the heavy caliber slug tore it apart. In one smooth movement he swung, settled and squeezed off another shot, this time taking a second creature full in the chest. It stopped like it had run into a wall, the heavy slug making the body cartwheel backwards. Screams of rage echoed and re-echoed off the canyon walls.

"Dyer!" Jackson called out. "Move! We have you covered." Dyer jumped up and scrambled and stumbled on the slippery ground the fifty meters to where the team was spread out. They were thirty meters from the base of the plateau and the protection of the trees.

"Two shots, two dead monsters," he stated flatly. "That should make them slow down some."

"You mean you hope it makes them slow down some," Hearst said.

"Go," Jackson shouted, "we have to get into the trees." They felt a rush of air compress their body suits, air that was being pushed and compressed by some huge force.

"Run!" Miller screamed.

Then the water was upon them!

CHAPTER 9
SECRETS

"The number of medals on an officer's breast
varies in inverse proportion to the square of the
distance of his duties from the front line."

—Charles Edward Montague

Ensign Marcie Chantella frowned at her bank of sensor displays. There it was again! The same faint, rogue power signature that she had detected before she went into orbit. It was located roughly fifteen hundred meters east of the secondary LZ, and kept fading in and out of the detection envelope of her passive arrays. Several times she had altered her orbit just enough so that her orbital path varied slightly in order to allow a little bit more of the electronic frequency being transmitted from the unknown power source to be captured by her sensors. It wasn't enough for a positive ID but her instincts told her it was the Caldarian attack shuttle supporting the Black Order Legionnaires who were pursuing Jackson. Chantella decided it was time to contact the Hunt.

She hesitated. If she transmitted, even on the encrypted secure circuit, she would be radiating, which meant she would be detectable to anyone with the capabilities to listen. She didn't want to be seen. After what she had experienced on the planet she didn't ever want to be seen again.

She set the sub-space encryption circuit and dialed in the frequency she knew the Hunt would be monitoring. She wasn't sure of the Hunt's call sign but she knew she would get their attention the moment the secure link blinked on the signal technician's 3D console.

"This is Shuttle One of the USS John Hancock calling the USS Hunt, over!" Her voice held no trace of emotion.

"Captain?" Ensign Paul Wazinski, manning the communications board, called. "Sir, we have an incoming voice only transmission on the encrypted

TAC net. It looks Confederate but I have no emission source."

"Authenticate."

Wazinski changed to the tactical net and spoke. "This is the USS Hunt. Please authenticate, over."

Chantella entered the shuttle's authentication code and palmed the transmit globe.

Wazinski watched as the authentication code was displayed on the cubic communication console in front of him. "It's the Hancock's attack shuttle, Sir, call sign Nightshade."

Middleton worked the com controls from his seat behind the helmsman. "Nightshade, this is Captain John Middleton of the destroyer USS Hunt, call sign Rescue-one, over."

"Ensign Marcie Chantella, USS John Hancock."

"Ensign, I'm transferring to the command link. Please give us a sitrep (situation report) on what happened here."

"Signal is starting to drift, Captain," Wazinski said. "We need to come about and go to stationary orbit or go to a polar track. She's in a geo-stationary orbit and she's low, so low that we can't see her in all the ionospheric clutter and geomagnetic interference."

"Clever girl," Middleton smiled tightly. "Helm, bring us about, polar track bearing three-six-zero, mark one-nine. Reverse course on reciprocating bearing at," he paused to view the holographic astral display, "grid three-four-six, mark four-three."

"Aye, Captain. Coming to course three-six-zero, mark one-nine, waypoint three-four-six, mark four-three laid in."

Middleton noted the helmsman's crisp reply, mentally flipping through her file. Fatima Doren Rast. She was a short, stocky female from the Floren home world of Fabre. She had graduated second in her class from the Confederate Naval Academy on Fabre and wore a signet ring that said she held a sixth level shield in tri-fan racing. A tri-fan was a short, low-slung, turbo powered vehicle capable of speeds in excess of mach one. The interplanetary racecourse was three thousand kilometers of the most treacherous terrain within three quadrants and competitors came from across the galaxy to win one of the coveted rings. Rast had won the title six years in a row and had been racing since she was three when she would sit behind her father in the open cockpit of their utility tri-fan delivering bauxite ore from the deep swamps and marshlands on the eastern rim of the Muldais Basin.

The signal cleared abruptly as the Hunt came about and Chantella's image on the view screen was as clear as if she were sitting on the Hunt's bridge.

"Sir, I was ordered to go in and pick up Mike Platoon, SEAL Team One. They had made contact and we were going to do a hot pick-up and flash run for the Hancock. Then something just blew the Hancock out of the sky. I rendezvoused with the team and proceeded to the drop point for the secondary LZ according to orders, then came back up to make a signal and maintain station to make the extraction run once Mike Platoon has completed their mission. We are under standard operating procedures Captain, no emissions. I'm to wait until I receive the extraction call, then move in. It was my idea, Sir, to stay in geo-stationary orbit over the secondary LZ instead of going polar. Sorry Sir," she added. There was no trace of guilt or concern in her voice and she gazed frankly at Captain Middleton. It was standard procedure to go polar once in orbit on a special ops insertion.

"Good call, Ms. Chantella," he replied evenly. "It's time to try and turn this situation around and recover the package. We have been briefed. We will continue according to your standing orders. We are here to assist and get out. The Imperial Japanese frigate Shirayuki and the HMCS Haida were sent as well. The Shirayuki has been destroyed and the Haida has sustained unspecified battle damage in an engagement with the same Caldarian cruiser that probably killed the Hancock. We believe that she was also damaged because she de-cloaked momentarily and then left the system. My hunch is that she left to repair her hull and will be back."

"I saw the fight, Sir," Chantella stated quietly.

"Then you know we can't fight her, especially since she has an Element drive system tied into her cloaking electronics."

"Yes, Sir."

"We're going to follow your example, Ms. Chantella. All we can hope to do is recover the Element and get it back to Confederate space. To do that, we need time and stealth. The stealth part is what worries me. They have something new tied into their cloaking. The minute you get the extraction signal, get in and get out. We're going to come in as low as we can and assume a stationary orbit, powering down everything we can."

"Sir, may I suggest you orbit these co-ordinates?" Chantella's image moved away from the view screen momentarily while she retrieved a set of map coordinates of the planet surface from her NAV system. Her face came back into view and she worked her NAV computer.

"Right along this fault line is a strong geomagnetic anomaly, some kind of giant conductor, Captain. It runs for eight hundred kilometers before it plunges into the mantle. There is also a string of volcanic ridges running roughly parallel. Sir, if you go into stationary orbit here and power down, they would have to be right on top of you to see you. Hopefully, it will buy you some time."

Middleton gazed at her in silence for a moment, his hard brown eyes going dark hazel as he thought.

Chantella stared back. She guessed that Middleton was about forty years old, his service stripes showing he had been in the navy for twenty plus years. He had a lean athletic frame and it was rumored on the beach that he had a passion for Zhondarian classical music and practiced tri-astral-algorithmic logic as a way to pass the time. The rumors were only partially correct. He had a passion for all classical music but since his wife was from Zhondra in the Perileus system, it was his preference by choice. The astral logic he did to keep his mind sharp.

It was sharp now and he knew she was right. This was no time to let pride or anger get in the way of doing the right thing, he thought. Without taking his eyes off of Chantella, he spoke to his exec, Commander Marshall. "XO, can we maintain contact with Ensign Chantella and watch the planetary approaches to the ground team without compromising our primary orders?"

"Yes Sir. We shouldn't have any trouble maintaining orbit along that track. The line is long enough to let us swing around without leaving the disturbed envelope produced by the geo-magnetic anomaly."

Middleton nodded. "Right then, let's get it done. Ensign, we'll monitor the team net and wait for your extraction signal. First we have to meet with the Haida and see if they can make steerageway. If not, we'll evacuate her crew. Good luck, Ensign." She'll need it, he thought as he signed off.

Three hundred and fifty kilometers below them and only three kilometers from Jackson and his team, Debra Lewis crouched in the wind and rain against the bole of a huge leaf cedar staring about her in the dark. She was scared. No, that was inaccurate. She was, she told herself, terrified. Her mouth was dry and she knew it wasn't from thirst. She had been sipping frequently from the hydration tube fitted inside her helmet. She checked her HUD display for the hundredth time. Still nothing.

Yet she felt a lurking menace drawing close. At times it was a soft despair filling her mind, building until it was a hard wave of evil rippling through her consciousness with its malice and lust for blood. At those times all discipline fled and she bolted, terrified and heedless, through the thick growth. She crashed and staggered until she was sobbing with fear, her lungs heaving as she gulped air. Whenever she stopped or tried to change her base course, the evil pushed her, caressed her mind and driving her on. She knew she was being herded in a specific direction yet there was nothing she could do to alter or stop it.

She cursed herself for leaving the pod. "I should have stayed, at least until dawn," she told herself. Once again, she felt evil, like vomit, enveloping her. She tried to squeeze it out but it wouldn't stop. She swung her head trying to shake the miasma free but it was so strong she could taste it on her lips and in the back of her throat.

And suddenly, with crystal clarity, she knew. It was coming from the creatures she had been briefed about, the nocturnal killers that had so terrified Green's team. He had alluded to how the team could feel or sense the creatures' approach and presence. And she knew instinctively that Green's initial guess had been correct—the creatures were empathic and used that ability to communicate with each other and herd their prey.

Now the feeling was so strong she could no longer ignore it. She staggered to her feet and in that instant, the world turned upside down. Two pairs of yellow eyes stared at her from a distance of four meters. She desperately grabbed for her particle weapon, knowing it was futile. The eyes came closer. A searing flash of dense particle fire cut the head off the first pair of eyes and then shifted and cut the other creature cleanly in two. There was a snarl of rage and the hovering evil withdrew into the surrounding forest.

Lewis bent to the ground as bile rose in her stomach. She unlatched the faceplate of her helmet, retching, her body shaking weakly as her stomach emptied.

The relief was only momentary. A dark shape materialized out of the blackness, a titanium gauntleted hand slamming her to the ground and reached for her throat. It clamped vise-like on her windpipe and slowly began to squeeze. Her vision narrowed and she knew she was going to pass out. The glove let go. She gulped air. A fist descended, smashing her faceplate and slamming her to the ground. Blood seeped from her nose and a gash on her cheek caused from shards of the broken lexite. A blade rang as it was drawn from a sheath and she felt the cold steel pressed against her throat through the fabric of her survival suit.

There was a hiss of escaping air as a battle mask released and a dark, green-painted face bent down to stare at her. "Welcome to Zilith, Commander Lewis. I'm Prelate Zirlin Medroth of the Ninth Cohort of the 12th Legion of the Caldarian Black Order. Please allow me to introduce you to the rest of my team," the voice mocked. Eleven forms materialized out of the darkness.

"Curan, Rysilis, take her back to the shuttle for the Centurion."

Curan knelt beside Lewis. He pushed a button on one of his armored gauntlets and a small compartment opened revealing three small syringes. Lewis watched in growing fear as he removed one of them and activated the dispensing head.

"Something to keep you quiet and still," Medroth told her. "We wouldn't want you to start thrashing about or trying to run off into the forest now, would we, Commander? This is a nerve agent, specifically synthesized for you humans. Not lethal in the dose you are going to receive, just enough to immobilize your motor functions and paralyze your vocal chords. You will be able to see but you won't be able to speak or move your limbs until the Centurion delivers the deactivation serum into your system."

The sleeve of her survival suit was roughly torn away and the head of the dart pressed against her arm. She felt a cold jab and within seconds her body went limp and her head lolled to the side. She willed her muscles to respond, anything, but it was no good. She felt her bladder and bowels release and could feel the soft trickle of the fluid as it flowed through the reabsorption tubing of her suit. Rage and shame filled her. Her eyes rolled and wandered aimlessly in their sockets, no longer responding to the neural transmitters in the retina.

"Curan and Rysilis, take Commander Lewis back to the shuttle. We will continue to our objective."

Curan lifted Lewis and threw her over his shoulder like a sack of grain. With his other hand, he gripped his rifle and disappeared, the legionnaire named Rysilis moving in front of him on point security.

Lewis' mind wandered, noting what they were doing and remembering what Lieutenant Jackson had told her once during a training exercise. "Always provide security for any detail, from filling hydration packs to setting out interdiction grenades. Never allow a team member to be alone. One to fill the canteens, the other to provide security."

Medroth slid the cover off his NAV display and checked his waypoint. Seven small, red dots formed a circle in the northwest corner of grid 01-34. He smiled a tight, hard smile. The SEAL team hadn't moved from the secondary LZ.

"We are standing on the edge of an abyss; history will mark this moment. Once we have located the source of the strange metal the Confederates found here, we will have control." Medroth paused. "What do you think of that, Warsilin?"

"Prelate, it is like a ripe Porthius pod, ready to be peeled and eaten. But first we must take a few wasp stings."

"Blood," Medroth whispered, "and who will die?"

He snapped the faceplate of his battle mask back in place, motioned with his arm and the team dissolved from view as their cloaking system went active. They moved deeper into the forest toward their objective.

Lewis tasted salt and felt blood and saliva trickling down her chin from her mouth. She tried in vain to close her mouth and tighten her jaw but there was nothing she could do but watch the dark ground that moved in and out of her vision and feel the movement as the legionnaire who was carrying her moved through the brush. She felt the occasional slap of a branch against her suit, could hear the wind moving and feel the rain that managed to penetrate the forest canopy seeping beneath her survival suit.

She sensed, rather than saw the small clearing where the Caldarian attack shuttle was sitting. There was the soft whir as the doors powered open and then a flood of red light as she was dumped onto a padded table in the center of the main crew compartment. Her helmet was removed and placed quietly on the deck. Her limbs were strapped down and a polished bar was fitted to her skull and locked in place across her forehead.

As her eyes rolled randomly, she noted the alien controls and instrumentation. A form wandered in and out of her vision but she couldn't stop her eyes' ceaseless wandering to get a good look at her captors. Words were spoken in an alien tongue. She heard the servomotors and felt the soft movement of air being released and knew from experience that a hatch had opened and resealed. A form moved beside her and once again she felt the jab of a dispensing hypo. Within moments her eyes blinked and she could feel her muscles contracting as her brain told her that they were once again responding to neural stimuli. She worked her lips and licked some of the spittle that had encrusted on her lower lip off. Slowly her eyes stopped their random circling and she gazed up into two of the cruelest eyes she had ever seen.

The Caldarian officer seated beside her was tall and his honor braid held two knots. He was dressed in full combat armor and except for the patch over his left breast, it was entirely black. He had no helmet but he still had his gauntlets on, and she noted that one of his gloved hands held a small silver globe that glowed and pulsed with a deep, green glow.

Oh, oh, Lewis, she thought, the shit is definitely getting deeper.

Her lips moved and she spoke in a hoarse whisper. "Those are outlawed by the planetary accord on humane treatment of prisoners," Lewis rasped. She was stalling. She knew she should keep her mouth shut, should say nothing, but her fear and the hopelessness of her situation made her garrulous.

The form beside her gave a thin smile that didn't reach his eyes and he motioned menacingly with the globe.

She averted her eyes and tried to control her emotions and maintain the proper façade. "Don't make eye contact. Don't try any of the stereotypical, holographic, hero bullshit," she repeated to herself. "Be quiet, silent and speak politely or it is going to make this a painful experience. No, that wasn't quite accurate. It already is a painful experience. We crossed that bridge way back!"

"Ah, Commander Lewis, I am Centurion Ensuris. We have very little time and I have no interest in playing the usual prisoner interrogator games. Let me make it clear at the outset that you are not going to live. The only thing we two will decide is how you die. There is no hope of rescue." He spoke in a quiet, accented voice that was as flat and emotionless as his eyes were cruel. He casually gestured to the bulkhead with the globe he held, noting that her eyes followed the globe.

"We will kill the rest of the SEAL team you were supporting. They inserted over," he paused, "what do you humans call it, the LZ? We have located their electronic signature and they will be dead within hours. What I need from you is the last piece of the puzzle, the ground coordinates of Dr.

Green's laboratory. We have surveyed the planet and run sweeps but have been unable to locate it. We initially thought it was the LZ but there is nothing there except for empty buildings and useless equipment. And we know that as the Hancock's senior navigational helmsman, you have the information we require. We have drugs that will make you talk but that procedure requires a trained psyche-technician and unfortunately, all you have is me...and this." He held the globe in front of her and smiled, seeing her tense.

"Ah, you recognize it then?" His thumb moved and the globe's pulsation shifted frequency, its color changing to a soft, pink hue. Instantly, Lewis' back convulsed in pain as specific neurons in her cerebral cortex were brushed by neural energy. He adjusted the globe and it resumed its green glow.

"We Caldarians specialize in more developed methods of extracting information. Blunt trauma is so prosaic, don't you think? We prefer the subtleties that the brain provides. It is a highly complex and powerful organ. The interaction of sodium and potassium ions across the brain cell membranes creates waves of biological lightning that pulse through the billion miles of nerve fibers and neurons to fully network together. They do this by extending branches of intricate nerve fibers called dendrites, which comes from your Latin word for 'tree'. These are the antennas through which neurons receive communication from each other. A healthy, well-functioning neuron can be directly linked to tens of thousands of other neurons, creating a total of more than a hundred trillion connections—each capable of performing 200 calculations per second. We have learned how to stimulate it in unique ways. Let me demonstrate again."

His thumb moved again and the globe's color reverted back to green and the pulsating ceased. Lewis' body relaxed but her forehead and lips were beaded with sweat.

"That was the absolute lowest setting," Ensuris said. "We have altered the device somewhat. It is frequency agile and we can also vary the amount of power. As you can guess, the variations are almost as numerous as the brain's neurons itself. We can isolate certain organs and muscles and alter bodily functions. It is even capable of multi-species stimuli."

In his other hand, he held a small glass box in front of Lewis' eyes. A small, fur-covered creature similar to a terran squirrel was inside. He moved his thumb and the globe pulsed and glowed. The creature began to writhe and a shrill, high-pitched cry came from its contorted mouth. Blood began to seep from its eye sockets and ears as it convulsed in agony. There was a soft popping sound and the head exploded, showering the inside of the glass box with red gore. It twitched and lay still. "That was a Veeth, one of the innumerable small creatures that inhabit this pleasant resort planet.

"We can also create sensory deprivation without needing to immerse you in a tank. Or program it for pleasure, pleasure beyond your wildest imagination," he spoke this last sentence softly.

Lewis was trembling. She knew that she would break and that everything she knew would be revealed. It was only a matter of time. She had to buy time. Enough time for SEAL Team One to recover the Element. The interior of the shuttle echoed dully with the crash of distant thunder and she could hear rain as it beat upon the hull plating. A distant part of her mind was glad that she wasn't outside, exposed, and then in the next instant, she wished she were outside being lashed by the weather.

"Commander Debra Lewis, United Space Confederacy, serial number three four three..." her voice cut off and a scream broke from deep inside her chest as the globe in Ensuris' hand began to glow violet and pulsate again.

Water from a hundred feeder streams swirled and flowed into the main channel that emptied into the ravine. The streams ebbed and flowed and followed channels that had been cut through the hard, basaltic bedrock eons before. As they reached the banks, the water spilled out over the edges and coursed across the top of the plateau, scouring the landscape. The streams became raging torrents and as their volume and speed increased, their ability to pick up and bear a heavier stream load increased proportionally. Soil, rocks and trees rolled in a dark mass like a giant ball mill, shredding and grinding softer objects into pulp.

The wall of water compressed the air in front of it, driving it downward. As the air compressed, it picked up speed, and the temperature dropped.

Jackson and his team stumbled and slipped toward the exit, twenty-five meters in front of them.

"Break left as soon as we hit the mouth," Jackson shouted above the roar of the approaching water.

Ten meters. The ground shook. Five meters. Open space! The team tore into the trees on the left of the fan-shaped alluvial debris field.

"Keep going!" he panted.

With a roar and a rush, the water exploded out of the ravine. It swept forward and crashed into the rocks and trees at the end of the slope. But once it was no longer bound within the close confines of the canyon walls, it rapidly spent its strength and collapsed itself, strewing a new line of debris across the mouth of the canyon.

The team lay on the ground, slightly uphill and a mere thirty meters from the opening. Jackson checked his wrist NAV. The waypoint for the secondary LZ was only three hundred meters east of their position.

"System status?" he asked.

One by one, the team verified that their URKS bio systems were functioning and they were green across the board. He could feel the warmth from his suit's climate system wicking moisture away from his skin through its inner membrane fabric and ducting it through the dispersal pores to the outside.

"Thank God for our suits," he said out loud.

"Amen to that," DeLuca replied.

Every non-essential system on their suits was powered down. The only systems operating were their helmet audio-visual inputs and the environment control systems. His voice whispered across the neural link, his calmness and control releasing endorphins that calmed the team even as he spoke, the empathic nature of the link bringing order and control.

"We're three hundred meters out from the secondary LZ. Strip your weapons out and make sure you get all the water out of the suppressors and the barrels. As soon as we arrive, we'll change out, set up our perimeter and then pull back to the northwest to that heavy line of cover where the scrub brush meets the LZ. The pods came down in a semi-circle around the central complex. We know the complex is empty but hopefully we can suck the Blackies into taking another look. We'll wait until we're within exactly forty-five minutes of the evening nautical twilight, then move in. It shouldn't take us more than fifteen minutes to switch out and start to pull back. It's going to get pitch black and I want us settled into position before then. Chief, you and Larsen move us in and make security until the rest of us gear up, then switch out. Questions?" There were none. All this time Jackson had been reassembling his MP-225. He finished and worked the bolt, stripping a round into the chamber. "OK, let's do it. Chief, give me a sweep before we move in."

"Going active now. All passbands are nominal, Sir. Nothing's moving except a few indigenous biologics."

They were on the western edge of the LZ and in the gathering gloom, the deserted buildings stood out in stark contrast to the fading forest around them.

"OK. Miller, Larsen—go!"

Cautiously, Miller and Larsen moved out, weapons at the ready.

"We're clear of the pods. Setting perimeter now."

Swiftly the others moved in and went to their individual pods located by the ID signature they picked up on their NAV. They broke the seals and removed the suit packs and particle rifle power modules. Turning on the suit pack passive sensors, they ramped up the power modules. Hearst and Dyer hit a switch on the side of their pod and a sliding door opened, revealing six olive green orbs and a spool of diamond ice detonation wire. The diamond braid was as thin as a cat whisker, completely transparent and had the strength of double-stranded durilium cable. Jackson withdrew a slasher and the hydration packs containing the thermite grenades, handing them to Hearst and Dyer. There were two sets of clackers, one for detonating the thermite grenades, the other for the slasher. Each pod also contained two days of TECRATS and two basic ammo loads to replenish what had already been expended in the encounter with the creatures. Hopefully it would be enough for what they knew would surely come that night.

They changed quickly, unlatching their helmets and setting them on the ground beside the extra suits. The pods still held an extra suit each and were armored against particle weapons. Jackson hoped that when the night was over they would be able to recover them. They each pulled a black watch cap over their heads and placed the stand-alone day/night goggles over the caps. They were small and only had enhanced night vision capabilities with no Heads Up Tactical display. That didn't concern Jackson. Their singular quality was that they were totally undetectable and passive and he didn't want the auto engage systems to override their intuition. He knew that the night would be won or lost based on training and intuition, not electronics.

"Switch," Jackson whispered. He and DeLuca moved up, weapons trained out, and the Chief and Larsen moved back to change.

"Dyer, Hearst. Set perimeter sensors. Larsen and DeLuca, deploy whiskers one and two."

Hearst and Dyer were already setting out the perimeter sensors in two patterns around a small cluster of rocks and broken trees, facing the small trail opening on the eastern side of the LZ. At that point, the base of the plateau and the debris field met the thick secondary growth tight against the edge of the cliff face. The trail wound and twisted all along the bottom of the plateau, at times hugging the cliff, at others swinging into the heavy cover along its base.

The green orbs were standard issue perimeter defense and locator monitors. They formed an interlocking array of motion detectors along with multi-frequency power and thoracic scanners that made it hard to move through once they were set up. Hard but not impossible. Each one was tuned to the other five in a pattern and any disturbance would sound an alarm on the control pack carried by the team member who was standing watch. Hearst and Dyer set two interlocking grids, an outer and an inner perimeter line. The outer perimeter was to give early warning and allow a fire team to orientate and control a firefight. The inner perimeter told them that it was time to move and fall back to their pre-designated fighting positions and detonate the slashers.

Hearst removed the safeties from the slashers. Each one contained eight hundred titanium fibers, each coated with a quick, time-degrading nerve agent. The fibers were razor sharp and when detonated, propelled outward in a sixty-degree arc, shearing through flesh and non-armored battle suits. The nerve agent ensured one hundred percent lethality within the kill envelope.

They moved the insertion capsules using the anti-gravity system, setting them down within the small circle of boulders and brush.

Larson and DeLuca ran to the trail entrance leading into the darkness on the eastern edge of the clearing. DeLuca felt his skin prickle as he looked up the trail. Trails were a lazy SEAL's death. Stay off the trails, his training told him "They're coming, both the Blackies and the monsters. It would be nice if the monsters met the Blackies. Then we'd only have to worry about the winners."

Cautiously they entered, DeLuca on point, Larson following. Fifty meters up the trail they stopped and DeLuca set a small, spiked object into the ground about two meters off to the right. He tapped a button on the top and there was a small thump as the sensing head deployed, driving the transmitter antenna a meter into the soft soil. They retreated and stopped one more time, right at the opening to the LZ and Larsen repeated the procedure on the left side of the trail.

"All done, Sir," Hearst said. "We've placed the six hydration packs in concealed positions within the inner perimeter close to the insertion pods, and the other three in a triangle pattern six meters further out. That should take care of their point element and the security force holding the outer perimeter."

"Good call, Doc. I have a feeling that whoever is leading that Blackie patrol won't commit all his resources to the point. He'll keep at least a third back just in case it's a trap." Jackson glanced around. "Suits in place, Chief?"

"Yes Sir. Four in prone positions and two propped up with a few branches. The one slasher we have won't do much if we don't know where they are."

"We'll chance it. If we're lucky, it'll make meatloaf out of their point man and disorient the follow-on force enough to give us an edge."

"I wish we could have salvaged a few of those 'blues' from the 363," Dyer responded.

"It would have been nice but we didn't have the time. What we have planned should be enough. I hope," he added as an afterthought.

"OK Chief, wind up arky and turn 'em loose!"

The chief knelt down, opened a side compartment on his pod and lifted out two small, metallic objects, placing them on the ground. He clicked a recessed lock on each one and small lids slid open, revealing miniature keypads. Quickly he keyed in a code and closed the lids. The chief watched as each arky deployed six tiny legs and scurried away, blending into the gathering darkness.

"I hope whoever is in charge hasn't seen a Confederate field simulator before because if he has, we're fucked," the chief whispered. "I set the suit power emulators a bit low, just so they don't think anything is amiss. We don't want them to think it's too easy. I've programmed them to move at our typical switch out intervals."

"Time, Sir," Larsen said. A gust of wind tore at them and they shivered involuntarily. But not from the wind.

"Feel that?" Dyer asked. "The same nuance of menace we felt last night on the plateau."

"Our friends are back," Hearst said.

"One dragon at a time," Jackson said. "First we kill Caldarians and then we kill the monsters. OK Chief, let's go."

The team moved across the LZ. Hearst and Dyer were last in line, trailing the diamond ice lead wire behind them. Night shadows enveloped them and they faded into the dusk.

They reached their hide positions overlooking the ambush site with five minutes to spare. One by one, they sank into position, forming a firing line. They were located directly north of the little cluster of boulders and brush on the incline slope in the rubble field at the base of the plateau. They were forty meters from the ambush site.

"Chief, deploy Mother Whisper," Jackson spoke quietly.

Miller unzipped a side panel on his pack and removed a device similar to the ones DeLuca and Larsen had inserted in the brush on the eastbound trail. He pressed his thumb and index finger into a shallow recess on the bottom and the top slid back, revealing a flat monitor screen with a small overlay map of the LZ. He depressed another button and there was a soft whump of compressed air as the receiver tried to deploy into the ground.

"Shit!" Six heads turned to watch.

"Ground's too rough here and all this debris is making it hard to deploy."

"Take your time, Chief," Jackson replied calmly. "We need that receiver in the ground or we're dead."

How the hell does he do it, Hearst wondered to herself? How does he stay so calm?

It was essential that the receiver have good ground depth in order to pick up the low frequency signal from the transmitters. Miller moved around several times before he finally found a piece of softer ground. He tried once more and the receiver probe penetrated the ground. A moment later, two small, green dots glowed on the screen, each representing the vibration detectors DeLuca and Larsen had deployed.

"Mother Whisper is active, Sir!"

They each took time to drink and eat, all of them knowing there would be no rest. Full night had fallen and it was total dark. Heads moved as eyes swung slowly, watching.

"Status, Chief?"

"Green board, Sir. All quiet."

"So far," DeLuca breathed.

The night moved on and it grew colder. Occasionally they saw stars through openings in the flying cloud rack that moved across the black vault above them.

"Check?" Jackson called.

"Two", "Three", "Four", "Five," "Eight", they responded one by one.

Time passed in agonizing slowness. Muscles cramped and the soft sound of boots and suit material moving could be heard.

A red light blinked on the tiny display Miller had switched on hours before. He tensed. "We've got telemetry from Whisper-one." The team came instantly alert. "Several objects moving in a westerly direction on the trail."

Jackson watched the trail opening across the clearing through his night vision optics. He zoomed in. Twenty-five power, nothing. One hundred power, still nothing.

"Get ready!"

Weapons came up and the barely discernable snick of safeties being pushed off could be heard. Dyer had his eye to his scope, its sensitive night optics making the trail appear as if it was bright day.

"We have telemetry on Whisper-two," the chief said tightly. "Confirm movement of several objects passing westbound on Whisper-two. Whisper-one is still transmitting telemetry, Sir. Same frequency and same rate of movement."

"Caldarians," Hearst said. "It has to be Caldarians. If it were monsters, the input signature would be random. This is too even, too well spaced."

"I agree," Jackson said. "Chief, what do the sensors show?"

"Nominal Sir, nothing showing. My bet is that it's the same hunter-killer team that hit us at the pick-up sight and then cloaked. Damn well cloaked. There's not a thing showing and if we had any kind of signature we would have picked something up, even on the passive array. Thank God we don't have our battle helmets on for this because this is a whole new ball game."

"Which means they have Element active suits," Larsen responded.

The small units that DeLuca and Larson had inserted on each side of the trail were motion and vibration detectors that used ultra low frequency transmitters to transmit through layers of rock. Each transmitted a single alpha letter that in turn was translated into either a blinking red light indicating movement or a solid green indicating no detectable movement.

"Whisper-one has gone green, Sir. Whisper-two is still sending telemetry."

"They're at the bottom of the trail where it opens up onto the LZ. Get set!" Jackson's gloved hand reached for the clackers to blow the grenades in the hydration packs.

"Nothing. No targets," Dyer said, frustrated.

"Patience, Robbie, patience." Jackson's thought echoed in their minds. "All good things come to those who wait."

CHAPTER 10
MOVEMENT

"You may talk o' gin and beer
When you're quartered safe out 'ere,
An' you're sent to penny-fights an' Aldershot it;
But when it comes to slaughter, you will do your work on water,
An' you'll lick the bloomin' boots of 'im that's got it."

—Rudyard Kipling

"The Confederates are still on the secondary LZ. Two are on watch. We've mapped their signatures and recorded their movement patterns. They're following standard procedure, Prelate. We've been monitoring them for the last cycle and a half, no pattern variation and standard sensor emissions." Jarrand, the first legionnaire, spoke over the Caldarian tactical net.

"Prelate, there is an overlapping security grid between the perimeters."

"Set suit chameleon grid to narrow-active and move in," Medroth whispered.

"Outer perimeter breach," the point legionnaire spoke. "Suit is being painted by multiple active sensors."

Medroth felt the salty sting of sweat dripping into his eyes.

"Suit has clean signature. Moving to inner perimeter."

With the exception of the Confederate signatures, all his systems were nominal. The tactical display on his battle mask, generated by the small thoracic signature radiating from each suit, showed the position of each legionnaire.

Inside the small clump of boulders and totally oblivious to the approaching killer team, a computer command executed and the two 'arkys' as they were referred to by the teams, extended their legs and moved to new positions. Their transmitters radiated a small envelope of electronic energy designed to emulate the power signature of a recon suit.

"Inner perimeter breach," whispered the point legionnaire. "Moving to assault position. We have movement within the zone. Repeat. We have movement within the zone. We show two movers."

Medroth checked his display and noted that the two on watch had each moved slowly about three meters along the inner perimeter.

The nine Blackies spread out and closed to within ten meters of what they thought was Jackson's team. The wind moaned through the grass, decreasing audio sensitivity by ten percent. But that was a factor that worked both ways, Medroth thought.

He checked his sensors one last time. The two movers had gone to ground. Good.

We could kill them all easily from here Medroth thought, but we need a few of them alive to obtain the location of the Confederate research lab, just in case the female we captured doesn't survive the rigors of the Centurion's interrogation. His left hand went unconsciously to his long blood knife. It would be far better to advance within arms length and use cold steel on them, as it should be done.

"In hold position. Ready on your mark," the legionnaire on point spoke. Medroth and the remaining two spread out so that there was a four-meter space between them as they faced the SEAL position.

"On my count!" His platoon stood ready to rush the SEAL position once the assault began. "Three, two, one, engage!"

Two searing shafts of light blinked out in a fan-shaped pattern that swept the position. As quickly they winked out, and the Blackies surged forward. A flicker of movement off to the point man's right made him pivot in that direction. His assault rifle was already raised and he fired at the movement. An arky exploded as it scurried along the ground. Particle fire ripped into the decoy suits and battle helmets exploded and fused into puddles of duralloy sludge. The smell of burning and melting electronic components filled the small clearing. The pods were undamaged.

For a heartbeat, Medroth stared at the burning suits and then comprehension dawned as a cold knot of rage rose in his heart, knowing that he and his team were dead. Medroth screamed into his COM.

Jackson's gloved hand gripped the clackers. The team was poised, ready to engage as soon as they had targets. On the left flank, Larsen had his primary weapon set on flechette mode and had ten 'slashers' in a drum feed. They saw the particle fire rip into the ambush site and watched as it swung and narrowed, reaching out and destroying the decoy suits.

Fingers tightened on triggers, eyes glued to their night optic scopes.

"Now!" Jackson breathed, and the night erupted in an avalanche of death and violence as he hit the clackers and blew the one slasher and the six thermite grenades.

Three legionnaires were standing directly in front of the slasher when it detonated, their bodies shredded to hamburger as eight hundred razor sharp titanium threads were projected up and out at a velocity of thirty-five hundred feet per second. They also contained most of the blast effect, saving Medroth and the other five legionnaires with him.

Medroth and the other legionnaires were enveloped in a pasty, reddish cloud of Chameleon epoxy when the six-hydration packs containing the thermite grenades detonated.

"Full sensor sweep, set suits auto detect, get ready to engage," Jackson spoke over the team net as the six figures materialized as if by magic, amidst the rubble below. But Blackies die hard and Jackson marveled again at their discipline and training as the remaining legionnaires pivoted and swung uphill to bring Jackson and his team under fire. They were no longer invisible but neither were the SEAL's. The moment the SEAL's went active with their sensors in order to track on the radar-reflective smudges the dye made on the Caldarians battle suits, they were detected.

Medroth heard the sonic whisper and crack of rounds as they whistled over his head. He and the other legionnaires dove and rolled for cover. There was a gasp and gurgling sigh as two of them were impaled by the flying titanium silk flechettes laid down by Larsen.

"Prelate, we've just been painted at close range by multiple Confederate sensors, low band tactical arrays. Threat axis bearing three-three-one," the legionnaire reporting cursed. "Kutar! Range forty metrics," he cried, desperation in his voice.

With a precision and smoothness that made the SEALs marvel, Medroth and the three remaining legionnaires rolled, increasing the distance between them as they began to flank Jackson's team. Rounds cracked and whined overhead.

Two legionnaires rose out of the dark and fired as Medroth and the legionnaire on the extreme left flank broke from cover and ran forward. There was the sound of rounds tearing flesh and one of the legionnaires providing suppressing fire twitched and danced and then pitched forward, his body stitched with jet ignited, high velocity rounds. The other legionnaire immediately rolled right as rounds tore into the ground where he had been kneeling. Medroth and his counterpart on the left flank surged forward, going to ground before the whispering dark hornets could find them. But each time, they drew closer to that darker point of shadow beneath the burning Rhodendis that concealed Jackson and his team. They moved relentlessly, each time dropping closer to the concealed SEAL fire team.

"Turn off sensors, nominal board, they have lock!" Jackson's urgent thought crashed and echoed across the neural link. Particle fire reached for them, hammering the rocks. The surrounding shrubbery burst into flame and glittering sparks rained down as the creosote rich sap ignited above them, giving a surreal glow to the alien landscape. The wind rustled and night vision systems compensated for the sudden brightness.

Medroth rose to move and something slammed him to the ground. He felt blood seeping down his side. He was beyond pain. Every ancestral strand in his DNA surged through his body. Three millennia of warrior tradition awoke and filled his heart and soul with the strength of Caldar, the dark warrior of his ancestral home.

"Sertoth Veth," he cried into his COM link. 'Death comes.' His left arm was numb. He reached up and there was a hiss of air as he unlatched his battle mask and tore it off. He flung it aside and with a gauntleted hand, tore away his battle suit, revealing a dark hole that was pumping blood low down on his left side. There was movement and glittering fire as the other legion-naires fired and moved, fired and moved, relentlessly advancing toward Jackson's team.

Medroth opened his battle pack, removed his field-cauterizing pliers and tried to pinch the edges of the wound tight with his left hand. Blood seeped between his fingers and he activated the cauterizer. He ground his teeth. He hissed and lowered his front canines. There was a click as the upper pair locked with the lower. He bit down, puncturing his lower lip and let the blood flow down across his chin onto his chest.

He laid aside his particle rifle and activated the electronics on his suit. He then threw it as far as he could, hoping that the electronic signature would draw fire. The electronics didn't but the movement and sound it made as it landed did. The brush and foliage around it snapped and cracked as rounds searched for it.

Medroth rose to kneel behind a huge Rhodendis dripping water from its lower branches. There was a whisper of steel as he drew his blood blade with his right hand. He worked his left hand. "Not much, but enough," he whispered to the night wind. With it he drew his secondary weapon, a hand darter. No noise, no signature. He chambered a cartridge and checked to make sure that the other six clips were in the auto feed tray.

"Time to feed, time to die," he said and moved into the night.

The firefight had degenerated into a stalking match between two roughly equal and similar foes. For each side, the electronics had done what they were designed and called upon to do—deceive, confuse and find the enemy. Each side had employed them and in their turn, neutralized the electronic threat facing them. The electronic fight ended in the blackness, each side knowing that so far, the Caldarians were the ones who had bled. That was about to change. Under the dark sky, the rich soil was about to taste alien blood once again.

When the slasher and thermite grenades blew and Jackson had turned on his sensors, he detected six signatures on his low band tactical radar. Two had gone down and then incoming fire had driven the remaining attackers to cover behind the boulders and trees. He knew what was happening because it was what he would have done himself if the situation were reversed. The Blackies were trying to flank their position. He was amazed that they didn't break contact. But he knew the reason for that as well. Neither team could let the other live. Not now, not here. It was no longer a matter of merely breaking contact and withdrawing. They had to be killed.

Jackson watched the ground in front of him, his eyes searching for any movement. He swung his head, paying attention to his peripheral vision. "They're trying to flank us," he whispered. Instantly, Miller and Hearst turned to face the rear, weapons up.

There was a searing flash and particle fire tore into their position. Dyer grunted and was flung back, his body twitching, his back arching as his suit absorbed and redirected the energy. He lay still. Jackson could still detect the neural energy from Dyer's brain. "Hang in there kid," his thought reached out and brushed Dyer's neural pathways. No one moved toward him. He would have to wait.

A brush of movement and two shadows rose and advanced. Immediately Jackson and DeLuca fired but couldn't tell if they had hit anything. Their night vision optics were overloaded with the blazing Rhodendis and the searing, arcing glow from the particle rifle fire. On the left flank, Larsen searched the darkness to his front, trying in vain to find a target.

All at once, a volley of fire stabbed out toward them. The particle assault weapons were on full auto, the cycling power system pushing the heat dissipation sinks to red line. The team cringed as the particle beams crashed and rippled across their position, searching for flesh.

"Watch out," Jackson cried over the net, "they're coming in, watch out!"

Hearst turned to her front, her eyes momentarily drawn to the flashing light, and fired at the flashes. She rose on one knee and fired short three shot bursts until the bolt clicked on an empty chamber. She went to one knee and hit the magazine release. In the darkness behind her, a blood-smeared hand reached out.

Larsen felt the blade go into his chest and tried to wrench free. He coughed once, blood bubbling up and frothing on his lips. The blade withdrew and an iron strong fist went around his throat. He tried to break the hold but he didn't have the strength. He gave a mighty heave and pushed forward but the blade went in again to the hilt and pierced his heart, and his body sagged in death.

Medroth withdrew his blade, blood running down the channel, and turned to his next target, Michelle Hearst. Some sixth sense warned her and she wheeled, fumbling desperately for a fresh magazine. Behind her, she sensed fear but it was buried, chained behind that door you never opened when in combat, but she dared not turn around. She could hear the whispered hush of the other's MP225's as they fired short disciplined bursts and the soft, chattering sound of spent brass hitting the ground, and she could smell the scorched and burning ozone smell left by residual particle ordnance. She hit the quick release buckle on her load bearing harness and her conformal pack fell away.

"Come on you motherfucker," she spoke to Medroth in Caldarian. He was startled to hear her curse him in his own tongue. He opened his mouth, revealing his canines. Hearst dropped her weapon and the sound of hard, tempered steel rang above the crash and roar around her as she drew her own blade, an eight inch dueling blade made of Ramillion black compolite steel. She watched his knife. He lunged in, attempting to pin her and swung his blade, reaching for her stomach, but she pivoted aside and slapped the knife hand away and immediately moved inside his swing, bringing her blade up as she did.

The steel sank in and she heaved with all her strength, tearing his chest open. Medroth staggered and Hearst wrenched her blade free, dropping it in the process. He twisted toward her and grabbed her by the neck with his left hand. Even with the wounds he had taken to his left side and the death cut to his chest, he held her and began to squeeze.

Hearst could feel his shoulders shift and knew that he was bringing his knife in to gut her, so did the only thing she could. With all her strength, she pushed her feet in and pushed herself over backwards and reached with both her hands for the incoming blade. As he brought it up, she caught it as they fell and twisted it away from her stomach and upward, the tip reaching for Medroth. With his own weight he drove the blade into his chest. They crashed to the ground, the glaze of death already in his eyes. His blood pumped out, covering Hearst who struggled out from under his dead body. Finding her own blade, she swept it up and turned to her front. Jackson and the chief were struggling with a lone legionnaire on the edge of the boulder circle. A blade glinted in the dark and the legionnaire went down. A sudden, numbing presence of fear assailed her. At the same moment, she sensed movement behind her and spun back around. "Too late," she thought.

Dyer cried out to her to get down and as she dove forward she felt the vicious whip-crack concussion of a large caliber weapon as he fired point blank into a form behind her. Hearst glanced back and saw Dyer on one elbow, the huge tango 51 in his hands. She looked at what he had been shooting at and her blood chilled. A creature lay on the ground. The heavy slug had taken it in the lower abdomen, the big .50 caliber slug turning everything in its path to strawberry jam. Hearst lay on the ground, her heart pounding. Silence descended. She was aware of breathing as lungs gulped air. Slowly she sat up and looked around her.

DeLuca, on the right flank, was down on one knee, watching the struggle between Miller, Jackson and the lone Caldarian. He was looking for a shot but realized he couldn't shoot for fear of hitting one of his teammates. He swung back to glance to the westbound trail and caught a blur of movement hurtling in. His weapon was already up and he fired, watching through his night optics as his rounds walked their way up the legionnaire's body. Jet-enhanced rounds tore him apart and DeLuca watched as something burst out of his neck amidst a spray of liquid. He stopped firing, his weapon up, and sighted down the trail.

"Check?" Hearst heard Jackson ask.

"Four clear," she said and listened to see who else was there.

"Three clear."

"Eight clear."

"Two," the chief said.

"Larson's dead," she spoke wearily.

"Perimeter," Jackson called. The team gathered their weapons and formed a tight circle around him.

"Sensor sweep!" They powered up their suits again and immediately picked up movement.

"Multiple tangos moving toward us from the east," DeLuca said as he watched his small tactical display. "The signature is not Caldarian. The thoracic signature is consistent with the creatures that have attacked us twice, Sir."

Jackson checked his display and noted the distance to the grid coordinates indicating the position of Green's field lab.

"Two kilometers west of here, at the base of the plateau, is our objective. The sun will be up again in a couple of hours. It's time to switch out. Pack away the 225's and break out our particle rifles. Set narrow beam, maximum cutting bandwidth. We're gonna un-ass, get the package and get the hell out of here," he finished. "Dyer, you OK?"

"Yes, Sir. The suit re-routed the particle energy but I think it burned out the main surge diodes on the dorsal array."

"We'll check it before we head out, Sir," the chief said. "If any of the pods are still intact, we have spares for that. We need to replenish our ammo for our primary weapons and Doc here is gonna need that extra suit."

"OK Chief, you and Doc take Larsen's body down and put it in his pod if it's still intact. Find every dead legionnaire and pull the power pack off his URK. We're not leaving those here for any follow-on force that may be in the neighborhood. Then check out the ambush site, get what we need and get back up here, ASAP. The rest of us will run a field check on our suits and cover your withdrawal. Ten minutes and we're out of here."

He glanced at the three dead Caldarians. Only two had uniforms on. The tall one that Hearst had killed had only his black insulated skin layer on. His battle suit was missing. Suddenly he tensed and drew in his breath. He moved to the dead legionnaire at the edge of the rock circle. Kneeling down, he grabbed at the patch over the left breast. It was torn and slashed but the unit designation was clearly visible and he wrenched on it, tearing it off the dead legionnaire's battle suit. He stood up, staring at what he was holding in his hand, his thumb stroking the unit embroidery. The team watched him, sensing the sudden transformation in the lieutenant's mood.

Hearst shivered. She had only seen Jackson really mad once. Normally, even in battle, he was cool, calling the shots and shifting the team as the tactical situation dictated. That was one of the reasons he was so good at what he did. Few men had the ability to lead men under the tremendous stress of battle, especially the type of warfare conducted by all the Confederate special warfare teams. But Hearst knew instinctively what it had taken the command structure two years to figure out, that Jackson was a natural leader, born to combat just as surely as a duck was born to water and she knew Jackson was a warrior. And she knew that buried deep beneath Jackson's cool, calm façade, was a fey mood that boiled over like an ancient Viking warrior who went berserk in battle.

Jackson stood and stared at the patch in his hand. He felt a terrible rage building inside him, rising like a dark flood, and a sudden twinge low down on his left side, the memory of a long ago encounter and a pair of dark, hate-filled eyes bending over him.

He smiled. "Centurion Mydris-Ensuris of the Ninth Cohort of the 12th Legion," he spoke softy. "We meet again."

"Sir?" Dyer asked. Jackson looked up.

"An old friend from an old encounter." He spoke evenly. "We should feel honored. The Ninth Cohort is the cream of the crop. They sent the best they have, folks. These people definitely won't go home without FOH!"

"FOH?" Hearst repeated. "What the hell is FOH, boss?"

"Foot on head, Doc. These folks aren't going to assume we're dead. They will keep coming and keep pushing until they see body parts. Mostly big body parts or unattached body parts, and they are relentless. Centurion Mydris-Ensuris is the platoon leader and you can bet your ass he isn't done with us yet. His name means 'he who kills by night'."

"Where did you find that out?" the chief asked incredulously. "We have very limited intelligence on the Caldarians and even less on the Legion."

"After my encounter with the Ninth of the 12th on Galdaris-One, I began to do some research. I scoured the fleet's intelligence records, the ones I could, and some that Commander Ortello was able to filter to me. Also, I began to study Caldarian history and culture. I found several file disks in the databank containing biographical information on prominent political and military figures, both past and present. One of them contained a thesis paper written by a research sociologist at the naval institute on Thebes. It contained the command structure of all the known line officers in the 12th Legion. One of them was a Centurion named Mydris-Ensuris and my gut tells me he's here on the ground with the rest of his platoon.

"Let's find that lab and get the hell out of here," he finished.

The chief and Hearst moved down into the ambush site while Jackson, DeLuca and Dyer locked out their particle rifles and got ready to move. They were covering the chief and Hearst as they came back up the slope with battle packs strapped to their backs. Hearst was wearing her spare suit.

They redistributed ammo, strapped on their packs and locked down their battle masks. The chief went over to Dyer and unlatched the control panel beneath his right armpit, exposing the dispersion diodes. The main diode was a blackened chunk of sludge. He used the diode extractor to pull the old one and replaced it with a new one.

"Suit check!" Jackson said.

Each member ran a suit diagnostic. Jackson got a green dot as each suit completed its check and sent a small signal to his bio-command overlay for the team.

"Good, we have a green board," he said.

"They're out there," Dyer spoke.

"Yup, but this time we'll burn their asses." Hearst gestured with her particle rifle. "Oh yea, we'll burn 'em good."

"Go Doc!" DeLuca exclaimed.

"All suits nominal, passive only. Chief, I want you on point with your sensors on low power, just like before." The team locked down and moved out.

Wind stirred and drops of rain fell on the sightless eyes of the dead Caldarian lying on his back close to the thick brush along the back edge of the trail he had used to try and flank the SEAL position. His torso had been hit by at least half a dozen rounds. The killing round had cut his carotid artery and he had bled profusely, his dark blood pooling beneath him. A scaled hand slowly extended five claws and reached for the dead legionnaire. The creature had watched the entire fight, knowing instinctively that there would be meat left here when the strange beings moved away. For a brief moment, it had stirred the left lobe of its cerebral nervous system but the strange creature that had killed the half-naked one had sensed something and it had shut its neural flow, cutting off the flow of energy. Its companion had been careless. It should have waited. It lay dead, its body only three meters from where it crouched beside the trail. His claws dug into the shoulder muscle of the dead legionnaire and he pulled the body effortlessly into the brush. The creature reached out and placed its left hand on the dead legionnaire's chest. Powerful muscles contracted and five long claws penetrated the chest cavity. The rain lashed down and lightning flickered and flashed. The sharp crack of ribs breaking was distinguishable above the rising wind. The claws dug deeper, seeking deep inside the exposed chest. Saliva glands within the creature's mouth responded to the stimuli from its olfactory organs and saliva dripped and ran down the creature's hard, calcified chin armor. It fed. Time meant nothing to the creature. Neurons flowed and potassium ions moved across his cortical nodes, channeling energy, and he bent his thought to others of his kind, summoning them for the hunt.

Jackson checked his NAV console. The waypoint marking the downloaded coordinates for Green's lab had turned a bright, solid green in the heads up display on his battle helmet. He looked around in frustration. An eight goddamn digit coordinate fix. It meant they were within meters of the lab.

"EH78530032," he read off the display. "An eight-digit grid location."

The team was stopped at a section of trail that narrowed down and was clogged with thick undergrowth and debris from the plateau far above. Boulders and huge tree limbs were everywhere and the thick undergrowth impeded their progress. They were close to the face of the cliff beside a small stand of dark conifers that grew along the trail edge. But there was absolutely nothing to indicate that there had ever been any human presence of any kind. No marks, no prints, no garbage or man-made debris.

"Shit," he said to no one in particular. Did they somehow get the coordinates wrong, he asked himself? What the hell was going on here? At that moment DeLuca, who had moved ahead about twenty-five meters to cover, spoke up.

"Boss?" DeLuca spoke. He had taken the point position to give the chief a break and was crouched down in the middle of the trail, bent over his small sensor display. He glanced up and read the numbers off of his HUD and scanned the terrain in front of him again. "Boss, you better have a look at this," he said to Jackson.

"I just picked it up. Everything was nominal and I flipped to scan mode in the fm band, the old guard frequencies we used to use for local training exercises, and got this." He tapped his display and a low carrier could be heard. He tapped his wrist again and a sharp waterfall of frequency could be seen cascading in a tight, even sine wave over the tiny screen. The frequency read 420.26 megahertz.

"That FM portion of the band hasn't been used in a hundred and fifty years. It's archaic and line of sight only, plus all the repeater shit you have to use to make it usable over any distance, unless you get an inversion, and then you don't know who you're talking to or who's listening."

"Put it up," Jackson said and immediately a low carrier beat could be heard over the team net. The team listened.

"Close," the chief said. "I'd say within five hundred meters."

"Maybe, let's keep going. Good work, Carl."

DeLuca resumed walking but he hadn't gone twenty paces before he stopped and went to one knee.

"It's gone!" he cried. "It just disappeared."

"That's impossible," Jackson said. "Check your system." DeLuca entered the command to run a diagnostic and waited.

"Everything is good, Sir." He reversed his direction and walked back from where he had come. The signal reappeared just as before. He stopped and moved off the trail toward the lava bed. Again he hadn't gone ten paces before the target carrier faded again. He moved back and instantly the signal resumed.

"Doc, switch to scan the FM band starting at one hundred and fifty megahertz and move up the band."

Hearst was about twenty meters behind and the team waited for her report.

"Nothing, Sir."

"OK, set your receiver to 420.26 megahertz and walk forward," he told her. "As soon as you get anything, stop."

Hearst moved forward. Ten meters from where the rest of the team was crowded around Jackson and DeLuca, she stopped.

"Right here," she cried, "It just pegged the signal strength display. Hang on a second. I'm going to adjust the calibration and set the gain so that the reading won't overload the display. If the signature is as narrow as I think it is, we should be able to pinpoint its location."

She bent over her display for a moment and then straightened and moved backward. She moved slowly. She stopped and began to move forward again. She stopped.

"Here! The signal is strongest here."

"Move back Doc, to where the signal drops off, and stop." She backed up a few meters and then stopped when the signal dropped off her display.

"DeLuca, calibrate your receiver and do the same thing." He moved forward and then back and then forward again. He looked at Jackson. Twenty meters separated him from Hearst.

Jackson stared at the chief. They both glanced toward the cliff wall and the dark stand of conifers.

"Chief, are you thinking what I'm thinking?" Without a word, the chief walked to the wall of thick cedar-like trees and disappeared, Dyer right behind him. Jackson had to grin.

"Habit," he said. "Never patrol alone."

"Sir!" the chief called. "You better have a look at this. I think we found what we're looking for."

Jackson pushed his way through the trees and five minutes later was standing beside Miller and Dyer. They were kneeling beside a dark, narrow opening in the face of the cliff. The chief had pulled back a huge piece of deadfall. It was so covered over that they could have walked past it a hundred times and never seen it. The narrow opening had been widened by a rock laser and meticulously covered to appear as though it had never been disturbed.

"DeLuca, Hearst, get back here." The sound of their suits scraping brush could be heard and then Hearst gasped when she saw the opening. She tapped her Wrist NAV and cried out as the shrill piercing beat of the carrier whistle overloaded her audio system.

"Pay dirt. The signal just went off the scale, boss. I think we just found your missing lab."

"We found something, but what?" Jackson replied.

The chief, cautious as ever, had moved away from the opening, his weapon trained out, eyes searching the forest. Suddenly they all felt it, a wave of fear washing over them, caressing them. It was stronger than before. As if in confirmation, the chief cried out a warning.

"Contact! We have multiple thoracic signatures, five hundred meters out and closing."

"In!" Jackson cried out. "Move!" The team needed no urging. They slipped inside the dark opening and instantly the feeling of malignant evil dissipated. The trail led down and soon it broadened to a path that two could walk abreast on. Their headlamps cast eerie shadows on the walls. The ground was sandy and their feet made no sound as they walked. After forty-five minutes of steady downhill walking, Jackson called a halt and they stopped, the darkness crowding them close.

"How deep are we?" DeLuca asked. The air was hot and after the rain and cool moist outside air, they could feel their suits' circulation systems switching from heat to cool as they drew off moisture from their bodies.

"We are three hundred and fifty-three meters below the surface elevation of the entrance," Dyer told them. "The ambient air temperature is twenty degrees Celsius, oxygen content is 20.9," he stated matter-of-factly.

"The signal strength has grown proportionally, Sir," Hearst spoke. "I've been monitoring it as we go. The deeper we go, the stronger it gets. It's incredible."

"OK, let's keep going," Jackson spoke. "Keep sharp. God knows what else may be in here." The team moved on. The left-hand wall fell away and they felt as if they were walking along a steep path. Their lights could no longer reach the ceiling or the far wall. Their feet told them they were moving downhill still. Suddenly, from up ahead, they could see a blue glow. The team stopped, hesitating to move forward.

"Now what?" Hearst whispered in frustration. Cautiously, they moved forward, weapons ready. The glow increased in intensity and seemed to pulsate and throb. They turned the last corner and stopped, dumbstruck by the sight before them. Their mouths gaped open, weapons sagged in their hands, muzzles pointing to the cavern floor. The blue light was around them, the walls alive with a deep azurite blue as the stringer veins of the Element throbbed and glowed. Workbenches and tables lined the walls and formed rows down the middle of the cavern. Banks of monitors and electronic equipment hummed and vibrated from the power flowing through them. A huge, coursing, pulsating arc of blue energy engulfed them.

"Sweet mother of God," DeLuca whispered. "Sweet, everlasting mother of God!"

CHAPTER 11
RECOVERY

"We gain strength, and courage, and confidence
by each experience in which we really stop to look fear
in the face...we must do that which we think we cannot."

—Eleanor Roosevelt

At first, Jackson thought they had walked into a trap. But if it were a trap, he would have been dead and not just lying on his back with the rest of the team around him. Then he realized that it was a trap, a security trap his team had activated when they crossed the threshold of the underground chamber.

It was the force and nature of the energy field that surprised him. They should have detected it, especially since it was a Confederate force field. He gave his head a shake.

"No. What am I thinking?" he said out loud. "Green was a spook. Why do I keep thinking that he will do all the predicable things? Give me a count. Everyone OK?" The team checked in, then stood up and faced the energy field in front of them. They were in a small circle, roughly ten meters in diameter. Dyer put his hand out and touched the shimmering blue wall. It zapped and he hastily pulled back.

Jackson was frowning, staring at his sensor display. It was completely green. "That's impossible," he whispered. "Totally, fucking impossible!" His voice held a note of incredulity. "No residual, no frequency spillover from any spectrum and no harmonics! What the hell is going on?"

Sudden comprehension dawned. "We didn't detect it because he set it up using the Element to power it. Damn," he said in admiration. "I like this guy more and more."

Chief Miller was about to make a comment but was stopped before he could say anything. On the floor in front of them, a full sized holographic image appeared.

"This is Dr. Winston Green. You have five minutes to enter the security code to deactivate the security envelope and turn off the power generator."

"And then what?" DeLuca asked the question that was on everyone's mind.

"Something goes boom and we fall down?" Hearst said.

"I think it will be a little bit more dramatic than that, Doc," Jackson answered.

As if in response, the holograph spoke again. "If the correct code is not entered at the end of five minutes, five fusion pod reactor cores enriched with military grade plasma rods will detonate. The feed loops and control circuits that communicate with the cores contain small conventional charges that will detonate and destroy all links to the command console. If an electronic peeper signature is detected, the pods will detonate instantly."

"Shit," Jackson said, "and I was just starting to like this guy! How the hell would he know about Caldarian de-coding peepers?"

"So what's the question?" Doc asked impatiently.

The hologram continued. "To deactivate the containment grid, please state what the Confederate training base on Deca-One is named after. The countdown sequence has been activated. You have five minutes."

Jackson blinked stupidly. He thought he was dreaming. "This is not happening," he spoke aloud. "This is just not happening. Not a complicated numerical or alpha-numeric code, not a DNA signature, not a retinal scan or a bio-chip ident, just a one word, god-damned, bullshit answer-type question."

"Great, just great!" Hearst said in frustration. "We travel to the outer rim of the galaxy to some God forsaken planet inhabited by psycho-monsters whose main objective is to shit you out their digestive track, and end up at the end of the dock playing ten questions with a holographic comedian. Great, just A-fucking great."

"No, this isn't a joke and it isn't some holographic science fiction thriller. This is real," Jackson said.

"But that's so simple, so stupid," Dyer broke in. "It was named in memory of Private..."

"No!" Jackson shouted and clamped a hand over Dyer's mouth. "I keep telling you that Green was a spook. And once a spook, always a spook. It's too obvious. It's bait to draw us in. Anyone who has access to a Confederate NAV pack would be able to access the historical archives and figure that out in a heartbeat. I don't want to even think about what kind of response a wrong answer would elicit but it probably wouldn't be, 'Sorry, best of three, try your luck again'."

"Yea, well the clock's ticking, folks," DeLuca said tightly, "so let's either answer the man's question or shake hands all around, bend over and kiss our asses good bye!"

"Four minutes to detonation," the voice said.

Jackson turned toward the holographic image of Dr. Winston Green. "Think simple, think simple," he whispered. "So what is so special about that particular base?" he asked rhetorically. Something no one but a Confederate would know. Something buried so deep, so arcane and so routine that it would be overlooked. Something that would never really be outdated and yet would be familiar to any Confederate who stumbled across his site. Codes change every eight hours as the duty watch rotates out and new personnel are constantly being added to the roster. No one in their right mind would send current security codes and algorithms on an open circuit, even a secure circuit, to the outer edge of the galaxy and absolutely not by courier bird. So the answer lies in his question. It's something we all know but because it's so common, we've forgotten it." He looked at his team. "I'm way open to suggestions here, folks."

"Three minutes to core detonation," a female voice intoned.

It's just like in the holo-views, Dyer thought detachedly, the dark, cave-like secret base, the sultry, female voice counting down to detonation. The only thing lacking is the heroine tied to a railroad track and the secret code written on a rock somewhere or in a bit of death poetry left by the villain. A small alarm was ringing in a deep forgotten corner of his brain and he was trying to recall it. Suddenly, he grabbed Jackson's arm.

"Sir!"

"Not now, Robbie," Jackson said, cutting him off.

"Sir, wait!" Dyer shouted. His grip on Jackson's arm was like a vise. Jackson looked down at the gloved hand gripping his arm, then up at Dyer's face.

"OK Robbie, run with it. What do you have?"

"It's not about who, it's about what! Don't you see? He didn't ask who the base was named after, he asked what! What does the base stand for, not who was it named after!" Suddenly, comprehension dawned and Jackson turned toward Green's image.

"Exdor," he said. Instantly, the shimmering blue energy field disappeared.

"Lieutenant Thomas Daniel Jackson, Mike Platoon, SEAL Team One, Earth Prime," he stated. The image turned to face him.

"Thank you, Lieutenant. Please follow me." The image faded and reappeared beside a series of tables and power monitors at the far end of the cavern. The team made their way across the hard cut floor, staring in wonder at the walls and equipment.

"How did you know the answer wasn't Private Verlin Haydren, Sir?" the chief asked in a low voice as they walked.

"Because originally the base wasn't named for Private Haydren. It was named to honor the engagement that was fought by the 4th Floren Marine Battalion at the siege of Exdor. That base was the first joint training facility built between the Floren Marines and the Confederate Navy. The name was changed two months before the base was commissioned when it was decided that it would be more appropriate to name the base after the Floren Marine private who wrote the poem, 'Darkness' before he was killed on the last day of the siege. That fact is not generally known outside of the Confederacy."

Green's holographic image waited until a sentinel subroutine loop detected motion within its movement envelope before it spoke.

"Since this holographic program was activated when you triggered the security field, it means that my team and I are dead. This program will address all its comments as if it were speaking to Lieutenant Thomas Daniel Jackson. If you wish to pause the program at any time, simply engage the thumb switch on your suit.

"It is UCT 247.0213 or if you prefer February 13, Terran year 2247. We have been on the planet for six years under orders from the Confederate Admiralty and under the direct supervision of Admiral Tra on Urilis. A Caldarian scout ship accompanied by a fleet class cruiser entered the system last month. They have crisscrossed the planet running multiple geophysical scans that we have detected, and they landed ground troops eight days ago. We now suspect that our security has been compromised. Possibly the Caldarians intercepted a slot buoy, we don't know for sure, but the fact that they are here conducting geophysical surveys confirms that they have gained knowledge of our project and are aware of the tactical and strategic significance of our find.

"We set up a decoy lab, leaving enough equipment and material on the surface so that it would appear to be the primary research location. We haven't used it for two and a half years. We detected particle detonations in and around the camp three days ago and have recorded troop movement along the path that follows the base of the plateau. I assume the Caldarians destroyed the decoy base in order to deny it to anyone else. Our research here is complete and we have been ordered to return to Confederate space immediately.

"Unfortunately, that is no longer an option but we will try. The Caldarian cruiser killed the Terra within twenty minutes of entering the system. We've plotted the orbital track of the cruiser and will wait until it is in shadow on the other side of the planet, but the fact that you are here watching this recording means that we didn't make it. All we have left to run with is a Class 4 courier shuttle and she doesn't have the speed to exit the system undetected."

The image smiled bitterly before continuing. "I guess I'll break one more order as well. When I leave, I won't be taking the completed drive and weapons modules with me."

Jackson paused the program and the image of Green froze.

"He knew he was dead," Hearst said softly. "Even a class four courier bird can't outrun a Caldarian fleet class interdiction cruiser, even with an hour or so head start to jump to star drive."

"No, and the residual ion trail from her propulsion system would point like an arrow to her base course unless she did some maneuvering before she left the system. My bet is that she didn't because it would have been just a waste of time," Dyer added.

"So he planned for that contingency even though it meant disobeying a direct order from the Admiralty. Smooth, very smooth," Jackson stated, his admiration for the man growing by the minute.

"And by disobeying that direct order he bought the Confederacy time," the chief added.

"Sir, look at this!" DeLuca, who had moved down the row of tables along the side of the cavern, called them over. The team walked over to where he was examining a wall of monitors. In a cut-away portion of the wall was a small nuclear power plant, the kind normally used by Confederate research teams. He was scanning the bank of displays and power conduits with the detachable wand off of his suit sensors.

"I'd call this god damn brilliant! Look at what he did! Absolutely genius class, this dude," he exclaimed. DeLuca snapped the wand back in place on his suit and turned to Jackson. "Sir, he re-routed the power conduits. No, that isn't entirely correct. He reprogrammed the security cloak and then re-routed the power feed to the security grid and set up a low powered FM transmitter to transmit a single carrier tone on a frequency of 420.26 megahertz. Brilliant!"

"OK," Hearst asked, "so do you mind telling us what's so significant about that, Dr. DeLuca, and maybe letting the rest of us bask in your superior electronic intellect?" There was a note of sly sarcasm in her voice.

He looked at her and blinked. "Right. Sorry, Sir." He pointed with one gloved hand and they all turned. "He shut off the conventional reactor core and powered it using Element crystals."

The team looked at him in stunned silence. It took them a moment to realize what he had just told them.

"Then it wasn't just a hypothesis or a working model, as we were told," Miller stated in a hard flat voice. The team looked around them and stared at the power monitors and rows of electronic equipment. What they hadn't noticed before was that every single piece of equipment was powered up and functioning. Not a single piece of equipment was powered down or in standby mode.

"The signal we detected was the key to the bank," Hearst said. "Every-one knows the Caldarians don't use FM. Hell, we haven't used it for over a hundred years and if DeLuca hadn't decided to scan down there because he was bored, we'd still be scratching our heads and wondering where we were."

"And because the transmitter is powered by an Element cored reactor, it could transmit virtually forever or until a component broke down," DeLuca finished for her.

"Let's hear what the good doctor has to say. It's time to contact Ensign Chantella and get out of here."

The team walked back to Green's holographic image and Jackson re-activated the program.

"I only took a very small sample of the Element with me, along with copies of some of my technical notes and diagrams. I left the finished Star Drive and weapons module here." Jackson had to pause the program again in order to digest this information before letting Green resume his brief.

"A functioning star drive and weapons modules!" His head reeled at the casual tone of Green's remark.

"The star drive module and weapon modules are in a man-portable transport pack behind the last row of instruments in a small cut-away. I assumed that when you got here, you would be in a hurry and the Caldarians would probably be up your ass, so I took the opportunity to ensure that you wouldn't have to waste time trying to find something to carry it with. The drive module will fit any standard Frigate or destroyer star drive coil from serial number 230.000 to 245.1231, and a weapons system with a serial number of 7852-874 to 8102-154, which should cover just about anything that was current in the fleet up until a year ago. The smaller drive module is a shuttle mod and will fit any standard Confederate shuttle. You will find that the drive modification will increase propulsion by a factor of twenty percent and there will be no residual ion particle signature or radiation dis-persion envelope.

"The weapons mod will increase standard bore destroyer particle can-nons to the rough equivalency of a Yorktown Class fleet cruiser. We haven't tested or run simulations on any other series of drive or weapons but I sus-pect the results will be pretty much standard across the board. Oh, and you don't have to run any modifications on the cloaking system. The Element's inherent ability to regenerate and sustain itself takes care of that.

"And last but not least, something I'm sure you will find useful are five assault rifle power packs modified with Element power coils. The beam is much denser. We tested it on a Bristol Mark-354G battle suit and it had no trouble cutting through the ceramic frontal armor with a 0.01 second hit. We were able to increase the density of the beam and narrow the band-width, which increased the range and widened the penetration envelope to fifteen degrees of deflection. Those suits are three years old and I assume that the armor is probably obsolete but that will give you an idea of what they are capable of."

Hearst whistled. "Oh, I gotta have one of those."

"I assume that you have met our scaled carnivorous friends already, Lieutenant. Dr. Alexander and Dr. Orlando were killed three days ago while transporting two Neuro-snoop antenna modules on the plateau." Green's image smiled wryly. "Once a spook, always a spook."

Jackson paused the program again. "That confirms it. If Green had a set of those modules, then he was definitely Confederate intelligence. Nobody, not even the teams, uses those antennas. They're considered part of the top-secret inventory. I wonder what else Green was up to down here?" he asked, more as a statement than a question. He resumed the program and Green continued.

"Don't underestimate them. They are extremely dangerous and cunning. No matter how we close the opening on the plateau, they always seem to manage to force it somehow. That's why we kept two guards posted there at all times. It was damn boring work but it was the only way we could be sure of the proper warning if they broke in. We had two of them get inside one night. They killed two technicians who were monitoring the charging coil array that was feeding the bleeder reactor to our hydroponic field in the west chamber. Remember that the security envelope is designed and programmed to keep people from getting in, not from getting out. The plateau exit is only used in emergencies and for secondary ventilation. We completed that raise two weeks before the Caldarians showed up and unfortunately, did not have the time to install the security envelope or place any charges. All we managed was an Epoxite collar and a grill made of plating we took from the Terra. It's hidden and cloaked but the creatures know where it is and won't stop trying to force it open.

"I don't know if you have noticed, but we suspect that they are empathic. I mentioned that in my last slot buoy transmission to Dr. Ralsus, the Ramillion anthropologist working at the University of Worlds on Rigulas-One. They use those abilities to herd or drive prey to others of their kind and to shock them into immobility. They hate bright light so don't even think of being caught outside after dark, especially alone."

Hearst snorted. "No shit! So tell us something we don't know." Jackson glared at her and she hastily apologized. "Sorry, Sir," she said meekly.

"Also, we discovered that their peculiar empathic abilities make them particularly sensitive to a neural transmitter. I suspect that a neural stimulation globe would be most effective in keeping them away.

"Well that's it, Lieutenant. Don't use the hidden raise we cut on the top of the plateau. We welded the locking mechanism shut before we left. We discouraged the creatures from snooping around there. We set up a neural array at the base entrance that...well, all we know is that it operates on a frequency way outside the aural envelope of any known species in the database. When we first found this place, we decided to move all of our research down here instead of transporting everything to the Terra. We figured that it was only a matter of time before the Caldarians showed up and if they stumbled on this like we did, it would be game over. Besides, it was far easier to rig a little surprise here and bring the roof down so to speak, rather than risk their taking the Terra and sifting through a scattering of space debris. This way, we hoped that they would at least have to bring in heavy mining equipment to expose the host rock again. Our hope was that someone from the Confederacy would find it first.

"The ore bearing rock plunges at a seventy-degree angle along the wall. We estimate that the actual planetary core contains more of this substance but we couldn't determine the extent of the ore body itself. It's just too complex. And we didn't come here to mine, we came here to build. One thing you can bet your life on is that this place is going to be a damn valuable piece of real estate once word gets out. The shaft we cut to the top of the plateau is at the rear of the cavern.

"And one last thing. You're probably wondering what happened to the Terra. She's dead," Green said in his hard flat voice. "It was the first thing the Caldarians found when they entered the system after breaching our security. There were forty-seven members of my team aboard when the Caldarians boarded. Dr. Reseren, our communications engineer, blew the pre-set scuttling charges in the engineering spaces and on the bridge. He took twenty-two Caldarian bastards with him.

"If you would be kind enough to see that the crew holo-message chips get delivered, it would be very much appreciated. When we realized that there was no escape, we each made a personal hologram for our families back home.

"Good luck, Lieutenant."

Green's image faded and Jackson and his team stood, the only sound the quiet hum of the equipment. Jackson stirred.

"We have to leave," he said softly. "Let's grab the modules and the holo-disks with Green's data.

"Shall I disconnect the FM transmitter boss," DeLuca asked? "We have the co-ordinates for this place."

"No," Jackson said. "Leave it on. We still have to get off the planet and back to the Lex. And there is still the rest of that Blackie platoon out there somewhere. Just make sure that you erase the location from your suit NAV systems." The team looked at him and nodded slowly. They knew what he was thinking. Better to leave the transmitter on and delete any reference to this location in case the Caldarians captured them. Jackson led them around the wall of the cavern behind the banks of equipment to where a small opening had been cut into the rock with a deep core mining scalpel. It was sealed with a piece of hull plating and a control panel had been tri-welded to it. The digital display showed the current date and time. Jackson didn't hesitate. He undid his battle helmet, removed his biochip Ident implant and clipped it into the small access slot and swept his palm over the command bar. There was a whir as servomotors worked and the door slid open. He removed his chip, put it back in its slot and locked down his battle mask.

"DeLuca, grab the pack, redistribute your gear and let's move."

DeLuca hit the quick release buckle on his harness and the chief redistributed its contents while DeLuca shouldered the pack. Jackson reached down and picked up the strip of assault rifle power packs.

"Here, let's switch these out before we leave."

Hearst and Miller switched out and then, once they had powered their weapons up again, the others did the same. DeLuca shifted the pack on his back.

"Congratulations Carl," Jackson said. "You just made the history books. You're the first Confederate combatant to carry the future of civilization on your back."

Hearst slapped him on the back and winked. "And you just became the prime target as well. You get to walk point."

DeLuca only grunted. The team filed back into the main chamber and stopped beside the last table and looked back. They were tired. None of them had slept for over twenty-four hours and fatigue was beginning to catch up with them. They were dirty and they stank of blood, powder and the acrid residual odor of particle weapons.

"Sir, maybe we should get some rack time before we head out. I'd feel safer here than trying to rest back in the open," the chief said.

Jackson desperately wanted to make contact with Chantella and get off the planet but he also knew that the longer they went without rest, the greater the chance was of making a mistake—and a wrong move now would be catastrophic. He was hesitant to make the team take their tri-Dexedrine tablets and only wanted to use them as a last resort. He knew if they took them too soon that, once the chemical wore off, they would black out wherever they were.

"You're right, Chief. We'll rest here." Jackson walked over to the table beside the converted reactor core and lay down on the smooth, polished floor. The team followed suit. They were asleep instantly, the hum of the electrical equipment softly singing them to sleep. They lay within touching distance of each other, one hand on the person beside them.

Hearst twisted and groaned in her sleep. She was falling. Her right hand was entwined in something and she couldn't pull free. She groped desperately and saw that her hand was imbedded in the chest cavity of a tall Caldarian. His dead eyes stared at her and a knife came up. She could feel the pressure of it against her rib cage but couldn't move. Her eyelids flickered and moved rapidly as her consciousness slowly surfaced out of the deep sleep that she had been in.

Her eyes opened. She was panting and her mouth was dry. She took a sip of water from her hydration tube and tapped the chin switch, bringing up her HUD from standby mode. She checked the time. She had been asleep for two and a half-hours. She tried to shake the image of the nightmare but her feeling of unease did not recede and her instincts told her that they should be moving.

Fifteen hundred meters above them, on the surface of the plateau, six huge forms moved in the night and glided silently to the edge of a small grilled vent set in Epoxite concrete. Epoxite has a compressive strength of ninety-eight hundred pounds per square inch.

A bent piece of rolled, dirillium plate armor that had fallen when the Hancock broke up in the atmosphere was wedged between the bars and five pairs of clawed hands began to twist and heave. The bars groaned in protest and slowly deformed from the tremendous force being applied. There was a rending screech and the concrete holding the bars cracked and broke. With the sudden release of pressure, the steel grill hurtled through the air and caught one of the creatures standing behind full in the face. There was a loud snap and the creature sank to the ground, its head hanging at an odd angle, its neck broken. The large alpha turned and stooped over the still form, flexing his cortex, searching for contact. There was none. Swiftly, he moved to the dark opening and peered down. His nostrils twitched and his mouth opened. The sweet odor of soft flesh flowed out of the dark opening. Without a second thought, the large creature climbed over the rim and disappeared into the darkness. One by one, the others followed.

Hearst stirred and the sleeping form of Chief Miller moved. He sat up and looked at her.

"What is it?" his thought echoed.

"I think we should move now!" she whispered urgently. The others, disturbed by the raw empathic energy emanating from Hearst, opened their eyes and sat up, hands reaching for weapons. In a heartbeat, they were grasping weapons and facing the dimly lit chamber. Jackson noted that they were all facing the rear. They all felt it. Fingers moved and safeties were thumbed off. Charging capacitors went active and a small diode on each weapon glowed a steady dull red, indicating that the weapon was up.

"Our friends are back," DeLuca said in a hushed voice. "Don't they ever give up?"

They looked toward the dark opening that led to the surface door underneath the Leaf Cedars.

At that moment, a red light began blinking on a monitor on the far side of the cavern. Five helmeted heads swung, drawn by the flashing light. A shrill scream cut across the cavern, echoing and reverberating before it faded into stillness. There was a soft sighing of dark movement and in the next moment, a rippling needle point of particle fire. The team spun toward the rear to see Hearst on one knee, particle rifle up, as she fired again. There was the searing, hollow snap of particle energy striking flesh as a creature slumped to the floor, its body cut in two by the heavy density beam. It was the huge alpha leader. She swung, and once more a particle beam reached out and took a second creature in the chest, shearing through its calcified layers and vaporizing a bank of monitors behind it. Immediately an alarm sounded and the ambient blue light began to pulsate ominously.

"Oh, I like it!" Hearst called out gleefully. "Gawd, let's buy some more!"

Their suit sensors immediately went red as they detected multiple signatures closing their position from the rear.

"They must have somehow forced the grill off the plateau entrance," Jackson said. "Chief, take the point. Let's go!"

The chief stepped out cautiously into the tunnel-like opening that led up to the narrow door beneath the cedars five hundred meters above them. "Nothing. Green board, Sir, to our twelve o'clock."

"Multiple contacts following. I show six thoracic signatures following but not closing, Sir," Hearst, as rear security, informed the team.

"Sir, this running is no good. We either have to stop and fight them or break contact with them," Dyer spoke. "And I don't think trying to break contact with them is going to work. They can follow our scent and will call others to wait for us in ambush somewhere ahead and I don't really like the idea of those power pack modules ending up in some hairy assed monster's stomach. I say fucking take 'em now. I'm tired of running. Let's take them in here before we get outside, before they call for help."

They were halted at a turn. They felt uneasy and exposed on the narrow trail. Jackson checked his HUD. All his systems were nominal and yet he was worried. Where were the other Caldarians?

"Chief, what do we have left?" he asked.

"We used up all our slashers on the Caldarians. All we have left are two anti-personnel darters and I don't know if they'll work on these things. Their hides may be too thick but I agree with Dyer. They're going to stay with us until they are either killed or they kill us."

He checked his sensors. It showed at least six of the creatures about one hundred and fifty meters back.

"OK, we settle with them. Around this corner and up that grade. If I recall, the path widens out a bit and that will be to our advantage. Darters need a bit more room than what we have here. This is going to be quick and dirty. Those darters each have six dispensing tubes. I want to trigger the first one and then wait until we hear that we hit some of them and then trigger the second one. Program the first one with two darts each for the three front movers. When they go down, we'll trigger the last one on the three in the rear."

The team moved up around the corner and Hearst noted that as soon as they moved out, the creatures did also. The path widened out and the right hand wall receded into the darkness. The hair on Jackson's neck prickled. He felt eyes on him. The chief knelt down and DeLuca opened a compartment on the chief's pack and took out the two thoracic grenades. He turned on their small power modules and allowed their tiny computer brains to paint and acquire their targets. When both grenades had blinked green, he set them in the center of the path. The team retreated. DeLuca monitored the creatures' movements as they followed the team.

"Come on, come on," he whispered impatiently. "Come and see what Uncle Carl has for you, my pretties!"

"The rest of you keep going," Jackson told them. "Dyer and I will stay here and detonate the grenades." Doc started to protest but Jackson cut her off. "Not now, Doc." I want you to keep moving and get out. If our neural signature goes flat in ten minutes Chief, the ball is yours. Contact Ensign Chantella as soon as you're in the open and then get the hell out. No hero bullshit. Get moving."

Dyer and Jackson sank to the ground behind several small crumpled boulders that had been heavily encrusted with calcium leaching from the cavern's damp air.

They could see on their sensors that the creatures were advancing. Jackson shuddered involuntarily as he watched the five thoracic signatures on his display advance.

"Heads up," he whispered, and he and Dyer transferred the output onto the tactical display on their battle masks.

"On my count," he said. "Seventy-five meters, sixty." Dyer raised his particle rifle. "Forty meters—get ready—thirty." He counted the five 'thoracics' on his display. "Twenty-five meters."

"Only five," his brain screamed at him. "Where's the sixth?" The second last signature in the line had faded and vanished from their sensors.

"Too late," Dyer shouted as figures rushed in and he chinned his lights. At the same moment, Jackson blew the first darter. The path lay in dazzling brilliance as the xenon lights drove the cavern darkness away. There was a soft, hollow pop as the darts ignited, followed by a sawing whir as Dyer fired his particle rifle. The three lead creatures staggered and fell backwards as the explosive heads in the darts made contact and detonated. The last crea-ture in line lay on the ground, his chest cavity cut open by Dyer's shot. Jack-son detonated the last grenade and once again, six darts tracked relentlessly in. The last creature crashed to the ground and slid toward Jackson, his clawed hand flexing and reaching for him, eyes glazing over. It stopped two meters away. The other four darts lost signature lock and slammed into the far wall, small pinpricks of light marking where they detonated.

Jackson had his weapon up, scanning the path, searching for the sixth creature. Where it had disappeared to or why it had not been detected made him distinctly uneasy. The xenon lamps timed out and their battle masks went back to nominal night vision.

Jackson and Dyer stood up and turned back up the path, Dyer occasion-ally turning around to check their six.

"Clear," he said, and was acknowledged by Hearst who was on rear security, watching for them.

They sprinted forward, anxious to catch up with the rest of the team. Hearst was bent on one knee, her particle rifle up, covering the rear as she waited, the optical sight of her rifle pressed into the concave-shooting cup in her battle mask. She watched Jackson and Dyer coming into view. She also saw a shadow dart out and reach for Dyer from the shadows on the right. Her mind cried out a warning and she squeezed off her shot, her eyes never blinking or moving from her target.

Dyer felt a burning in his right shoulder as powerful muscles clamped and claws tore through the fabric of his suit. He cried out.

Jackson swung his weapon up but was flung back by the passing, sear-ing heat of a particle beam, Doc Hearst's shot searing his left arm. There was a howl of rage and Jackson chinned his light. Another bolt of particle fire reached out and the creature fell, a perfect circle burned through its chest. The left arm was severed between the elbow and shoulder, claws still grip-ping Dyer's shoulder. Doc's first shot had taken it off as clean as a surgeon's blade.

Blood was seeping from Dyer's shoulder and he grit his teeth as he stag-gered to his feet and stumbled forward, collapsing a few meters behind Hearst, who never took her weapon or her eyes off the downward leading path. Dyer was cursing in a steady monotone as the chief searched the wound, applied the antibiotic nano-particle and sutured the wound. "Good luck, Robbie," he said when he was finished.

"Nice shooting, Doc," Jackson said.

Hearst blew on her gloved nails and brushed them against her suit and winked at Dyer. "You owe me, sailor boy. Your ass is mine when we get back to the Lex."

"I'm still way ahead of you, Doc," he growled through his pain.

"Fifty meters more and we're clear," the chief said. The team moved out. There was a faint stream of daylight filtering through the thick cedars at the mouth of the entrance. One by one, they exited and stopped short of the trail, examining both directions before leaving the cover of the trees. They were about to move out when Jackson raised his right fist and knelt back down. Alarmed, the others sank down automatically, training their weapons out. They were tired and bone weary, and knew that they were at the ragged edge of their endurance.

Jackson's head was lowered and a look of disbelief crossed his face. He held up three fingers on his left hand and quickly scrunched them three times. The team switched to the command net.

"Stalker, Stalker, this is Nightshade, over," said the voice of Ensign Marcie Chantella.

CHAPTER 12
SIGNALS

*"The most effective indirect approach is one that
lures or startles the opponent into a false move—
so that, as in jiu-jitsu, his own effort is
turned into the lever of his overthrow."*

—Sir Basil H. Liddel-Hart

The Pegasus drifted in the black interstellar void between Battle Group Six and the Caldarian right flank. Her systems were powered down and her reactor coils were in standby mode. She was as invisible as current technology could make her. Her hull bore no external ridges or plate lines and her Chameleon plating was a thin layer that had been applied using a fusion reel that melted the epoxy and made it as smooth as glass. A computer checked her position three hundred and sixty times a second and a light-emitting grid work as fine as silk, imbedded in her coating, flashed and twinkled in an exact holographic representation of what the stars would look like to anyone visually searching that particular section of space. Her EMF (electro-magnetic field) replicators shifted and altered her magnetic field so that whatever returns a monitoring patrol vessel received would look like background clutter. Her hull was a compressed oval and her engine nacelles were mounted internally to reduce her overall sensor signature even more. She had no armor or weapons. Her mark 6F series star drive was capable of outrunning anything in the Caldarian fleet.

She was an ELINT bird. The acronym stood for Electronic Intelligence. Her sole purpose was to record and report any movement and electronic traffic that was passed to and from the Caldarian fleet, poised to smash the Confederate center and sweep in and envelop the four home worlds behind them. Three days ago, a Caldarian patrol squadron had passed within ten kilometers of her position. The crew had shut off everything that could be shut off and held their breath as the third and fourth Caldarian frigates in the patrol line swept toward her. The inboard frigate closed to within one kilometer. The crew of the Pegasus watched their passive sensor monitors as Caldarian sensors washed and played over their hull. Would they detect her? Would her advanced Chameleon grid really absorb and re-configure the electronic fingers probing for her? The patrol line moved on and the crew let out their breath.

"Damn!" technician Kelly Ruderman breathed. "Did you see that? I could count the seams in her hull coating, she was so close."

"She also had her starboard gun ports open, her weapons in standby mode and the charging capacitors at one hundred percent. If she had seen us Ensign, we wouldn't have had time to blink—in case you didn't notice that part," Captain Haste Osno replied cheerfully.

Captain Osno of the Pegasus was a short, stocky Hadarian who held a PhD in pulse plasmatic electronics. His close-cropped black hair glistened with the traditional coating of Selesian herb oil that Hadarian males applied each morning. His face always showed a five o'clock shadow from the thick facial hair that grew at a phenomenal rate and his muscular frame rippled with benign energy. He had two daughters and wrote them every evening before settling in for a few brief hours of rest. His favorite picture of his wife and daughters having a tea party was mounted on the overhead bulkhead above the battle bunk in his small stateroom. The Hadarians were a gregarious, exuberant race who put great stock in families and family tradition.

Genealogy is almost a genetic passion, Kelly Ruderman reflected, smiling at the thought of the burly Captain having tea in the family garden with his wife and two small daughters. In a galactic society where the entire commerce of certain planetary systems was based solely on philandering and prowling, the Hadarian belief in celibacy and conjugal fidelity was a most singular trait, Ruderman noted. Whenever shore leave came, most of the crew scattered to one of the dozen planets that catered to every known avaricious bent the heart could conceive. The Captain almost always stayed onboard or went to one of the intergalactic university institutes to 'rest' as he called it, reading the latest research journals on pulse induced electronics.

"Yes Sir. Good to know all this high tech smoke and mirrors stuff works, Sir. I'd really hate to end up in a Caldarian cargo hauler doing time for eavesdropping on their battle fleet."

"Somehow Ensign, I don't think we would ever see the inside of a cargo hauler," he replied laconically. "I think they would have something a little more high tech, as you call it, in mind for us."

"Yeah, like watching our skin peel off inside an acid tank," Technician First Class, Jacin Antonavich retorted.

"Whoa! Now there's a highly objective and intelligent observation, Mr.

Anty-dick," Ruderman retorted.

Antonavich flipped her the bird without taking his eyes off his bank of surveillance monitors.

"Yeah, I know, your old man is a member of the old Russian inter-planetary parliament and the 'vich' was added to your name by Tsar Elizaveta Petrovna in 1758 and your IQ is 184. Big deal! So tell me, if you're so smart, what the hell are you doing on a spook bird, bustin' your balls on standard Caldarian ELINT traffic with us blue-collar trash instead of in a nice, safe research office on Earth Prime making time with an admiral's double D's, Comm Tech?"

Antonavich turned and glared at her. "Because I like what I'm doing, and the food is so-o-o good."

The bridge crew laughed at the sparring exchange between Antonavich and Ruderman.

"The cloaking works, too well at times, Sir." Tom Mallone, the Executive Officer, said as he stood up and stretched.

"That's why the Mercury is in space dock, XO. You can't go playing sneak and peak with a trash hauling Hadarian cargo freighter carrying dry chemical for the mining colony on Pandara-Four and not expect to get bumped in the process."

"Expensive way to see if your cloaking grid is working Captain, even if it was supposed to be a training run. Those damn bulk carriers don't exactly stop and turn on a dime. Even when the Merc realized she was going to get hit and put her hard over with the 'pedal to the metal,' it still took way too long to clear the friction envelope along her starboard side. And because we don't really exist by any form of scan or sweep (or even on any ship registry with a clearance lower than ultra), Mercury drifted for two days making emergency repairs before she could limp back to the O'Brien for overhaul. I'll bet that trash hauler's captain is still scratching his balls, wondering what the hell happened."

A sudden waterfall of color on one of Kelly Ruderman's monitoring scopes intruded on her listening and brought her back to immediate focus. She worked her data screen, moved one of her forward lateral arrays, and the signal definition peaked and then vanished as quickly as it had appeared. She frowned.

"Captain," she called, "you'd better have a look at this, Sir. I just picked up that rogue signal again."

The captain came over and Ruderman's hands flicked over her control console as she quickly built the three-dimensional picture from her narrow band data-stream and tapped the control nipple on her palmer. A bright yellow dot appeared at the left-hand edge of the display and she paused it for a moment.

"This is the first occurrence," she said, holding her right index finger over the small point of light. "We picked it up shortly after arriving on station and four hours after the Caldarians punched through the Sixth fleet's outer perimeter." Her hand worked the log display. "We lost three frigates and the cruiser Sussex in the initial shit throw. Oops! Sorry, Sir." Ensign Ruderman had a tendency to forget where she was and who she was when she got excited, and rank etiquette often got thrown out the window.

"No problem, Ensign, please continue," the captain said.

Again she worked the controls. A three dimensional astral array appeared over the holograph.

"When we first picked it up, I took no note of it and passed it off as routine Confederate traffic because of its signature envelope. But we've clocked it every day at the same time for the past eight days. We've been able to locate its source. We used our base course as the baseline and fixed its position each time. It was hard the first few times but once we identified it we knew what to look for and because it transmits at the exact same time every eighteen hours, we scooped it."

"And?" the captain asked.

"Eighteen hours is the length of Terran time in one Caldarian dayra or twenty-two Caldarian cycles, Sir."

"Which is the equivalent of one earth day," Osno said, finishing the thought. He felt a cold knot of dread forming in the pit of his stomach. "Where's the signal source, Ensign?"

"Sir, its point of origin is within the debris field where the Sixth is holding station in the Degus system." She paused for a moment before continuing. "It's coming from the Sussex, Sir."

Osno stared at the display in blank astonishment as the realization of what he was looking at struck him.

"A covert Caldarian surveillance team of Blackies," he said. He had been briefed on them several months ago when he was first assigned to the Pegasus but only half believed the intelligence reports, thinking that it was just another myth to be separated from fact concerning the Black Order. "Are you sure, Ensign?"

"Positive, Sir. Watch."

She called up the signal log and overlaid each transmission on the display. The yellow dot grew and became several yellow lines that radiated out from one point and then converged again where they terminated at the other end. The lines curved across the astral grid in a graceful arc that ended where Ruderman was pointing with her finger again.

Her finger was hovering over the center of the Caldarian battle fleet.

"And we have this, Sir. After the second occurrence, I spooled it to Technician Antonavich and he was able to strip away the external signature and found this beneath it, a Caldarian pulse transmission bead. It's sort of like an old zipped file, Captain. Just a small kernel of electronic data on a plasmatic pulse bead, but once he unzipped it or 'watered' it as the saying is, Mr. Antonavich was able to detach the self-destruct loop from the bead. When he did, we got this."

She tapped her control board and a dense pattern of electronic code began to scroll down the screen.

"We haven't been able to decipher it yet because it's something we haven't seen before. We're electronic specialists, not cryptographers, especially not Caldarian cryptographers. But my bet is that if they thought it that important to plant a surveillance bird, then whatever they're re-routing has to be some shit hot important. Sir!" she added as an afterthought.

Osno released the magnetic clamps on his hover seat and drifted up to his bridge seat where he reattached and spoke into his COM. The Pegasus didn't have artificial gravity dampers. Gravity dampers radiated a tremendous amount of low frequency, electronic emissions that acted like a beacon to anyone with the ability to detect them. Shielding was heavy and complex, and did not totally conceal the gravity field. So the Pegasus and her sister, the Mercury did without.

"XO, it's time to move this expensive bucket of bolts and earn our pay. We have to call this one in. Code it black and send it as soon as we move off our base course and are finished executing pattern Delta and clear the envelope."

"Captain, when we make our last course change with pattern Delta and open that bleed valve off the starboard nacelle for the ion dump, we'll be about as stealthy as a Rygillian cargo box. The ion stream is going to lose spatial conformity real quick since the plasma coil doesn't induce it, and it won't be as elongated as a real ion stream produced when we jump to light."

"I know, XO, but any tracking vessel still has to follow the sensor track in order to plot our jump point. I'm betting that will give us enough of a lead to break contact and run for the envelope edge. Then we'll come about and head back in to our patrol station unless there're search drones out or multiple picket craft. Then it's gonna be a cast iron bitch to break clear," Osno replied.

"Pulse signal ready. Standing by to execute pattern Delta on your mark," Mallone said.

"Captain," signal technician Duris said, "we're coming up on the first line of Caldarian pickets. Four Serpent class Caldarian frigates steaming in a diamond pattern bearing four-three-two, mark four-nine. Coming abeam of the trailing frigate now, Sir."

"Helm, engage Delta on my mark. Now, Ms. Jamison," he said.

"Engaging Delta. Aye, Sir," Lieutenant Brenda Jamison replied. The Pegasus heeled over and began to execute her egress maneuvers.

"We don't operate this way," Mallone murmured, half to himself and half to the bridge in general. "We normally move and transmit clandestinely and remain on station."

"Agreed, but we need to make sure this one gets out and the only way to do that is to move out of the Caldarian envelope and send the pulse transmission from clean space. Don't worry," Osno said, "we'll be back on station in a heartbeat and you can go back to beating Mr. Antonavich at Duvarian chess."

Because of the curtain of electronic surveillance, communication was accomplished on a very strict schedule and the pulse transmission was programmed with its own series of course changes and maneuvers so that if it was detected, it could not be traced back to its source—in this case, the Pegasus. This took time. To clear the envelope gave them a hole shot at the Lex without the need for the egress course maneuvers. It also put the Pegasus at risk. She was virtually invisible when she wasn't moving. But once she engaged her engines, she started to radiate. Not much but radiate nonetheless.

Mallone smiled. "Well Captain, since Mr. Antonavich has beaten me seven straight, I don't think I'm really looking forward to that prospect."

The Pegasus passed like a black hole between the starboard and trail patrol frigates as she cut across the diamond.

Kelly Ruderman watched her threat board, comprised of three special systems that recorded and countered any electronic threat depending on their level of intensity. Her monitors were going crazy. The amount of electronic energy that was painting the Pegasus would 'cook an Arkansas warthog in its own fat' she thought.

Computers cataloged the electronic sensors sweeping over them and determined which threat posed the greatest danger to the ship and routed power to the cloaking grid and 'shimmer screen' accordingly.

Her boards were red but the systems were coping. She was just about to breathe a sigh of relief as the ship passed between the port side frigates when a light began to flash on the monitor that operated the port array. She paled.

"She's going to light off—she's going active! Captain, we've just been painted by the frigate on the starboard edge of the formation. She's altering course, Sir. I think she has us."

"XO, open starboard nacelle and dump ion stream."

Ruderman watched her monitors as the ion field dispersed and the dump valve sealed on the starboard nacelle.

"Helm, come to new course, set two-seven-eight, mark four-nine and engage star drive," Osno said. The Pegasus wheeled and pivoted as the powerful vectoring thrusters along her hull fired, settling her on base course.

"Sir, the port frigate has just powered up her weapons and is still closing. She's ignoring the ion dump, Captain. The other frigates are heeling over and coming to a new base course. The lead frigate is swinging wide. She just cloaked! Repeat, she just cloaked. Residual signature indicates ion flux. She's trying to flank us! There she goes!"

"Coming to new course two-seven-eight, mark four-nine, star drive engaging now, aye!" the helmsman cried out. The Pegasus jumped to star drive and the stars twinkled, blurred and then came back into focus as the ship settled to her run.

"Frigates are closing, Captain, range five thousand kilometers, signature lock! They have lock, the lead frigate just launched on us. We have three incoming torpedoes; look like standard Caldarian fusion disrupters," the tactical officer said.

"Two minutes to envelope breach, Captain," the XO said. "Time to impact, two minutes, fifteen seconds. They're fanning out. It looks like they're going to try to radiate the envelope edge, Sir."

"Prepare for pulse transmission," Osno said, his voice tight. "Engineering, as soon as I say the word, I want full power on that drive coil!"

"Aye, Captain," the chief engineer replied.

Suddenly, the tactical officer cried out a warning. "Sir, we have a vessel approaching from zero-four-four, mark one-one. It's the other frigate, Captain. They must have known we were heading for the edge."

"Envelope breach in five, four, three, two, one. We have breach! Send the pulse!"

"Pulse away," Mallone called out.

"Bring us about and launch the MOSS! Get ready for crash stop!" Osno cried out.

"MOSS away," the tactical officer replied.

"Crash stop rig for ultra quiet," the captain called. In the engineering compartment, electronic orders were given and the Pegasus decelerated and dropped out of light. She slewed to a full stop as her bow thrusters fired. A shrill screeching filled the COM system as the Caldarian torpedoes lost lock and the frigates went storming past. She drifted dead and dark in space. The term 'ultra quiet' was an anachronistic carryover from a bygone age. In the vacuum of space, there was no sound. It was the electronic probes the crew feared.

"There's a Ramillion saying that goes, 'We don't fear the Caldarians but we do fear their sensors,'" Ruderman stated.

They knew their systems were good but not perfect. And it was that little bit of imperfection that worried Osno.

"Sir, I have a plant signature close aboard, two point eight kilometers. It's the frigate that tried to flank us, she dropped out of light seconds after we did," Ruderman said.

"Ms. Jamison, give me steerage way using the thrusters very gently. Bring us about, course three-three-one, mark eight-six. The moment we're on course, I want you to punch it. We're going back in. Put the view screen up."

The object of a snooper vessel was to evade contact. Doctrine dictated that if patrol craft approached, you were to power down and shut down as many systems as possible, the premise being that if you weren't radiating, you couldn't be detected. That was true up to a point. However, unlike on land, there were no bushes to hide behind or thermal layers to sink below. All you could do once you had powered down was hope the other side's sensors weren't as sensitive as yours were and that their electronic warfare technicians were tired, fatigued or more or less semi-comatose from staring at a monitor screen for several hours. It really was a game of smoke and mirrors. The crew of the Caldarian frigate sitting broad on their port beam was neither fatigued nor were their onboard sensors any less sensitive than those on the Pegasus.

"Aye, Sir," Lieutenant Jamison said. Slowly the bow of the Pegasus swung about. Twenty-eight hundred meters away and facing directly toward them, bow on, the form of a Caldarian frigate could be seen. It was still and silent. Or so it seemed. Ever so slowly, its bow began to swing parallel to the Pegasus.

"Aspect change!" the tactical officer cried out. She's swinging about to bring her weapons to bear, Captain!"

"Now, Ms. Jamison," Captain Osno spoke. There was a sudden convulsive rush and the Pegasus was gone, jumping to star drive a millisecond before the frigate's starboard particle cannons fired.

"Frigate is in pursuit, she's just fired a full spread of fusion torpedoes," the tactical officer cried out. He was sweating profusely from the intensity of this one-sided match. He felt like a mouse that had run out of holes to duck into.

"Bearing change. Torpedoes are spreading out. We have an opening bearing on all incoming," the tactical officer said. "Damn it all to hell and gone, I wish we had something to fight back with," he spoke to the bridge in his frustration.

"We do," Osno said. "OK, Peg," he breathed as he patted the crash bulkhead beside his chair. "Let's see what you got! Time to stretch your legs, sweetheart! Let her go helm, everything we have. If ever we needed it, now is the time."

Like a racehorse sprinting for the finish line, the Pegasus gathered herself and accelerated. In a blink she was gone, a glimmer receding and fading into the further stars.

"The Caldarian frigate is falling back, Captain," Ensign Ruderman said as she watched her sensor arrays. The frigate vanished off the scope. "She's gone, Captain. Long rang sensors are clear out to full sweep," she said, relief flooding her voice. "Yea, go Peg!" she chortled.

"Helm, hold this course for another five minutes. Then come to our base course and bring us back on station and power down all active systems. I want passive only. Well done, people."

In the USS Lexington's electronic control station, the senior duty officer, Lieutenant Commander Jack Wilson, sat in his chair on a raised platform above the twelve technicians processing the mountain of electronic information flowing in from hundreds of sources. The technicians looked like they were asleep and but for the quiet hum of the environmental system, all was still. He stood and moved to the servo tray and poured himself another cup of hot, black tea. Most of the crew drank coffee while on watch but Wilson preferred tea after several hours of processing signals. He moved back to his chair and sat down.

An icon appeared on his command screen and he watched as the authentication code identified the signal as coming from the Pegasus.

This is unusual, he thought. This isn't routine traffic. He put down his mug of tea and ran his palm over the alert icon and the script header identified the signal as 'code black.' He entered his security ID and ran the complex algorithm that deciphered the transmission. His tea was forgotten.

He swung around and tapped a key on his COM console. "Commander McGivens?" There was a momentary pause and then Admiral Greig's Aide, Tom McGivens' face appeared on the holo display.

"Good evening, Commander. What keeps you up so late?" he asked.

"Signal from the Pegasus, Sir. Code black. I thought the Admiral should see it right away. It's not a routine transmission." He paused. "Captain Osno must have thought it was damn urgent to break silence. By the looks of the pulse, he ran to the envelope edge to fire it off. I hope he made it back. I ran it through the deciphering loop and I've already passed it up the line. You should have it now."

"Thanks Jack, keep me posted. If anything else comes in, notify me immediately."

"You got it, Sir," Wilson said and signed off.

McGivens left his quarters and walked the short distance to CIC where Admiral Greig and Captain McMann were going over the tactical overlay. Greig and McMann turned towards him as the door closed. Several officers and technicians were manning the consoles and the huge tactical display showed the position of every Confederate and Caldarian vessel for three light years.

"Signal from the Pegasus, Admiral. It just came in, code black. Commander Wilson ran it through the decryption code and sent it up."

Greig looked over at McMann. "Thank you, Tom."

"Aye, Sir," McGivens said and left the room.

Greig flicked his palm over his console and opened the message script. There was no audio or video feed. Signals sent by stealth intelligence platforms were kept as short and brief as possible to lessen the possibility of the signal being detected and captured. The shortest pulse burst possible was used. It was like a shutter opening that took a nanosecond to send and then the window was snapped shut again. A holo-shell would take considerably longer to send and would be easier to break open if the data stream was captured.

UCT 247.0820 0400 GALACTIC
TOP SECRET BLACK
FR:USS PEGASUS
TO:ADMIRAL GREIG USS LEXINGTON
INFO: COMSPAC
1. INITIAL ROGUE SIGNAL DETECTED UCT 247.0813 GRID 357-MARK 49. SUBSEQUENT SIGNAL DETECTED EVERY EIGHTEEN TERRAN HOURS AT 0200 GALACTIC. GRID LOCATION INDICATES DEBRIS FIELD FROM ENGAGEMENT 247.0813. APPEARS TO BE ORIGINATING FROM THE HULL OF HMS SUSSEX.
2. TERMINAL POINT OF ROGUE SIGNAL GRID 356-MARK 49. TERMINATION POINT THE SHIMMERING WIND AT CENTER OF CALDARIAN BATTLE FLEET.
3. ASSUME ROGUE SIGNAL INITIATED BY BLACK ORDER SUICIDE SURVEILLANCE TEAM INSERTED DURING ENGAGEMENT.
4. RETURNING TO STATION.
5. RUNNING

Greig read the message again and looked at the last line.

"Running! That means she was detected. The Caldarians must have been expecting this and they got a twitch or they just got lucky, I don't know."

"UCT 247.0820—that's today. She must have just sent this," McMann stated. Greig called McGivens. "Tom, will you ask Commander Weir to come to CIC, please?"

"Right away, Admiral."

Greig swung around and spoke to Colonel Jim Thomas, the tactical officer standing at the holographic display. The door opened and Commander Weir entered the darkened room, sat down and read the message on the TAC display.

"We can play this two ways," Greig said. "We go in and get those bastards and take them out or we play our pair of deuces. If we try to take them, it's going to cost us. They'll either let us get close and then detonate whatever they have wired or they'll do it the moment they realize we're on to them, which will only alarm the Caldarian fleet and possibly precipitate action that we aren't ready for yet. I don't want to force their hand yet but I do want to grab their attention."

"And the deuces?" Weir inquired.

"We fuck with their heads," Greig replied flatly. His fist came down on the table and the coffee mug jumped. Every eye in CIC was on him. The months of defeats and reversals galled him. Images of twisted hulls and broken bodies filled his mind. "I want these bastards dead meat. I don't want any of them to go home alive! And I don't just want to kill the black team; I want to kill them all. But to do that we have to make them respond to us. This is a golden opportunity to do just that."

He walked over to the plot. "Colonel Thomas, can we monitor the traffic the Blackies are sending?"

"Yes, Admiral. Now that we know what to look for, we can capture the signature envelope when they transmit."

"Good. We'll get the code boys working on breaking it immediately but for now it's enough that we know they are there. Next, I want a coded signal sent to Regent Kandor on our right flank, ordering him to deploy the Myloen battle group and move in a sweeping end run around the Caldarian left in sector 15-25. Next, signal the Essex, Kharkov and the Hiryu to break station and move across our front to the center position just as if we were getting ready to hit them on a three parsec front. I want them to think we're coming for them. Lots of signals, lots of movement. We have to distract them and give Mike Platoon a running chance to get out. I want it to appear and sound like a goddamn Terillian bar fight after the inter-galactic Super Bowl."

"Is the Myloen cruiser Dark Wind still on station?" he asked Commander Weir.

"Yes, Admiral," Weir answered.

"And is that company of Myloen Marines still on board?"

"Bravo Company of the Second Imperial Myloen Marines? Yes, Sir," Weir grinned. He knew where this was going.

"And are they still ape shit pissed off looking-for-a-fight?" Greig asked again.

McMann spoke up. "Admiral, those boys were on the Carrier Brightness when the Caldarians boarded. They fought them hand to hand and only left when Admiral Aulis Ra ordered them to retreat so they could fight again. Ra had a Caldarian darter pressed against his head and the Caldarian centurion holding him thought he was going to tell them to surrender. He was wrong. Instead, he told the marines to take the last attack shuttle that was locked to the aft escape hatch and to take egress route one. They watched as his head was blown off. Oh yeah, they want to fight alright."

"And what happens once the Blackies signal the Caldarian fleet that we're moving, Admiral?" Colonel Thomas asked.

"Simple," Greig said, "we kill the bastards."

CHAPTER 13
SUBTLETY

"There is nothing glorious about war.
War is dirty, violent, ugly business.
Courage surfaces in places we think not to find it;
ordinary people facing situations and predicaments
that demand action, and the realization that if
they do nothing, others will die."

—cb

"Stalker, Stalker, this is Nightshade, over," said the voice of Ensign Marcie Chantella. Jackson listened for a moment, his senses momentarily disorientated. The team knelt in position around him, their weapons training out, watching the surrounding bush. Jackson's neural link switched over to the conventional encrypted circuit, he opened the command frequency and spoke.

"Nightshade, this is Stalker, over!"

"Stalker, I've made contact with Captain Middleton of the USS Hunt. He arrived in the system with a relief force seven hours ago," Ensign Chantella stated.

"Lieutenant Jackson, this is Captain John Middleton of the USS Hunt. What is your status, Lieutenant?"

"Sir, we lost three of our team members, two in fire-fights with a platoon of Black Order Legionnaires and one to the creatures Dr. Green mentioned in his brief."

"Lieutenant, the frigate Shirayuki was destroyed and the destroyer Haida damaged by an unknown Caldarian cruiser class that we assume is supporting the legion ground team. We damaged her cloaking and she jumped to light before we could re-engage. Our assessment is that she left the system to make repairs and will be back any time. We are in grave danger and need to get you and the remainder of your team out immediately." Middleton paused before he asked the most important question he would ever ask. "Is your suit nominal, Lieutenant?"

"Sir, I have a green board," Jackson replied flatly. This was the pre-arranged signal that would tell Middleton that Jackson had recovered the Element. If Jackson had said he had a red board, then it would mean they had failed to recover and the mission was to be aborted. But now they could get the hell off this planet and go home. They would come back for Wicker's body later, if it was still there. It would be hard to leave him, and it went against every grain and instinct Jackson had.

What he heard next surprised him.

"Roger, Lieutenant. We have one final task for you before extraction. Ensign Chantella detected two signals while in her hide position. One was a faint power signature that we believe is a Caldarian attack shuttle located roughly fifteen hundred meters east of the secondary LZ. We need you and your team to get there on the double and sanction the remaining Black Order legionnaires."

Jackson was stunned. Chief Miller turned his head and Jackson could feel the chief's eyes on him, waiting for a response. Jackson smiled grimly at Middleton's euphemistic use of words. Yeah, sure, he thought, easier said than done.

"What the fuck?" Hearst said, her voice tight with anger. Jackson held out his gloved fist toward Hearst before she could continue.

Middleton ignored the comment.

"Captain, why can't you just radiate the shuttle's location with particle fire? That would destroy the shuttle and whatever is left of the Blackie platoon," Jackson asked.

"Because we detected one other signal," Middleton said. "The other signal was a Confederate personnel distress beacon. It went off the air soon after but its last position was the same coordinates as the attack shuttle."

Jackson felt a cold knot form in the pit of his stomach.

"The Ident signature of the beacon belonged to Commander Debra Lewis, helmsman of the dead Hancock."

Hearst let her helmet move until she could see Jackson out of her peripheral vision. Although Jackson thought no one knew how he felt about Lewis, with a woman's intuition Hearst knew that Jackson's feelings toward the Commander went beyond a mere casual barroom encounter.

"Do you know what a neural manipulator is, Lieutenant?" Middleton asked quietly.

"Yes Sir, I'm familiar with the device," Jackson replied in an even voice. He knew what was coming.

"Commander Lewis was with Captain Zhao and others of the Hancock's bridge crew at Admiral Greig's brief. She knows the location of Green's real lab and everything she knows will be extracted, Lieutenant. If we radiate the site and kill everyone except one Black Order legionnaire who just happened to step aside to take a piss, then when that cruiser comes back and picks him up, we've lost and they'll locate Green's site," Middleton finished.

"Ensign Chantella will rendezvous with you at the secondary LZ so you can tank. Then she'll go into 'hover and hide' and wait for your signal. The moment you're 'clean', the extraction will take place and we leave."

Jackson knew what Middleton meant by tank. They would drop off the power pack DeLuca was carrying and if everything else went to hell in a hand basket she would at least have a chance at getting out with the package. Jackson motioned with his left hand, raising two fingers and dipping them twice, switching to the team net.

"Chief?" Jackson's mind flared in an urgent question. "I want to be on that LZ in thirty minutes. That means we have to haul ass from here, so I want you on point with DeLuca in the middle. Doc, you have the rear. When we get there, we tank and move out. If anyone thinks we should abort, I want to hear about it now, otherwise, we work the plan. Robbie, you OK with this? I need that tango and you're the shooter, but if your shoulder's gone south we'll switch you out and Doc here will show us what she can do."

"Shit, Boss, you know Doc can't hit nothing if she ain't hosing targets with that spray can she carries with her. I'm OK, Sir," he added in a serious tone. "The chief here fixed me up pretty good. I'm sore but it ain't affected my aim none."

A loud snort told the team what Hearst thought of that. Jackson switched back to the command channel and spoke to Middleton.

"Captain, if the shuttle is radiating enough signature to make her detectable, then it means it has no Element system. That means the Caldarians only had a small sample to work with, enough for that cruiser and the URKS the Blackies are wearing. But that's all."

"That's correct," Middleton replied. "Sensors show no active arrays, no emissions, so you should be able to get in close, at least close enough to see the shuttle itself. We will give you a direct path ion pulse as we swing over their hide position. The pulse will saturate their electronics and when they go active momentarily to flush their systems you should be able to see them or at least lock onto the signature to get a shot."

"No," Jackson said. On board the Hunt, the bridge crew looked up in shocked surprise. Middleton's mouth compressed in anger and he was about to respond but Jackson cut him off. "Captain, if you do that you'll be in their crosshairs. If they kill you they can sweep us up at their leisure or just leave us to the planet. Kind of like leaving someone in the desert, Sir, and letting them die of thirst and sun stroke. Only here, I don't think that would be the worst case scenario. Secondly, the Caldarians will be expecting that. It's SOP

(Standard Operating Procedure) and it will only tell them that someone is coming for them and that is exactly what they want. These guys don't play by the rules. They want us in the open and locked in. If we do the normal routine, we're dead."

Middleton frowned at the COM system. "What do you have in mind, Lieutenant?"

"Captain, do you have any insertion pods onboard?" Jackson asked.

"Yes, we have twenty-two Mark-135 standard insertion pods. They're not armored, as you know."

Jackson knew. They were standard airborne dump pods used to insert an airborne line company from orbit. Under a normal drop, the ground attack flight elements provided cover and electronic cloaking to cover the drop.

"Captain, I'd like you to make a standard drop with six of those pods. Push them out the launch bay just like you were inserting a platoon right over that attack shuttle, but stagger them at ten second intervals. That will give us six minutes, eight tops, to get to the shuttle and get inside."

"And how is that going to help you, Lieutenant?"

"Captain, you may have made a jump or drop in one of those pods during a training exercise but do you know how it feels to make a hot jump? It's a grunt's worst nightmare. Where would you rather kill an airborne company, Sir, coming in helpless or on the ground once they've deployed?" Jackson let his words sink in. Goddamn think about it, Capain Middleton, he said to himself.

"I see your point, Mr. Jackson." He shuddered at the thought of what that implied, and then smiled to himself. He was beginning to like this young lieutenant with the brains.

Jackson continued quietly. "When those pods come down, those Blackies are going to be pissing all over themselves trying to kill them before they land. That's when we'll take them. If we don't make it at that point, we aren't going to. Once we're inside their perimeter I'll send a single digit—a zero for abort or a one to begin your run."

Middleton smiled. "OK Lieutenant, we'll wait for your signal. After that, we have to get to the Haida and see about her people. That should give Ensign Chantella enough time to make her extraction run and rendezvous at the grid location to make our jump and start our dash for home. Good luck, Lieutenant," he added.

"Thank you, Captain," Jackson said and the link went dead.

Hearst chuckled. "Damn, Boss! If I didn't have this helmet on and you weren't so ugly, I'd kiss you!"

"That would be construed as a gross breach of military conduct, Weapons Specialist Hearst, and grounds for a general court."

Hearst raised a gloved hand to her battle mask and saluted. "Yes Sir, Boss Sir! Wouldn't want to breach that starched military conduct...SIR!"

The trail lay deceptively quiet in front of them. To the west they could make out a long volcanic ridge that merged with the lava fields that stretched out as far as the eye could see away to the south. The wind stirred and the huge cedars groaned and swayed in their ceaseless dance. The team was reluctant to step out into the open again.

Far above them, Ensign Marcie Chantella disengaged her auto pilot and began her descent, entering the coordinates and taking her time in order to go in undetected. She wasn't too worried about being detected. The Caldarians were in passive mode only and the shuttle was all but invisible with her Chameleon cloaking on.

She watched out her armored windscreen as the LZ came into view. "Stalker, Nightshade is hard contact, ground zero, waiting your authenticate."

Jackson and the team watched from their positions on the edge of the LZ as a blurry image hovered and then slowly sank to the ground. Jackson tapped his chin switch and transmitted the team's authentication ID.

"Confirm authentication, turning off Chameleon now." Chantella powered off the Chameleon grid and put the system in standby mode.

The team watched as the blur took on sharp lines and the shuttle came into view. The chief and DeLuca dashed forward, the rest of the team covering them. The hatch hissed open and they took position on either side, covering the rest of the team as they moved toward the shuttle, alternately sprinting and going to ground as they covered their approach. Jackson was uneasy. All of the bodies of the dead Caldarians were gone. Even the bloodstains are gone, Jackson thought, washed away by the rain that had started just after the firefight.

Chantella entered the crew compartment and stared at what was left of Mike Platoon, SEAL Team One. It was the stench that hit her. The team had been in the field for seven days without a change or wash. They looked like they had been wrestling in the mud and she didn't even want to think what the other darker stains were. They took off their battle masks. Their eyes were sunken and rimmed with black circles and held a sharp, feral gleam that Chantella recognized as the look of hunted creatures.

She reached into the cockpit and pulled out a small utility dispenser and held it up for the team to see.

"Is that what I think it is?" Dyer asked, his eyes gazing at the flask.

"Yup! Real, honest to goodness, high grade, Raxillian coffee." She filled five mugs and the team gulped the strong, dark brew with a look of ecstasy in their eyes. Hearst closed her eyes and held her mug in her gloved hands under her nose and inhaled the rich aroma.

Jackson looked up. "Sorry we can't stay for the party, Ensign. We have to move."

Chantella glanced at the pack DeLuca was leaning on. "Is that it?"

He nodded.

"We'll put it in the weapons locker before we leave." Jackson tapped his NAV. "Are these the coordinates to the Blackie shuttle?"

"Yes, Sir," she answered.

Jackson called up the display on the terrain imaging display and then overlaid the tactical grid.

"Chief, we're going to take the trail until we get to this point and then we're going to cut across this stand of cover and spread out. I suspect their perimeter will be about fifty and then twenty. The sentries will be just inside the second line," he paused, "just like we were. Before we start, let's move Larsen's pod into the insertion port. At least that way he'll get off if we don't," he said quietly. The team nodded slowly.

"Time to see if all this high-tech underwear works," Dyer said.

"And if they don't?" DeLuca asked.

"Then we all learn to like Vash," Jackson said. The team laughed.

"Oh my God. That pasty shit is about as entertaining to eat as the acoustical paste we use for deck sealant. And probably just about as nourishing," Hearst ventured.

Jackson put his battle mask on and lifted a gloved hand to lower his faceplate. "Time to kill some Blackies. Kill them as fast and as violently as possible, from a distance or close up, it doesn't matter. But you never, ever give the bastards notice or a chance to react." Jackson's mind strayed to an image of Debra Lewis and then it snapped shut. "Not now," he whispered.

"Good luck," Chantella whispered to the empty compartment.

A swirling orb of blinding pain flowed and coursed through Debra Lewis' body. Her head felt like it was going to explode. She had never in her entire life felt such pain. Every time she felt herself blacking out, the pulsing globe in the tall Centurion's hand would change frequency and her body would go limp with relief that was only momentary. That was the most terrifying part of the nightmare. With a blinding surge, the pain would return and she would scream. The front of her torn survival suit was covered in vomit and bile as her stomach heaved and emptied. There was nothing more there but she still heaved.

"Mary had a little lamb," she whispered. "Its fleece was white as..." A choking scream broke from her lips and she bit her tongue, blood seeping out the corners of her mouth.

"What are the coordinates?" the impassive voice whispered again. "Tell me and I will kill you quickly and end this."

"Grid, grid, Echo, Hotel. White as snow..." she screamed. The gauntlet moved and the globe shimmered and glowed a deep, angry red. "Please, please make it stop," she whispered through split lips. Her back arched and she felt herself slipping into darkness.

Jackson was lying prone beneath a thick layer of ferns inside the first electronic perimeter, the sticky underside of the shrubs dripping onto his suit. They had come to a small stand of thick honeysuckle and devil's club-like thicket and turned on their suits' sensor absorption and dispersion grids. Jackson knew they were radiating but he hoped not enough to register on the attack shuttle's passive arrays or anything else they might have outside. He watched his HUD. It had gone slightly nuts when the first multiple hits touched him but the suit had re-established the laser beam and absorbed and washed the infrared.

"One down, one to go," he whispered. He felt a tapping on his battle mask and started, almost lunging to his feet, until he realized that it was only starting to rain again. Soon the tapping became a steady beat that drowned out sound. That's a good and a bad thing he thought—good for the monsters, bad for us. He was glad they had decided to go in with their MP235's instead of the particle rifles.

His neural link went active as the team checked in, hard, disciplined thoughts of focused neural energy. Dyer had the furthest to go to get into position. But if he reached it before the shooting started he would have a clear field to provide over watch. If Jackson wanted anyone to have a clear field of fire when the shit hit the fan, it was Weapons Specialist Robert Michael Dyer.

"Five in position, target acquired, green board," Dyer's thought echoed over the neural net.

"Good boy," Jackson whispered to himself. He could feel the coldness of the rain even through his suit's thermal coils, and he could feel his body sinking in the muddy ooze as he crawled slowly forward.

"Two in position, green board. The shuttle is hard," the chief thought, informing the team that the shuttle had no cloaking electronics on. "Must be powered down to just about nothing. Well, almost nothing. You can bet your ass that cockpit has a Blackie pilot sitting at the controls, ready to jump to orbit in a heartbeat."

"Three in position, green board," Hearst's mind whispered. "One, I have movement at my two o'clock. I have eyeballs on a Blackie! Repeat, I have visual contact. One, they aren't cloaked," her mind whispered.

Jackson could just detect a subtle expectancy in Hearst's thoughts, a prodding flow of energy that heightened her reflexes and acuity.

"Four in position, green board," DeLuca spoke across the neural link. The eyepiece of his MP235 was pressed tight against the optical cup in his helmet and the crosshairs of his night scope were trained on the dark figure of the legionnaire kneeling ten meters behind the shuttle's rear crew compartment hatch.

The rain pounded the ground. Jackson inched forward. Suddenly he stopped. His HUD display informed him that a Caldarian peeper, a small robotic creeper that roamed at random within the inner perimeter, had just painted him in a low powered sweep. His threat board was red.

"Go away," he breathed, "just go away." There was a soft scurrying sound above the pound of the rain and his HUD went orange and then slowly faded to green. He let out his breath and inched forward. Jackson and the chief's tasks were to breach the shuttle hatch as soon as the five remaining Blackies outside had been terminated. Ten minutes later he was in position inside the inner perimeter. He could see the black, oval shape of the attack shuttle clearly through his optically enhanced faceplate.

"One in position, green board." Almost time, he thought.

"One, I have movement, confirm, movement. I have visual on two Blackies," DeLuca whispered.

"Roger, movement, confirm targets," Jackson whispered.

"Confirm five movers," the chief said.

Jackson changed over to the command net and punched a single number. A short, single digit burst of electronic energy was sent. A warning diode flashed on a signal technician's console on the Hunt and he entered a command. The outer door of the launch bay opened and there was a puff of venting compressed air as six oblong objects were ejected at thirty second intervals to begin their descent. The Hunt swung about and altered course as she accelerated away from her low track, heading for the Haida.

The six pods fanned out and descended rapidly in a staggered formation, their auto-NAV systems engaging as they headed for the Caldarian attack shuttle.

"Let them engage," Jackson said. "The pods will be lighting up the pilot's sensor scopes and if they don't engage he'll know something is wrong and he'll jump." Five fingers reached up and there was a barely discernable snick as five safeties moved to the off position.

In the darkened cockpit of the Caldarian attack shuttle a warning tone sounded. The three-dimensional display on the pilot's threat board suddenly lit up with multiple inbound bogies. A feeling of foreboding washed over him. He immediately switched to active and watched as the image displayed altitude, angle of attack and speed.

He realized that they were coming in too shallow to be bombardment weapons. They could only be one thing, he thought, insertion pods. The Confederates are sending in another team. His fingers worked and another set of sensors went active and swept the night sky, illuminating the six descending pods with electronic energy. He had to inform Centurion Ensuris but he didn't want to distract him from his interrogation of the Confederate prisoner. From the sounds echoing from the crew compartment, he could tell she must be either almost dead or at the breaking point—in which case she would soon be dead anyway. *I wonder if he will play with her once he has his information,* he thought, and instead of killing her quickly as he had promised, will see how much pain she really could take. He hoped it was the latter. It would be entertainment and would break the boredom. Without thinking, he hit a button and the hatch to the crew compartment opened. He stood but stopped at the threshold, gagging at the smell of vomit and excrement. "Kalosh," he said to himself!

"Centurion, we have inbound contacts heading directly for us. They have been identified as Confederate insertion pods. They are sending in another ground unit."

"Our perimeter watch will destroy them before they land," he replied without turning around. "Continue to monitor."

"Yes, Centurion," he said and returned to the cockpit. He reached a gauntleted hand to the hatch control but his hand stopped and he hesitated.

Why not, he thought. He withdrew his hand and sat down in his armored battle seat. He left the hatch open so that he could listen to the 'entertainment'. *He could do both,* he thought, never realizing that in that simple decision he changed the course of history.

Dyer watched the image of the Caldarian legionnaire through his scope, totally oblivious to the pounding rain and the surge of electronic energy his sensors told him were descending from the sky. He held the crosshairs of his scope on the right eye socket of the legionnaire's battle mask. "I will shoot straighter and faster than my enemy. He will not prevail, for my hand is sure and my aim true, so help me God," he whispered to himself.

The Caldarian reached up and took a swipe at his helmet and shook his head as if trying to shake the rain off. Suddenly all five Caldarians pivoted and went to one knee, pointing up at the rain-soaked sky as their threat receivers fed them information about the inbound pods. Their particle rifles tracked, waiting.

The pods slowed and spread out once more. At two thousand meters they took on a layered formation with two hundred meters between each one. Suddenly five dense beams of particle fire arced upward, ripping the darkness away as the five legionnaires took the first two pods under fire. The lower pod was cut in half, its fuel cell exploding and adding it's burning to the night sky. The second pod cart wheeled and crashed into the upper canopy a hundred meters north of the shuttle.

Dyer watched his target. "Don't worry about the rain, asshole," he whispered. "Worry about the hole I'm going to punch in your forehead."

"Now!" Jackson said.

"Tap, tap," Dyer whispered and squeezed the trigger. Instantly the legionnaire's head burst and he toppled forward. Dyer swung to his next target and squeezed off a second shot. Again a legionnaire died.

Another kneeling behind the shuttle slumped forward, his chest torn open by three silenced rounds as DeLuca had stitched him.

The chief's target went down without a sound, the round entering his right ear canal.

The last legionnaire had been off to the side of the shuttle and Hearst shot him through the right eye socket at a range of three meters.

Jackson and the chief rushed to the rear entrance of the shuttle, their chests heaving as they gulped air. Jackson stooped for a moment over the slumped form of the dead Caldarian. A blade whispered as it was drawn and Jackson grabbed the dead legionnaire's right hand.

Hearst and DeLuca ran to the dead Caldarians they had shot, picking up the particle rifles and training them on the remaining four incoming pods.

Dyer shifted slightly, ignoring the glittering arcs of fire, and provided over-watch security while Jackson and Miller approached the rear of the Caldarian shuttle.

The chief knelt and tapped a command into his tactical assault field computer, entering a single numeric character. A snooper algorithm began to run. It blinked once, paused and then flashed a green dot.

"Snooper loop locked in, shuttle's external sensors are in repeat mode; we're in!"

"Come on, come on," Jackson panted. The arcing ripple of particle fire could be heard above the rain.

"Two minutes," the chief said. Jackson searched desperately for the insert laminate of duralloy on the inside of the gauntlet between the thumb and index finger of the dead legionnaire. He found it and his knife flashed once, twice. He leapt to his feet and ran to the rear of the shuttle where the chief was kneeling, covering him.

The pilot watched his sensor display and the three-dimensional tactical holograph. The pods were dropping off the display. He could see the rippling arcs as the legionnaires outside destroyed the pods. There was a searing yellow flash and the fourth pod detonated and careened over the shuttle, almost scraping the upper hull plating before it crashed into the thick brush behind it.

"Two more," he said to himself in satisfaction. He checked his external displays, noting that the legionnaires were where he had last seen them. He turned back to watch the destruction of the pods. Something in the back of his mind noted that the positions of the legionnaires outside was subtly out of place but another part of his mind was listening to Centurion Ensuris speaking to the prisoner in a low voice and the soft, whimpering sobs of the human female.

Ensuris walked around the table Lewis was strapped to, coming to her left side. He glanced up and noticed the pilot sitting in the cockpit. Momentarily irritated that the hatch was open, he considered the circumstance. "It is a minor detail," he told himself. "I will deal with his misdemeanor later."

Lewis came up out of the black pool her mind had sunk into and realized that someone was dribbling a cool liquid over her lips.

Water, she thought, opening her mouth and desperately trying to reach for the precious fluid. The stream of water moved and she drank and gulped as it trickled into her mouth. The trickle stopped. "Please," she gasped hoarsely, "please water," her voice cracked and tears streamed from her eyes.

Ensuris was pleased. She was tough, far tougher than he would ever have imagined but the end was near. He sighed. And I have barely increased the power, he told himself. This is indeed going to be enjoyable, seeing how tough she actually is. He had no intention of killing her quickly. He wanted to push her, see how long she lasted, how much pain she could endure before the end. "Oh yes, this will be most entertaining," he whispered.

"Tell me the coordinates of Green's camp, Commander," he said in a soft, soothing voice, his hand caressing the globe as it pulsed ominously. Lewis trembled. She had felt that dark caress and knew she was finished.

"Thirty seconds," the chief said.

Jackson laid aside his weapon and took out the darter he had taken from the legionnaire Hearst had killed. He checked the cylinder and primed the mechanism. Now all he had to do was point and pull the triggering device. With his other hand he held up the bloody ID disk he had taken off the dead Caldarian, holding it over the access panel.

"Snap shot, Chief. This is going to be quick and dirty. You ready?" Jackson wanted to do this as quickly as possible. He would have simply attached a demolition charge and blown the shuttle but the one thing stopping him from doing that was the fact that inside that shuttle there was a Confederate officer. He knew the cockpit door would probably be battle sealed and had brought a bulkhead charge in order to force the door and kill the pilot as swiftly as they could. The romantic notion of allowing your opponent to turn and fight or giving him an opportunity to defend himself was just holo-screen horseshit. It looked good on the screen or read cute in a disk-novel but it was nowhere near the truth.

"As ready as I'll ever be, Sir," he said and thumbed his selector switch to selective fire. He took a step back and raised his weapon to his eye-port.

Lewis was trembling uncontrollably. She saw her death reflected in the Centurion's eyes and the sudden realization that he had been lying to her all along hit her like a fist. She wasn't going to die quickly. They were going to squeeze her like a ripe melon until she burst. From deep inside her the last vestiges of her iron will surfaced with the realization that she was at death's gate. Rage gave her strength.

Her swollen lips moved and she rasped, "Fuck you, asshole!"

"Here we go," Jackson said. He pressed the bloody disk into the access panel and the shuttle door hissed open.

With sudden desperation the pilot realized what was wrong with the external picture and the position of the legionnaires. They hadn't moved. He lunged to his feet even as out of his peripheral vision he saw the rear hatch hiss open.

Ensuris bent over Lewis. He felt the soft inrush of damp air and realized that the weapon fire had stopped. Good, he thought. We've killed the team the Confederates just sent in. At the same moment, out of the corner of his eye he saw the pilot turn and lunge out of his seat.

"You won't get away with this," Lewis croaked. "He'll stop you."

Ensuris held up the globe and smiled at Lewis, his cold, dead eyes mocking her. "And just who would that be, Commander?"

"Me," a voice behind Ensuris spoke.

With the speed of a striking snake, Ensuris instinctively spun and moved. It was that instinctive move that saved his life. He saw two battle-masked figures wearing strange battle suits that looked vaguely familiar. The tall one had stepped inside and immediately taken a step to the right of the hatch and the other one was standing just inside the entrance. A part of his mind recognized the device the tall one was pointing toward the cockpit and for a brief millisecond wondered how he had come to be holding a Caldarian darter. And then time seemed to stop and everything slid into a whirlpool of black slow motion.

In the same instant, the pilot reared up, clawing desperately to bring his particle pistol up.

Even as Jackson pulled the trigger, a part of his mind was analyzing the tactical situation inside the shuttle, hoping the chief could take Ensuris down and end this quickly. As so often happens in that first second of close quarter combat, things don't go the way they are anticipated or planned.

The pilot realized in that final, flaring moment of comprehension that he was dead, even as five explosive darts tore his chest apart. The instrument panel was splattered with the pilot's blood as he fell backward and as he died, his finger convulsed reflexively on the trigger.

In the same instant Ensuris pivoted and the three shot burst the chief had snapped at his head went whispering by like deadly hornets, sparking and hammering into a storage locker.

The chief tried desperately to line up for a second shot. He saw Lewis lying on the table but before he could realign on Ensuris for another shot, the pilot's particle bolt hit him in the shoulder.

Jackson was working the chambering feed of the darter as Ensuris lunged.

"Time's up," he told himself.

CHAPTER 14
REPAIRS

*"Of all the tools the Navy will employ to control the
seas in any future war, the most useful of the small types
of combatant ships, the destroyer, will be sure to be there.
Its appearance may be altered and it may even be called
by another name but no type, not even the carrier or the
submarine, has such an assured place in future navies."*

—Fleet Admiral Chester W. Nimitz

The Haida drifted dead in space while repair crews swarmed over her
outer hull frantically attempting to fix the hull breaches and patch the underlying network of Chameleon conduits before the Sipedesis returned, while
engineering crews worked to restore power. The Hunt had moved into a low,
geo synchronous orbit and had, with the combination of her Chameleon
cloaking and the geomagnetic anomaly, totally disappeared off what remained
of the Haida's damaged sensors. That had been several hours ago, and Captain Mark Nolan was beginning to feel distinctly uneasy. He felt terribly exposed with no power and no ability to energize his cloaking array. He knew
it was only a matter of time before the Caldarian cruiser returned and in the
state his ship was in, they would be sitting ducks.

"Commander?" Chief Petty Officer 1st Class Tadara Sheenan called.

"Go ahead, Chief," he replied.

"Sir, we have sub light and the weapons systems are back online but we
only have five turrets on the starboard side."

Turret was an anachronistic carryover from a vanished age. Along the
sides of the vessel there were openings the crew called gun ports but which
were in reality, openings that contained the charging coils for the weapons
array. These were tied into the ship's Corealus Combat System (CCS), which
integrated the ship's sensors and weapons systems to identify and engage

threats. The CCS had a federated architecture with four subsystems comprising an AN/SPY-251 multifunction phase sensor, a Command and Decision System (CDS), a Corealus Display Module (CDM) and the Weapon Control System (WCS). The CDS received data from ship and external sensors and provided command, control and threat assessment. The weapons system received engagement instructions from the CDS and interfaced with the weapon fire control systems. There were six charging coils on each side of the ship lettered from port to starboard.

Destroyers also had six torpedo tubes per side and carried three different types of torpedoes. Ion fusion torpedoes tracked on the residual ion trail like old time sidewinder missiles. They had a small warhead and were designed to interrupt the power envelope of a drive system and stop them dead. Then there were disrupter torpedoes intended to disrupt and kill electronic sensor platforms like the anti-radiation missiles of the 20th century. Lastly, there were the plasma torpedoes whose goal was plain and simple—to kill and cause maximum damage at long range. They were named after the Imperial Japanese 'long lance' torpedoes used so successfully by the Japanese during the Earth conflict called the Second World War.

"The second hit took out 'K' turret forward of the bridge section but the port side is fully functional. We expended two Mark 215's, so we pretty much still have a full load, Skipper."

"We should have used lances," Nolan stated, "instead of the fusion ones."

"But we didn't know what we were up against and those two tubes were loaded with a standard war shot, Sir. It should have stopped him, would have stopped him, if it had been a line cruiser. But she isn't. We know that now. Next time we'll bag 'em and tag 'em, as the airborne says."

Nolan grinned to himself at the chief's pithy sarcasm directed at the ground pounders. The Navy traditionally thought of themselves as the upper crust of the military structure. Deep down he knew that if the ground pounders didn't cut the mustard and hold the ground, they all might as well head for the Omega quadrant now and look for a nice, quiet, M-class planet to hang out on for the next three thousand years.

"Good work, Chief! How are the hull repairs coming along? Or are we going to have to trade in this bucket of bolts once we get back to space dock?"

Chief Sheenan grinned to herself. "Well, Sir, I have good news and I have bad news. The good news is that the damage isn't as bad as we had initially thought. The initial particle beam was re-routed and deflected but when that second one hit us it overloaded the shield generator coils and shut down. The fourth discharge had a sensor detection pulse attached. It hit us hard, Skipper, and nailed our acquisition arrays. When that happened, we were as good as blind."

Poke out our eyes and knock our teeth to hell and all we are is a 400,000 ton lump of scrap iron, Nolan thought.

"That's what caused the hull breach, Skipper. While the system was working to capacity we took multiple detection pulses and she couldn't handle it. It caused a rogue power surge that spiked the targeting array but it's been reset and is functioning normally again so we can fight when it comes down to a shit throw."

"You think you've tagged all the damage?" Nolan asked.

"Sir, the engineering spaces are buried deep in the center core of the ship. We're generally well protected from a seeker pulse and our back-up systems will go into shunt mode within nanoseconds of envelope breach. We should have been able to re-route that particle pulse and redirect it on the return bearing but we had no signature lock. Hell, we didn't even get a shot at their halo array, they were so damn close."

"I know, Chief. And we can't afford to get hammered like that again. Our long suit is stealth and speed. We need to get up close and personal, fire a spread of Mark 235s and get out. We can't get involved in a bar fight, Chief. Not with whatever is out there stalking us." It would be a damn site better to be invisible and get close and then slit their throat without quarter, Nolan thought. "And the bad news?"

"The bad news is that the detection pulse overloaded our system. The second hit came right in and fused our drive crystals. Those Uridian crystals get brittle if they get overloaded and the anti-matter flux-damping field is at all disrupted." The chief paused but when Nolan remained silent, she continued. "The inner shielding grid between the inner hull and the ballast matting didn't even slow it down. We didn't just lose one shunting node, we lost them all, Skipper, and that's damn surprising. We've been hit by Caldarian particle fire before but never anything like the hits we took today, Sir."

"How so?"

"The shunting nodes should have re-routed the incoming particle energy, Skipper, and they didn't. Hell, we've been fighting these bastards for almost two years and in that length of time we've managed to catalogue every weapons signature they've had. The shunts are specifically designed to take multiple Caldarian hits and still maintain the grid. Ours went down within seconds and not just one or two. All of them blew at once."

Nolan felt that needle of worry turning into a hard, hot blade of dread. "And?" Nolan ventured, not really wanting to hear the 'and' part but knowing he needed to anyway.

"That means the Caldarians have something we've never seen before and if they've managed to re-ordinance their fleet, we're totally fucked, Skipper," Sheenan stated flatly.

"How many people did we lose, Chief," Nolan asked softly.

"When engineering was vented, we lost three people.

"If we hadn't already been at battle stations, it would have been the whole watch, Skipper."

Sheenan paused again before continuing. "So, unless we can find a new drive module, Sir, it's gonna to be a long walk home."

"How about doing a hot change-out with the Hunt? A bit slower maybe but we both can fight and we both get home."

A Confederate star drive module held sixteen Uridian high-grade power crystals. The modules were interchangeable. By connecting the crystals in series and shutting down all auxiliary systems, a ship could go to star drive and get home. The catch was that it was like running an ancient automobile on a small sized spare tire. You could only do it for so long before the tire failed or in this case, the drive coils went critical and made a small dark hole in the vastness of space.

"We can try, Skipper," was all she said.

"Thanks, Chief. Keep me posted and I'll toss it to Captain Middleton when he gets back. If we can't fix her, we'll have to abandon ship." Nolan broke the COM link and looked around. He walked between the rows of bodies laid out along the port bulkhead on C deck and watched the damage control parties working on sealing a section of hull plating that had buckled and melted inward from the particle blasts of the Sipedesis. A hatred for all Caldarians was boiling inside him.

A nice, clean war in space! Yeah sure, he thought bitterly as he looked at the splattered gore on the deck. There hadn't been time to do anything but bag the bodies and move them to the side, out of the way of the damage control teams.

At least, he thought, it's not like in the old days when dog tags were halved into two pieces. One piece was placed between the teeth, if there was a head, and the jaw slammed shut, clamping down on the metal tag. The other half went into the captain's box to be used for notifying the next of kin.

Now instead I have a box of bio-chips, electronic signatures downloaded into a slot buoy that can be sent to the navy to notify the next of kin if the Haida is destroyed. Nolan had sent a lot of bio-chips in the last eighteen months.

The attrition rate is staggering, he mused. We're being bled white at a rate that will depopulate entire systems of all military age personnel within the next two years, he remembered from an intelligence briefing eight months earlier. That thought filled him with the deepest sadness he had ever experienced.

"Captain? Bridge."

"Go ahead," Nolan said wearily.

"Sir, the Hunt is approaching. We lost her for awhile when she settled into that belt of disturbed electromagnetic clutter but she just reappeared on the starboard array. Captain Middleton is ferrying over on a shuttle. He'll be here in five, Skipper."

What the hell is going on, Nolan wondered, more than a little taken aback. From what he knew of Captain John Middleton, he wasn't the type to get spooked into doing something rash like leaving his bridge. Nolan's gaze fell on the bulkhead to the empty plate where the Haida's commissioning plaque normally hung. He sighed. It had been a long time since he had personally taken that plaque down and sent it on a class four courier bird, along with every piece of personal rank and unit designation of every crew member, back to the Confederate military headquarters on Earth prime. "A long time," he said to himself. Now all that's left are our biochips. I don't think the Caldarians are overly concerned with notifying our next of kin, he thought as he made his way to the shuttle bay.

The shuttle bay depressurized and Captain John Middleton stepped out of the shuttle. He had a Mark 341-S battle EVA suit on and the armor-plated rib plates made him look like the Michelin man, the trademark of an old company that had survived the transition to space and now produced mining equipment. Wordlessly Nolan led him to his day cabin and as the door hissed shut he raised an inquiring eyebrow.

"How goes it, Mark?" Middleton asked.

"Sir, sub-light has been restored and we have weapons. The cloaking grid has been repaired and the hull patched but our star drive is toast."

"SEAL Team One has recovered the package," Middleton stated flatly. "I didn't want this going over any sub-space frequency, even the secure Tac net. Lieutenant Jackson confirmed our initial suspicions about a security breach. The Hunt will go back to cover-mode to extract the team once Mike platoon takes care of one last item. The Caldarians have a platoon of Black Order Legionnaires on the ground and they've captured the Hancock's chief navigational officer, Commander Lewis."

Nolan's slate gray eyes always took on a deeper, darker hue when he was angry. He was angry now. "Which means all the legion ground elements need to be eliminated, including Lewis if she can't be rescued," Nolan finished for him.

Middleton sighed. "That's about it, Mark. According to Confederate intelligence, the Caldarians don't have any qualms or guilt about using a neural manipulator." Nolan knew what that meant and therefore the reason for the termination order Middleton had given to Mike platoon.

"Poor bastard," Nolan thought.

"There won't be any need to do a 'hot Mod' on your drive system. Apparently Dr. Green wasn't just mining. He managed to build a standard drive and weapons module. Jackson has already delivered both to Ensign Chantella, the Hancock's shuttle driver. She's on the ground now, waiting to pull Mike platoon as soon as they call for extraction."

Nolan stared at Middleton in silence, waiting for him to continue.

"I've already read your damage reports and seen your status board. Once she makes her pick-up run, I've instructed her to head for the Haida. When she's onboard, you install that power module and get out, Commander. That cruiser is due back any moment. The Hunt will try to run interference for you. All I require of you is that you get back with that module and the tech cube Jackson is carrying. We should be able to buy you enough time to exit the system, and with the Element module you shouldn't have any trouble getting back to Confederate lines."

Nolan started to protest but Middleton raised his suited arms to silence him. "No Commander, we are not going to stick around and try to take on that cruiser. We've no experience with this thing. They have. There's too much at stake here. If Mike Platoon gets out before that cruiser returns we both run balls to the wall for home but you get the lead position and you run no matter what the hell happens to us. If that cruiser follows, we'll fall back and see if we can buy you some time. She can't ignore us. She'll have to swing about to engage."

He held out his gauntleted hand. Nolan reached out and reluctantly took the small cube Middleton had been holding in the palm of his gloved hand. He smiled thinly.

"You and I both know we're expendable," he told Nolan. "That's why they sent us. At least our families will have that, something the Hancock's crew didn't have time for."

"Yes, Sir," Nolan told him quietly.

Middleton cleared his throat. "I understand that your repairs are almost complete. As soon as I leave, I'm taking the Hunt back down to the hide position we were holding, to the coordinates that I've had downloaded to your NAV system. We'll continue to communicate through normal channels once I'm back on board the Hunt."

"Is there anything we can do?"

"Yes. Get your people back inside and power absolutely everything down. Turn off all your systems and put your drive and weapons systems in standby mode. Then I want you to jettison every single escape pod you have and leave your shuttle bay doors open with your distress beacon set on the standard Confederate sub-space guard frequency. I'm sure he's heard lots of those in the last two years. As a matter of fact, he's probably heard so many of them that he won't even think twice about taking a closer look."

Nolan stared at Middleton with a questioning look.

"Where's the first place that ballsy Caldarian bastard is going to come back to? He's going to come back and make sure the Haida's dead before he does anything else. He doesn't want a wounded badger crawling up his ass while he recovers his troops and secures the package, no matter how stealthy his systems are, so he'll come to make sure you're dead first. When he detects the pod ejection residuals and sees your bay access door wide open, he won't even stop; he'll just keep coming in."

Nolan was nodding now.

"I'll signal you as soon as that cruiser appears and then you start your run," Middleton told him. "No matter what goes down, as soon as that shuttle docks, you're out of here Commander, no questions."

"Sir, how are you going to know when the cruiser is back?"

Middleton chuckled. "Because she'll be shooting at us. The Hunt is going to be in that hide position. The Caldarians are going to come back and bombard the secondary LZ in the hope of killing our recon team. The moment she fires we're going to power down our chameleon grid and let her acquire us. That's your signal to un-ass, Commander. The Hancock's shuttle will be heading for you, Mark, not the Hunt."

Nolan nodded. The two looked at each other in silence for a moment. Middleton shifted and looked around the cabin.

"Are the King's ships still wet, Commander?"

"Yes Sir, that they are," Nolan chuckled. He walked over to a small cabinet set in an inboard cubicle beside his desk, opened the door and took out an old bottle. He held it up to the overhead lights. The amber liquid glowed golden.

"My father gave this to me when I graduated from the academy fourteen years ago. I've carried it with me on every vessel I've ever been on, starting as a cadet on the old MacKenzie. God, what a tight-assed whore that ship was." Nolan took out two tumblers and set them on the desk. "He told me to save it for a very special occasion. He said that whiskey was to be drunk seriously and not for pussy puckered idlers who sit in cozy cast towers made of Ramillion glass and thermalite concrete. I suppose the occasion is serious enough, wouldn't you say, Captain Middleton?"

"Yes, I think it is, Commander." Middleton laughed.

"This is a very old, very good, single malt whiskey, a Glendronach. Did you know that the term 'whiskey' is derived originally from the Gaelic 'uisge beatha' or 'usquebaugh', meaning 'water of life'? I believe they were right," he sighed, opening the bottle. He poured a finger into each tumbler and held one out to Middleton. Nolan looked at Middleton. "Who should we drink to, Captain?"

Middleton raised his glass. "To Mike Platoon, SEAL Team One."

"To Mike Platoon, SEAL Team One," Nolan replied softly and drained his glass. He winced as he swallowed the fiery, amber liquid, wondering if he was toasting the dead.

They stood in silence for a moment again, knowing this would be the last time they met.

"I'll walk you back to your shuttle, Captain."

At the door of the shuttle, Middleton put his helmet on and turned toward Nolan. "Do you remember Fleet Admiral Terelus at the Academy on Perilius?"

"Yes, Sir. He addressed the graduating class every year for forty-five years before he died," Nolan said.

"Do you remember those lines from Kipling about the Choosers of the Slain he quoted every year?"

"No, Captain. I'm sorry, I don't. That was a long time ago."

"That's us, Commander. We're going to kill those Caldarian bastards when they come for us."

He turned and boarded his shuttle. Nolan watched from behind the transparent alumina-matrix window as the shuttle bay was depressurized and the doors slid open and then made his way back to the bridge.

"Hull repairs are complete, Skipper. The last of the hull plating has been installed, the crews are back inside and we've re-molded the internal bulkheads. It doesn't look pretty but she's ready whenever you give the word, Sir," the Executive Officer Jason Crichton said.

"I'm not interested in pretty XO, just in fighting and moving." Nolan opened the shipboard communications and spoke.

"All hands, this is Commander Nolan. First, well done people! You completed those repairs in record time. I want everyone in their battle suits. That cruiser is coming back and we're going to play dead and hope that she leaves us alone, at least long enough for Mike Platoon to get off the planet and rendezvous with us. The Hunt is going to try to draw them off while we make the jump."

All over the ship, crewmen looked at each other. They knew what that meant for the Hunt.

"We're going to jettison the escape pods and the docking shuttle and power down. I want everyone in their EVA's with their thoracic damping circuits powered up and on. I know we've been at stations for the past twenty hours so I want a hot change. Each watch section is to shift out and grab a bite to eat and drink. Make sure your hydration dispensers are full and relief bags empty. I don't want anyone getting dehydrated. I have also instructed the galley crews to fill a hot pack with your hot beverage of choice for you to take with you when you go back to your battle stations. Hook up your suits and stand to. We have a few rough hours ahead of us, folks. Once your stations are manned, I want you to sleep in shifts. Power nap, full gear."

Nolan paused, searching for words. What can I tell them, he thought? They're magnificent! Most of them are just kids barely out of the academy.

"I can't tell you how proud I am of what you all have done. We were hit by what appears to be a new class of Caldarian cruiser and we're still here. We have power and we have our claws back." He tried not to think about the biochips on his desk or the bodies lining the passage on C deck. "Good luck to us all," he finished.

Then he keyed his com link. "XO?"

"Go ahead, Skipper," Crichton responded.

"Check the battle log. I want you to recover our initial attitude after that cruiser hammered us, before attitude control came back online. Once you have the information I want you to enter the data into the control computer and project our attitude and drift since we were hit to where the ship would be now if we had abandoned her. Still with me?"

"Aye, Sir."

"Good! Then I want you to move us to that position ASAP, turn off the artificial gravity field and use the attitude thrusters to put us in the exact attitude and position we would be in based on the computer projections from the data model. And XO, we have a special package that is going to be arriving with Mike platoon. It's a drive and weapons power module," he stated flatly. "When they get here, we're going to be moving and probably running, and that cruiser is going to be looking to kill us. I want you to get those mods in and get ready to punch it, no questions asked. We won't have time to break her in easy. I just wanted to give you a heads up."

"You got it, Skipper," Crichton said.

All over the Haida, men and women prepared for what was coming. That the cruiser would return was without question. Each man or woman put the thought of what that implied out of their mind and went about their assigned tasks. Crewmen went to the galley and ate, picked up their hot packs and moved back to their battle stations. There was very little talk.

Weapons Officer Sub Leftenant Jack Stacey sat at the main tactical console and watched the data stream scroll across his holo viewer. He worked his palm control, calling up his astral navigational display and watched as a yellow line appeared on the display. A small, red destroyer representing the Haida appeared at the initial point of impact and he watched as it heeled over to starboard and stood on its bow. He winced when he saw the projected axis and attitude the ship would be in if still disabled. Getting damn close to atmosphere breach, he thought.

"Skipper? I've programmed the CCS and I'm standing by to initiate attitude burn to bring us to projected track and attitude. We're going to be tumbling on our 'Z' axis so everyone is going to have to make sure they're locked in and have their clamps set," he said.

"Roger, attitude burn on my mark. Three, two, one, mark!" Nolan called out. "Chief, cut the gravity generator, all hands rig for zero 'G'".

The ship accelerated and moved, slowly heeling over in response to the electronic instructions from the CDS system. Thrusters aligned and burned, making minute adjustments. The bow began to take on a steep angle as it nosed down. Stacey watched his display as the digital clock ticked down to zero burn. The destroyer icon tilted and pivoted on its axis and came to rest at the exact spot he had programmed.

"We are at zero burn, program execution terminated," he called out.

"Roger, zero burn. Chief, shut down all systems, open shuttle bay doors and start auto pod eject sequence," Nolan said.

Hull hatches blew open and the Haida shuddered through her length as thirty-seven escape pods were ejected and descended to the planet surface. The bridge crew watched the pods and the shuttle descend on the view screen.

"Pods away, outer doors open, Sir," the chief called out.

Nolan reached across his Captain's console and flipped the cover off of one last computer pad. Now for the really hard part, he told himself.

"We commend their spirits to you, oh Lord. Blessed be the LORD my strength, which teacheth my hands to war and my fingers to fight."

He pressed the switch and from seven emergency escape hatches seven small objects were ejected. They didn't accelerate or move away from the Haida. Instead they formed a small orbital cloud drifting alongside the skewed vessel. They were bodies. Two had standard EVA suits on, the other five were helmetless.

"Chief, did you get those pieces of hull plating arced in place like we talked?"

"You bet, Skipper. Seaman Spate even had the forethought to splash a little Chameleon epoxy on them and heat them with the ion welder before he uh, attached them, Sir." Nolan had instructed the repair crews to use the arcing welder to fabricate patches from some of the leftover hull plating and pieces that had been damaged in the fight, attaching them to the hull where the particle fire had hit them. Wouldn't want that cruiser to come back and see the hull repaired, he thought.

"Nice touch, Chief. Tell Seaman Spate that I owe him a six-pack when we get back."

The chief laughed. "Aye, Skipper, I'll pass the word."

Nolan looked around the bridge. "All right you bastard, come and take a look. And if you so much as fucking twitch, I'll blow you to Mars!"

The Haida drifted. She appeared dark and empty, fully visible with her Chameleon cloaking powered off.

The Sipedesis—Grid R-433, mark 47

"Consul, our repairs are completed and all systems are fully functional. We ran system checks on the cloaking grid and ship's weapons. We can return immediately," Legate Dra said.

"Cut the drones and take us back to Zilith. Make for the co-ordinates of the damaged Confederate destroyer. We'll check her status and see if she's dead. If not, we'll finish her first and then move to the rendezvous coordinates for the ground team," Va said.

"Yes, Legate," Dra answered. The Sipedesis came about and held station momentarily as the perimeter drones were cut loose. Helm orders were given and her image shimmered, blurred and vanished as her chameleon grid energized.

Twenty minutes later, her star drive disengaged and she went to sublight, moving to where she had engaged the Haida. Dra watched the view screen. The section of space where the fight had taken place was empty.

Well almost empty, he thought. Pieces of hull and other debris floated in a small field.

"Hmmm. Principal Narisn, plot the Confederate vessel and extrapolate with her last known position from our engagement. Project for impact displacement from multiple hits and display on the astral overlay."

Narisn's hands moved over his tactical board and a line and a dot appeared on the overall three-dimensional display.

"There." Va pointed at a bright orange dot. "There is where she should be if she's dead. Helm, move us in. Stand by, weapons. Give me a full sweep." The Sipedesis' powerful sensors energized and reached out.

"Contact bearing, three-two-seven, mark eight-seven," the technician spoke.

"Helm, match bearing and bring us about," Dra spoke from his command seat overlooking the tactical plot.

"Magnify," Va said.

Instantly the image of the Haida filled the view screen. "Five thousand kilometrics and closing," Narisn spoke. "Four thousand."

"Helm, bring us alongside at five hundred metrics and scan for bio's. Weapons, stand by on my mark," Va said.

Slowly the Sipedesis drew abreast of the Haida as her sensors reached out and painted her again. "Nominal bio signs, Consul. Scans show hull breach and residual vented atmospherics where our weapons hit her."

"Principal Narisn, focus on the hull section we hit directly over the engine compartment and magnify."

"Zooming now, Legate," Narisn responded.

A curled and blackened section of hull plating swam into view. Dra sat back in his chair, his eyes narrowed as he concentrated. He could see several bodies floating around the dead destroyer but he knew that meant nothing. The shuttle doors were standing open and there were numerous round and rectangular hull openings.

"They abandoned ship. Those are the escape pod recesses and the other debris are the hatches," Dra said. "Shall we fire, Consul, just to be sure?"

Va pondered a moment. Narisn's hand hovered over the firing button, waiting for the order to fire.

The Haida

The executive officer, Jason Crichton, was watching his threat board. Suddenly he stiffened and his face paled as three of his warning displays lit up. "Skipper!" Crichton whispered in a hoarse croak. "Something just painted us, bearing one-four-seven, mark five-two. He's at our six. It just appeared and vanished, Sir. No source, no residual signature."

"Easy," Nolan whispered, "easy. We'll know in thirty seconds what his intentions are. Either our spoof works or we end up dead. Either way, we'll know in a heartbeat."

"Bio scan! We've just been scanned. Standard Caldarian bio sensor envelope has just swept us. This one's close, has to be almost touching our hull," Crichton said.

This is eerie, Karen Gabriel thought to herself. The view screen showed nothing yet something had scanned them twice now and was just about kissing their hull plating. The moment seemed to hang as the bridge crew held their breath, waiting to see what would happen next.

Nolan had tactical control and had overridden the command system. He was going to shoot a full spread the millisecond he detected any incoming. He hoped he would have time.

The Sipedesis

"No," Va said. He watched the Haida tumble on her keel axis as she drifted. "The Confederate vessel is dead. Her distress beacon is transmitting and if she is alive, she isn't going anywhere. We killed her and she crawled away to bleed to death. Move us to the rendezvous coordinates."

"Aye, Legate. Moving to course zero-eight-seven, mark nine-eight, standard sub light."

The Sipedesis swung away from the Haida and in toward the planet's surface in a long spiraling descent.

❧❧

The Haida

The clock display in the bottom right hand corner of the view screen on the Haida's bridge ticked off the seconds. Thirty seconds, one minute, two minutes. The clock moved forward. "Five minutes," Nolan breathed. "I think he's moved off." He smiled grimly and spoke to the people on the bridge. "So now we wait for the other party guests to arrive."

❧❧

The Hunt

"Captain," the electronic warfare technician on the Hunt spoke, "the Haida has just been illuminated from long range, source unknown. No residual signature, Sir."

"Our turn," Middleton said tightly. "Get ready. This is going to be quick and dirty."

～～

The Sipedesis

The Sipedesis was in a stationary orbit directly above the Black Order attack shuttle. All attempts to contact the shuttle or the ground attack team had failed. Consul Va felt a choking rage building inside. He stalked the bridge, his hand straying to his darter with every second step.

"They have failed in their primary mission," he stated angrily. "Somehow the Confederates killed them."

"Consul," Dra spoke evenly, choosing his words with care, "it could be that they cannot respond. We should give them more time before we go to condition Durak." Durak was the Caldarian order to radiate the Black Order position with particle fire and wipe out any trace or remaining presence before re-committing follow-on ground forces. The word actually meant 'terminal', in the rough Confederate equivalent but the word conveyed the idea of disgrace and dishonor to a house name. Caldara Prime was a hostile world that was very unforgiving. The weak, the forgetful and the unwary died hard on Caldara.

It makes us strong, Va thought. Destiny is ours, has been ours since the tribal feuding stopped three thousand years ago.

"No, we will initiate Durak now and then send in the eighth cohort as planned. Centurion Ensuris has failed. If there is anything left after we radiate when the eighth arrives, his body will be sent home and dismembered so the High Council can discipline his house according to tradition."

"Co-ordinates locked in, weapons ready," the warfare principal stated calmly.

"Fire."

CHAPTER 15
WARFARE

"The Guns, Thank God, The Guns."

—Rudyard Kipling

In one smooth movement Ensuris flung the globe at Jackson, drew his blood blade with his right hand and struck out with his right foot. Jackson instantly dropped the darter and drew his own blade even as he blocked the kick and stepped in a circular movement toward the hatch. He had to get Ensuris outside. From the corner of his eye he could see Commander Lewis but he dared not take his eyes off of the Centurion. Ensuris solved that problem for him. Without warning, he swung his blade and moved in. As the blade came in, Jackson blocked it with an outside forearm block and pivoted, grabbing Ensuris' arm. He used the momentum and the leverage to slam him into the rear of the shuttle and then stepped outside, pulling the Centurion with him. He drove a gloved fist into his kidney and swept his blade up but with practiced ease, Ensuris broke contact and rolled away. Jackson reached up, unlatched his battle mask and tore it off.

"Centurion Mydris-Ensuris," he whispered softly, "I will kill you now," and moved in.

Ensuris' face went white beneath his battle paint at the shock of hearing his real name being spoken by this Confederate SEAL. Slowly comprehension dawned, and Jackson saw the fear in his eyes and smiled.

"Yes, it's me."

They moved in. Hard steel rang as they parried and fought, trading blows. Jackson felt the hard jab of a flat hand in his ribs and staggered. He ignored it. He had scored Ensuris across his left arm, the special blade parting the fabric of Ensuris' battle suit like it was tissue. He quickly extended his right arm, palm raised, hoping to break the Centurion's nose and drive the cartilage into his brain but the Centurion didn't even flinch, blood gushing as he moved in. Jackson blocked kicks and punches as they both sought an opening.

Jackson felt himself fighting like he had never fought before. He was hurt, he had been kicked and punched, his right cheek had been laid open and his right eye was swollen shut but he smiled. He knew now. He had taken everything Ensuris had to give and he was getting his second wind. Something deep inside him surfaced, some ancestral chord that had lain buried, waiting for such a moment as this, came boiling and crashing out. He border shifted with his knife, tossing it to his left hand, and moved to the attack. Ensuris retreated, his chest heaving as he gulped air. He swung his blade and Jackson blocked it but his left smashed Jackson in the chest, staggering him. Jackson locked his leg behind Ensuris, threw him to the ground and fell on top of him, their blades locked together.

Jackson rolled away. "I have to end this, I have to take the blade," he told himself.

Ensuris circled, watching him. "You weren't good enough last time, Lieutenant, and you aren't good enough now," he gasped between swollen lips.

Ensuris feinted suddenly and Jackson's intuition told him it was now or never. He moved into the blade. It caught him in the left arm but instead of moving away, he pulled himself in, the blade going into the flesh on the outside edge of his biceps. Too late, Ensuris realized his mistake and tried to disengage but Jackson drove his blade into his stomach with all his strength. Ensuris fell and Jackson heaved on the blade, tearing open his chest cavity. He staggered back, blood seeping from his left arm, his chest heaving as he gasped for air. Jackson reached down and pulled his knife out of Ensuris' chest. The Centurion's eyes flickered briefly before death took him.

"Yes I am," Jackson said softly.

He blinked. Suddenly he realized that it was quiet. His team stood transfixed, watching him as if he had strange magical powers.

"The chief?" he rasped.

"I'm here," the chief said through clenched teeth. The particle blast had burned clean through his left shoulder and his left arm hung useless at his side. He clutched a particle pistol in his right hand.

"Deb," he whispered as he staggered back to the shuttle and entered the crew compartment. "Security, now," he hollered. The team rolled into defensive positions. The globe had fallen against a bulkhead after it had struck Jackson. It was pulsating and glowing a deep blue. Lewis' body was convulsing in pain. He threw the globe outside.

"Shoot it," he cried. Hearst lowered her MP225 and the globe disintegrated as the rounds tore it apart. The bar around Lewis' head instantly stopped pulsing and her body lay still. Jackson un-strapped her and unlocked the head manipulator across her forehead. He pulled her off the table and fell in a heap on the floor. He couldn't support her. He felt weak and he could feel a hot, sticky warmth seeping down his left side.

"Doc!" he shouted. "Inside! I need you!" Lewis groaned and opened her eyes, looking up at Jackson. She blinked and tears began to trickle from the corners of her swollen eyes.

"What took you so long, Jack?" she rasped hoarsely as she weakly tried to smile.

"It's these Caldarian radio operators, Commander," Jackson replied. "Always getting the signals mixed up." Lewis tried to laugh but began to weep silently as her body shook. All at once she relaxed and went limp.

Doc Hearst was bent over her, checking her bios with the wand from her sensor system. "She's going into shock," she whispered. "We have to get her out of here. Now!" She hit the quick release buckle on her pack and tore open her medical field kit. She took out a syringe and a small bag of blood expander and saline and connected the auto pack to Lewis' arm. The bag detected a body temperature of thirty-seven degrees Celsius and the conformal wraps extended and fastened to her arm. Hearst pressed the head of the dispensing dart against her and hit the trigger. Immediately, a small diode light on the bag turned green and began feeding fluids into Lewis' unconscious body.

"We need an evac," Jackson said. He reached with his right hand and put his suit COM system in manual override mode and keyed the transmitter on the tactical net.

"Nightshade, Nightshade—Stalker, over."

At once, the voice of Ensign Chantella replied. "Stalker Nightshade copy."

"We are at condition Zulu and we have casualties. We are on egress route but need evac."

"Wait one, Stalker." Fifteen hundred meters west of where Jackson sat, Ensign Marcie Chantella frantically looked at her tactical display and the topographical overlay of the terrain between her hide position and Jackson's team.

"Fuck!" she cried in frustration. Her eyes searched the trail. Suddenly she stopped and pointed a finger. "Right there," she said triumphantly, "three hundred meters west of that Blackie shuttle." She hit her COM switch.

"All Stalker elements, make for grid echo—hotel—seven—eight—five—two—niner—niner—seven," she stated.

"Roger, confirm, echo—hotel—seven—eight—five—two—niner—niner—seven," Jackson replied.

"It's just a small clearing. Looks like some windfall damage but I can't land. I'll have to hover and pull you out with the link rigs through the auxiliary loading hatch on the bottom, Sir," she told him.

"Roger, Ensign. Stalker moving." Suddenly the Caldarian shuttle was filled with a foreign language and a light flashed on a display panel in the cockpit.

"Oh, oh!" Doc said. "Something tells me the shit is about to get deeper." The voice called again and even though they couldn't understand the language, the tone of voice left no doubt in anyone's mind that whoever was calling was pissed.

"You're absolutely right, Doc," Jackson confirmed. "That's whoever is upstairs supporting the Blackie platoon we just finished off."

"And?" Hearst asked.

"And," Jackson said, smiling and struggling to his feet, "we are about to be bombarded with particle fire."

"Fine bunch, these Caldarian bastards," the chief growled. "Let's go!"

"Dyer, DeLuca, grab the commander and let's un-ass. Doc, take point. Drop everything but your weapons. We don't need anything else and if I miss my guess, if we don't get out of here immediately or sooner, that's not the only thing we won't need." They hit the ground outside the shuttle running, with Doc in the lead.

"Three hundred meters," Jackson grated through his clenched teeth. "Just three hundred giant steps and we're out of here," he told himself. They came to the small opening on the west side of the small clearing and lumbered frantically down the trail, Commander Lewis slumped in the makeshift litter Dyer and DeLuca were carrying between them. They hadn't gone sixty meters when a seesaw sound that raised the hair on the back of their necks ripped behind them. There was a thundering detonation and the canopy above them swayed and bent in the back blast.

"The Blackie attack shuttle just blew," the chief cried out. "Go! Run! They're going to systematically radiate the entire trail section on both sides of that clearing, hoping to kill everything in a five hundred meter line on either side."

"They're gonna go east first," Dyer panted as the team stumbled in a shuffling semblance of a run toward the extraction site. More particle fire came in as the Sipedesis worked the shuttle site over, turning the clearing into a smoking, charred crater.

❧❧

The Hunt

The threat board in front of Ensign Paul Wazinski lit up and a cascade of electronic data spilled across his tactical display. His throat tightened. He desperately tried to get a lock but there was no signature envelope. When the firing ceased, his systems went green across the entire spectrum.

"Captain, sensors just picked up that same halo signature that killed the Shirayuki and then everything went nominal again when he stopped firing.

Particle fire! Captain, he's firing again. He's bombarding the planet's sur-face, Sir! He's radiating his own position!" The frustration in his voice was evident.

"Plot, put it up on the screen. Time to ring the bell and join the party, folks," Middleton said.

"Helm, nudge us up slowly out of this disturbance and prepare to en-gage. TAC, the next time he fires, match the projected bearing on his residual halo signature and shoot. I want him dialed in. You are weapons free."

"Aye, Sir," Wazinski replied.

"Helm, as soon as we fire, come to course zero-one-five, mark two-seven and bring us about. Cut chameleon system to ninety percent output. I want that bastard to see us and come running."

The Hunt nudged up from the geo-magnetic clutter that she had been hiding in. On their view screen, the bridge crew suddenly saw the searing, arcing flash of heavy particle fire stabbing at the planet surface and then vanish again.

A millisecond later, the Hunt fired and then fired again, her port batter-ies reaching out and converging on a point they hoped was where the Caldarian cruiser would be.

"Now helm, bring us about," Middleton spoke.

"Coming to course zero-one-five, mark two-seven, chameleon system at ninety percent. Aye, Sir," Rast replied. Even in the twenty-third century, with all the automation, the different bridge stations still confirmed every helm and tactical order verbally.

"XO, prepare to launch the MOSS. Set her signature to match and her chameleon at ninety percent. Set her on an intercept course aft of the last bearing we have to their particle fire. Once she's away, bring our chameleon grid to one hundred percent and come to two-eight-five, mark six-one and go to three quarters sub."

"I hope this works," the XO said tightly. "We already buffaloed him once with this. Think he'll fall for it again, Captain?"

Middleton smiled tightly. "Worth a shot XO, you know what creatures of habit most sentients are, don't you?" It never failed to amaze Middleton that no matter how many fleet exercises they took part in, the flight attack elements and the 'warfare wizards' as he called the carrier countermeasure technicians, always went after the MOSS unit, even when they knew one was deployed.

"Bridge? Helm! Moss unit away, course two-eight-five, mark six-one laid in, Captain, chameleon at one hundred percent."

∽≈

The Sipedesis

Her hull shuddered at the sudden impact of incoming particle fire and there was a stab of orange fire that washed across the view screen and then faded into the darkness as it swept past. The helmsman immediately engaged his battle thrusters and the Sipedesis stood on her tail, did a one eighty and came about, ready to engage the threat.

"Consul, sensors show residual particle fire bearing zero-one-five, mark two-seven. We have a vessel closing aft on the same bearing," the electronic warfare principal stated.

"Prepare to engage. Bring us about," Captain Dra cried. The helmsman was about to bring the Sipedesis about when Consul Va spoke.

"No. It is not the Confederate destroyer. It's another of their decoys. There's too much signature. Ignore it. Bring us to course three-one-five, mark one-two," Va stated.

The Sipedesis came about, breaking off from her bombardment of the planet's surface, not realizing that in doing so, she was giving Jackson's team the one chance they needed to escape. The two vessels were closing in a one-sided game of catch me, kill me. The Sipedesis was invisible and the Hunt, although cloaked and with her chameleon systems working at one hundred percent, was detectable.

"Full sensor sweep on the front array," Dra said. The tactical officer's gauntleted hand energized the frontal array and an invisible grid of electronic energy swept the seemingly black emptiness of space in a sixty-degree arc to the front of the Sipedesis. Most of the probing electronic fingers found nothing but empty space and Dra was just about to switch to the port side array and try again when the electronic warfare principal cried out a contact. Both ships were on a collision course but the Hunt was still just outside the Sipedesis' envelope, off her starboard beam. The outside edge of the searching fingers on the starboard side illuminated a shimmering, shifting object closing at high speed.

"Target!" The electronic warfare principal cried out. "Shimmer shadow bearing zero-four-seven, mark two-three," he cried.

Instantly Dra saw what was happening. "Fire! Emergency attitude vent now! New course two-two-five, mark two-three," he cried out. There was a blinding shaft of light that reached out and the Sipedesis rolled to starboard and stood on her head as her powerful 'fencing' thrusters burned. As she heeled over, her port battery fired at a shimmering image that blurred past at a range of five thousand metrics. The power envelope around the Hunt flashed and rippled as it tried to redirect and absorb the staggering hammer blows from the Sipedesis. Her image wobbled, corrected and then slowly came into sharp relief as her cloaking grid went offline. Instantly, the Sipedesis came about and headed relentlessly in. She fired and another broadside reached for the Hunt but missed. The Hunt engaged her own 'fencing' thrusters, radically changed course and went to full sub-light, heading for the northern pole on the other side of the planet, hoping to draw the Caldarian cruiser after her. Just before she spun on her axis, her own particle cannons reached out to the projected bearing, hoping to at least hit the cloaked cruiser.

$\approx$ $\approx$

The Hunt

Wazinski watched his threat board and his passive arrays. His skin was crawling. He knew that cruiser was out there and was hoping that it would go after the MOSS. The bridge crew watched the attack clock as it ticked off the seconds in the bottom right hand corner of the view screen.

"He should have had it by now," the XO breathed. He was sweating even though the environmental system maintained the ship's ambient temperature at twenty degrees Celsius.

"He didn't buy it," Middleton stated flatly. His admiration for whoever was giving the helm orders on that cruiser was growing, despite the fact that whoever he was, was trying to kill him. "He's one smart bastard," he commented tightly. "He knows we're trying to spoof him and right now he's wondering what we would do." His face tightened as comprehension dawned. "He'd do exactly what I would do. He'd close to knife fighting range. Helm," he cried. There was a note of tight desperation in his voice. "He knows we came in last time and he knows he can't ignore us, he has to engage.

"New course, zero-zero-three, mark two-six. Take us right over the pole and down the planet's axis. Weaps, get ready to fire the moment you have anything," he said.

Before the helm could be put over, Wazinski cried out a warning. "We've just been painted by multiple sensors at close range, no bearing. It just swept us and vanished, Sir, no residual signature. I couldn't get a bearing. Sorry Sir." His young voice held a note of frustration but a nuance of something more Middleton thought, even as the rest of his mind made tactical decisions. At that moment, a shocking series of muted crashes tore into the shielding envelope. The Hunt reeled. A bypass shunting diode located in a panel beside the tactical officer's station exploded, showering the bridge with panel shards and pieces of melted electronic components. Wazinski grunted as shards bounced off the ribbed armor of his EVA suit. He cursed in a steady, fierce monotone, ignoring the ache.

"Fire," Middleton cried out. His six port particle coils discharged, reaching for her unseen antagonist. The Hunt tilted on her axis and spun so she could bring her starboard guns to bear and went to full sub-light, heading for the safety of the other side of the planet. Just as she fired, a blinding flash went stabbing past aft, missing her by five hundred meters.

"That was close," Rast said tightly as she worked her NAV controls.

"Captain?" Wazinski called. He watched his Chameleon monitoring displays with fatalistic finality. The display told him the story. They were dead. "Captain?" he said again, his voice level, no hint of the fear he felt as he spoke.

"Chameleon is down, Sir. That last broadside that just missed us didn't really just miss us. One jet hit us and three detection pulses breached the shield envelope." He looked directly at Middleton. "The detection pulses didn't even slow down," he said quietly. "They should have been re-routed and redirected but they blew every shunting diode ship-wide."

Every head on the bridge turned to look at him. "We're visible, Sir," he said.

"Weaps, get ready to launch a full spread of 235's on our reverse bearing, set spread for sixty degrees," Middleton said. "Sure as hell is a busy day," he told himself. "Punch it, Ms. Rast," he said. The Hunt leapt forward.

"Six plasma torpedoes leaped out of their launch tubes and streaked away, their sensors sweeping, searching for anything that would tell their electronic brain that there was a target out there. The Hunt streaked flat out for the pole.

❧❧

The Sipedesis

"Pursuit course," Dra ordered. "Bring us about and close."

"Incoming torpedoes," the tactical principal screamed out a warning. "They are in search and acquisition mode. Consul, they are passing us. Torpedoes are passing aft."

"You see?" Va said. "They can't see us. Close that destroyer and kill it before she drops over the top."

"Yes, Consul," the warfare technician replied. The Sipedesis leapt forward and closed the distance rapidly. The image of the Hunt loomed in the view screen. She sunk lower toward the planet, attempting to chop distance as she dropped into the upper atmosphere, reaching for the other side.

"Fire at will," the captain said. Charging capacitors flushed as the electronic command to fire was executed and ten dense lances of light reached for the Hunt and missed as she dropped over the edge and sank momentarily out of view.

Va brought his fists down on the view screen as the Hunt dropped away from them. "Kill them! I want to see their dead bodies floating in space and then I want you to target the bodies one by one and shred them with the high energy, close support, particle cannons," he screamed. He was beyond reason.

Dra stood up. "Consul," he began, but was cut short as Va whirled, darter up, and with one step, pressed the dispenser against Dra's forehead.

Dra stood rooted to the ground in sudden fear.

Va's eyes glittered with smoldering rage and malice and he lowered his canines.

"Do not distract me, Captain Dra, or I will shred your body with my bare hands and feed your heart to the bridge crew if you so much as open your mouth against me again." The bridge crew watched in stunned silence as the black order officer lifted Dra off the floor and held him with one hand suspended in the air. He pulled Dra close and hissed. "That is your last warning." His canines snapped and ground as he trembled with rage. He dropped Dra to the ground and as Dra lifted his head, Va backhanded him with a gauntleted fist. Dra's head snapped back and he fell to the bridge floor unconscious, blood seeping from his broken nose and jaw.

꿈ꝯ

The Hunt

"Come on, baby," Rast whispered to herself as she gently stroked the helm board. She was cutting it close, she knew, dropping down dangerously close to the atmosphere but she thought it was better to let the hull warm up a bit than to get blown apart by that Caldarian cruiser.

"Drive it like you own it, drive it like you own it," she whispered to herself. Once, after she had racked out her father's family turbo tri-fan while attempting to fly the Tularian Canyon at Mach 1.2, her father had only made one comment as he surveyed the destroyed tri-fan and looked at his frightened daughter. He had walked back to the mining fan, a hulking machine she called a garbage scow, and motioned for her to take the driver's seat. Frightened and more than a little disconcerted, she had frantically shaken her head in an emphatic 'no'. He had said only one thing to her. ·

"Drive it like you own it, Rasty," he had said, and then strapped himself in. She had reluctantly gotten in the driver's seat and driven at a slow speed back to the outpost. Only years later when she had won her very first ring, did she understand what her father had meant. "Drive it as if you are the master because if you don't, if you're afraid of it or show any hesitancy at all, it will kill you," he had told her afterwards.

She was driving like she owned it now. The Hunt dipped below the edge only just in time.

꿈ꝯ

The Sipedesis

The Sipedesis spiraled in after her, attitude thrusters lowering the nose and pivoting her so that the moment she made polar breach she could bring her weapons to bear. Just as she went over the top, the Electronic Warfare Principal made a standard sensor sweep of their six o'clock position to check for a vessel attempting to sneak in and get a stern shot, when he detected movement. He adjusted his aft array and punched the energize button. He blinked. There must be something wrong, he thought. Once again, he manipulated the transmit control and once again, two objects were painted—one small and one large—on his display. He read the ID signatures and his hands trembled as he spoke.

"Consul," he cried out. "We have two contacts on long-range scans at the southern polar edge." The consul whirled to face him, a fire glinting in his eyes. "They have been identified as the stricken destroyer we initially engaged and a small shuttle, closing at speed. They are docking now," he said as the two signals blended into one. Immediately the dot went to maximum sub-light and began to move out of the system, vanishing as it slid behind the outer planet, Zelkor.

A scream of rage broke from Va's throat at the realization that the Confederates had deceived him again. He raised his darter and fired five explosive darts into the unconscious form of Captain Dra. He worked the chambering mechanism and fired again into Dra's already dead body.

"Helm, bring us over the pole and prepare to engage the moment that destroyer is on sensors."

"Yes Consul." They didn't have to wait. With a rush, the Hunt came spiraling up and let loose a full spread of plasma torpedoes. She couldn't see the Sipedesis but she had felt the probing caress of her sensors as she approached the pole, knowing she was close.

"Fire!" Va cried.

᠅

The Hunt

The Hunt was visible and she took a full broadside of particle cannon on her port side. Bulkheads collapsed and she immediately slewed and began to rotate from the force of the blows.

"Fire," Middleton shouted. "Target that discharge." The Hunt fired and then fired again. The huge shield envelope surrounding the Sipedesis displaced and shimmered as the blows hit her but nothing got through the envelope. A crashing blow struck the Hunt, throwing Middleton to the floor and breaking his collar bone. His helmsman, Ensign Fatima Rast was dead, her body slumped over her helm controls. An overhead grid support had been cut in two and had crushed her when it fell. The bridge was vented to space and she slowed. The WCS was off-line and Middleton reached a gloved hand to the weapons board and triggered the particle cannons. He couldn't tell if he was hitting the cruiser or not. A shocking series of blows slammed into the Hunt and the captain found he was lying on his back. His ship was gone. Odd he thought, how did I get down here? Darkness began to close in on him and with his final strength, he palmed his Com switch and switched to the Command frequency.

"Good luck, Haida," he choked, blood bubbling up from his lungs. His suit was punctured and he was dying. A piece of shrapnel had penetrated the ribbed armor of his suit and gone through a lung. "Sorry we weren't much of a distraction, Mark. Have a shot of that Glendronach for me when you get back to the Sixth." He slumped forward and died. The Sipedesis kept firing, heedless of the debris and distress beacon broadcasting. The Hunt blew apart under the staggering blows, shredded to space dust by the orders of an enraged Black Order Consul named Dedra-Va. He never knew that his actions bought the Haida an extra seven minutes, long enough for Chief Sheenan to install the Element modules.

༄ ༄

Mike Platoon

Experience was proving that Dyer had no future as a prophet. The creeping particle fire was working the westbound trail. Jackson stumbled and fell in his weariness. Hearst fell back and knelt beside him. They could feel hot ashes being blown by the wind upon their cheeks as the particle fire ignited the rich, creosote-soaked resins in the alien trees. Jackson lay on his back staring at the trees. Hearst reached down to grab him but he slapped her hand away.

"I'm OK Doc, get to the extraction coordinates, now!"

"Begging the lieutenant's pardon, fuck you, Sir," she said. Jackson struggled but Hearst heaved him to his feet where he swayed, trying to maintain his balance.

"Goddamn it, Lieutenant, you're gonna run or I'm gonna shoot you in the ass and make you run," she hissed. "Now run!" He tried. Hearst grabbed his right arm and pulled/carried him along.

Ensign Chantella stared at her passive monitoring systems. "I don't believe this, I truly don't believe this," she said as her sensors detected the incoming particle fire. "Just another day in paradise," she told herself. Her cloaking was at one hundred percent and with her small electronic silhouette, there was no way they would see her. Or so she hoped. She engaged her engines, rose above the trees and moved slowly to the coordinates she had given Jackson and his team for the extraction pick-up. She was literally scraping the tops of the trees as she brought it into hover two hundred feet over the site. She hit a button and there was a whirring sound as the emergency entrance hatch on the bottom of the shuttle opened.

"Warning, shuttle security compromised on keel axis," the soft female voice of the auto warning system intoned.

"Yeah, yeah, I know," Chantella growled. "Why don't you go and get a manicure or something," she told the voice. Her hands flew over the keys as she entered the commands to deploy the link rigs. From small compartments just on the upper edge of the floor of the open emergency hatchway, six wire thread leads with large snap buckles descended. Each was weighted with a smooth, tear-shaped weight that allowed the line to penetrate the thick canopy.

Abruptly, the detonations and the buzzing rip of the particle fire ceased.

"How far?" Jackson asked.

Hearst checked her NAV plot. "Twenty-five meters—almost there," she said. They could hear the whispering sound of muted shuttle engines hovering over them. They stumbled the last few meters to where the others were crouched on the ground below.

"Stalker, this is Nightshade, over," Chantella called over the tactical net.

"We have you on visual," DeLuca said. He reached out and grabbed three of the dangling lines and unlatched the weights.

"Put the Commander between the two of you, that way you'll be able to cover her as we get pulled up," Jackson said. Hearst helped the Chief and Jackson with their load-bearing harnesses. She snapped the leads on the D-rings on them and then spoke into her COM.

"Nightshade, lines away," she said, "haul away." Two hundred meters above them, Marcie Chantella hit the re-spool button and watched her underside camera as the lines slowly came up.

"Come on, come on," she whispered. "We need to get out of here before that cruiser starts shooting again." She knew that Captain Middleton had probably exposed the Hunt, drawing the cruiser off. Part of her was sorry for the Hunt but another part of her was glad that it wasn't her taking the particle fire. She watched her camera as Hearst, the lowest and last one, entered the small cargo area of the shuttle.

"Confirm six clear," Hearst shouted.

"Nightshade away," Chantella declared and punched the engine controls. The shuttle leapt skyward even as the hatch was still closing and locking in place. Dyer went over to the dispensing cabinet, pulled out several MED kits and went back over to where Commander Lewis lay. She was still unconscious but her breathing had deepened as if she was just sleeping deeply. Hearst tended to Jackson, applying an auto tourniquet spool on his left arm and putting an IV self-dispensing pack on his right arm. He waved off the Dexaclorafate she was going to give him to kill the pain.

The cockpit hatch hissed open and they could see the dark blue sky gradually change to velvet black as the shuttle entered orbit. They didn't have time to waste. Chantella was streaking flat out for the Haida which had drifted to the upper edge of the atmosphere above the planet's South Pole. The Haida had flattened out her ostentatious false attitude and pitch and was now moving slowly away from the planet toward point Delta, their egress route out of the system. As Chantella approached, she saw that the Haida's shuttle door was open and she set her glide receiver on the same frequency as the bay nodes located on the inside of the shuttle bay. She had a green board and was getting ready to dock when her threat receiver went off, telling her that she had just been painted by long range Caldarian scanners.

"Oh shit," she said. At the same moment, her intercom came alive as the voice of Haida's Weapons officer, Sub Leftenant Jack Stacey, broke the silence.

"Nightshade, this is Rescue Three on egress route Delta. This is going to have to be a hot jump, Ensign, we have company coming for dinner," he said.

"Yeah, any more good news?" she said to herself. "Roger Rescue Three, engaging auto docking lock-out now." She entered a command and eight small, black nodes on the shuttle's exterior hull plating swiveled and locked into place, each seeker head rotating until it had located the corresponding signal from the Haida's shuttle bay.

"Rescue Three, override engaged. You have helm control," she stated flatly. The shuttle altered course as the computer's docking system made a minute course correction. They all felt the vibration as the shuttle picked up speed. Chantella glanced at her chronometer.

"Passing one hundred thousand kilometers per hour and accelerating," she stated flatly. "I hate hot jumps. I really, really hate hot jumps."

Chantella checked her sensors and her face went white.

"Sir, we've just been painted by an unknown narrow band, Caldarian sensor array. By the intensity of the sweeps, she's closing. She has lock!" she cried out, feeling fear rising inside her like a black tide. Her mouth was dry.

"Come on sweetheart," she breathed.

She glanced at her sensors and then at the waypoint clock and did the math. "They can't catch us, even that ugly cruiser can't catch us before we dock."

"Lieutenant, we have seventeen minutes before that cruiser is in range. She can't jump until we do because she'd overshoot us by at least three parsecs. Override in three—two—one, the Haida has helm control."

The shuttle was pulled, almost by magic, into the Haida's shuttle bay. She heaved a sigh of relief. The bay doors closed and crewmen and technicians swarmed forward as soon as the bay was pressurized.

❧❧

The Haida

"Welcome to His Majesty's ship, the HMCS Haida," the Executive Officer, Leftenant Jason Crichton, said. He stopped short as he stared at Mike Platoon. Or what was left of a platoon, he thought. Medical corpsmen gently laid Commander Lewis on a servo table and rushed her to sickbay.

"Chief, will you please take Lieutenant Jackson and the rest of his team to sickbay as well? There are some other casualties here that need to be tended to."

"Yes, Sir," Chief Amanda Russell replied.

"Leftenant, you need to get this module installed right away or we're not going anywhere," Jackson said. He pushed the pack containing the drive and weapons module to Crichton. Two crewmen had already grabbed it and went racing for engineering.

"Chief," Crichton called into his intercom.

"Go ahead, XO," Chief Petty Officer 1st Class, Tadara Sheenan, said. "The package is on the way Chief; we have fourteen minutes before that cruiser gets here."

"No problem, Sir. The switch-out will only take five. I've already pulled the old pack on both the drive and weapons systems and I've flushed out the ion damping coils, so all we have to do is snap it in place and hit the big red 'D' for drive, Sir," she finished.

"Good, Chief."

"Sir?" Jackson said.

Crichton turned toward him and stared. Something about his eyes, he thought as he looked at Jackson, like a Sylashian snow leopard stalking. He shivered.

"Sir, would it be possible to go to the bridge? I'd like to see the Commander and be there when that cruiser arrives." He asked politely but his eyes held a cold finality that said in no uncertain terms, "if you say no, I will rearrange your anatomy."

"Follow me please, Lieutenant," he said and strode briskly from the shuttle bay.

"Not without me, you're not," Doc Hearst said. Crichton motioned with his hand and they followed him. As Jackson walked down the halls, he noted that every crewmember had on their class four EVA battle armor. A moment later, the bridge door opened and Jackson and Michelle Hearst were ushered in.

"Welcome to the Haida, Lieutenant. And?" He raised an inquiring eyebrow in the direction of Michelle Hearst.

She came to attention and raised a filthy gloved hand in a salute. "Sir, Weapons Specialist Michelle Hearst, Sir."

There was a flicker in Nolan's eyes and a ghost of a smile on his lips as he returned the salute. "Welcome aboard the Haida, Weapons Specialist Michelle Hearst."

Jackson's eyes swung to the view screen. The blackness of space filled the screen but he knew they were being followed.

"Yes, he's gaining, if our sensors tell us anything. We can't see him but every once in a while he energizes his sensors and we feel the probe. We can't detect the signature or the source of the signature but we feel it when it hits us," he said.

"Skipper?" Chief Sheenan spoke. "That weapons module is in place and by the looks of the power monitors, we got us one hell of a drive mod."

"Roger, Chief. Here's how we're going to play this hand. He doesn't know what we have and we're not going to let him in on our little secret until we're ready to. XO, are those two MOSS units warmed up yet?"

"Aye, Skipper."

"Good. I want to jump to light and when we do, we'll eject them both. Then we're going to change course and swing out parallel to the second MOSS and see what happens."

"And then what?" Jackson asked, wincing as the medical corpsman worked on his left arm.

"Then we're going to let him know what it feels like to watch his ship die," Nolan said.

CHAPTER 16
VORTEX

"Friendly Fire Isn't."

—Unknown line grunt

Master Seaman David Petrie, the Haida's electronic warfare technician, watched his control board and three-dimensional displays. He looked at the spikes that told him that somewhere over the planet's North Pole a Confederate vessel was firing her particle weapons, the bright waterfall display of peaks flashing and arcing like lightning across a dark sky.

The Hunt, he thought, and by the pattern and frenetic nature of the particle discharges, something's up close and in her face. Overriding the Hunt's frantic firing was a steeper, wider profile that flickered and vanished once it had discharged, indicating a Caldarian fleet class battleship. But he knew from the Haida's first encounter with the Caldarian craft that it was a cruiser. He was unable to obtain a signature reading on the particle fire emanating from the unknown vessel, but from the visual size of the discharge halo, he knew that the Hunt was dead.

He winced as a final cascading spike of fire emanated from the Hunt, followed by a few random discharges that told him that the ship's targeting and acquisition systems were down.

The Haida was slipping behind Zelkor, the third planet in the system, on her egress route to begin her run for Confederate lines. The bridge crew had watched the one-sided fight between the Hunt and the Caldarian vessel on the long-range view screen.

"Signal from the Hunt, Skipper. It's Captain Middleton," Petrie said quietly.

"Put it through," Nolan replied. The Hunt's outboard sub-space antenna arrays had been swept away in the first crashing volley and she was using the internal backup loops that ran along her keel line. Since she was five hundred and eighty thousand kilometers away and the gap was widening swiftly as the Haida accelerated, the signal was breaking up and wavered in and out as her attitude and drift affected the radiated signal lobes coming from the antennas. The crash and roar of heavy incoming particle fire could be heard as Captain Middleton's helmeted face came into view.

"Good luck, Haida," he choked, blood bubbling up from his lungs. "Sorry we weren't much of a distraction, Mark. Have a shot of that Glendronach for me when you get back to the Sixth." They saw him slump forward as he died.

The bridge crew watched the final moments of their sister ship in silence as the particle fire vaporized her.

"Our turn," Jackson breathed.

"Chief? I need our star drive; how long?" The tension in Nolan's voice was evident.

"Five minutes, Skipper. We already have the weapons module in. We just have to reconnect the plasma injectors on the drive and we'll be ready to jump."

"That's about how long it's going to take for that cruiser to get here. Let me know the second it's on line."

"Aye, Skipper." She turned back to her displays and controls. She was trying to skim the information on the Holo-cube that Jackson had given her. It contained all the technical specifications on the Element drive and weapons modifications from Dr. Green. She kept shaking her head in astonishment, the further she read. "That's impossible," she kept repeating to herself in disbelief, "absolutely impossible. Nothing's capable of these kinds of power levels."

'Disconnect the plasma venting from the ion scrubber and re-route into the main intake manifold,' she read. She blinked and took her eyes off the display. "That's totally nuts!" she cried. "If we do that, then we'll be feeding directly back into the main plasma intake feed and she'll go Nova instantly. What the hell is he on about anyway?" she asked herself in frustration.

Sheenan was a tall, stout-figured redhead from Toronto, in the North American Alliance. She pulled absent-mindedly at the short tufts of hair on the back of her neck and swore. She always pulled them when she was stressed. She was stressed now. She hated protocol with a passion and detested any interference with what she considered were 'her' engines.

She had a degree in Vortex engineering from Queens University in Kingston and had gone on to earn her doctorate in applied Star Drive Engineering at the MIT campus on Kandar, a busy system in what was called the 'Regent Envelope' on the lower extension of the Ectesian spiral.

As if in response, Green's image appeared on the view, superimposed on the complex piping and flow diagrams for the drive hook-up. "If you hesitate to try and figure it all out first, you'll be dead," Green's image stated. Sheenan looked at the viewer. That wild looking recon lieutenant had told her tersely that she was to ask no fucking questions and to hook the modules up immediately if she wanted to live through the next half hour chunk of time.

And now, here was a holographic image of a goddamned dead physicist, telling her the same thing. "Only with just a marginally more polite tone of voice than the lieutenant," she growled to herself.

"Just hook it up," the voice said, "you can read the technical minutia and figure out the why later, but hook it up now and charge the system or you're dead." Sheenan shivered. There was a quality and intensity in Green's eyes though, that convinced her.

"Chief?" Electrician's Mate First Class Christensen called. "We're ready to do the final snap in. Everything's cold." The engineering space was quiet as they watched her. She hesitated; everything inside of Sheenan told her this was crazy. She looked at the diagram behind Green's image and slowly nodded her head.

"Right," she said. "Check the board. Disconnect the plasma venting from the ion scrubber and re-route into the main intake manifold." They blinked at her in confusion. "Just fucking do it," she shouted. "I don't understand it either but we haven't got time to play twenty questions. There's a pissed-off Caldarian cruiser that just killed the Hunt coming this way and we're next on her breakfast menu. So let's just get this done and hit the big red button. I mean, worst case, what's it gonna do? Kill us?" Her crew grinned at her.

"How we going to play this, Skipper?" Executive Officer Jason Crichton asked.

"Once XO," he said grimly. "We won't get a second shot at this. Mr. Petrie, what was the signature distance on that cruiser's engagement with the Hunt?"

Master Seaman David Petrie, the electronic warfare technician, stooped over his monitoring console and worked the palm control before speaking. "Skipper, it's tough to say because we haven't been able to get a lock on that cruiser. All we get is the halo-flare when she fires and then it snaps shut when she's finished, but we got a pretty good fix from the way she chewed the Hunt up, Sir. I'd say she was close, fifteen hundred meters tops when she killed the Hunt."

"And why would a cruiser that has a stand-off kill capability of five hundred kilometers move in that close?" Nolan asked. No one spoke but they were all watching him intently.

Rene Girard, the medical corpsman who had accompanied Jackson to the bridge, finished her suturing, clamped a sub-atomic restoration unit in place and activated the wand. "All set, Lieutenant," she told Jackson. "Give that twelve hours and you'll be as good as new. I'd give it a few weeks before you do any vine swinging or Holo-humping when you get back to the Lex though Sir, to let the muscles and ligaments re-align and fasten properly. Her lewd comments didn't go unnoticed by Doc Hearst.

Girard looked at Jackson with frank appraisal. Her eyes held a blatant invitation that made Jackson wary. He had seen that look too many times before. On board, regulations were strict when it came to male—female interaction and conduct. Although the military didn't care who you screwed on the beach, woe betide the unfortunates who were caught engaged in what was considered inappropriate conduct while on board.

Rene Girard knew the rules but enjoyed pushing the envelope, and had a bad habit of wearing her 'poopie suit', as her blue medical fatigues were called, a size 'just short of plastic wrap' as the saying went.

Doc Hearst watched from where she sat against the bulkhead by the tactical console, and felt her ire rising. Her legs were pulled up and her arms were wrapped around her knees. She was about to uncoil her legs and say something when she saw the startled look on Girard's face as she turned and without another comment, left the bridge.

Hearst smiled to herself at the oily, offended look on Girard's face as she left. "Bitchzoid," she said to herself. She brought her attention back to the bridge crew and the Caldarian cruiser that was stalking them.

"Somebody on that cruiser thinks like a Marine," Nolan said. "One shot, one kill, get in close and hit them once, so hard that they haven't got a chance to respond." The bridge was totally quiet.

"I don't know about the Hancock but he killed the Shirayuki at close range, then he moved in and hammered us at, what?" he paused and looked at the XO.

"One thousand, seventy-four meters, Skipper," Crichton replied. Nolan turned back to the bridge crew. Jackson, Hearst noticed, was unconsciously flexing his left hand and trying to rotate his shoulder, the tissue restorer already beginning to work at the molecular level.

"The exact same way he killed the Hunt," Nolan stated flatly. "So my bet is that he's going to move in close to finish us off, and we have five minutes to figure out what our response is going to be. We want to initiate and get him to have to react to us," he stated.

"By now he knows we're not dead, he knows the Hunt was just a decoy and he also knows that we've killed his ground team and recovered the Element. If he hasn't already done so, within the next half-hour, he'll launch a slot buoy to inform the High Admiral that he's failed and that we're coming. If that happens, the fleet units in front of the Sixth Battle Group are going to engage and send an immediate interdiction squadron here."

"Why here?" Jackson asked, ignoring the stares.

"Because they believe that if they can hit first, they'll destroy the Sixth and hopefully us in the process and," he paused, "to put a ring around the planet and deny us access. First they'll try to keep the planet within their control and if all else fails, they'll kill the planet rather than let it fall into our hands." There was stunned silence on the bridge.

"Think about it," Nolan replied. "They're already beating the shit out of us. They don't need any new technology or new substance to do that. If they could kill us all without being detected by using Element drive capable ships, it would only be the icing on the cake.

"But even if we get back and survive the carnage that would ensue, if they control or destroy the planet, there's only one of us. And in time, we would make a mistake or end up surrounded, and with the odds a thousand to one, even an Element powered and cloaked ship couldn't fight those odds. We'd be killed.

"The only thing we have going for us is the Caldarian's extreme paranoia of failure. They won't admit failure until there's absolutely no way for them to succeed. What we have to do is kill them quickly before they can transmit that one signal. We close to a thousand meters and we kill them," he finished.

"And how do you propose we do that?" Crichton inquired.

"As soon as we get the word from the chief, we're going to jump to light. Then we're going to exit the system without executing any egress jumps. XO, when we settle on our base course, I want you to get ready to eject two Mossies."

"Why two?" Jack Stacey asked.

"The first one is going to continue right along on our base course, just as if we were flat-lining for home, radiating a slightly higher detection level. Not much higher, just enough to give him a twitch and let him pick it up. The second one will make a hard course change and come to course..." (Nolan paused momentarily to check the tactical overlay) "...zero-four-five, mark four-nine. We're going to set the detection levels on that one exactly like they were when he picked us up the first time."

Jackson chuckled suddenly and they turned to look at him. "Commander, once we get home, I think you should put in for a transfer and come on over to the teams. Your talents are being wasted here, flying these overpriced Gudak cans."

Nolan laughed. Middleton had mentioned that this recon lieutenant wasn't afraid to use his head or speak his mind. Nolan continued. "Whoever is driving that cruiser is sharp. We spoofed him once and then he picked us up with everything set as tight and quiet as we could drive her. The Hunt tried and he ignored the decoy and moved right past it and killed her too. He has something new. Not only is he cloaked using the Element but his detection and acquisition arrays must be an upgrade that we haven't seen before. We don't know if that upgrade has anything to do with the Element but either way we need to get the frequency specs back to Confederate intelligence ASAP."

Crichton broke in. "And that cruiser will see two standard Confederate signatures, one slightly stronger than the other, and he'll ignore the stronger one and move right in on the second one to kill it," he finished, a little breathless at the realization of what the tactical projection looked like.

"That's what I'm banking on," Nolan stated flatly. "I'm thinking that when that quiet 'Mossie' alters course to starboard, he'll turn to match speed and bearing on the starboard side so that he can bring his port weapons to bear."

"And where will we be, Skipper?" the XO asked.

"We're going to be paralleling that MOSS on her starboard side at three thousand meters. That gives us a little bit of leeway so that our envelopes don't touch. And when he fires, we're going to kill him." Nolan glanced at the clock on the view screen. "Four minutes and thirty-seven seconds. Good," he said. "Time to go to work, folks."

Chief Sheenan looked up. She had just finished re-routing the main intake manifold. She stood at the main control station that monitored the critical components that made the star drive what it was. Her crew had worked frantically and had accomplished their assigned tasks in less than five minutes, just as she had promised. The bulkhead clock said four minutes, twenty-seven seconds.

"OK," she breathed.

She lifted the heavy transparent alumina-matrix cover off the main power bus bar and each person on the watch removed their lockout tags and locks. Sheenan wrapped her gloved fist around it and pushed it forward. There was a solid clunk as it locked in the online position. Every eye in the compartment was watching the main power panel monitors and the digital flow back feed grid. The display immediately went to normal one hundred percent on the plasma coils and continued to climb. The crew gasped. More than one of them had expected something to overload as the vented plasma and spent ions were routed back into the feed chamber.

"Easy," Sheenan said. "That psycho Holo-doctor said to ignore the power readings. He said that until we re-calibrated according to the revised schematics, it would climb way out of the normal envelope."

The values continued to climb until they slowed and then stopped when the shunting overload capacitors were fully charged.

"Shit," one of the technicians said. "Look at those readings. Do you know what that means? We just made history. We're the first Confederate vessel in the fleet, no wait, the first Confederate vessel ever to move the power envelope to twenty-seven percent over the emergency design specs. Not," he added, "the capacity override but the emergency envelope that no one except us is supposed to know we have. And it only stopped because the overload capacitors are containing the field. God knows what this will push us at," he said in awe.

Sheenan slapped him on the back. "Let's just hope it does the same thing for the charging coils on the weapons."

The intercom came alive as Nolan's voice broke in on their collective introspection. "How we doing, Chief?"

"All done, Skipper. Everything's on line and in the green. We can punch it anytime you want. I don't know what it will give you but my gut feeling is she's gonna get up and boogie when the time comes." She winked at her crew.

They grinned back at her, half in relief that the ship was still moving, the other half grinning at her covert referral to the collection of vintage blues and jazz cubes she carried and played at every opportunity. Often, during the night watch, the engineering spaces were filled with the melancholic, mesmerizing sounds of B.B. King and Stevie Ray Vaughn.

"Great work, Chief," Nolan said. "XO, sound general quarters, close her up." Once again, the piercing, strident sounds of 'all hands to station' sounded throughout the Haida, as men and women moved to their stations.

"We have a green board, Skipper," the XO said. "All stations manned and ready."

"Helm, bring us about. New course three-three-five, mark two-zero. Prepare to engage star drive," he said.

Coming to course three-three-five, mark two-zero—aye, Skipper," Karen Gabriel replied from the helm. Her right arm had been cast after their first fight with the cruiser but she refused to go to sickbay. The entire crew had their EVA battle armor on and was plugged into the secondary life support system. In case of a hull breach or damage to the ship's environmental systems, they could still function and fight.

"Engage star drive on my mark—three, two, one, mark!" Nolan cried out. The Haida leapt forward, streaking for home. "Mr. Stacey, launch the Mossies and reload with standard mark 235 plasma torpedoes."

Stacey pressed the digital actuator controls and the Mossies in tubes two and four on the port side were ejected. In the weapons launch bay, computer sub-routines took over, the blast door on the Haida's magazine was opened and two mark 235 plasma torpedoes were selected from the magazine and put on the munition lift. The weapons technicians manning the tubes engaged the compression controls and the torpedoes were fed into the tubes, the warheads armed and the safeties set as the arming nodes that were mounted in the forward section of the tubes scanned them. When the technician had a green control board, he tapped a small control nipple on his wrist console and a signal was sent to the bridge informing Stacey that the tubes were 'up' and clear. The entire process had taken less than thirty seconds.

"Sir, MOSS one is radiating at ninety percent and is flat-lining on three-three-five, mark two-zero. We have an opening bearing on MOSS two at zero-four-five, mark four-nine, Skipper. We just lost her on the forward array. She's operating at one hundred percent Chameleon. We were able to expand the shimmer envelope on her enough that she'll still look like a cloaked destroyer, Skipper. They'll have to get real close before they can see through the cloud enough to distinguish her outline."

"And hopefully by that time, we'll have killed her," Nolan said.

"The operative word of course, being 'hopefully'," Jackson remarked wryly.

Nolan glanced at Jackson and Hearst standing beside the tactical console. They looked grungy and dirty in their battle-scarred URKS. Jackson's left sleeve was ripped and torn where Ensuris' knife had been driven through it into his biceps. Nolan motioned with his armored hand toward a storage locker marked 'Emergency EVA'. "Lieutenant, why don't you and Weapons Specialist Hearst see if you can grab yourselves an emergency EVA and suit up. I'd hate like hell to have you come this far and have to put you in cold storage over a simple oversight on our part."

"Aye, Sir," Jackson said. He and Hearst opened the locker and fumbled amongst the ordered clutter looking for something that would fit.

"Helm, bring us about. New course—zero-four-five, mark four-nine. Keep us abreast of MOSS two at four thousand meters."

"Coming to zero-four-five, mark four-nine, holding station at four thousand meters, Skipper," Gabriel told him.

"OK Chief—show time. Engage the Element grid and let's see if we can bag us a Caldarian cruiser." Nolan glanced at the clock. "Eight minutes and fourteen seconds. Thank you, Captain Middleton," he said softly to the bridge crew.

⚜

The Sipedesis

Va looked impassively at the body of Captain Dra. He worked the chambering mechanism on his darter and holstered it. It wasn't the first time he had killed a subordinate but he knew he needed to control his rage and focus it on the ones responsible for his dishonor, that Confederate destroyer he had thought was dead. Shame filled him. He had never before been thwarted of his prey. He intended to make them pay for the disgrace they had brought to his house name. The execution of the Captain hadn't raised an eyebrow.

They went about their duties while two of the legionnaires from the Eighth cohort removed the body.

"Consul, the Confederate shuttle has docked and the destroyer has engaged her cloaking. She is moving out of the system, Sir," Weapons Technician Parthen Hedra said.

"Is there any residual ion trace?" Va asked.

"Yes, Consul. Bearing three-three-five, mark two-zero."

Va gave his helm orders. "Bring us about, pursuit course, match bearing."

The Sipedesis came about and began to overtake the Haida. Hedra watched his sensors. Two small red triangles moved out on the astral grid. He pressed a button and the tactical plot expanded, showing space out to three light years. "Consul? The Confederate vessel's base course indicates that she's engaged her star drive and has started her run." The battle clock said eight minutes and twenty-seven seconds had passed since they had begun their pursuit.

"Sensors detect two signatures, Consul. One is holding on three-three-five, mark two-zero, the other signal is lower density and is very low, almost nominal. Bearing is opening on second contact at zero-four-five, mark four-nine," Hedra stated. "Course laid in to engage forward bearing, energizing port weapons array," he called out.

"No," Va said. "It's a decoy. The signature is too strong. Whoever is in command on that destroyer is trying to draw us in while they make their escape." He pointed an armored finger at the three dimensional tactical plot.

"That's him," he said, "the one that has changed course. Helm, match bearing on the second target and bring us abeam his starboard quarter. We'll engage with our port cannons. I want you to close the distance to exactly one thousand metrics before we fire. We will engage with a full broadside on the port array. I want you to continue to fire until there is nothing left but dust. Once the destroyer is dead, we will return to Zilith and the Eighth cohort will continue the search. We know we are close. It is only a matter of time before we find what we are looking for."

"Yes, Consul," Weapons Technician Hedra responded. "Range closing, eight thousand kilometrics. Systems nominal, no aspect change on target."

"You can't see us," Va whispered. "This time there will be no stopping us."

The Sipedesis closed the distance. In one respect, Commander Nolan was wrong. Her enhanced sensors had nothing to do with the Element crystals powering her drive and weapons systems. Before she had been commissioned, the Caldarians had captured a small, unmanned Confederate snooper drone. Each side employed drones for a variety of tasks but the problem with drones was fundamental to the necessity for teams and people like Jackson.

No matter how complex the electronic programs or the snoop and shoot algorithms were, they could be deceived or avoided.

This particular drone had been flying a complicated loop in an attempt to draw close to the Caldarian home system and find strategic locations for an alpha strike. It was a risk but a risk the Confederate high command had thought worth taking. Unfortunately, the drone had been detected, ironically enough by another drone, a Caldarian patrol drone that was working the outer perimeter envelope to the Caldarian home system. The Caldarian drone had recorded the unknown electronic sensor signature and relayed the information to a frigate that was patrolling within the sector. The frigate had closed, expecting to find a vessel. Instead it found the snooper drone. The drone had turned out to be an unexpected watershed of stealth information for the Caldarians. Its onboard electronics and stealth systems had been systematically reverse-engineered and the drone itself had been used in fleet training exercises. The result was a suite of upgraded sensors for the Sipedesis, before commissioning, and upgrades that would be made in the fleet as ships rotated out to service docks for re-calibration of their cannon coils.

"One thousand kilometrics." Hedra called out the distances. "Five hundred, one hundred. Consul, we are drawing abreast. The shimmer envelope is just becoming visible."

"Prepare to fire on my mark."

"Twenty-five, fifteen, five kilometrics! Drawing abreast and holding station at one thousand metrics on the target's starboard beam, weapons are locked in."

Ten particle cannons tracked the target. Va didn't want to kill them at long range. At a range of one thousand metrics there would be nothing but a cloud of dust when he was finished.

"Now," Va said. Ten searing shafts of particle fire reached out and vaporized the MOSS.

✥◈✥

The Haida

The sudden appearance of the arcing halo from the particle cannons lit up the threat board on Sub Leftenant Stacey's control display and the CCS immediately identified the threat as a Caldarian battle class weapons signature. The bridge crew was under tremendous stress. The initial fight, the destruction of the Hunt and the creeping fear that a lethal killer was stalking them took its toll on their emotions. "Particle fire close aboard, bearing two-seven-zero, mark…. Fuck, he's nominal, repeat—he's nominal, Skipper." He watched his display. "WCS engaging, we have residual halo lock."

"Fire," Nolan shouted, completely unaware that he was shouting. He was totally absorbed in fighting his ship and utterly lost in the battle. "I can feel you, you Caldarian bastard," he breathed. "Weapons free, you are weapons free."

The Haida fired, cycled through and fired again.

In engineering, Sheenan and her crew watched the weapons system as it cycled through its firing sequence. "Holy shit," Sheenan whispered in awe.

≫≪

The Sipedesis

The Sipedesis shook and staggered as particle fire tore through her shield envelope, impacted on her reactive armor and raked the cruiser the full length on her starboard side. For a moment, the bridge crew stared at each other in stunned surprise. Another broadside hit her; the shield envelope rippled, flexed and parted as the Element powered particle fire tore into her.

"Consul, we've been hit! No residual signature but the halo is cruiser class bearing..." His face went white before continuing, "...bearing zero-nine-zero, range two thousand metrics." He staggered as particle fire found them again.

But this was no unarmored Carillian privateer manned by a dozen drunken, undisciplined mercenaries.

"Emergency rise on the forward thrusters, new course zero-nine-zero, mark zero-nine," Va shouted. The Sipedesis decelerated and stood on her tail as the powerful attack thrusters responded to the helm. When the bow had lifted to a ninety-degree angle, she fell off and twisted laterally and fired. The Sipedesis swept up beneath the Haida, visible now like a black cloud but she still couldn't see her antagonist.

"The first contact had to be the damaged destroyer," Va's mind was telling him, "and they must have called for reinforcements after our initial engagement. A cruiser but why can't we see her? No matter, we'll kill her too."

≫≪

The Haida

In engineering, Sheenan watched in awe as the charging coils fired, rotated through their recharging cycle and fired again. The compressed particle coils hadn't even gone to stand-by mode, firing within nanoseconds of the initial discharge. She had never before seen such a massive power discharge from destroyer coils. She guessed that the broadside had the weight of a fleet cruiser and then some.

The bridge crew watched as pieces of the Sipedesis' hull plating suddenly became visible as they separated from the main hull, the cloaking grid spiking as it flared, died and went nominal. Her last broadside went wide as the Sipedesis maneuvered clear.

"She's visible, target is visible. We've damaged her cloaking, Skipper," Stacey cried out. Suddenly the Sipedesis fell away.

"Goddamn it, stay with her," Nolan cried out. The Sipedesis swam back into view as the CCS tracked her and locked back on. He watched. Suddenly he knew what the Caldarian was going to do.

"Helm," he shouted, "two-eight-five, mark zero-four."

"Two-eight-five, mark zero-four, aye," Gabriel spoke through clenched teeth. The Haida heeled over. "Come on sweetheart," she breathed. The two ships closed. Cannon muzzles moved and tracked on the closing Caldarian cruiser.

"Coming abreast," Stacey said.

"Fire," Nolan cried.

They watched as their particle fire once again raked the Sipedesis, chunks and pieces of plating bursting outward as her reactive armor detonated. As they drew away they were hit and the Haida staggered under the blows. There was a pop, like glass breaking and then a soft, sighing hiss as a bright bead of particle shrapnel, three millimeters in diameter, impacted on the bridge console beside Gabriel. A red light flashed on Stacey's threat board.

"Warning. Multiple hull breaches on decks four, twelve and alpha one," the flat metallic voice said.

"Section alpha-one," Gabriel thought, "that's the Battle Bridge."

"Chief?" Nolan asked on the fly, "we OK?"

"Dust transients Sir, nominal damage, all systems green."

"Skipper, that last broadside breached their hull. The detection pulse found an opening and must have damaged her tracking systems because that last shot was wild." He broke off. "Here she comes," he shouted. "She's matched our halo signature and altered her course, bearing is closing."

❧ ❧

The Sipedesis

The sickly sweet smell of melting flesh filled the bridge. They still had no target. What do the Confederates have? Va thought. The last broadside had come right through and breached the hull. They were venting from the port nacelle and it was only a matter of time before she dropped out of light and went to standard drive. The environmental system was offline and already the CO_2 levels were climbing. "What do they have?" he asked again.

Va reached for the control nipple on his battle seat and moved the control wand. His helmsman and weapons principal were dead. The last broadside had contained a search pulse that had overloaded the targeting system. The following jet had cut through the hull and a portion of it had deflected directly into the bridge where dampers had absorbed the residual energy but not before it had seared and burned through his helmsman, consuming the flesh as it neutralized.

He watched his sensor grid. Va called up the tactical sensor display and entered a command. Characters and numbers began to scroll down the display. The display paused and one line of numbers turned red and began to flash, the frequency of the residual halo envelope from the Haida's particle fire.

He knew that when a particle weapon was fired, the searing flash of light at discharge, called a halo, bore a unique power signature that could be tracked if a vessel was equipped with a full spectrum corona array used to monitor and record sunspot activity and radio magnetic distortions.

They were used primarily in research vessels but when it was discovered that they were capable of recording the frequency that was emitted when a particle weapon discharged, they became standard equipment on military vessels. They were rarely used, since both sides had far more sophisticated targeting and acquisition sensors, and had been more or less forgotten until now. Va didn't have anything else to go on. He entered the data into the auto engage system and programmed the weapon control system to override the standard sensor array and engage the moment the array detected the halo.

He entered the last known coordinates that had been detected from the Haida's halo signature and altered course.

⁊ᔢ

The Haida

Nolan watched the Sipedesis closely. He was about to swing in to meet her head on when the intuition that only battle can breed made the hair on the back of his neck rise. Something's wrong, he thought. He can't see us. He has no sensors and yet the bearing is closing. An icy ball formed in the pit of his stomach as he suddenly realized what whoever was conning the cruiser was about to do.

"You cunning bastard," he breathed.

"He's dialed in, Skipper. We'll finish him on this next pass," the XO stated.

"No!" Nolan shouted, desperation in his voice.

"Chief, power down the charging coils now."

"Sir, if we..." Sheenan broke off as Nolan cut her off.

"Just do it, Chief, now or we're dead."

"Helm, bring us about. Disengage. Emergency pattern tango X-ray!" Gabriel cringed. Emergency pattern tango X-ray was a radical course and attitude change designed to give the smallest possible cross sectional profile to a pursuing vessel.

212 • CHRISTOPHER BESSE

"Sir, it will tear us apart. She can't tolerate that kind of shear force at this speed. We need to drop out of light first," Crichton said.

"He has halo lock on his spectral array. The moment he closes to ten kilometers, he's going to fire and every particle cannon he has will be focused on our particle coils," Nolan said. Crichton paled.

"Weaps, open the outer doors on all six starboard tubes and set for delayed detonation and remove the safeties. As soon as we come about, I want you to fire. Helm, on my mark, execute pattern tango X-ray."

"Aye, Sir," Gabriel said, her voice tight.

In engineering, Chief Sheenan took the cannon capacitors off-line. She watched as the power monitors sank until the only display was the stand-by light. Her crew watched her in silence. "That's it," she said.

The Sipedesis grew in the display as the two vessels closed. Amazing, Nolan thought. Here we are, hurtling through space at maximum light speed, careening and clashing in giant, curving parabolas, completely disconnected, yet a part of the universe all at the same time.

"Three, two, one, mark," he said. Time stood still. Nolan watched in slow motion as Karen Gabriel's fist came down on the triangular disk that would execute pattern Tango X-ray.

The Haida groaned in every seam and joint as she heeled over and stood on her tail. Her gravity dampers were overloaded and shut down at the tremendous forces that were being exerted on the damping field grid. All over the ship crewmen suddenly found themselves weightless at the sudden loss of gravity. Magnetic cleats took hold on decking and servo battle seats suddenly went active, holding station keepers relative as the ship radically changed attitude.

Time moved. "Pattern tango X-ray complete," Gabriel said breathlessly.

There was a soft, shuddering sigh as six long lance torpedoes were ejected and raced away.

"Torpedoes away, outer doors closed," Stacey said. They had successfully executed an extreme breakaway maneuver and they were still alive. The bridge crew watched the aft view screen, each pair of eyes alternating between the cruiser and the clock that was now counting down the time to impact.

❧

The Sipedesis

"No," Va shouted in rage.

He couldn't see the Haida but the moment his sensors had detected the incoming torpedoes, he knew it was over. He set the command and control systems to emergency evade and tried to maneuver clear. In the last moment before impact, he reached for the control yoke that would deploy the slot buoy that had been preprogrammed before they left Caldara Prime, its one message that the Sipedesis had failed in her mission, at which point the Caldarian fleet was to attack Battle Group Six. His hand closed on the handle and he pulled. A small hatch blew out on the port side on the aft keel line and a small black cylinder was ejected. It immediately cloaked and went to star drive. Its destination, the Caldarian Command Ship 'Shimmering Wind' and High Admiral Corack-Va-Morlaris.

The first torpedo sheared through the outer hull and detonated inside the battle bridge. Va's body turned to ash and then the heat consumed his residual molecules. One torpedo would have been enough. Six turned the Sipedesis into molecular space dust. The last five torpedoes slammed into the Sipedesis on her starboard side and tore her apart. Torpedo four detonated in the engineering spaces and when her plasma conduits ruptured, she novaed.

⋦⋫

The Haida

"Eat shit and die, asshole," Stacey breathed.

"Helm, bring us about. Set course for residual debris cloud, bring us in alongside and give us a full spectrum sweep," Nolan said. "I want to know if anything got out before we killed that son of a bitch."

Michelle Hearst took a deep breath. She was clutching the titanium crash bar in front of the tactical console with all her strength. She blinked. Slowly she looked around the bridge. "I take back everything I ever said about you squids being a bunch of slack-assed transport pukes," she breathed.

Nolan turned toward her and smiled. "Well, Weapons Specialist Michelle Hearst, I'll take that as a compliment."

"Sir," Stacey said. "I have a residual ion signature bearing three-three-five, mark two-zero. Signature is consistent with a standard Caldarian slot buoy. Stacey paused, his voice stony with dread. "It's heading for the main Caldarian battle fleet in front of Battle Group Six, Skipper."

Jackson looked up from where he was sitting beside the tactical display.

"Helm, come to course three-three-five, mark four-nine," said Nolan, watching the debris on the view screen.

"Coming to course three-three-five, mark four-nine, aye, Sir," Gabriel replied.

"XO, send a pulse transmission to the Lex, code it black, and let them know that we killed the Caldarian cruiser but they got a slot buoy away before she died."

Jason Crichton punched a single key on his control console. "Transmission sent, Skipper. All systems green."

Nolan looked up at Jackson and Hearst. There was something in Nolan's eyes that made Hearst's heart suddenly go cold. Oh no, please no more. We've done everything they asked of us and then some, she thought to herself.

"Mr. Jackson, would you kindly gather your team and meet my Executive Officer and I in my ready room please?"

"Yes, Sir," Jackson replied.

"Thank you, Lieutenant." Nolan paused momentarily to call Chief Sheenan. "Chief?" I'm on my way to engineering to have a quick look at our new module, and then please come to my ready room. I need your input."

"Aye, Skipper," Sheenan replied.

Nolan turned back to Jackson. "Unfortunately Lieutenant, there's only one way to stop the Caldarian fleet from immediately attacking the Sixth once they get that slot buoy."

"How, Commander?"

"By assassinating the High Admiral," Nolan replied.

CHAPTER 17
ABRASION

"Retreat hell! We just got here!"

—Unknown officer, Sixth Regiment Second Marine Division,
United States Marines, Chateau-Thierry June 1918

Everyone's tired and it's beginning to affect them, Jackson thought. The regular joking and horsing around that preceded and accompanied a mission was gone. It had been replaced by a tight silence that could be felt. A deep undercurrent of dread seemed to permeate the Haida. The word was out that they had been way too damned lucky so far and that it wasn't going to last. The Haida was a flying wreck, undermanned and outgunned, and yet Nolan was suggesting they walk right into the heart of bad guy territory and attempt a phoenix hit.

No one had ever been inside a Caldarian battle group, let alone attempted to board a command ship, and yet Jackson knew that Nolan's assessment was correct. As wild and inconceivable as it sounded, it just might work.

Surprise and complacency, he thought. That's what's going to pull this off. It's never been done before. No, that's not right, it's never even been attempted before, he corrected himself. We've been fighting the Caldarians for almost two years and we've never breached their security envelope and we have always retreated. Do the unexpected, do it quickly and get out, and we may get away with this.

We came out here basically expecting a normal mission and we've seen too many friends and comrades blown away. Twenty-five hundred men and three ships gone as if they were never there.

They had been stalked and chased for ten days. Three team members killed: one horribly by creatures that moved like shadows and struck with terrible rapacity and the other two in firefights with Black Order legionnaires. In the back of everyone's mind was the nightmare picture of the team member they had had no choice in leaving behind and what had probably happened to Jamie Wicker's body. Jackson had never, ever before left anyone behind.

"But Zilith is different. This mission is going to be the one that goes into the books, that will break all the old rules and standards," he mused out loud.

Jackson knew the team was walking the dark side of the edge. Sustained combat was tremendously stressful. Recon was a totally different ball game. It wasn't like going out on patrol and coming back every morning to a base camp, to sleep and relax in relative safety or at least what was considered relative safety. The constant need for being one hundred percent focused and observant, and then being relentlessly hunted in the darkness had had a heavy impact. And swirling in and out of your thoughts was the knowledge that there was a hunter-killer platoon of Blackies waiting somewhere ahead to ambush you. It all took a tremendous toll on a person's ability to make quick, objective decisions.

Hearst made her way down the passageway to engineering with the suit packs they had taken from the dead Blackies. She was on edge. She found herself cringing at doorways and hesitating to pass dark shadows. The soft, ambient, red battle lighting, glowing softly from the glow panels on the bulkhead, did nothing to ease her tension.

There was a brush of movement behind her and she reacted instantly to the perceived threat. She dropped the modules, immediately pivoted on the balls of her feet, and with her right hand, drew out her knife. With her left, she blocked and deliberately moved her hand in and it closed on fabric. Without thought or thinking, she spun and kicked. There was a thud and a startled grunt and the next thing she saw was a pair of terrified eyes looking up at her and her knife against his throat. Her mind swirled and she came back. Dyer was beside her.

"Easy Doc, easy." His right hand inched its way down Hearst's arm until it was over the hilt of the knife. "It's OK, Doc," he said gently. Hearst blinked and looked at him. Slowly she relaxed and then sagged against him. There was complete silence in the passageway. He pulled her close and she began to weep silently, her body heaving and shaking as her emotions crashed and stormed to the surface.

She looked at the terrified crewman who hadn't moved. Because all rank and designation had been removed from his uniform, she couldn't tell where his station was. He was young she thought to herself, probably no more than nineteen or twenty, young and innocent. She sheathed her knife and then reached out a dirty gloved hand that was stained with blood and dirt and ever so gently, touched him on the cheek, letting her hand rest there for a moment.

Tears rolled down her dirty face. "I'm sorry," she whispered, "so very sorry." Slowly the fear in the young sailor's eyes faded and he relaxed. He pulled himself out from under Hearst, put a hand out to the bulkhead and used it to pull himself shakily to his feet. "It's OK, Ma'am," he said, "I understand." And he moved off down the passageway.

"I almost killed him, Robbie," she whispered. "I—I heard this noise and suddenly I was back in that awful place under the trees in the darkness, feeling those eyes on me, and I felt those horrible stalking thoughts of killing and blood. And I could see Roger's body hanging on that knife, and I watched the life go out of his eyes while I just stood there. And I couldn't stop it, I couldn't bring him back and I was thinking that, if I had had a particle rifle, I could have cut that bastard in two and maybe saved him. But instead, I was standing there with an empty 235, the bolt locked open." She sagged and started to weep again.

"Michelle, there was nothing you or any of us could have done," he said softly. "We were all fighting. If it hadn't been for you, that Caldarian probably would have killed us all, or that creature behind him would have. Look at me, Michelle, look at me." He shook her gently. Hearst raised her eyes and looked at Dyer. His eyes were like cast obsidian. It caught her breath. This was a different Dyer, older, harder. He was only twenty-three but he had the eyes of an old man. She saw the fear but she saw something else there too, a determination.

He's looked over the edge, she thought to herself. He's seen what's calling from the blackness below. She shuddered. I wonder if I'll ever have the courage to look, she thought.

She smiled and choked on a laugh amidst her tears.

"No one's ever said that before."

"Said what?"

"Michelle. No one's called me by my real name for years. It felt good, like a memory of sunshine and trees." For a moment longer Dyer held her and searched her eyes. Like electrons that pass through an electronic circuit passing information, they both felt the empathic energy pass and wrap invisible fingers around them.

Dyer stood up and reached out a hand. Hearst looked up at him and slowly lifted a gloved hand. He pulled her to her feet. "Come on," he said softly. "I'll help you pick these things up and walk you to engineering."

When Hearst and Dyer entered engineering, Sheenan looked up from her work monitoring the plasma coils. She was about to make a smart-assed comment but the look in Hearst's eyes warned her off. Suddenly she felt uneasy but it angered her too. This was her ship and these arrogant, cocky mud-pounders filled her with a seething resentment and smoldering enmity. Now the skipper's intentions to take the Haida into the heart of the

Caldarian battle group were the last straw. Already, scuttlebutt was flying and the rumor mill was rampant. Throughout the ship and in mess rooms crewmembers sat in small groups and spoke in whispers. Fear seemed to flow like a vapor and ooze out of the bulkheads. Nerves were drawn taut and old rivalries and tensions that had long been buried were about to come out.

"The Haida is my ship," she thought fiercely to herself, "my ship."

Irritated, she turned to where Electrician's Mate First Class Paul Christensen was replacing a power coupling that had shown signs of stress on the high-speed emergency maneuver during the fight with the Sipedesis.

"Goddamn it, Christensen! Aren't you finished with that coupling yet?" she bellowed. "You were supposed to have that finished an hour ago. What the hell do you think this is? A goddamn Rysilian cruise ship?"

Christensen cringed as if he had been struck. "Give me a break, Chief. I'm going as fast as I can. We're working sixteen hour watches and we're undermanned."

Sheenan started. His words cut her like a knife. She had lost three people in engineering when they had been hit by the Sipedesis' initial attack. His words stung her to fury. She felt responsible for every life that had been lost and her mind flashed back to that awful moment when the hull had been breached and three of her crew had been sucked out into space. The last one had been Coil Specialist Third Class Giselle Park, a pretty, petite, first tour technician fresh from the academy on Perilius-Prime, whose armored battle suit had been punctured by a piece of particle shrapnel. She had clung to a valve assembly and screamed at Sheenan to save her, eyes wild and terrified as her lungs decompressed and exploded. With a gurgling cough, she had let go and been sucked out into the vacuum, her eyes never leaving Sheenan.

In one stride she was upon Christensen and her huge, rough hands were around his throat, choking him.

"You fucking little piss ant," she hissed. "Where were you when we were hit? Watching Park and the others die while you hid behind the drive shield in your EVA suit? Why didn't you help?" A part of her mind told her that Christensen's regular battle station was in the drive cell and that he was desperately moving forward to assist when the hull had been breached, but she was beyond reason.

Christensen was shaking with rage. He brought his forearms swiftly up and broke Sheenan's hold on his throat. As her arms flew up in the air, he brought his hands in and with his hands cupped, he boxed her ears. She howled in rage and doubled forward. As she did, Christensen brought his knee up. There was a sharp crack when her nose broke as it made contact with his knee and she staggered back, blood flowing freely down her coveralls. Enraged, she swept up a pair of coil pullers and was about to attack when the shocking crack of a conventional sidearm brought the entire engineering space to a standstill. The eerie, careening whip snap of ricocheting shrapnel was heard before it buried itself in a portable lift tray. In the dead silence that followed, a harsh voice rang with authority.

"The next person to move gets one in the head," Nolan bellowed from the catwalk above the deck. "This is a Confederate military vessel under wartime conditions and so help me, I'll kill the next son of a bitch who so much as twitches."

The gun in his hand was rock solid and his eyes didn't waver. He moved his left hand momentarily and tapped his COM link. "Security to engineering on the double, code blue. Repeat, code blue." Nolan moved down the ladder and walked up to Sheenan. He lowered his sidearm.

The only sound was the quiet hum of the equipment in the background and the soft splat as blood dripped from Sheenan's broken nose onto the deck. The tension seemed to have vanished like smoke in a wind. Nolan stopped a foot away from Sheenan and holstered his sidearm. He looked around the compartment. All eyes were on him. He spoke into the ship-wide COM link.

"All hands, this is Commander Mark Nolan. I haven't got time for bullshit, so I'm going to give this to you straight.

"There is a piece of earth history I want to remind you of. From November 14th to November 17th, 1965, the First Battalion of the 7th Air Cavalry Regiment, led by Lieutenant Colonel Hal Moore, was engaged by an entire division of the regular North Vietnamese army in the Ia Drang Valley. Cut off and surrounded, they fought them off for four days. They had no help. All they had was each other. In the heat and chaos of battle, all they could do was trust that the person behind and beside them would watch out for them. At one point, they were ordered to fix bayonets because they were down to the last of their ammunition.

"That's the way it is right now. We've come through a major engagement and what you have heard via the grapevine is true. We're going into harm's way once again. We don't have a choice. Neither do the team members of Mike Platoon SEAL Team One. All we have is each other. There are no reinforcements coming to bail us out or guard our flanks. We're alone. We are going into the very heart and center of the Caldarian main battle fleet and members of Mike Platoon are going to attempt to board and kill the High Admiral on the command ship, the 'Shimmering Wind'."

All over the ship, heads raised and crewmembers looked at each other in stunned silence.

"I can't promise you we will get out of this alive. I can only promise you that if the Haida goes down, we will do it fighting and we will take some of these Caldarian bastards with us. I need your help. We need each other right now like never before, because ladies and gentlemen, you and I are all we have. No banners, no bullshit. The Haida's been hit and they've marked us but we've still got fangs and mark my words, we're going to make the sons of bitches bleed. Nolan out."

For a moment there was dead silence. And then, like an ocean swell from all over the ship there came a deep echoing roar as every single person cheered and began to chant, "Haida, Haida, Haida!"

Nolan turned to Sheenan and Christensen. He gazed at them in silence for a moment. "I'm going to forget this ever happened due to the nature of the circumstances and the situation we are in." He turned on his heel and began to walk away. He stopped and turned to Sheenan.

"Don't worry about the nose, Chief," he said with a ghost of a smile on his lips. "It'll give you character. Think of the action you'll get on the beach once word of this gets around," and he left the compartment.

Sheenan started to walk away and heard footsteps behind her. She stopped but didn't turn around. She felt drained but oddly enough, she felt better. There was anger but it was focused. She wanted to kill Caldarians.

"Chief." It was Christensen. "I'm—I'm sorry, Chief," he said and then stopped, not knowing what else to say. He turned away.

"Paul, you did good in there when that Caldarian cruiser hit us. If you hadn't been in the plasma control cell, this ship would have gone nova when that particle blast found the conduits. Thanks."

Christensen didn't turn around. He heard the echo of the chief's footsteps as she left but the tight brightness he felt in his chest made him catch his breath. He looked at his armored electrical gauntlets and felt a surge of pride. "OK," he whispered, "let's get that plasma coil back online."

The Haida had been hit hard. There were blackened streaks from her cannon ports and her hull looked like someone had taken a giant can opener and randomly raked it down her sides.

Jackson reached over and hit the COM switch located on the console. "Chief?"

"Go ahead, Sir," Miller replied.

"Grab the others and come to the Commander's ready room now if you can, please."

"On the way, Sir," the chief said and the COM link went dead.

When the team was all gathered and seated, Nolan began. "I wanted to brief Lieutenant Jackson first but events have dictated otherwise." He turned to a tactical display. "It's roughly a forty-six hour run, flat out, between here and the Caldarian envelope but the slot buoy is going to get there about two hours before we do. The Caldarians will need at least four hours to make their plans before they attack. That maybe gives us enough lead time to stop it from happening but unfortunately, the only way to stop that attack is to assassinate their High Admiral."

The team looked at Nolan in silence. "Don't look so shocked. You practice 'black ops' and routinely train for phoenix operations," Nolan said to Jackson.

"Why?" Hearst asked angrily. "Why can't you just move in close and fire a spread of long lance torpedoes? They're more than capable of taking out a Caldarian fleet class capital ship."

"For a number of reasons. First, for the same reason you had to go in and take out the remaining members of that Black Order Platoon. Even if we move in close and kill the 'Shimmering Wind', the Caldarians have a fail-safe device built into all their command ships that will override all other systems. Where do admirals spend most of their time?" Nolan asked rhetorically. "On the bridge or in the CIC. Both of those places are built adjacent to the admiral's quarters. They're heavily armored and shielded, and the moment that fail-safe condition is breached, the admiral will eject in a specially designed escape capsule built around his cabin. In that way, he escapes and simply transfers his flag, even though doing so means the destruction of his ship."

Nolan's face took on a hard set. "The most important reasons are the cultural factors involved." The team looked confused. Nolan could see them struggling with the idea of the complexity of Caldarian culture. How do I make them understand, he asked himself?

"You need to grasp the fact that the Caldarians' entire culture is built on a warrior, military mentality that permeates every level and every person in Caldarian society. They are not like us in ideology or practice, neither are they like any sentient race we have so far encountered in all of our travels and exploration. Every single Caldarian for three thousand years has had one purpose and one purpose only. That purpose is to become a fully functioning part of the Caldarian military empire. Nothing else matters. They believe that High Admiral Corack-Va-Morlaris' destiny is to lead Caldara to its appointed place of ruling the galaxy. It's totally irrelevant what you or I think or believe because as long as he's still alive, they'll continue to build up their forces and drive relentlessly to the attack. They will never stop. Killing him means that the Talachra or 'Telling' he received during the fall terminus at the great gate on Caldara Prime, was wrong." He paused and looked at Jackson and his team.

"If that happens, the entire Caldarian fleet will have to withdraw back to the Caldarian frontier in order to choose another High Admiral. He saw sudden understanding dawning on the tired faces around him. "Do you know what 'Corack-Va-Morlaris' means?"

"Yes," Jackson nodded. "The rough translation is 'Vortex'."

"It's a rather simplistic title isn't it, for a person with such a high destiny as you say," Crichton, the executive officer said.

Nolan smiled grimly. "That's another thing you need to understand about

Caldarian names and culture. It's a sign of great honor and station to have a very simple hidden name. As a Caldarian matures, his name shortens but it contains the complete prophecy of his destiny. As far as we have been able to determine from our sources within the Caldarian system, the association of his name means 'he who pulls into darkness."

"Like a dark, black hole, pulling everything in," Michelle Hearst whispered.

Nolan nodded. "Exactly."

"We have sources within the Caldarian system?" Jackson asked incredulously.

"The Caldarians have billions of slaves and many hundred slave planets," Nolan answered him. "It stands to reason that someone somewhere would decide to try and communicate with anyone engaged in fighting them. We have been so contacted."

"It's not the operation I'm worried about," Jackson said. "It's our ability to complete such a mission that worries me. With all due respect Commander, we've been in the field for almost ten days, I've lost three of my people and the only ones who haven't been wounded are LPO DeLuca and Specialist Hearst, Sir. We're already stretched to the limit."

Nolan nodded slowly. "I understand Lieutenant and no one can force you on this one but if we don't do it, then no one else can. There isn't time for Greig to plan and execute such an operation and they would never be able to approach anywhere near that ship anyway. The only people mission-capable on this are the Haida and Mike Platoon. My chief can install the power module for the shuttle and if we can manage to adapt the suit power units you stripped off the dead Blackies to fit your battle suits, we might just be able to pull this off. But you are the ones who have to plan the mission. We're just a taxi service, remember?"

The team chuckled darkly.

"It's not like phoenix operations are something new. In earth year 1941 the British sent a commando team led by Major Geoffrey Keyes to kill General Erwin Rommel in his headquarters in North Africa. Unfortunately, Rommel was at the front inspecting his troops and they failed in the attempt.

"And certainly your own military background had its origins in what the historians call the Vietnam era of the mid-twentieth century, Lieutenant. MACV-SOG was the joint service high command unconventional-warfare task force, engaged in highly classified clandestine operations throughout Southeast Asia. It was given the title 'Studies & Observation Group' as a cover, as you well know," Nolan said quietly.

The door to his ready room opened and Chief Sheenan entered, her nose bandaged. The others turned toward her and she gave Mike Platoon a hard, appraising glance. Jackson merely nodded and turned back to Commander Nolan.

"Some of those highly classified specific tasks were kidnapping and assassination." Nolan let his last comment hang in the air.

Jackson looked around the room before he spoke. His team stared at him and he could feel the misgivings and fear emanating from them like vapors. But there was something more, a nuance or undercurrent of resentment.

"We'll need new suits," he said, "and this will only work if we can adapt the power supplies from the ones we took off the Blackies."

Nolan glanced at Sheenan. "Chief?"

In answer she reached into her coveralls and tossed a small object to Jackson who caught it and held it up for the team to see. It was an URK power pack. He examined it and then glanced at Sheenan with a questioning look.

"Yup, it's a standard Confederate field power module for all standard issue Special Forces and Marine force recon URK's," she stated flatly, "with one very small and very significant difference. It's Element powered." Before anyone had time to react, she tossed another small object to Jackson. "That's one of the power modules you pulled off one of the Blackies. Look at the two of them together." Jackson held them both up. Except for color and a slight difference in size, they were virtually identical.

"You guys steal a key to the Caldarian patent office by chance?" she asked with a wry smile on her lips. "Because those packs are almost identical, even down to the insert hollow under the right armpit." The team stared at the power modules.

"You brought me seven packs. I've changed out four of them already." She looked over at Jackson. "So Lieutenant, have you ever had to whack anybody on one of these special operations we hear rumors about all the time?" Jackson looked at her. He knew she was baiting him.

"I'd tell you but I'd have to kill you, Chief," Jackson deadpanned.

Sheenan laughed. "So why aren't I surprised at that answer?"

Nolan cleared his throat and stared hard-eyed at Jackson and Sheenan.

"Right," Sheenan replied. "We can change out the power pack on the shuttle and it will be undetectable by anyone as long as you don't do anything stupid like energize a sensor array or fire weapons. Otherwise, you should be able to crawl right up that command ship's ass and they won't even know you're there."

"We'll follow standard boarding procedure," Jackson said, "just as we've trained and practiced, except we'll be making history—we'll be going in one hundred percent cloaked. Commander, do you have any sections we can look at and maybe rig up a mock Caldarian day cabin with the adjoining passageways in the holo-simulator?"

"Boss, who's going in on this?" Dyer interrupted before Nolan could answer.

"Doc and I will do it," Jackson said. DeLuca began to speak but Jackson cut him off. "No. We've run VBSS (Vessel Boarding Search and Seizure) missions as a team but this is one instance where we have to go in with the absolute minimum. A full assault team would increase the odds of compromising the mission."

"If by sections you mean, do I have any diagrams of a Caldarian fleet battle ship, the answer is no," Nolan stated. "However, we do have layout schematics of Caldarian vessels we have destroyed and managed to examine. They seem to have the same basic layout."

Nolan turned to his data link and tapped in a command. A three dimensional cutaway of a Caldarian cruiser appeared on the display and slowly rotated. He tapped the keypad again and a small red triangle appeared slightly forward and center of the vessel's midsection. A thin red line could be seen leading from the main docking bay to the triangle. The team gazed at the display.

"Let's set it up," Jackson said. "Chief, I want you and Dyer to rig a mock-up of this in the cargo bay. DeLuca, you go back to engineering with Chief Sheenan and get those suits ready. Doc's suit is OK but I'll need whatever you have that will fit. Our battle suits are good for short duration exposure to vacuum and with any kind of luck, we'll be in and gone like thieves before they even know anyone was there. Once they do figure it out, it's going to shock the living hell out of them."

"That's exactly what is going to buy the Confederacy time," Nolan stated emphatically. "At least time to regroup and get ready for the escalation this is going to produce."

"You mean the blood bath this is going to produce, don't you, Commander?" Hearst asked.

Nolan turned to her. "Yes," he replied quietly, "that's exactly what I mean."

"How long do we have Commander, before we get to the Caldarian security envelope?" Jackson asked.

"Forty-six hours, give or take," Nolan said.

Jackson looked at Hearst and then at the rest of the team. "We practice it until we have it cold and then we take our Zirlaxin and power sleep for three hours."

"The Haida will bring you in close, release the shuttle from inside their security envelope and then wait at the downloaded grid location for your signal. From there, it's just a short jump to the Sixth," Nolan said.

"This is all very interesting but time's wasting and we have a mock-up to build," DeLuca said, bringing everyone's attention back to the immediate task at hand.

Jackson smiled and nodded his assent. He turned his attention back to the diagram.

"See this docking skeg right here?" He pointed his finger to a small section of hull plating that had a ninety-degree bend facing forward of the main docking bay.

"The shuttle will latch onto the hull just above and slightly behind the docking bay on this corner. Ensign Chantella, do you think there's enough room to hover and hide at that point?"

Chantella studied the diagram and slowly nodded her head. "Yes, Sir, that shouldn't be a problem. What worries me is that somebody might get close enough to bump us. They may not be able to see us but if they physically touch us, then it's game over and I don't even want to think about the amount of electronic energy that will be sweeping over us.

"Only at the envelope edge," Nolan spoke. "Once you're clear of that and inside, it should be relatively calm."

"Yeah, calm like the eye of a hurricane," Hearst growled.

"We have to take that chance," Jackson told her. He looked around the room.

"According to the little intelligence we have, if you're detected while in the docking bay, the doors will begin their auto-shut down sequence." Nolan paused and looked Jackson in the eye. "That means you'll have about six minutes to get out, maybe eight, max, before the bay doors shut and they pressurize the interior."

"Which means we're dead," Hearst stated flatly.

"That's why they pay us the big bucks, Doc," Jackson drawled.

Sheenan hesitated, and then spoke. "What are you going to take for weapons, Sir? If you go in there with a particle weapon of any kind, it's going to light up every internal security net on board."

"We take two hand pistols," Jackson responded, "one a conventional phase pistol, the other a silenced Glock 341. We bring the conventional particle pistol as back up. The Glock is a special issue stealth pistol used by the 4th battalion of the Ramillion Marine recon regiment. The Ramillion military purchased a patent to the original Glock 340 and tailored it for their own specific needs."

Jackson didn't elaborate on what those 'specific needs' were but Nolan thought he had a pretty good idea of what they entailed.

"The body is molded from a single piece of Kevalum composite epoxy and just before they lay the barrel, a Chameleon underlay is bonded in place. It runs off a very small stealth power cell and is virtually invisible."

"I notice the barrel is smooth. How do you sight?" Sheenan asked.

"The targeting optics are linked into the HUD display in the battle mask," Jackson replied evenly. "Each pistol issued has a matching silencer tube which is good for the life of the pistol." He glanced sidelong at Hearst. "And they stay in their suit holsters until the last moment," he added.

"And how do you see each other if the suit's cloaking works as good as you claim it does, Lieutenant?" Sheenan asked.

"In order to stay in sight when the suit's cloaking electronics are on, a very small thoracic signal is emitted through a lens-like opening, called a peep aperture, on the suit's dorsal array. Everyone has a distinct thoracic signature, Chief," Jackson said.

"Before deploying, the suits are programmed with each team member's specific thoracic signature. When we cloak, the suit sensors detect those signals and the electronics in the battle helmets project a holographic image of each team member on the HUD. The signal is extremely narrow and ultra low power and the aperture can be set to localize the signal even further in extreme cases, or open it up and increase the distance as field and terrain dictate.

"When we go in, we'll have the aperture set narrow and detection distance to one meter. If necessary, we can change that on the fly or set it on auto or even momentarily turn it off, if the suit detects movement or a sweeper loop," Jackson told Sheenan. "But we will be going in with all active systems in standby mode. The only electronics that will be emitting are the Element cloaking circuits and the absorption and dispersal grids. We know the suits work, from our contact with the legion platoon on the planet's surface," he finished grimly. And I have three dead team members and I've only retrieved two bodies, Jackson added to himself. He looked at Sheenan. "What's on your mind, Chief?" he asked when he saw the questioning look in her eyes.

"What about pressure plates in the deck and bulkheads? If you set off any of those, it won't matter that you're invisible. Any of those weight sensitive squares set in the deck or bulkhead panels would set off an alarm once their weight detection threshold was compromised."

"No, not on board a ship. A fortified ground installation would no doubt have them in place but it would be too difficult to have them set up in passageways on a ship and most navies consider themselves," he glanced sidelong at Nolan, "safe from intruders in space. We plan to prove that theory wrong," he finished flatly.

"Right then," Nolan said. "I'll start the log. Lieutenant, could I have a word with you before you leave?"

Jackson turned back and saw the Commander looking at him with a frank expression on his face and he tried to frame an answer for the question he knew was coming.

"Mr. Jackson, are you up to this?" Nolan asked.

CHAPTER 18
THE VALLEY

"…'E's the on'y thing that doesn't give a damn
For a Regiment o' British Infantree!
So 'ere's to you, Fuzzy-Wuzzy, at your 'ome in the Soudan;
You're a pore benighted 'eathen but a first-class fightin' man;
An' 'ere's to you, Fuzzy-Wuzzy, with your 'ayrick 'ead of 'air—
You big black boundin' beggar—for you broke a British square!"

—Rudyard Kipling

"Sir, Doctor Fitzpatrick told me that fourteen hours on the tissue re-structuring beam and my arm will be as good as new," Jackson told him.

"No, that's not what I'm referring to. Your arm should be fine by the time the mission goes down. Are you and your team OK?" he asked pointedly.

Jackson felt the heat rising from deep inside but he checked himself before he let it get the better of him. He knew the fine line he was walking here and what the impact of his words and emotions could have if he wasn't careful. He chose his next words carefully.

"Commander, none of us, including your crew and yourself, ever expected this mission to go the way it has. We have all seen and done things that we hope we will never ever see or do again and that will haunt our darkest nightmares for the rest of our lives. And yet from all you have said, this is just the beginning and these are the opening rounds in an escalating conflict that we have no means of winning without the Element. Our people are tired, your people are tired. But it's more than just simply being physically tired. This tired is deeper than all that. Tired people make mistakes and they tend to focus and lash out at whatever is closest. Right now, what's closest is one another and that could very well prove to be a worse enemy than the Caldarians." Jackson stopped, struggling to find the right words before continuing.

"From what you said to the crew, including my team, and I think it was the right thing to say and the right way to handle the situation." Jackson looked at Nolan and there was a dark glitter in his eyes that made Nolan go cold. When Jackson spoke there was a hard edge to his voice.

"Commander, my people are ready. I'm ready. Doc Hearst is one of the best field operators I've ever worked with. We call her the Ice Queen, Commander because she's so calm when the shit hits the fan that she doesn't even blink or break a sweat. She's been in more fire-fights and black OP strikes than anyone else with the possible exception of the Chief. I'm taking her in because she wants to go and I know that whatever goes down, she'll be rock steady. So if you don't like that, I suggest you send a priority black pulse bead to Captain Ortello back on the Lady and ask that I be relieved. But you better hurry Commander, because you're pissing away valuable time with this rah-rah bullshit warm and fuzzy question game!" Jackson and Nolan stared at each other for a hard moment and then Nolan nodded, a small smile forming at the corner of his mouth. "Right then, let's get to work. We have forty-six hours."

"OK, let's run it again, Doc," Jackson said. They were tired. They had been going through the mockup they had built using the Haida's small holo-generator, as she streaked for home. That was thirty-two hours ago. The first time through the scenario, they had been detected and executed by a remote cutting laser before they had gone ten meters. They had made adjustments to the suits' filtering parameters and had made it to the admiral's door, only to be blocked trying to enter his cabin.

Jackson's arm ached and his head felt like two needles were being driven into his temples.

"The only way in without detection is to wait until someone else goes in and then slide in right behind them," Hearst said. She had been thinking about this for several hours and knew it was the only way.

Jackson nodded wearily. "You're right, Doc. That's the way we'll work it. It's the time factor I'm worried about. Let's run it one more time and if we get a green board, we'll call it a night and get some rack time." They ran the simulation once more and got a green sweep on the CFSIM (Combat field simulation) board. Jackson looked around at the team. "Thoughts? Suggestions? Comments?"

"One point," DeLuca said. "I think you had better take two extra clips with you."

Hearst winked at Dyer and said, "Somehow, Inspector Gadget, I don't think two extra clips are going to be much help should we be found that deep in bad guy land."

Jackson looked at her. Something had happened to her in the last twelve hours and she was almost back to her old, irascible self again. He saw the exchange between her and Dyer and had to control the smile on his face.

"OK," he said. "Rack time."

The team put away their gear and left to eat and get some rest. They had no trouble finding bunks. There were plenty of empty ones. The chief lingered behind and sat down with his back against the shuttle. Jackson came back out of the crew compartment and sat down beside him.

"How's the shoulder, Chief?" he asked.

"It's coming, Sir. Doc Fitzpatrick repaired the bone and muscle but it will take special treatment on the Hopkins to restore it to pass the certification board." They were silent for a moment, each occupied with their own thoughts.

"What's your gut on this one, Chief?" Jackson asked quietly. The chief sighed. He took a sip of his Raxillian coffee before he spoke.

"I've been in the teams for twenty years, Sir. I was with Whiskey platoon when that hunter killer team was waiting for us and stalked us for six days on the frontier world of Griffon. That one was bad. But nothing has been as bad as the one we just completed. There's something about Zilith that is going to give me nightmares for a long time. It wasn't the Blackies. We've been dealing with them for a long time. No, it's the planet. It feels—I don't know—evil. You can feel it when you enter the system and it just gets stronger. It chases you, pushes you. We didn't know at first what it was and just brushed it off as stress and worry or whatever you want to call it but it's the planet. This one is going to break all the old mission records Sir, believe me." Jackson nodded in agreement.

"There're so many variables on this one it's tough to gauge which way it will go. What if all our intelligence is wrong? What if the Caldarians have more security inside their fleet security envelope than we think? What if the layout is all wrong and you get lost in the command ship? It's not like you can call for an extraction bird and we'll come and get you. Once you're inside you either do what has to be done and get out or it's over. End of story. Too many 'what ifs'." His voice trailed off.

Jackson swirled the dregs of his lukewarm coffee around his mug and gulped it down. The two men sat silent for a moment longer, each lost in his own thoughts. Finally, Jackson rose.

"Thanks, Chief. I think you're right but we have to try. It's all we got. Get some sleep." Jackson left and went to his bunk.

Jackson heard a soft whimper and paused beside the small curtain enclosure where Ensign Chantella lay. Nightmares he thought, and continued to his own small cubicle deciding not to awaken her.

Fog and mist were creeping across the ground and small tendrils were winding around the landing struts. The lights on the shuttle were not working. Every time Chantella ran a full diagnostic, she got a green board but still the lights refused to come on. The darkness outside was almost complete. There was just enough ambient light for her to see the creeping fog. It only increased her anxiety. She could feel fear like a blanket, sucking her life away but she couldn't move. Something was wrong with her battle harness and it held her fast in her seat. She squirmed and moved, fighting against the restraint, but it only tightened. The door to the crew compartment was open but the lights weren't working. She could make out the sleeping forms of the team but they weren't sleeping. They were dead. Each one's chest cavity had been torn open and the heart had been ripped out. She could reach her controls but they wouldn't respond to her commands. She could turn her head just enough to see the rear hatch. The fog reached higher and the wind began to tear at it, making it shift and twist as if tortured souls from some hellish abode were trying to break away from the planet that held them prisoner. And then she heard the noise. It was soft at first but grew steadily louder, and suddenly she realized what it was. She twisted her head and watched the rear hatch. Something was trying the opening mechanism. "Oh God no, please no," her mind screamed. She twisted and pulled desperately at the harness but it held her in its grip. The handle on the hatch began to twist and move slowly, inexorably, to the open position. She screamed and swung her head wildly from side to side and then her screams changed to a soft, whimpering sob. "No, please no, Nanna, please no." The lever continued to move.

Chantella sat bolt upright in her bunk and stared wildly at her surroundings. She was soaked with sweat. She blinked vacantly and her racing heart slowed. Without warning, her stomach heaved and she reached for the waste bucket she kept close and wretched. She was having trouble keeping anything down and the nightmares were getting worse. Tonight was the worst yet. She wondered what would happen if the hatch ever opened. She desperately hoped it wouldn't. Maybe she should go see the Haida's doc and see if she could get something to help her sleep. She reached for her water flask and took a sip, then drank a little more, the cool liquid trickling down her throat. She lay back down and closed her eyes. She hoped the nightmares would stay in the shadows for the rest of the night.

They called it an envelope even though it was a dense, outer perimeter of patrol craft with overlapping fields of coverage. But the coverage was so complete that it formed an electronic wall that was as impossible to get through undetected as if it were made of terillium steel.

"Commander?" Petrie, the electronics technician, called.

"Go ahead, Mr. Petrie," Nolan said.

"Commander, we'll be at envelope breach in ten minutes, all systems are nominal and the cannon coils are offline," he reported. Every electronic system except essentials was shut down. They were on passive only.

"Wild," Stacy thought. "If we misjudge by a nanosecond, then wham, space dust."

"Roger, envelope breach in ten," Nolan replied. "OK, let's see what we're up against. Put it on the viewer and set for long range."

The viewer came alive and as it zoomed out, every person on the bridge gasped. Immediately in front of them, all along the envelope edge, were frigates, destroyers and robotic patrol drones in every direction, and deeper in toward the center, hundreds of larger vessels.

"Envelope breach," Stacy called out. "Another eight minutes to shuttle launch, Skipper."

Ensign Karen Gabriel gazed at the view screen. "Oh, my God. We're fucked—totally, completely, turkey-ass fucked."

"Sir, there are three picket lines converging on us. Eight patrol frigates and four fleet class destroyers are crossing abeam. All arrays are picking up multiple sensor sweeps. My God, I've never seen anything like this. We have a straight red board, Skipper," Petrie said, his voice tight with tension.

"Helm, drop us to full sub-light. Set course one-five-five, mark four-two and take us in nice and easy," Nolan said. "Set helm controls for emergency attitude evasion and watch your TAC display, Ms. Gabriel."

"Aye, Sir, full sub-light engaged, coming to course one-five-five, mark four-two," Gabriel responded without taking her eyes off her display. She was focused, her initial shock at the sight of the vast armada forgotten. The bridge and the people on it were fading into the twilight area that surrounded her when she was driving. It was like her senses were heightened, her acuity sharpened. She heard every command, could almost anticipate the course changes and attitude corrections. Her responses were so smooth and instant that Nolan marveled at her intuitive precision.

"I was born for this," she whispered to herself. "Let's rock!"

On the tactical display an astral grid displayed every vessel and drone out as far as the far envelope edge on the other side of the battle group. For the moment, she wasn't concerned with anything that was beyond the envelope. It was cluttered with moving, twisting, hostile craft, each one lashing out with active sensors. She had set the combat navigational system on auto and it catalogued and identified each contact, maneuvering according to which one it interpreted as the most threatening. She would only override the system if it was overwhelmed by the number of contacts and went 'petulant' because it couldn't decide which contact posed the worst threat. She had never seen the system overwhelmed but she had never been in the heart of a Caldarian battle group either. There was a first time for everything.

You could feel fear and tension on the Haida. Every crewmember was aware of it and in their own way, dealt with it as best they could.

In the shuttle bay, Jackson and Hearst sat in the crew compartment with their battle harnesses strapped tight. They had spent the early evening meticulously going over their suits and integrated load-bearing harnesses. They checked and then had the chief and DeLuca go over every square inch of the suits to ensure that there was nothing that would rub, rattle or make the slightest sound as they moved.

"What's the point of being invisible if, every time you take a step, you sound like a servo-tray with an out-of-synch gravity damper?" Jackson had growled.

The cockpit hatch was open and Jackson could see Ensign Chantella sitting at the controls. He hesitated, then unbuckled his harness and strode to the cockpit entrance. Jackson put a gloved hand on her shoulder and gave it a light squeeze. She started.

"You OK?" he asked.

Chantella hesitated and then nodded. "I'll be OK, Sir. Just tired, that's all."

Jackson watched her. She's coming apart, he thought. Calm on the outside, breaking up on the inside.

He nodded his head in understanding. "I know what you mean. I've been having trouble sleeping myself. Every time I fall asleep, I find myself back on Zilith and can feel something stalking me. I run but no matter how fast or how far I run, it's always behind me, getting closer. Then I wake up."

"He has them too," she said to herself and a wintry smile touched her lips. Chantella stared at him, her eyes like huge saucers.

How do I reach her? I have thirty seconds, he thought desperately. "But then I realize it's just a dream. We lost people, good people, and if I fold now, I'll be letting them down. And I just won't let that happen, Marcie. You're a good driver, one of the best I've seen. You hung in there when we were ass deep and you pulled us out." He stood up and looked down at her. "You looked over the edge, Ensign, and you're still here. Don't believe the whispers. I learned long ago that they are all lies."

Jackson stepped back down into the crew compartment and strapped his battle harness back in place. In the cockpit, Chantella felt as if she was coming out of a dark dream and the clouds were starting to part. Not much but enough to realize that it was going to be OK.

"Chief, turn off the gravity dampers, all hands rig for zero 'G'," Nolan called out over the ship COM system. All over the ship, servo seats and cleat plates went active, ready to maintain attitude relative to the ship's skew or roll. It was something they practiced and drilled on a regular basis.

"Aye, Skipper, gravity dampers nominal," Chief Sheenan replied.

"Sir, we just passed through two picket lines. We are approaching the inner horizon," Petrie said.

The Haida rolled and her bow lifted suddenly. Everyone tensed and there was dead silence.

"Come on, sweetheart," Gabriel whispered to herself.

Why does every helmsman I've ever flown with talk to the ship as if they owned it, Nolan wondered as the bow went vertical and the Haida skewed to port.

"Whoa," she cried, "that was close! Here comes another one. Down we go, breaking to starboard. Axis skew!" she cried out gleefully. The Haida slewed around on her axis and did a tumble as she maneuvered clear. "Over the river and through the woods, to grandmother's house we go," she sang softly to herself.

"We just passed through, around and over a squadron of robotics, Skipper. Damn, this invisible shit works! They didn't even blink or change course, 'cuz if they had, we'd be crow bait." She broke off as the Haida heeled and came about again. "Sorry Sir, we just passed through another ring of drones, two Cadak-class patrol frigates approaching from the port beam. They're sweeping. Coming abreast, passing aft, Sir. They missed us. Yeah, baby," she cried out.

"God damn it, Ensign, can't you at least keep your chortles and inane babbling to yourself?" Nolan growled, more in relief than in seriousness. He grinned. It was working. He could sense the mood on the bridge shifting.

"Inner perimeter breach, we've passed inside, boards are going nominal, Sir. Shuttle release in two minutes. Sir, the Shimmering Wind is coming up on our port side, her screening vessels are probing," Stacy exclaimed.

"OK, time to make like a hole in the water, to coin an old saying," Nolan said. "XO, start the clock. Helm, initiate pattern Hotel-Tango. That'll bring us to within fifty kilometers of the Shimmering Wind and let us take whatever evasive maneuvers we need to stay clear of attending vessels and patrol craft."

"Initiating pattern hotel-Tango, aye, Commander," Gabriel breathed.

Nolan swiveled in his battle chair and hit a closed command link on his COM console. "Lieutenant Jackson?" he called.

"Here, Commander," Jackson replied. Ensign Chantella was in the cockpit, her hands hovering over her controls, waiting for the Haida's helm override to disengage. The shuttle doors were open and they were hovering in standby mode. Jackson and Hearst had taken their Zirlaxin and slept for three solid hours. They had received their briefing along with the rest of the team in CIC, on the Haida's bridge.

"Good luck, Lieutenant. See you at the Lex."

"Thank you, Commander," Jackson replied.

The Haida continued on her course toward the Shimmering Wind, rolling and tumbling as her auto NAV systems took over the flying as they passed picket vessels and altering course to try and stay away from the densest concentration of patrol craft. The bridge crew watched in breathless awe as the towering shapes of two interdiction cruisers approached. Instead of heeling over, the Haida headed inward to drive between them as Ensign Gabriel overrode the NAV system.

"God, I hope Gabriel knows what she's doing," the XO breathed. What the hell, he thought, in for a penny, in for a pound. I might as well sit back and enjoy the ride.

They held their breath. No one moved. They would either make it or they wouldn't. It was too late now. The cruisers closed. Stacy watched in horrified fascination. He could see the epoxite seams on their Chameleon grid coating and could even make out strange, alien hieroglyphics along the side. He was counting small, round openings on the side, thinking they looked vaguely familiar, when he realized that he was looking at gun ports—fourteen of them. He shuddered.

Nolan read the harsh, alien-looking writing. He knew enough Caldarian to make out the names on both vessels.

"The cruiser Kutarak and..." suddenly his face tightened and went dark with anger, "the Drudaris 'Darkness' and 'Wind of Storm'. The Wind of Storm was one of the cruisers that helped kill the Sussex. She moved in to close range and hammered her long after she was dead," he said tightly.

The bridge crew breathed a collective sigh of relief as the cruisers receded astern.

"That was fun," Stacey grated. His hands were locked in a death grip on his weapons console.

"Five hundred kilometers and closing on the Shimmering Wind, Commander," the XO called out.

"Shuttle away," Stacy called.

"Affirmative," Nolan breathed. "OK people, let's stay sharp. We may be invisible but that doesn't mean somebody won't try to fly through this particular piece of space were sitting in. XO, start the clock." He watched as Crichton punched a key and the clock in the bottom, right hand corner of the view screen started counting down. "Oh, and by the way, congratulations. We're the first Confederates to see the heart of a Caldarian battle formation and lived to tell about it."

"Let's hold on the 'lived to tell about it' part," Gabriel said.

"Three hours," Nolan thought, looking at the clock. "Three hours to Armageddon."

Jackson and Hearst caught glimpses through the alumina-matrix windscreen as the shuttle twisted and spun toward the Shimmering Wind. Chantella was flying the shuttle manually. At one point, she had reversed course and stood the little shuttle on its tail to avoid three robotic sentries that were weaving back and forth from the Shimmering Wind in long, slow, S-loops. Jackson winced and closed his eyes as two small drones converged and grew large in the windscreen, only to pass below the shuttle as she streaked in.

"OK, here we go," she called out. "The docking bay is coming into view. We have telemetry on Whisker One and Two, all systems are nominal. Docking Whiskers One and Two are passing horizon zero. I'm moving us in." She watched her threat board. It had gone completely red the moment they had left the Haida. Now it started to change color and the lines indicating several different sensor passbands began to shrink and recede. "Passing shadow horizon," she cried out. "We have a residual board, all systems are nominal."

They had entered beneath the Shimmering Wind's envelope of electronic surveillance. They were in. The shuttle looked like a flea beside a Dudarian Grondak, a huge pachyderm in the Dudara system.

"Easy," she breathed. "We don't want to bump you, honey, we just want to spend a few parking tokens, that's all. Then we're going to fucking kill you, you black bitch. But life sucks, I know," Chantella said tightly.

Jackson and Hearst shared a glance and Hearst winked at him. He shook his head and smiled. "Goddamn shuttle jocks," he whispered ostentatiously.

"I heard that!" Chantella said from the cockpit. "OK boys and girls, time to party!

"We are at station lock and in hover and hide mode. Stand-off distance is two meters," she reported. Chantella gazed out her view screen and for the first time was hit by the sheer, massive bulk of the Shimmering Wind. Even fleet carriers would be dwarfed by this thing. Her mouth was dry and she felt her skin crawl.

"Roger your hide and stand-off of two meters," Jackson confirmed.

But at least we're in sensor shadow and in relative darkness, Chantella thought to herself. She still couldn't believe where they were.

Jackson thumbed his NAV display and set the clock. "OK, Doc, three hours, let's go."

He hit the release button, the rear hatch opened and he stepped out. He drifted two meters over to the hull plating and his magnetic cleats took hold. A moment later, Doc Hearst joined him. For a moment they stood and stared. Jackson felt Hearst's hand on his shoulder and caught the faint sound as she gulped air. He watched his bio-scan. They were both hyperventilating. He didn't blame her. Nothing in Jackson's experience or wildest nightmares had prepared him for the incredible vista before him. The dark hull of the Shimmering Wind stretched above and below them as far as he could see and vanished into the utter dark of space. She was so vast that the curvature of her hull was invisible. Even the brilliant arc lights surrounding the huge docking bay looked small and insignificant from where they were standing. He felt lightheaded and, for a moment, thought he was going to pitch forward and float away as the sheer mass and presence of the vessel overwhelmed him. He put a hand out to touch the hull and steadied himself. His head reeled. Steady, he told himself. He reached a hand out and gripped Hearst, moving his helmet so that it was touching hers and risked a transmission.

Jackson clutched her helmet. "Doc, Doc. Focus. Look at me. We're both hyperventilating. Relax and breathe with me. Doc, don't look down or up, look at me! It's just another ship. We've done this a hundred times. Breathe!" he hissed. Slowly their breathing stabilized and they relaxed. She patted his arm twice.

"OK, I'm OK," she said. "Let's do this and go home."

They moved out. The door to the docking bay was fifty meters below them. They had exchanged their normal suit gauntlets and boots for specially designed infiltration gear. They were double cushioned and had magnetic suction concaves that could be used in magnetic clamp mode or as suction manipulators, allowing them to scale non-metallic surfaces without radiating an electronic signature.

Jackson led toward the open maw of the docking bay and then lowered himself slowly until he was at the lip. He adjusted the peep aperture that allowed him to see Hearst, so that she was just within the passband at one point five meter's distance. He could hear his breathing echoing in his ears and told himself to relax.

Suddenly he tensed and held up his right fist. Behind him, Hearst froze in place and looked around, trying to identify the threat axis. She watched as Jackson took a step back, then another, and lifted his right leg in the air. She looked down and grinned in relief. A hull spider, a small robotic tracking drone, had scuttled away right under Jackson's legs, totally oblivious to the presence of the two SEALs. Hearst heard Jackson let out his breath and grinned behind her battle mask. She was about to make a comment but checked herself.

It was like being a mouse trying to tiptoe through a room full of sleeping cats. You know if one wakes up, it's going to be a fight, and if he catches you, that's it, Hearst thought to herself.

They reached the bay opening, knelt down and peered over the edge. The bay was relatively empty. They were between cycles and it was the midnight watch, according to Caldarian time. That should be helpful, Jackson thought. No, I hope it's helpful, he corrected himself. He pointed toward the rear of the docking bay. Hearst nodded her head and made a circle with the thumb and forefinger of her right hand. His first fear was unfounded. He had worried that the shuttle would have an energy shield and that the entire cavernous bay would be pressurized but it wasn't. There was an air lock at the rear of the bay that provided access to crews and personnel boarding or disembarking.

They slid over the edge and sank down. Jackson used the outer edge of the bay opening to launch himself inside and down toward what he hoped was the exit to the corridors and passageways leading into the ship's interior. There were several vessels inside, disembarking passengers and two Class IV courier birds that Jackson recognized from intelligence photos. The hackles on the back of his neck rose as the realization of how close they were to the enemy flooded in. The soft rubber of their boots made contact with the deck and they came to a halt, both of them panting.

Now comes the hard part, Jackson thought, playing dodge ball with a ship full of Caldarians. He slid along the wall and watched the people moving in and out. There was no security. The air lock doors operated on a simple lockout mechanism that was operated by a palm pad on the side.

Complacency. Thank God the Caldarians think they're invincible. Well, we're going to help them change that attitude real quick, Jackson thought grimly.

He and Hearst inched forward and stopped, waiting for a lull in the stream of traffic. Giving the signal to climb, Jackson and Hearst reached up and their boots took hold. They climbed until they were two meters above the ground, where Jackson could just reach the door switch by leaning out and down with his right hand. They were just in time. The doors hissed open and a squad of legionnaires came out, heading for a courier shuttle. If they had stayed where they had been, they would surely have made contact as the squad went past. Jackson waited five minutes before moving again.

He checked the time. It had taken them twenty minutes to get to the air-lock doors.

"Now or never," he said. Jackson reached down and hit the button and the air lock doors opened. They slid over the lip, clinging to the bulkhead and felt gravity return and the brush of air on their suits as the air lock was pressurized and the interior doors slid open. Moving as quickly as they dared, they slipped over the edge and dropped to the corridor which was lit with a soft red glow from the overhead and bulkhead glow panels. They must rig for circadian rhythms the same way we do, Jackson thought. They were inside the Shimmering Wind.

They pressed themselves tight against the bulkhead walls. Every single nerve ending in Hearst's body was screaming at her to bolt and run. The alien script on the walls and the occasional sound of an announcement tore at her senses. The lighting was dimmer and less intrusive than the night lighting on Confederate vessels. Every fifty meters or so there were small enclaves or indents in the walls and Jackson couldn't figure out what purpose they served until several Caldarians came around a corner, two of them pushing a servo tray in the opposite direction. As they went by, the two pushing the tray pulled into an alcove, allowing the others to pass.

As Jackson and Heart passed corridors branching off and fading into the heart of the ship, they felt a mounting panic. They passed turbo-lifts and closed doorways, hoping and praying that no one would enter the corridor they were in. They both watched anxiously as the ghostly red line on their HUD display indicated that they were to look for a right turn that would lead them to the turbo-lift, which would take them to the command deck and the passage that held the High Admiral's quarters. Without warning, a hatch opened and three Caldarians exited, walking directly toward them. Each held a darter and one had a sniffer box that he held at arm's length in front of him as they walked. Jackson and Hearst hurriedly scrambled up the bulkhead and clung to the deck lexite. Jackson tensed as the three unsuspecting Caldarians passed directly beneath them.

Jackson let them pass and waited for them to turn the corner. But the last Caldarian in line stopped and turned, gazing back down the passageway. He said something to the others and they turned, weapons up.

Oh shit, Jackson thought. His arms ached and he could feel sweat trickling out of every pore of his body. His left arm was beginning to tremble from the strain. He glanced at Hearst. At first he thought he was hallucinating as he watched Hearst's right hand slowly inching downward toward her holster. He watched in horror as her hand reached the flap.

"Don't do it!" his mind screamed at her. "Stop!"

Suddenly the Caldarian with the sniffer box said something and made an obscene gesture with his hand toward his crotch. The others laughed and they turned and continued on their way.

Jackson looked for Hearst. He couldn't see her. He searched desperately and was about to use the COM, when he noticed a shadowy blur crouched in a recess. He dropped silently to the deck and moved to her side.

"I'm OK, I'm OK," she repeated. "I was losing my grip and I had to get down and the only safe place was this recess in the bulkhead."

"We're almost there," Jackson told her. "We just have to take the turbo-lift and we exit on the command floor."

"What an understatement," she stated flatly. "Just take the turbo lift, whack the Admiral and we can go home. Do you wanna ring the bell or should I?" she asked tightly.

Jackson tapped her on the shoulder and pointed. "Right there, Doc," he said. It was the turbo lift.

It was when they entered the turbo lift that they felt like caged rats waiting to die. The ride to the command deck took eight seconds but it was the longest eight seconds of Hearst's life. She thought her heart was going to burst. She was tired and couldn't blink the sweat out of her eyes. Hearst felt that shadow of deep calm that always descended upon her in battle. Her heightened acuity made every sound and object seem sharply etched. She and Jackson had backed up against the wall on opposite sides of the door and had pressed themselves as flat as they could. They had to get into the corridor before the doors closed. She tensed.

The lift stopped and the door opened silently. They waited. A guard stuck his head in and his eyes scanned the elevator. His arm held the control panel and kept the door from sliding closed. Jackson averted his gaze as the guard looked directly at and through him to the bulkhead behind him. The guard withdrew, shaking his head, and Jackson and Hearst made their move. Swiftly they passed through. Hearst felt the pressure and brush of the door's magnetic seal as it closed behind her.

They plastered themselves against the wall to catch their breath. Jackson gazed at the guard who was standing no more than three meters away. He was acutely conscious of the smallest detail. Jackson marveled at how clean and crisp the guard's uniform was compared to his own and wondered how he would feel if he was in flag country, then realized in a perverse sort of way that he was. He checked the time. One hour and thirteen minutes had passed.

It took ten more minutes to make their way to the door leading to what they hoped was the High Admiral's cabin.

"Thank God, there're no door guards," Hearst whispered to Jackson. They were close enough that they could exchange muted whispers but Jackson held up his fingers in front of his battle mask, signaling Hearst to be silent.

They waited. They dared not move or attempt the door. Around a corner a crewmember approached, pushing a servo tray. In front of it strode a huge Caldarian dressed in a captain's uniform. Jackson tensed. Something told him this was it. He motioned to Hearst and they both drifted to the other side of the corridor, waiting. The uniformed Caldarian entered a code and the hatch slid open. Hastily Jackson and Hearst glided in behind them as the hatch hissed shut. They immediately separated and moved along the walls to take up flanking positions on either side of the room.

Jackson stared at High Admiral Corack-Va-Morlaris. His honor braid held a single knot entwined by a brilliant blue sapphire thread, a mark of the highest honor.

The steward bowed and exited.

Jackson knew they had no time to waste in listening and loitering. They hadn't come here to gather intelligence, they had come to assassinate the High Admiral and get out. He reached down to his holster and could see Hearst, across from him, doing the same thing. They had already briefed how it was to go down. Jackson was to take out the Admiral and Hearst was to act as security and take out anyone else in the room.

"Captain Dercelus, thank you for coming on such short notice," the Admiral said. His voice was hoarse and deep. The captain bowed. "I have the attack plans ready," the Admiral said. "The Sipedesis has failed. I shall download the plans to your command console and we shall attack as soon as helm orders are given. We have sat idle too long, I fear. It is time to kill these Confederates. Once we destroy the forces in front of us, the assault ships, along with the attending flight elements, shall move on the home worlds."

"Now," Jackson said to Hearst. They opened the peep aperture on their suits just enough to let the High Admiral and the Captain obtain a visual. Yes, we want you to know who it is, Jackson thought.

There was the softest whisper of sound as they drew out their silenced weapons and in that instant, the High Admiral and Captain Dercelus looked up to see the two shapes that had materialized like death shadows on either side.

"I don't think so," Jackson spoke softly in Caldarian, pulling the trigger twice.

The High Admiral's head snapped back and his body fell to the deck. He lay there, blood seeping from his empty eye sockets where two nine millimeter rounds had entered his skull. His face looked like there were crushed cherries where his eyes had been. The back of his skull had blown out as the rounds had expanded and exited, splattering the room with a fine mist of red and gray.

Captain Dercelus' lifeless body joined the Admiral's, the front of his face and skull blown apart by two similar rounds from Hearst's weapon that had entered the rear of his skull.

Never taking her eyes off the two still forms, Hearst spoke. "Tap, tap," she said softly.

Jackson reached down, picked up the two spent brass from his weapon and placed them gently on the Admiral's chest.

Jackson looked at the clock. Two hours and eight minutes had passed since they had left the shuttle.

"Let's go home, Doc," he spoke softly.

They moved cautiously down the corridor but found that they were almost running in their haste to get away, now that it was over. Not good, Jackson thought. He reached back and made contact with Hearst. They stopped and took a moment to catch their breath in a small recess. They could see the guard and the turbo lift in front of them.

He brought his helmet close to hers and opened the COM link using the helmet amplification system only. "We need to do this by the book, Doc, nice and slow, one step at a time, just the way we rehearsed it."

Hearst nodded her head in understanding.

They walked down the hallway. All was quiet and still, the only sound was the quiet hum of the environmental system and the air moving through the ventilation ducts. Just as they took station beside the turbo lift, wondering if they would have to kill the guard and take their chances, the door opened and two high ranking officers got out. As they passed, Jackson stared at the unit patch over the left breast on their uniforms.

Jackson and Hearst leapt into the lift. Jackson moved close to Hearst and grabbed her arm.

"We're in trouble. Those two Blackie officers are going to the Admiral's quarters."

"How in the hell do you know that?" Hearst whispered.

"Because the insignia on their fatigues is the Ninth Cohort of the 12th Legion, the same platoon we whacked on Zilith, and they aren't coming to drink tea."

"Oh, this is too rich," Hearst hissed, her voice taut with rage, fear and an overwhelming sense of despair. "It just keeps getting better and better. What is it with you, anyway? Are you a disaster magnet or what?"

"Doc, when we get out of the lift we need to move as fast as we can. It should only take twelve minutes to get back to the shuttle," he said, ignoring her anger. The door opened and they peeked out.

"All clear. Now for the last run. Let's go."

Jackson took off in a shambling run, following the shrinking red line on his HUD, willing it to go faster. They ran. As they turned a corner, Jackson pivoted and leapt for the ceiling, reaching out with his palms up. They gripped and held. He groaned as his arms took the weight. Hearst was flattened against the far bulkhead. Three legionnaires in full battle dress went boiling past.

They could see the docking bay through the clear alumina-matrix plate of the air lock. They ran. Suddenly, from all around them, an alarm klaxon began an incessant, brash clamoring. Doors flew open. There was chaos in the passageway.

"Too late," he whispered.

CHAPTER 19
LAST RACE

"Fall seven times and stand up eight."

—Japanese proverb

Legate Merethe Tranis was not looking forward to this 'interview' with the High Admiral. He cringed inwardly. Centurion Ensuris had failed, as unbelievable as that seemed to him, and it was a stain on the battle honor of the 12th Legion. High Legate Porlan Norst had called him a cycle ago and informed him that he had been summoned to the High Admiral's presence at once. He had dressed in full battle armor as befitted the request. He hoped he would not dishonor himself.

"Mind your words, Legate Tranis. Your life depends on it," High Legate Norst whispered as they approached the High Admiral's door. "Remember, it was your suggestion that we only send in Ensuris. Your fate hangs by a thread right now and a lot will depend on how you conduct yourself in the next half cycle." Tranis nodded but did not answer.

Norst pressed his palm against the door hollow and the door opened. They stepped in and the door shut silently behind them. Blood pooled and ran in little rivulets to their feet. Tranis and Norst stood and stared at the carnage in total, uncomprehending disbelief. Tranis blinked and stood rooted where he was standing.

Surely I'm dreaming and this is an awful nightmare. I'm in a punishment cube and they are testing my allegiance, he thought. Tranis took a faltering step, two, and looked down at the bodies. It was then that he noticed two small, shiny objects sitting on the High Admiral's chest. He stared at them in total confusion, and then comprehension dawned. Trembling, he reached down and lifted one of the spent brass in his fingers. Only once before had he ever seen such an object, but he remembered the event well. It was at an ambush site on the outpost world of Galena-One. He remembered walking through the site as part of the immediate reaction team sent as a follow-on force. There were hundreds of these small objects all over the ground in the thick cover a few yards off the trail. There were also fourteen dead legionnaires sprawled out on the trail.

He began to shake. His mouth worked but no sound came out.

"Tuva linsalis," he roared. It meant 'death marked'. He had recognized the small object for what it was but his mind refused to accept the reality of what those two small objects implied. It filled him with fear, a terrifying, choking fear that he had never before felt or experienced. Someone had accomplished the act but he did not yet know how they had executed it.

Probably some traitorous serving scum who had been paid by the Confederates to do this shameful, cowardly act, he told himself. The thought that their security had been breached and the Shimmering Wind penetrated did not yet enter his head. He hit a large triangular emergency response panel on the wall and raced from the compartment.

He never did find out how wrong he was.

Harsh alien words could be heard. The doors opened and a platoon of Blackies swept past as Jackson and Hearst dove through the air lock doors. Sounds gradually receded as the atmosphere was sucked out. Jackson motioned Hearst to climb. The hatch opened and they climbed out over the lip, into the docking bay. Lights were flashing overhead. Jackson and Hearst raced along the bulkhead and launched themselves upward onto the wall, where they began to climb frantically for the open bay doors and the relative freedom of space. Something in Jackson's peripheral vision drew his attention and he reflexively turned his head toward it. Several small lexite panels had been detonated by deployment charges and the broken lexite was lazily billowing outwards in a dense, red cloud of sifting powder that swirled around and engulfed them. Jackson recognized it immediately.

"Oh shit," he cried. "It's reflective epoxy. Someone blew the emergency locator nodes and it's filling the bay. Hurry," he shouted, "we're visible."

He looked up. He knew it took time for the chameleon circuits to absorb and adapt to the suit's outer layer and wondered if the advanced Element cloaking systems would adapt quicker. They were twenty meters from the bay doors.

"Climb," his mind screamed at him, "climb!"

Desperately they climbed, reaching for the doors. A brilliant arcing glow of light sparkled and rippled three meters below them. Particle rifle fire. He could see Hearst as she climbed. She looked like a bright red fire ant. Ten meters. The swirling red cloud of reflective resin was throwing off the legionnaires' aim on the deck. That won't last long, Jackson thought.

He had to admire the duty officer on night security. Complacent they may have been but the swiftness and intelligence of their response impressed him. He looked toward the doors and could see the brilliant glare of the vapor lamps and beyond them the dark, star-studded blanket of space. Something struck him a glancing blow on the leg and he looked down.

A legionnaire in full battle armor had launched from below and had struck the bay wall just below him. Hearst had reached the lip and was kneeling above him, her phase pistol in her hand, looking for a shot. He could see the outline of her helmet and then felt an iron fisted grip grab his right leg.

He looked down and saw the visored face of the legionnaire and his arm raising a particle pistol. Jackson could only watch. Time slowed and his vision narrowed to a small cone of light. The universe shrunk to a five-meter section of bulkhead panel in an alien ship under a backdrop of brilliant, artificial lighting. The center of that small universe was the right hand of an armored legionnaire and the high-density particle pistol he was bringing up. He could see the pistol coming up and he could see a dozen more legionnaires ascending toward him. He knew what that dense beam would do at this distance and exactly where the legionnaire would target the beam. He hoped it would be swift. He didn't relish the thought of dying by space decompression if the legionnaire's aim was off.

He was slipping.

"No-o-o-o-o!" Hearst screamed. The sound echoed and hammered through his COM link.

Then as he watched the legionnaire, his suit fabric glowed blue for a brief instant and vanished. There was a look of startled fear in the legionnaire's eyes as he released his grip on Jackson's leg and was thrown backward, cut in half by a particle beam.

Jackson stared unbelievingly. He looked below him and saw several bodies spinning and tumbling, their battle suits ripped open, their bodies cut in half or dismembered by the heavy fire.

"Move your goddamn ass, Lieutenant, we haven't got all day here," Chantella shouted over the tactical net. She was holding station just outside the docking bay with the attack shuttle, the particle cannon sawing back and forth as it laid down suppressing fire.

The hatch was open and Hearst was kneeling in the doorway, the eyepiece of a particle rifle locked in the sight cup of her battle helmet. Jackson pushed off and tumbled through the hatch as Hearst stepped aside. He felt the hatch hiss shut and felt the motion as the shuttle went to full sub-light. They were gone.

An electronic warfare technician stared at his display board. He couldn't believe what had just happened in the shuttle bay. The emergency locator nodes had detonated and suddenly two forms were detected high up on the docking bay wall, heading for the open bay doors. A reaction force had immediately gone after them and then something had just materialized in front of the docking bay like a specter and opened up with a particle cannon, a heavy particle cannon. He was just getting signature lock when the two small forms disappeared as if through a black hole, and all his displays went dead and the phantom image disappeared. It was like a window had momentarily opened and then snapped shut.

Jackson lay on the deck plating in a heap, hardly believing that he was alive. Hearst had broken the seal on her helmet and then helped Jackson remove his. She was slumped across from him with her back against the bulkhead, her particle rifle gripped tight in her gloved hands. Her eyes were shut tight and she was gulping air into her lungs in long gasps. Jackson struggled to his knees, crawled over to her and slumped beside her. Her left hand reached out and took his right hand and held it in a hard, tight grip. There were no words, only two weary, battered warriors who had looked over the edge together and had seen the reflection of their own fears.

In the cockpit, Chantella entered a single alpha letter into her communications console and hit the transmit button.

"First star on the right and straight on till morning," she whispered.

∽∾

The Haida
Nolan watched the clock. Two hours and forty-seven minutes had passed. If Jackson was successful, they should be receiving the single digit signal indicating they were away and breaking for Battle Group Six, now only minutes away. This would allow him to complete his part of the mission before they themselves broke for the Lex. The shuttle had long enough legs to get there on her own.

"Helm, one quarter sub, come to course zero-seven-two, mark zero-zero," he said.

"One quarter sub, coming to course zero-seven-two, mark zero-zero, aye, Sir," Gabriel said.

"Four hundred kilometers," Stacy breathed. "Two hundred, one hundred. Sir, we are holding station at fifty kilometers."

"Sir!" Petrie cried out, "I have a signal from Nightshade. Green board. Say again, green board."

Suddenly, a massive spike of electronic energy lit up his master control display, which was monitoring power fluctuations emanating from the Shimmering Wind. His face paled. There was only one thing that would cause such a massive power surge. The Shimmering Wind was getting ready to jump.

"Transients, we have power transients close aboard. Target has just charged her star coils, she's going to jump, Skipper!" he cried. Nolan cursed.

"Weaps, open outer doors on all tubes and standby to fire. Helm, attitude tango-x-ray on my mark," he shouted. "Skew roll, engage full sub now!"

The Haida moved in, her teeth bared. The order took milliseconds to execute.

"Fire!" Nolan shouted.

The Haida fired and her powerful fencing thrusters rolled her to starboard. Nolan could have fired all twelve tubes at once but he wanted each side to 'see' the target. The moment her port tubes were unmasked, she fired again. Twelve long lance mark 235 plasma torpedoes, with a stand-off kill range of five thousand kilometers, closed on a stationary target at a range of fifty kilometers.

In the massive engineering spaces on the Shimmering Wind, a dozen pairs of black gauntleted fists locked down the star drive main bus line. There was a momentary pause and then the huge charging capacitors discharged their stored energy into the plasma relay conduits. A dozen gold-visored helmets turned at the pulsing brilliance that suddenly blossomed along the starboard bulkhead. In the next instant, their bodies turned to ash and were consumed in the expanding heat wave as the long lance torpedoes found their mark.

The Shimmering Wind didn't have a chance. The moment the torpedoes ejected, every ship in the Caldarian fleet detected them. Threat boards went red and hundreds of pairs of uncomprehending eyes stared in disbelief. A few captains issued helm orders and sensors lashed out, searching for a return contact bearing and finding none. All they could do was watch the end of their honor as the twelve long lance torpedoes bored in. They ripped the Shimmering Wind her entire keel length. All twelve torpedoes had special penetration charges designed to defeat hardened ringed armor to a depth of fifty meters. They cut through the Shimmering Wind's belt armor like a knife through butter. Three penetrated to her reactor spaces and she novaed.

"Helm! New course one-nine-five, mark two-one, now!" Nolan cried out. "Chief, bring the particle cannons online, prepare to fire on my mark."

"Coming to one-nine-five, mark two-one, aye, Sir." Crichton looked up. "Sir? We just rolled out and hammer-headed back in. Where are we going?"

"Just a small detour, XO. We're going to kill a cruiser. Mr. Stacy, plot the track for the 'Wind of Storm' and give me a closing bearing."

Stacy watched his board. "Sir, she's come about and is heading for the Shimmering Wind's debris field." He looked up. "She's closing, Sir."

"Bring us in tight. We're going to pass directly below her and rake her the length of her keel line. Then I want to do an attitude roll-up and when we hit our base course, we're going to hit her again along her dorsal line and open her up like a tin of Ramillion Gudak. Chief, as soon as we fire, get ready to hit the big red button. We're going to jump and break for the Lex."

"Yuck," Gabriel said, "I hate Gudak."

The two ships closed.

"Steady, get ready, fire!"

The Haida dove and closed to one thousand meters below the unsuspecting cruiser. She rolled to starboard to bring her port cannons to bear. Six dense particle beams reached out and raked the Caldarian cruiser her full length. She didn't have her battle shields up, only her debris disrupters, and she reeled under the sudden onslaught. The Haida came about and closed once again, this time on the damaged cruiser's dorsal line.

On the Wind of Storm, the captain and bridge crew lay dead. The totally unexpected attack had caught them unprepared. The electronic warfare technician recognized the halo signature.

"Confederate line cruiser, close aboard," he shouted.

He was about to engage but then his tactical display went nominal. An ominous fear gripped him. Something told him they were dead.

He was still wondering how a Confederate battle cruiser had gotten through the security envelope when he died, as once again six dense particle beams cut the ship like a welding torch down her dorsal line. The stricken cruiser broke in half and came apart. The dense beams had cut several longitudinal support girders and the increased stresses on the remaining bulkhead supports were too much.

There is no air friction in space, no wind to tear at ripped hull sections or pressure squeezing a pressure hull as it would if a submarine sank below its crush depth. There are however, hundreds of kilometers of conduits, cables and piping, all part of the intricate and complex systems that power a starship. Despite redundant back-up systems and automatic damage control devices designed to keep a vessel moving and fighting, there were limitations to what they could do. Particle fire was designed to destroy those systems and consume power conduits. The inevitable chain reaction was an internal detonation that caused the main star drive components to nova. It was a crewmember's darkest nightmare.

The broken halves began to tumble, displaced by the impact of the particle fire, still on course, closing the huge debris field left when the Shimmering Wind had novaed.

Nolan watched the dead cruiser through the aft view screen. "That's for the Sussex," he said. "Helm, set a course for the Lexington."

"Now, Chief," he said. The Haida vanished. In a twinkling she was gone. She passed through the chaos and carnage she had created, slipped through the outer envelope and headed for the frontier between the two fleets.

❦❦

The USS Lexington

Senior Duty Officer, Lieutenant Commander Jack Wilson, sat bolt upright in his command chair in the Lexington's electronic warfare center. His threat board had just turned completely red.

"Oh shit," he cried. Every technician in the Corealus Combat System center was shouting out warnings as their boards went active across the entire spectrum. Wilson punched the direct COM link to Admiral Greig.

"Admiral, something just happened in the Caldarian center. We have target and acquisition arrays going off the board and..."

There was silence before he spoke again. His voice held a note of disbelief.

"Admiral, you're not going to believe this but residual ion scans indicate Confederate long lance torpedoes. Fuck! Something just hammered the shit out of the Shimmering Wind at close range, Sir. The Caldarians didn't even have time to evade. She just novaed. Admiral, the Shimmering Wind just blew apart. Something got up to knife fighting range and slit her throat, Sir."

"We have increased drive emissions on every Caldarian fleet unit."

In the Combat Information Center, Greig and McMann stared at each other in stunned silence.

"Admiral, we have movement along the entire sector. The entire Caldarian battle fleet is coming about," Wilson said, his voice shrill with tension.

Greig looked at McMann. "Here they come, Mitch."

He swung around. Greig hit a switch that opened his command circuit to every ship in the Sixth Battle Group.

"All flight elements, this is Condor One. This is not a drill; repeat, this is not a drill. Battle formation sierra-whiskey, launch strike craft now. Admiral Perseus, you've got the left flank. They're going to try and send in that squadron of heavy cruisers. We've nothing more out there and our line is spread thin. I'll try and swing the Hiryu your way but right now they're going to try and kill us first. If they manage to nova the center, then we're split and they can kill the rest of us at their leisure. Good luck and good hunting. Condor One, out."

Behind him McMann was giving helm orders.

Like a Yularian swamp slug, the formation shifted. Ships moved. The center changed shape as the screening cruisers and battleships moved up to their battle stations.

Three decks above, on the Lexington's massive flight ring, on four levels, two hundred and ninety Prometheus strike craft and three hundred Dark Ice fighters began their launch sequence. The formation swarmed like a stirred up hive of hornets as clouds of attack craft and fighters set course for the approaching Caldarians.

As the TAC officers adjusted course and prepared for the onslaught, the approaching Caldarian vessels swung away. Entire squadrons disappeared as they engaged their star drives. McMann watched the tactical plot as the Caldarian fleet vanished off every sensor array in the battle group.

"What the hell?"

A young electronic warfare technician in CIC screamed out a warning. "Contact bearing two-seven-zero, mark zero-zero, close aboard. There's a vessel de-cloaking one thousand meters off the port nacelle. Correction, we have a second vessel de-cloaking as well. It looks like some kind of shuttle."

"Target acquired, you are weapons free," McMann replied instinctively.

"Belay that!" Greig shouted. It had taken only a nanosecond for him to realize what was happening. He grinned. "This is Condor One. Abort, abort, abort."

He entered a single alpha character into his override command console and hit the enter pad. A signal was immediately encrypted and sent to every vessel and flight element in the fleet. It was the command authorization code to abort the mission and disengage.

Captain Chris Patterson watched his tactical plot. He was the lead element of Squadron VF-241, attached to the Lexington's fighter wing, the Black Falcons. On the starboard engine nacelle, just abaft of his armored alumina-matrix bubble, were painted nine small red serpents. He was almost a double ace. He had killed nine Caldarian Partharic attack fighters. He was about to call 'Tallyho' when he saw the abort code flash on his tactical display. He breathed a heavy sigh.

"Roger control, acknowledge abort, authentication code away. All Falcon elements replace safeties and break off. Another day people," he spoke quietly.

He knew it was lousy radio discipline and that the air group commander would no doubt tear him a new asshole, but what the hell, he thought. It isn't every day you get to watch an entire Caldarian battle fleet disappear and have a chance to look at life again. He worked his controller, rolled out to a one eighty and headed back to the Lady. Seven flat, black shapes followed him.

On the Lexington's view screen in the Combat Information Center, a shape slowly came into view. Every person in CIC stood to their feet as the shape solidified and the Haida's Chameleon dampers de-energized. They stared at the scarred and blackened hull of the HMCS Haida as she de-cloaked.

Greig hit his COM link. "Welcome home, Haida."

≈≈

The Haida

The shuttle floated into the Haida's docking bay and the doors closed. Jackson and Doc Hearst sat on the bench, their helmets off, eyes staring at the bulkhead. As the shuttle doors hissed and the cockpit hatch opened, Jackson turned to look at Ensign Marcie Chantella. Her eyes had dark circles beneath them as she stared back at Jackson but she was grinning.

"Looks like I saved your ass again, Lieutenant. Honestly Sir, I think you're getting a little too old for all this gung-ho shit, don't you?"

Jackson and Hearst laughed. They both felt their bodies giving in to the sudden release of tension and knew they were going to crash big time, in short order. But they didn't care. They were safe.

"Thanks for the lift, Marcie," he said softly.

She winked. "Anytime, Sir."

The team swarmed in and Jackson felt a swelling warmth as he looked at the familiar faces. Dyer grabbed Michelle and gripped her fiercely. She didn't resist. Her powder stained fingers entwined in his hair and pulled him close, feeling his emotions stir across the neural link.

"Don't ever die, you sweet mother-fucker," she said, and then kissed him full on the lips.

The COM light blinked and Captain Mark Nolan spoke.

"Welcome back, Lieutenant. Admiral Greig has called over and is sending a shuttle for you and your team. He wants to debrief within the hour."

"Aye, Sir. I have to make one stop first and I'll meet you back here in the shuttle bay."

"No problem, Lieutenant," Nolan said and then the COM link went dead.

Nolan watched the view screen. Already, courier shuttles filled with technicians and engineers were on the way over. He didn't care. He palmed the ship-wide PA system.

"All hands, secure from battle stations, prepare for docking auto sequence. The Alberta will be here at 17:00 hours galactic. Rotation will commence at 07:00 hundred hours tomorrow." He paused. "Good work people, damn good work. Nolan out."

Nolan left the bridge and entered his ready room. He hit the switch that opened the battle shield on his small viewing window and watched as the Myloen cruiser, the Predator, crossed his line of sight. He opened a drawer and lifted out a small lexite box with a hinged lid. From another drawer, he drew out the bottle of Glendronach and a tumbler, and placed them on his desk beside the lexite box.

He turned to his command computer and entered a password, and the image of the Haida's battle crest filled the screen. He opened his command personnel database and started to reach for the lexite box but instead his hand went to the bottle of amber liquid. He poured the tumbler two thirds full and held it up to the light. The golden liquid swirled as he rolled the tumbler between his fingers. He took a long drink and felt the whiskey burn like dense smoke as he swallowed. He set the tumbler down and, opening the lid on the lexite box, he reached in and removed a small round disc that was encrusted with a dark stain. He turned to his computer and began to type.

"Dear Mr. and Mrs. Poulin,

My name is Commander Mark Nolan. I was Anthony's commanding officer on the HMCS Haida. It is with deep regret and sorrow that I must inform you..."

In the Haida's sickbay, Commander Debra Lewis sipped her water and felt the warmth of the bed's heated underlay surrounding her. The door to sickbay hissed open and she turned her head. She caught her breath. Jackson was standing in the doorway watching her.

"Hi," she whispered. He looks awful, she said to herself.

His eyes were deep pools and the walls were momentarily down. She gasped. She had never seen such raw, naked pain in her entire life. For a moment, she gazed through the window and saw to the deepest corner of his soul and then the window snapped shut.

Jackson moved to her side before he spoke. He reached tentatively for her hand and their fingers entwined in a quick, hard grasp.

"Hi," he answered softly.

EPILOGUE

"The river is nothing. The water is everything."

—cb

"This is Dr. Winston Green. You have five minutes to enter the security code to deactivate the security envelope and turn off the power generator. To deactivate the containment grid, please state what the Confederate training base on Deca-One is named after. If the correct code is not entered at the end of five minutes, another countdown will begin. There are five fusion pod reactor cores set in deep exploration shafts along the edge of the cavern you have entered. The safety mechanisms have been removed and the cores have been enriched with military grade plasma rods. Once the countdown starts, there is no way to stop the pods from going critical. The feed loops and control circuits that communicate with the cores contain small conventional charges that will detonate and destroy all links to the command console. If an electronic peeper signature is detected, the pods will detonate instantly."

"The countdown sequence has been activated. You have five minutes."

The four creatures snarled and hissed at the holographic image standing impassively in front of them. They had followed the scent of the strange creatures and come once again to the small opening beneath the thick stand of leaf-cedars along the cliff face. At first, they had been reluctant to try the entranceway. Previous attempts to access this particular cavern through this entrance had caused excruciating pain in the creature's cerebral cortex and it had taught them to stay away. The scent and lure of soft flesh had gradually overcome their fears and they decided to test the entranceway again. They had cautiously approached, sniffed the air and tentatively stepped inside. They stood in the entrance, flexing the nodes of their cortex but they sensed and felt nothing. Cautiously they made their way deeper down. They came to several bodies of their kind and paused. There was no answering neural traffic, so they moved on.

They turned a corner and instantly a pulsing blue sheen of light enveloped them. They raged and hissed as spittle and froth spattered the ground, arcing as it vaporized on contact with the invisible wall of energy holding them back.

A clock at the base of the holographic image ticked down the final five seconds. A signal was sent and five monitoring nodes sent a signal to firing circuit loops on five enriched pod reactors buried three hundred meters below the chamber floor. Triggers closed. A huge detonation shook the chamber. The host rock within a three hundred meter radius of ground zero turned to glass from the intense heat, a weak fault line ruptured and what was once the chamber began to fall.

It fell nine thousand miles and the molten conglomerate mix of rock and alien ore plunged into the core magma chamber. Far above, the ground was rent open and lava vomited forth from the new vent and flowed over the blackened remains of the dead Caldarian shuttle. Rain and wind lashed the sluggish lava as it began to cool, forming a new debris field.

A thin blue stream of denser material coalesced and flowed within the magma chamber, stubbornly refusing to be assimilated. A thin tendril reached across six thousand kilometers of swirling magma and slowly, with infinite care, wound itself around a harder, older pillar of alien metal suspended in the churning, turbulent sea of liquefied rock. The tendril morphed and shaped itself into a finger and depressed a small recess. A sentient guardian portal was opened and a shrill piercing burst of energy emanated from the strange pillar.

The energy rose, resisting the tremendous heat and pressure until it breached the surface and welcomed the darkness and cold of space which it hadn't seen in one hundred and fifty-three million years.

The stars were strange but something within its infinite memory triggered and it responded and altered course, bending its mind toward its primal origin.

The journey was immeasurable. But it was patient. The guardian had awakened.

It was time...

About the Author

Chris Besse has a diploma in geology and a degree in theology, and is currently working in engineering systems at a large petrochemical facility. He has been an avid shooter since age fourteen and is a passionate motorcyclist who also practices traditional Shotokan Japanese karate. All of his life, Chris has been a student of history in general and military history specifically.

Chris has worked the science that paints the background for *Element* for many years, and his study and continued interest in theology has been a unique microscope with which to observe and study human nature and social behaviour on every level. He is currently working on book two of his *Element* trilogy.

Chris and his wife, Pat, live in Red Deer, Alberta, Canada and in his spare time Chris enjoys playing with his granddaughter and four grandsons.

Visit Chris' official website at www.elementscifi.com.

Printed in the United States
95336LV00005B/43-60/A

9 781594 264740